# CHAPTER 1

*Tuesday September 20th 1586*
*The twenty-seventh year in the reign of Queen Elizabeth I*
*Lincoln's Inn Fields, Holborn, London*

The hurdles clattered across the cobbles on their way up the hill. The crowd was restless. Some threw rotten vegetables, but the atmosphere was sour and brooding. The soldiers were nervous and twitchy; many of them had drawn their swords or lowered their pikes. It wasn't usually like this, but they knew the prisoners had friends still at large. The sky was heavy and promised rain before they reached the gallows.

The narrow streets meant the crowd was uncomfortably close. Close enough to see into people's eyes. Some of them weren't friendly or encouraging. There were shouts and curses, but it wasn't always clear who they were cursing. Of course none of them mentioned the Queen.

The men strapped to the hurdles were hardly conscious; those that were groaned or called out piteously. Although they were tied to the hurdles, none of them could have got very far. Broken legs, mangled arms and wrecked backs.

Out in the fields a weak autumn sun shone on the pale stalks of the harvested barley. At the gallows it was an awkward business. It wasn't as if they tried to escape. It was more that they had to be half carried up the steps or picked up when they collapsed. Amidst it all one of the youngest, who seemed to have escaped the worst of the torture, climbed the steps with some dignity. His expensive clothing was torn and dirty, his long curls uncombed and knotted, but his chin was up and his eyes burned bright.

Only two of them struggled against the tightening ropes. He wasn't one of them. The other three were past caring. It took more than one or two buckets of water to revive them. One had to have smelling salts thrust into his face.

There were some soldiers who were hardened to the drawing process. They worked like butchers, except butchers knocked their cattle senseless before using the hooks to pull out the sweetmeats and giblets. Here the same tool was used, but the humans were conscious. The screaming which seared into his head had lived there since that day. Catlin fought those around him to get away. A hand held his arm. He turned to take one last look. The young man's eyes were closed. He'd escaped – gone to his heaven or his hell.

### Wednesday June 3rd 1981

'Bloody typical!'

'Mick!'

'First holiday I've been on since…'

'What is it?'

'They've moved that bastard Castle's trial to this week!'

'And?'

'They want me there on Thursday.'

# A Ripple of Lies

Rick Lee

2QT Limited (Publishing)

First Edition 2012

2QT Limited (Publishing)
Burton In Kendal
Cumbria LA6 1NJ
www.2qt.co.uk

The author has his own website www.attheedge.eu/

Cover design by Martyn Davis
www.marengo.cc

Typesetting by Dale Rennard

Printed in Great Britain by Lightning Source UK Ltd

This is a work of fiction and any resemblance to any person living or dead is purely coincidental.
The place names mentioned are real but have no connection with the events in this book

A CIP catalogue record for this title will be available from the National Library
ISBN 978-1-908098-77-1

# Acknowledgements

*I'd like to thank my friend Carola Makowitz for once again providing enthusiasm, encouragement and support.*

*Kate Edwards for asking the awkward questions!*

*Karen Holmes again for her critical analysis and making me face up to my tendency to use a metaphor when telling it straight is far better.*

'That's tomorrow!'

'Is it?'

'I don't believe you.'

Laura snatched the telegram from Fletcher's hand.

He walked to the window and stood looking out over the sea. The Mediterranean Sea.

They'd been here a week and a half and Fletcher was just getting used to the idea: you didn't get up till you felt like it, sometimes you had sex in the morning and after that you had breakfast: fruit juice, coffee, croissants. By then it was time for a swim, but soon enough it was lunchtime. More swimming. More sex. Playing on the beach. Aperitifs. Dinner under the stars. More sex. Sleep. He'd died and gone to heaven and now they wanted him back. Bastards. He knew it wouldn't last. He'd disconnected the phone and given the receptionists strict instructions to say he wasn't in – for anyone.

A hand stroked his neck. It was replaced by a kiss. The hand went elsewhere. So did the lips. They made the most of the last few hours.

\* \* \* \* \*

Later that afternoon they were looking down from the departure lounge at Nice airport. Below them was a huge noisy crowd, lots of shouting and whistling. The arrivals door opened and the noise came to a crescendo. Out of the doorway into a cocktail of light and sound came a small figure dressed in green. Her hair was full bodied and dark, she was wearing a big smile; this was her moment of fame. Fletcher, who hardly ever watched the television properly, didn't recognise her; but Laura said she'd seen her in something and, in any case, she knew who she was from the Festival news, which she'd avidly followed for the last week or so.

'It's Cheri Lunghi,' she laughed. 'She's Guinevere in *Excalibur*.'

'Um,' said Fletcher.

'Just your sort of woman, eh,' she nudged his arm.

He had to admit that she had a lot in common with the nudger. Laura wore her hair long again after trying out various shorter styles. More to do with the women Fletcher was working with at the time than her own preferences but her self-confidence had gradually returned during the last six months – not least because the problems with her daughter Grace had faded away. They'd left her at home revising for her A levels.

Mick turned to Laura and kissed her full on the lips. 'I'd better go through,' he said.

They kissed again.

'I'll see you on Friday,' he whispered.

Laura was less than convinced that this would happen, but whispered a promise in his ear. His eyes went wide.

'Madam,' he said. 'I don't think you should use language such as that to a grammar school boy. I'm not even sure I know what you mean.'

She grinned.

'Don't worry. I'll be gentle with you.'

Half an hour later she watched the plane take off into the purple sky. A sudden evening breeze ruffled her curls. She thought of the film star and decided she didn't envy her at all.

\* \* \* \* \*

## Wednesday 26th June

'Cora! It's ten past eight. You're going to be late for school.'

'OK! OK! I'm coming!'

'Bloody typical!'

'What?'

'Typical of your father.'

'Why? What's he done now?'

'Says he's too broke to pay his maintenance.'

'Well, he's lost his job, hasn't he?'

'And whose fault is that?'

'I don't know, do I?'

'It'll be him. Too big for his boots, thinks he knows best, always arguing with the boss.'

'And you don't?'

'What's that supposed to mean?'

'You're always slagging off your boss.'

'That's different, she's a cow!'

Cora's mother ripped open the other letter she'd retrieved from the hall floor.

'Who's that from?'

'School.'

'Aw – no.'

'It says you've been jigging it again. Three times last week.'

'Shows how much they know.'

'What?'

'Nothing.'

'It says they're going to take me to court if you keep missing school.'

'No they won't, Mum, they're just trying to frighten you. It would take ages and I'll have left next year. Just ignore it.'

'Don't you tell me what to do! You'd better get to school; I'm the one who'll get fined.'

'Don't be stupid, Mum. You haven't got any money anyway.'

'Don't call me stupid, you little cow.'

'Well you are; you never went to school did you? Not according to what dad said anyway. You were always getting into trouble, so don't preach at me.'

'And you believed him – that liar.'

'Oh leave it out, Mum. Your needle's got stuck.'

'Not as stuck as that bloody Kate Bush tape. You're going to wear it out.'

'Well that'll be my problem, won't it?'

'I'm sick and tired of you and your music and your answering back. Why don't you go and live with your precious father?'

'You think I wouldn't, don't you? Well maybe I just will.'

'You really think he'd have you. Not if that slag he's shacked up with has anything to do with it. She wouldn't like the competition.'

'Are you calling me a slag?'

'Well, what d'you look like? Short skirt showing you haven't got any knickers on, going round with those smack-heads.'

'Oh don't start that off again. If there's any slags about then you're the ultimate role model. I mean just look at your hair!'

Cora's mother flies round the table and slaps her daughter hard across the head. Cora falls to the floor. The doorbell rings. They both freeze. The doorbell rings again. Cora struggles to her feet.

'One day you're going to regret that.'

'You and who's army? You little coward. Go on, get to school. Tell your dancing friends what a cow your mother is. Fat lot of good it'll do you. GO ON! GET OUT!'

Cora and her mother look long and hard at each other. The doorbell rings again. Cora picks up her school bag, walks to the door, turns. Her mother glares. Cora opens the door and leaves. Her mother screws up the letter, tries to tear it up – but she can't. She leans against the table and sobs.

* * * * *

### Friday June 5th

Consigliere Emilian Luca sits at his usual seat under the awning outside Al Mangia with the view of the Palazzo Pubblico. It is raining, not heavily, and the sun is making intermittent attempts to break through the clouds. He is reading *Der Spiegel*, as much to keep his German up to scratch as paying attention to the news. He is wearing a Brioni cream silk suit, rose-coloured linen shirt and purple silk bow tie, with soft leather Ferragamo purple shoes. An empty espresso cup rests on the table before him; a few crumbs of amoretti biscuit litter the white tablecloth.

He looks up as a shadow passes in front of him. A fellow customer takes his hand. Civilities are exchanged. The other man enters the interior of the *ristorante*. Luca's attention is momentarily held by the silhouetted figure of a young woman a few tables away. Her dark hair falls across her face. She catches his eye and stares. He looks away, squinting into the sudden glare of sunlight shining onto the *campo*. When he looks back at the woman she is smiling at him. He smiles back, but turns to the pages of his newspaper.

A waft of rather heavy perfume drifts past him. He senses the figure standing to his left. He looks up to meet the dark gaze of *la padrona*; she looks out at the *campo*.

'*Buon giorno dottore.*'

'*Buon giorno*,' he replies, looking the same way. The young woman has gone.

'*Il sole sta arrivando.*'

'*A suo tempo una buona.*'

'*Sempre.*'

Without making eye contact she bends forward and picks up the coffee cup and saucer.

'*Un altro?*'

He stares at the small receipt she'd placed on the table.

'*Si, per favore.*'

She slips away as silently as she'd arrived.

He looks across the expanse of chairs under the awning. Three people he recognises: then there are two tourists and a group of dark suits having a business meeting. Nothing to trouble him. He picks up the receipt. Apart from the usual words and numbers, he sees that there are some pencilled marks.

'CroCus10302006.'

He frowns and places it back on the table. He stares into the sunlight. His coffee arrives.

He watches as the sun brings out more tourists and the street sellers. Ten minutes later he folds his paper, leaves some coins on the table and walks slowly out of the *ristorante* and heads off towards one of the alleys leading away from the *campo* into the *contrada* Leocorno. If someone had been following him, they would have found it either fascinating or irritating. Fascinating because he seems to know an awful lot of people: some of the conversations in fluent and very rapid Sienese go on for five or ten minutes. Most of them are about the weather, local gossip and of course the latest Palio developments. Irritating if you just want to know where he is going or if you are trying to tail him.

Finally he turns down an alley and stops about halfway along, takes out a key and unlocks a rather nondescript door in a long wall of medieval four-storey terraced buildings. Anyone catching up at that point would have only seen him enter a darkened space. He is through and inside in a matter of seconds, the lock mechanism clicking smoothly into place. Inside the entrance hall he pauses for a few moments and listens intently, before opening the inside door and entering a space full of light.

The house is very old and had belonged to a very prestigious Sienese family of goldsmiths. Luca stands and looks at the courtyard. The living quarters occupy three sides, but the heart of the house is this exquisite space, filled with light and the perfume of orange and lemon trees. Light and shade are harsh in the Tuscan sun, creating dislocated angles and shapes, but Luca loves it all. He walks along one side and opens a door into the main entrance. The cool interior is in marked contrast to the heat generated during the last hour outside. He stands listening to the silence. There are no clocks ticking. No creature stirs.

He sighs with pleasure and walks up the marble staircase. On the first floor he stands and looks towards the east wing. Not a sound. They didn't come back until dawn this morning, so he isn't expecting to see them until much later. He turns to walk the opposite way, but can't resist the lure of their presence. He removes his jacket and drops it onto the floor, takes off his shoes and abandons them as well. As softly as he can, he makes his way along the corridor, moving from light to shade as he passes each opening. He comes to a double door. He stops. The door is ajar. He pushes it open with two fingers and stares into the shadows.

The room is large. Heavy curtains block the sunlight, but he can make out the shapes before him. There is a large bed against one wall. He holds his breath. On the bed lie two figures. One is spread-eagled face upwards like a starfish, the other coiled like an ammonite in the arc of the other's right arm and leg. They are both naked. He marvels at their beauty, the contrasts between them, their symmetry and asymmetry. He wants to step forward and touch them, but doesn't want the picture to dissolve and come to life. Life that he knows will entrance him further, will terrify and enthral him with its energy and virtuosity and laughter. He steps back. Back from the edge.

In the corridor he leans against a cool pillar and gathers his breath. His shirt is soaked and sweat is streaming down his legs. He staggers back along the corridor, gradually regaining control of his limbs. He goes along to the other wing and enters a similar room – his bedroom – and collapses onto the bed.

He doesn't know how long he lies like this, eyes closed, breath and pulse gradually returning to normal. He doesn't hear anyone come into the room and flinches away what he thinks is a fly, only to find it is a soft hand, stroking his hair. The hand moves swiftly to his mouth, before he can speak.

'*Occhi chiusi,*' whispers a voice.

Obediently, with mounting excitement, he keeps his eyes shut. His pulse begins to race again. He feels a hand travelling down his chest, slowly unbuttoning his shirt. Two hands deftly undo the buttons of his trousers. He can hear breathing other than his own. The two hands expertly release his erection from the enclosing silk. His whole body dissolves as he falls into ecstasy. Soft lips envelop him. Soft hands gently stroke and finger him. It takes time. Nothing is rushed. The explosion, when it occurs, is a heavenly release. The fingers trace back up his naked chest and touch his lips – to be replaced by another's lips. The kiss is long and warm and wet. He feels a slight draught as the figure retreats and is gone. He opens his eyes and weeps tears of joy and despair.

\* \* \* \* \*

*Thursday June 4th*

Fletcher paces up and down. He's outside the courtroom. The jury has gone back in. The word is that they've reached a decision. His head is bursting.

A door clatters open. The first person out is a local journalist, who rushes past Fletcher, before he can stop him.

Staring in frustration, knowing that the little runt knows but he doesn't, he feels someone grab his arm. He turns round ready to fight, but it is Irene. She looks him in the eyes. He knows. He whoops with relief. The two of them do a little jig, much to the amusement of others streaming out of the courtroom.

They head to the stairs.

'The first three are on me,' Fletcher yells.

Halfway down the steps he stops and grabs her, hugs the breath out of her and kisses her full on the lips. They stand in this embrace for just too long. He can feel her thin body against him. She can feel his. They let each other go, eyes locked. He licks his lips. She copies him. They laugh and continue running down the stairs hand in hand. At the bottom they stop again, look again and laugh again.

'We did it,' he said quietly.

'We certainly did. Life. Minimum fifteen years.'

Fletcher's eyes widen. Irene looks over his shoulder.

'Although I think the celebrations might have to wait a while.'

Fletcher swings round, half expecting to find Laura glaring at him. Instead, standing in the middle of the entrance hall is Louisa Cunninghame: trademark blue suit, cascading blonde hair, cold blue eyes boring into him.

'Louisa? What are you doing here?' he mutters.

'I'm a magistrate, Michael. I work here sometimes. I just heard your news. Congratulations.'

He notices she hasn't as much as glanced at Irene. He nearly blushes.

'Well thank you.' He pauses, feels a hand squeeze his. 'Oh, sorry! Hey. This is Detective Sergeant Garner. Irene. It's as much her success as mine.'

'Delighted to meet you,' says Louisa, stepping forward and offering her hand.

Irene smiles.

'I've heard a lot about you, Mrs Cunninghame, and thanks for the tip off.'

'The least I could do. I understand this helped you gain promotion as well.'

Irene nods, glancing at Fletcher.

'Richly deserved,' adds Fletcher.

'I imagine,' smiles Louisa, 'working with Michael.'

Irene grins.

'Would you mind if I borrow him for a few moments, Sergeant? A personal matter.'

'No problem. I'll go and order the first round.'

Irene smiles at her again and looks meaningfully at Fletcher. 'I'll see you in a few minutes.'

He nods; she walks down the steps and disappears. Louisa takes Fletcher by the arm and leads him round a couple of corners into a small cafeteria.

'Get yourself a coffee and an orange juice for me,' she orders and heads for a corner table.

'Yes ma'am,' he says under his breath.

Two minutes later he places the juice in front of her and sits down.

'So what's the personal business? Have you been caught speeding again?'

'Don't be facetious Michael. This is important.'

Fletcher is perplexed.

'First there are a few conditions. As we seem to be constantly bumping into each other, you will please get rid of that disgusting coat. Secondly, you must promise not to get drunk or tell tales about certain exploits which I wish to keep private. Thirdly, you will not wear a kilt.'

The light of understanding begins to dawn in Fletcher's astonished mind. 'You mean . . . ?'

'Yes. Against my more sceptical instincts, I have decided to invite Laura, Grace and you to my wedding.'

She produces a large white envelope from her handbag and offers it to him. He knows his mouth is flapping open like a fish on a slab, but can't come up with any response.

'"Thank you" would be sufficient, Michael,' she says, getting to her feet and giving him a stern look. 'You've two weeks to get some decent clothes and a haircut. Do NOT embarrass me. Is that understood?'

'Yes,' he murmurs. He looks down at the envelope.

She turns at the door.

'And remember Michael. I owe Laura. You be careful. "Temptation, misfortune, danger, upsets" – yon slinkit lassie has a wickit edge.'

Before he can question this, she's gone.

He finds 'yon slinkit lassie' in the Horse and Farrier surrounded by journalists. He watches as she glitters in this company. Half of them fancy her and the other half know they've no chance. There are a couple of women reporters, but he can tell they aren't enjoying themselves. She glances over and grins, sees his face and shakes her head.

'Here's the man you really need to talk to,' she says pointing at him.

Fletcher's heart sinks. The two women reporters' eyes brighten as they head towards him. He puts his head down and makes his way towards Irene. He glares at her, she smirks.

'Don't ever do that again,' he growls.

Turning to face the mob, he bellows for silence.

'Right, you lot. That's it. No more. You've had your fun. If you print anything my colleague said, I'll find out where you live and send out party invitations to all the teenagers in town. Got it! You know damn well there's a correct avenue for you to follow – stay on it. Now get out of this pub before I have it raided.'

The publican is about to question this, but can tell Fletcher means it. He puts beer mats on all the pumps and rings the bell.

They don't go willingly. Lots of grumbling about freedom of the press and police heavy handedness, but eventually the pub empties. The publican takes off the mats and begins collecting up all the glasses. Throughout all this Fletcher has steadily put away two pints and now wants a third. He hasn't spoken to Irene. She apologises, says it was just a bit of fun, no response. She's just beginning to think she'll have to find another way home, when he speaks.

'You know what, Irene?'

She shakes her head.

'The last thing Louisa said to me was to beware of you.'

'What?'

'She actually said "yon slinkit lassie has a wickit edge".'

He turns to look at her. She returns his gaze: hazel eyes, cropped blonde hair gelled into a small quiff. Tight leather jacket over tight-fitting red top; short black skirt and black ankle boots. She doesn't look like a cop.

'She also invited me, Laura and Grace to her wedding in a fortnight's time.'

'Bully for you.'

'Got to get my hair cut and some new clothes.'

'Can't argue with that.'

They both look into their drinks.

'Do you want another?'

'I'm with you. Your car. Remember?'

'Um.'

He nods at the landlord. 'Sorry about earlier,' he says.

'No problem: pain in the arse, reporters.'

He puts two more pints on the bar.

'So do you think I'm wickit, sir?' she asks.

He looks her full in the face. 'Of course I do. Just remember I'm off your list, yeh.'

'What makes you think you were ever on it? Sir?'

He raises his eyebrows at her. She punches him on the shoulder.

'Don't even think it!' she laughs.

\* \* \* \* \*

Twelve hours later he was lying on the bed next to Laura. She'd lied to him. She hadn't been gentle at all. He thought it might have a lot to do with showing her the wedding invitation straight away. Anyway, he'd survived the onslaught. She was leaning up on one elbow tracing her fingernails down his back.

'So where's this place she's getting married?'

'Dunno. Somewhere in the Borders, at his estate, a big Gothic castle on the banks of the Tweed, I expect.'

'And that's where her family comes from?'

'Think so.'

She laid back, ideas and questions surging through her head. 'God knows what I'm going to wear.'

'She didn't say you couldn't wear a kilt.'

She slapped his naked bottom.

'More, more,' he squealed.

'Seriously though, Mick, it's going to cost a lot of money.'

He turned over, sat up and looked out of the window at the velvet night sky. 'I don't care how much it costs. The three of us are going to look like movie stars. I'm not having any of her stuck-up friends looking down their noses at us.'

Laura hesitated and cleared her throat. 'We could get our stuff here. There are some amazing shops in Nice and Cannes.'

Fletcher smiled at her. 'You're on,' he said, 'on one condition.'

'What?'

'That you repeat tonight every night until the wedding.'

'Deal,' she replied. She put her head on his shoulder. 'Are you as happy as I am?'

He kissed her hair. 'More than I can believe.'

\* \* \* \* \*

### Saturday June 6th

The next evening Luca took them to a trattoria in a small village near Arezzo. The tables were outside; the food was peasant food – the *padrone's* own lambs, vegetables and wine. It was slow, but the customers were not peasants. Gold and silver flashed from every quarter: young girls in short gold skirts and tiny bolero jackets, hair huge and sprayed solid, shining lipstick, heavy bracelets on bronzed arms and legs and high heels sinking into the soft earth as they got out of the BMWs and Porsches.

His two dark angels were dull in comparison, unless you made the mistake of looking into their deep, raven eyes or noticed they both wore the same scarlet lipstick. Marko's hair was a lustrous mass of Medusa black curls, while Tsura's ebony mane was slicked back into a tight ponytail. They always wore black, unless they were performing. Both were bare-footed and moved with an effortless grace, which made the gold and silver parade look not only gaudy but vulgar. They hadn't given him any questioning glances, but sat and watched.

Occasionally one of them would put their head close to the other and mutter some comment. This would produce the ghost of a smile which vanished like a melting snowflake and was replaced by their customary stern demeanour. It wouldn't have mattered if they'd spoken out loud. They spoke a language no-one else, other than Luca, would understand.

The target hadn't arrived yet, but Luca had it on good authority that he liked to think that this was his true home. The man was rich and felt himself to be untouchable. It was true that many of the other *ricchi* in Florence were afraid of him, but that was to be his downfall. Too much is too much. He had to die. Luca had the contract. It didn't specify how or when or where, but here he was out of town. He'd bring his praetorian guard with him, but Luca suspected he'd think the others didn't know about this place – didn't know about his humble origins.

'. . . and wrinkled lip and sneer of cold command,' breathed Luca into the warm night air.

Marko touched his arm. Another BMW had crept along the farm track and slid in amongst the others. Two slim figures appeared from behind the house, presumably dropped off further away from another car. They circled the lit space like hyenas. The car door opened to disgorge a much larger and taller man who came slowly into the light. He walked past everyone and entered the cook's house. His presence caused a ripple of excitement and fear. He reappeared and walked back to the car. Three more men got out of the car. Only one of these men wasn't dressed in a dark blue Berber *haik* and *chalwar*.

But he made up for it.

He outshone all the girls in their gaudiness. He wore a turban of spun gold and rubies. His *haik* was blood red, encrusted with gold braid and his voluminous red *chalwar* billowed in the evening breeze. If this was his way of returning to his roots, he'd failed, as was made very clear by the appearance of the *padrone*. He'd made no such effort: tattered jeans and dirty t-shirt, wiping his hands on an unhealthy looking cloth. But they met like brothers. Four kisses. Lots of excessive greeting words, before the man turned to the assembled crowd and announced that he would be paying for everyone tonight and no-one was to leave unless they were drunker than him. Most of the company greeted this with cheers and whistling. Luca glared at his companions until they managed to stand and raise their glasses. Tsura even gave them a few seconds of Berber ululating.

The rest of the evening passed in an uproar of eating, drinking, singing and dancing except for the eight people who didn't drink, although three of them had to make it look like they had.

Tsura and Marko entertained the crowd with their love songs – full of longing and revenge – their wild flamenco dancing, their exhilarating tumbling and fire-eating. The man in gold insisted that they should come to his house in Florence the following weekend. They agreed and promised to bring the rest of the troupe. As they'd made themselves the centre of attention for much of the evening, no-one missed the older man in the dark suit who quietly slipped away to make critical alterations to the two cars. One of the reasons he had for keeping up with his German was to make sure he could read the damn car manuals. He'd also opened the boots and made minor adjustments to the weaponry, so as to even the odds up a touch.

The evening ended at dawn. The majority of the customers had taken the man at his word. They were either unconscious or still drinking. Luca appeared to have made it to his car before passing out over the driving wheel. The two entertainers were entwined together beneath one of the tables. The ground was littered with gold and silver bodies. The man in red and gold picked his way through these bodies and allowed his guards to help him into the car. He took one look back at the wreckage he'd caused and signalled the driver to take him home. Within minutes he was asleep, snoring like the fat cat he was.

The drivers knew that it was only a few kilometres to the nearest *autostrada* and were pleased to see the quickening light. The evening had passed without incident. How were they to suspect the ferocity of the carnage which was about to erupt?

The first sign was the appearance of a following vehicle in

the second car's rear mirror. The driver, who'd recognised the car, spoke quietly to his companion who picked up the radio to pass on the information. The information was passed but not in the way he'd intended. The car exploded, veered to the left and thudded to an abrupt stop in the nearest ditch. The driver in the first car calmly changed into manual and accelerated away from the inferno . . . or would have done if the gear stick hadn't come off in his hand. He stared at it in disbelief, without considering the consequences of keeping his foot on the accelerator pedal. He realised his mistake a second too late as the sound of the engine reached screaming pitch. His second mistake was to instinctively put his foot hard on the brake. The car was utterly confused, so it turned round and stalled.

To be fair, the two remaining bodyguards were out of the car fast, on their feet and looking for targets. The following car was behind the smoke billowing from the back-up vehicle. They waited. It wasn't a great shock to suddenly see two motorbikes hurtle through the smoke and head at warp speed towards them. The smaller of the two men had taken the sub-machine gun from the boot of the car before they left and had checked the magazine. He waited until he knew he couldn't miss and squeezed the trigger. Nothing happened. He looked at it questioningly. A hole appeared in his forehead and he toppled forward, still puzzling why his gun didn't work.

The bigger man read the runes. He rolled over the car's bonnet with practised alacrity and aimed at where he calculated the bike would pass if it followed its current trajectory. It didn't. He heard it hit the top of the car and readjusted his aim, but too late. The bike landed, swerved sideways and a burst of gunfire ripped his body into lumps of meat. The driver, meanwhile, had slipped out of the door and was cowering by the front wheel. The second bike swerved to a halt, showering him with a spray of grit and soil. Rubbing his eyes he saw a pair of dark eyes staring into his. He didn't see the gun or hear its retort. What remained of his head fell onto the gravel.

The noise and smoke subsided. The man in red and gold struggled out of the back door. He couldn't see anyone. As a figure appeared from the smoke, he levelled his gun. His hand and the gun disappeared: the pain shrieked up his arm, blood spurting from the end of his severed arm. He screamed. The scream stopped – his mouth had been severed from his lungs. His eyes gazed with astonishment as the sun burst the line of the horizon.

Marko recovered from the crouch position and sheathed his sword. Luca took five photographs, while Tsura picked up the severed hand and placed it in a police forensic bag. Marko was already astride his bike. She put the bag in her pannier and pulled her bike upright. Luca was back in the car. They drove away in convoy. At the *autostrada* the car headed south to Siena. The two motorbikes headed towards Florence along the minor roads.

The hand was left at the agreed drop point. The photographs arrived by mail the following morning. Five hundred thousand lire arrived in a Swiss bank account the same day.

# CHAPTER 2

***Wednesday June 24th***

Barrow-in-Furness has little in common with Siena apart, perhaps, from a spectacular town hall, but the resemblance ends there. Same colour bricks but different material. Cora passes it every day on her way to school although she'd be hard pressed to describe it in any great detail. She's more likely to be on the look-out for Nellis and his gang or some other threat. But it is where she meets her friends or rather the other girls who are as dance crazy as she is.

Round the corner out of the brisk wind huddle Farah, Olga and Rachel. Cora joins them, producing a packet of ciggies which she offers around. They all shake their heads. Defiantly she lights up and ignores the superior look Farah is giving to the others.

'Where's Gina? We're going to be late again; that'll be the second time this week.'

'Who cares, Olga, you swot,' sneers Farah.

'Was that your mum shouting at you again, Cora?' asks Rachel.

'Yeh, so what?'

'Just asking.'

'Rachel's mum wouldn't shout at you, would she Rachel?' laughs Farah.

'No cos I'd shout back and then me dad would start.'

'That's mean, Farah.'

'What?'

'You know.'

'What she means, Farah, is that you shouldn't mention fathers because mine has run off with the local tart and you might upset me.'

'So has he then?'

'Yeh.'

The girls look at each other, but say nothing.

'But I don't care cos I'm probably not going to be around much longer anyway.'

They stare at her.

'I'm thinking of taking off.'

'Where would you go?'

'Does it matter as long as it's as far away from this shit-hole as I can get?'

'What about Robbie?'

'Well, he'll just have to make a decision for once, won't he?'

'Here's Gina, at last.'

'Hey. Are you waiting for me?'

'No, we're waiting for the bus to Fame School.'

'Come on. We've got to get there in time to get some lunch passes for our dance rehearsal.'

'Are you for real, Olga, or have you come through some time warp from the fifties or something?'

'I don't know why you're still doing dance practice, Farah. You never stop complaining.'

'Yeh, well, she's right. I mean, does Miss Prescott think she's dead cool or something, getting us to do Kate Bush numbers?'

They all laugh and head off leaving Cora deep in thought.

'Come on Cora,' shouts Gina.

She slowly makes her way after them.

* * * * *

The day doesn't get any better for Cora: two detentions by first break. The only thing that keeps her there is the rehearsal at dinnertime. They're dancing to 'Breathing' until Tricia angrily stops the tape.

'Farah! You've ruined it. You can't keep time at all.'

'What?! Me? What d'you mean! You stuck up slag!'

'I mean you dance like a pig and you're the only slag round here.'

'Listen, you tart, if it wasn't for me you wouldn't even be here.'

'How's that then?'

'Because I told Miss Prescott that you were reliable when she'd heard you weren't.'

'You lying bitch.'

'Don't call me a bitch.'

'Or what?'

Tricia grabs Farah by the hair and pulls her this way and that. Farah is screaming and lashing out with nails and feet. The others try to stop them. Miss Prescott arrives.

'Girls! Stop that at once!'

They stop, but stand glaring at each other.

'What's this all about?'

Nobody speaks.

'It's nothing, Miss, just a bit of an argument,' offers Tina.

'I can see that, Tina, but I'm not having you girls fighting when you should be practising so we'll cancel today's session and perhaps Farah and Tricia can come and explain to me why they've let me and themselves down so badly.'

They all gather round her. 'Aw, Miss. No, Miss. Sorry, Miss.'

'No, my mind's made up. All of you, out now. I'll see you tomorrow.'

The girls go off grumbling, blaming each other. Cora stays.

'Cora, I meant everyone.'

'I said I'd meet someone here, Miss, after practice.'

'Oh, I see. Still going out with Robbie are you?'

'Sort of.' Cora wanders over to the window, her back to the teacher.

'How are things at home?'

'Alright. Well actually, I'm in trouble again, for jigging it.'

'Yes, well, I heard Mrs Trencham saying she would have to write to your mother again.'

'Yeh, she has, hasn't she?'

'She's only doing her job, Cora.'

'Yeh, I know, but she doesn't have to enjoy it so much, does she?'

'I don't think . . .'

Miss Prescott is unable to finish the sentence as Robbie slips into the room. She uses it as an excuse to leave.

'Where are all the other girls?' Robbie asks.

'Why?'

'I thought you were having a dance practice?'

'Well we're not.'

'Right.'

He waits; doesn't know what to say or do. Cora continues to stare out of the window.

'What's the matter?'

'Nothing.'

'Nothing?'

'Are you deaf or something?'

'Sorree.'

'Yeh.'

He waits; gives it another shot. Not a good idea. 'Have I done something wrong?'

'I don't know. Have you?'

'Well, obviously you think so.'

'It's obvious, is it?'

'What d'you mean?'

'I mean everyone knows but me.'

'I don't know what you're talking about.'

'Course you don't.'

'Look, I don't know what anyone's said but I'm not seeing anyone but you . . .'

She says nothing. Still has her back to him. He takes a step forward. 'Has someone said something? One of them girls? Was it Farah?'

She shrugs. He crosses the room and reaches out to touch her shoulder, but she twists away.

'Look . . .' he starts to say.

'Don't touch me,' she yells.

'OK! OK!' He backs away.

She moves to another window. 'Just don't touch me.'

'Alright.'

Silence fills the room. The distant noise of the school hubbub fades, to be replaced by the harsh ringing of bells. He waits till it stops. 'Cora?'

'What?'

'I . . . I . . .'

'What?'

'It doesn't matter.'

'Let go. Let go. Let go. . .' she sings under her breath.

He shakes his head and walks away.

She turns. 'Rob?'

He's gone. She sighs, walks over to the tape, puts on 'Breathing'. She dances until it finishes. She stands in the final pose, back to the door. Mrs Trencham comes in and stands looking at her, arms folded.

'Cora Beck. I want a word with you.'

Cora freezes, but doesn't turn round. 'I know.'

'Where were you last Tuesday afternoon?'

'Can't remember.' She begins swaying to an imaginary soundtrack.

'And last Thursday and Friday?'

'I've just told you. I can't remember,' she sings as she dances.

'That's not true, is it, Cora?'

Cora stops abruptly and turns to face the teacher. 'Are you calling me a liar?'

'You know exactly where you were Cora. You were with the Nellis gang down in the sea shelters.'

'Are you hiring private detectives now then?'

'Don't be cheeky to me, Cora Beck. I know you were there.'

'So who told you then?'

'I'm not going to tell you that.'

Cora walks up to her. 'Because if Nellis finds out someone's grassed him up, they're dead.'

Mrs Trencham stands her ground. 'Don't exaggerate, Cora. I'm not afraid of that young thug and I don't think anyone else is. My advice to you is to stay away from them and get yourself into school.'

'Your advice! Why do you think I'd want to listen to your advice?'

Mrs Trencham reaches out towards her. 'Because I care about you Cora.'

'Don't touch me!' says Cora through clenched teeth. 'Care about me? Ha! That's a good one!'

'But I do, Cora,' says the teacher. 'You could do really well if you put your mind to it.

Miss Prescott tells me you're very determined when you want to be and Miss Ridgeway says your poems are really quite exceptional.'

'Do they? Well all of you can get lost! I'm going and I'm not coming back. You stupid cow!'

'Cora! Don't you dare speak to me like that.'

Mrs Trencham grabs at her arm. Cora twists away.

'Don't touch me! Get off!'

Cora pushes her backwards. The teacher falls and her head clunks against the wall. She groans and her head flops to one side. Cora sees that she is lying still, goes to her, touches the back of her head – there's blood on her hand. She looks up, horrified, then she runs away.

Two other girls walk past the open door. They see Mrs Trencham. One of them runs off for help. The other kneels down next to the teacher. She feels for a pulse as she was taught at Girl Guides. Her hand goes to her mouth. Teachers come running. She watches with her friend as Mrs Trencham is carried away. Other teachers hustle all the other kids back to their classes. The two girls are taken to the main office. Questions are asked. An ambulance arrives. The rumours begin.

\* \* \* \* \*

## Tuesday June 23rd

Roger Skeldon looked at his watch: plenty of time. He was determined not to be late on his first day, so he had left home just after seven even though at that time in the morning the short journey from Barrow should only take him half an hour. He wasn't entirely sure of the last few miles to the house, but on the map it looked about five minutes.

However, as he turned off the main road at Haverthwaite, he was a bit concerned because the tide had brought a damp sea fog up the estuary. His fears increased as he headed down towards Cark. He knew from the map he needed a turning on the right after a couple of miles, but the fog was getting denser. He was reduced to driving at about fifteen miles an hour, which was just as well because otherwise he would have definitely hit the figure that leapt out of the bushes and ran briefly down the road in front of him before jumping the ditch and disappearing into the woodland on his right. Skeldon slammed on his brakes and did well to keep his car on the road.

He got out and peered into the thick fog. He could only see as far as the first lot of trees. The fog also had the effect of deadening sound, so he couldn't hear anything either. He thought of shouting but couldn't think what to say, so he stepped back to the car. As he bent to get back in, he heard a noise. He looked back towards the wood. Nothing. But he was certain what he'd heard. A deep-throated laugh. Well, if someone wanted to play silly buggers at that time of day then more fool them. He got back in the car.

The rest of the journey passed without incident. He found the turning and arrived at the Hall at five to eight. It appeared like a giant warehouse out of the fog. He knew that it was a big building, constructed according to its owner's instructions. He'd also heard that the locals had objected strongly to it and he could see why. It didn't look anything like the local grey stone houses.

He pulled up on the wide expanse of gravel where several other cars were parked. He knew that his new employer had a lot of staff. The secretary had sent him a list to help with his duties, so he knew there were at least six people in the kitchens, four gardeners and various odd job people and gamekeepers. There were also four nurses who worked shifts and two other security officers. That was apart from the owner, his wife and his full-time personal assistant. Roger had also been told that there were frequent visitors to the house and sometimes larger functions which required considerably more part-time staff.

He got out of the car and adjusted his new suit. He'd got two the same, as instructed, and had the bill tucked in his wallet which they had assured him would be reimbursed. Although the fog was at its thickest here near the estuary, the building filled the surrounding area with an enormous forest of light. There must have been twenty windows flinging their gaudy yellow interiors out into the gloom, as well as a host of outside lights which gave the whole scene the feel of a football stadium – except there wasn't a soul to be seen or heard.

Roger walked up to the front steps and tried the door. It opened onto an entrance hall, which was identical to many of the modern hotels in which Skeldon had worked. Across the marble floor was a reception desk and sitting behind it was a young woman who looked up from what she was reading and smiled at him.

'Mr Skeldon, is it?' she said, standing up behind the desk. She had a strong Barrow accent and long, very straight dark hair which fell to her left shoulder. The other side was pulled back with a clip. He made a mental note to add 'very attractive receptionist' to his list.

'Yes,' he replied approaching the desk and offering an outstretched hand. Her slender hand had a strong grip.

'I'm Shirley Thomas, pleased to meet you. Miss Ridley has asked me to send you straight up to her office. If you go through that door to the left, up the first flight of stairs and turn right, her office is at the end of the corridor.'

He thanked her and followed her instructions. Two minutes later he was sitting in Miss Ridley's large office. The woman was on the phone when he walked in, but she indicated the chair and the coffee machine. He helped himself. She wasn't saying much at her end of the conversation and looked straight at him as he sipped his drink. Occasionally she said 'Yes' or 'I see', but otherwise concentrated hard on what was being said to her.

Skeldon broke the eye contact and looked around the room. It was spacious and fairly empty: a large desk, very tidy, no photographs. Behind her was one of the many big windows throwing its light out into the fog.

Over to one side was a bookcase filled with what looked like business and management books. Next to it was one brand new filing cabinet. It was minimalist and cold, which seemed to fit very well with its main occupant. Skeldon looked back at her. She was still looking at him. He held the gaze for a few seconds, but couldn't sustain it. She was wearing a dark-red, square-shouldered jacket over a crisp white shirt. Her brown hair was short and cut like a man's, brushed back from her face. As she listened she twirled an expensive looking pen between her fingers. Red nails to match the jacket.

She was finishing the phone conversation. 'Yes. I understand. I'll get onto to it straight away.' She stood up. 'Certainly, sir.' She walked towards the coffee machine. Black trousers. Red high heels. 'Yes, sir. He's here now.'

She turned to look at Skeldon. 'I will, sir.' She listened. 'Of course, I'll be here when you get back.'

She put the cordless phone down and poured herself a coffee, took it to her desk, shook his hand firmly and went to sit down.

'Welcome Roger. We hope you'll be happy here.'

'Thank you,' he replied. 'I'm looking forward to it.'

She looked at him hard. Acid-green eyes. 'Good. We run a tight ship here, Roger. Do your job well and efficiently with the minimum of fuss and Mr Hadden will be satisfied. Any problems, come to me first. Understand?'

'Yes . . .' he hesitated, unsure how to address her.

She stood up.

'Miss Ridley,' she made clear. 'Follow me. Quick tour, then you're on your own. We expect our employees to fit in as quickly as possible.'

'No problem,' he said, getting to his feet and following her out of the office at a brisk pace.

It was indeed a quick tour: first-floor offices, meeting rooms, large conference room, library, a door leading to Mr Hadden's private quarters and a staircase up to the second floor; down on the ground floor: kitchens, storerooms, workrooms and garages – back to reception.

'Shirley will help you with any domestic problems. Mr Hadden will show you his own rooms and his wife's suite when he returns this afternoon. Have a nice day, Roger.'

She shook his hand again and was gone, heels clicking all the way up the stairs.

'Phew,' he said when he knew she was out of range.

'You're not wrong,' whispered Shirley. 'She is one scary lady. My advice is to not have any problems, eh?'

'I think you're right.'

After a few more words with Shirley, he decided he'd better get himself acquainted with the rest of the staff as quickly as possible. That took him all morning. By lunchtime, he considered he'd got his head round the layout of the building although of course it would take a lot longer to see the whole estate. One of the gamekeepers said he'd take him out in the afternoon.

The tide had retreated and taken the fog with it. A weak sun was beginning to reveal the woods and estuary. He'd not realised how close to the water they were. The house sat on a slight rise, but was only three hundred yards to the nearest ditch. As he stood waiting for the gamekeeper's van to arrive, his eyes focussed on another building further up the estuary. When the fog lifted he could see that it was the ruins of a large grey stone house.

The van came to a halt behind him; its seat springs groaned as Jim Birkby got out and came to stand with him.

'That's the old hall,' he said, 'built during the fourteenth century. The story goes that the family got on the wrong side of the Tudors and ended up in the Tower. The house and land were given to someone else. It's been a ruin for a very long time. Comes complete with ghost. Black Jack. Beard and a long black cloak.'

Skeldon nodded. He wasn't very interested in history. Not one of his better subjects. And he didn't believe in ghosts.

It took a couple of hours for Birkby to show him round the estate. His family had been in the area for four generations. He told some long-winded stories and said to be wary of the tide. Skeldon didn't think he would ever need to go out onto the broad stretch of sand and mud which now was lying baking in the hot afternoon sun. From the level of the house you couldn't see the river or the many channels Jim was warning him about.

When they got back, there was a large black Mercedes parked outside the front entrance.

'His lordship has returned,' said Jim.

Skeldon got out of the car and made towards the entrance.

'Rather thee than me,' said Jim to himself as he drove the van away.

As Skeldon closed the door behind him Shirley looked up. 'Library. First floor. Third on the right.'

He thanked her and took the stairs at a run. He knew he wouldn't be out of breath when he got to the top. He worked out regularly and had kept up his karate practice. He marched purposefully along the corridor, straightening his tie. Before he could knock at the open door, a deep voice told him to come in.

Thomas Hadden was standing looking out of the window.

Skeldon waited.

'I never tire of watching the estuary. I love its regularity, but also its mischievousness. Always trying to catch you out. Just when you think you know it, it changes.'

Skeldon didn't know whether any of this musing required a comment, so kept his mouth shut.

It seemed like an age, but was probably only a few seconds before the big man turned and faced him. 'Roger Skeldon, I presume. Security officer?' He didn't offer his hand, kept them behind his back.

'Yes, sir,' said Skeldon. He was finding it difficult to make out the man's features: dark hair, dark eyes, dark suit and dark shirt.

'Not good, Roger.'

Skeldon frowned, uncertain.

'Standing with your back to a window. Any decent teacher or management guru would tell you that, especially if your audience includes deaf people. They wouldn't be able to read your lips.'

He didn't move. Skeldon realised he was squinting.

'Sergeant. Cyprus. Eleven years. Honourable discharge.'

'Sir.'

'Fourth dan?'

'Er . . . yes, sir.'

'I prefer tai chi, myself.'

'Yes, sir.'

'Found your way around already?'

'Yes, sir.'

'Had to listen to old Jim Birkby's fairy stories.'

'Yes sir, most entertaining.'

'Don't be fooled. He's not an idiot; he knows the estuary better than any man alive.'

Hadden still hadn't moved from the window. Skeldon moved two steps to the left so that he could see him clearly.

'Good, Roger. Took your time. Balanced respect against personal safety.'

He walked towards Skeldon, who tensed instinctively. There was a lot of physical presence in this man.

'Follow me,' said Hadden, and left the room.

He showed Skeldon round his personal quarters. The rooms were large. Everything was white. There were no mirrors, not even in the bathroom. The minimalist style adopted by Miss Ridley matched his rooms: cold and empty like a show house. No photographs, no paintings. No ornaments of any kind. Black Bang & Olufsen hi-fi system. No television.

'So you see, Roger. I live a simple life. Your job is to make sure it stays like that.'

Hadden stood at the huge window looking out. 'The tide has turned,' he whispered. He stood watching for a few minutes. Skeldon waited.

Suddenly Hadden turned towards him. 'You're not married, Roger?'

'No, sir.'

'Homosexual?'

Skeldon's eyes widened.

'No. I didn't think so.'

Skeldon couldn't think of anything to say.

'I am. Married that is.'

'Yes, sir.'

'Let's go and see her.'

Skeldon followed him back through the hall and through a door he hadn't noticed on his way in. It led onto a small landing. In the opposite wall was a lift. Hadden took a key from his pocket and inserted it into a lock. They got into the lift and Hadden pressed the button. It ascended silently then stopped. Hadden slid back the cover on a small screen in the wall and pressed the button repeatedly. Each time he did this, Skeldon could see a different room; sometimes the same room, but from a different angle. In the fourth picture he saw a woman sitting in a chair. Hadden turned the screen off and pressed the door button again. The door slid open. They stepped out onto a thick carpet, unlike the polished wood floors below.

Skeldon followed Hadden as he walked through the suite. A woman in a white uniform was in a kitchen washing some plates. Hadden nodded at her. She gave him a blank stare and continued with the plates.

'Nurse Birch, Skeldon. Not to be trifled with.'

Skeldon didn't think this required acknowledgement and, in any case, he was trying to come to terms with where he was. Here there were paintings, expensive oils, but no mirrors and no glass on the paintings. He recognised one of them as a romantic rendition of the ruined hall the gamekeeper had told him about. The furniture and walls were soft pastels. Everything was muted. They came to the room where the woman sat in a chair. Another woman in white was brushing the woman's straight blonde hair.

'Thank you, Miriam,' said Hadden and took the brush from her hand. The woman disappeared without a word.

Hadden walked up to the woman in the chair. He stood behind her and began gently brushing her hair. 'I've brought someone to see you Stephanie,' he said. 'He's called Roger. He's the new security man.'

Skeldon smiled politely.

The woman didn't seem to have heard her husband, but now she turned to look at Skeldon. Her eyes were dark brown ovals set in a featureless white face. They were close set and incredibly piercing. Skeldon was unnerved. He couldn't take his eyes off her.

'As usual, Stephanie, you've frightened the man. Don't stare so hard, you'll bore a hole in his head.'

Hadden put his hand over her eyes. She took it to her mouth. The pale lips opened and she fastened her teeth over the side of his hand.

Skeldon looked at Hadden. He was smiling. He didn't try to take his hand away. She took it and held it against her face. Her eyes closed. He brushed her hair. This went on for some time. Eventually Hadden prised his hand from her grip and backed away.

'We have to go now Stephanie. I'll come and see you later.'

He ushered Skeldon out of the room.

Back in the library, Hadden poured himself a brandy. He didn't offer Skeldon one, but pointed to the slim file on the table.

'I had the doctor write a brief account of my wife's condition and what you need to know in case of an emergency. The most important part of your job is to see that she does not leave the suite upstairs. The consequences for her would be catastrophic. The consequences for you would be terminal.'

Skeldon looked at him.

'I mean, of course, that you would lose your job. Instantly.' Hadden smiled. 'I believe your shift is over now, Roger. Take the file home. Read it carefully and bring it back tomorrow morning. Goodnight.'

Skeldon walked.

He'd had a strange day. In the car, he glanced at the file on the passenger seat.

\* \* \* \* \*

Stephanie remembered the tiny fingers and toes. Pink warm worms. For no reason they'd suddenly spasm. The blue eyes would flicker.

She stood by the window. The water was slithering across the sand towards her. She backed into the room. Her breathing became laboured. She saw one of the nurses out of the corner of her eye. She sat down, sat still. She didn't want the needle. He said he'd come tonight. She would be ready.

There was another man today. Roger something, with very short hair. She looked round. The nurse had gone. She felt down the side of the chair. The knife was still there. She folded it into her sleeve and waited.

She was asleep when he came. She felt the kiss on her head. She opened her eyes, felt the hardness of the knife. He lifted her from the chair and carried her through to the bed. Suddenly he threw her down onto her front and jumped on top of her, forcing her arm up her back until she cried out. His fingers prised the knife from her grasp. He flung it across the room, got up and turned her over. She stared at him in terror; she knew what was going to happen next. He crossed the room and found the knife, stood for a few seconds to control himself. When he turned he had that smile on his face. She whimpered.

'Please. Don't.'

He laughed. A deep sardonic growl.

He opened a drawer and took out the tape and the bracelets. She tried to get off the bed, but he was too quick. He grabbed her, pulled her to her feet and slapped her hard across the face, once, twice, before grabbing her by the throat and forcing her back onto the bed. While he held her so tight that she could hardly breathe, he flipped open the bracelet in his other hand. Before she could wriggle free, he clipped it onto the ring on the bed head. Breathing heavily, he stood up again and looked down at the woman who had now gone limp. She turned her face to look at him. Her right cheek was red and swollen, but her eyes burned into his.

He gave a soft laugh, went to pick up the other bracelets, but decided the tape wasn't necessary. She didn't resist as he fastened her other wrist and both ankles to the other three corners of the bed, so that she was spread-eagled, arms and legs stretched tight. He used the knife to cut away all her clothes. After a few seconds looking at her naked body, he left the room. She looked at the ceiling. He came back – also naked. He was already aroused.

Without hesitating he first used his fingers before forcing himself into her. It didn't last long, but it was brutal. When he'd finished, he withdrew and stood above her, his chest heaving with effort and excitement. Throughout it all, she hadn't made a sound, shutting her mind away from her body so that it was as if it wasn't happening to her. Now she continued to stare at the ceiling. He leant forward and twisted her left nipple until she gasped with pain. He laughed.

'You felt that, didn't you?'

She looked at him.

'I'm going to kill you,' she whispered.

He laughed again.

'I doubt it, Stephanie. I think it's more likely that I will tire of this game, this punishment. It may be another year or two before I do to you what I did to him, slowly, giving you time to remember his dying, his agony.'

She looked back at the ceiling. He left the room. She didn't cry. She wondered about the new man. Roger.

* * * * *

The new man had stopped for a drink on the way home. He sat in a corner and read the file. Afterwards he finished his pint and went home to his flat in a large tenement building near the docks. He took off his suit and changed into a tracksuit and running shoes. Out of the building he turned left, crossed the bridge and ran down to the sea. The tide was up, so there was only a thin strip of sand to run along. He didn't stop until he was nearly at the northern end of the island, where he could see the tidal bore sweeping up the river. He watched as the swell rose and formed a wave.

He thought of Thomas Hadden watching the estuary. He thought about what the doctor's notes told him. How the wife had lost a baby in childbirth and the resulting descent into hysteria and madness. How Hadden had persuaded the doctors to let him care for her in his own home. The warning that she could appear calm and sane one minute and a wild animal the next. The look she'd given him was certainly not normal. He turned to look back the way he'd come.

Marcus hadn't said anything about the wife. Devious sod. Marcus Pole. Roger knew him from his brief spell in Belfast. Eighteen months ago now. Roger had been one of the lucky ones. They were ambushed. It didn't last long. Hail of bullets. Captain Keane's shouting cut short. Bodies all around. Someone screaming. But Roger didn't have a mark on him. They'd sent him straight back home and insisted he had a number of sessions with a shrink.

Marcus turned up a few weeks back and told him some bollocks about working for Special Branch and needing someone he could trust to do some undercover stuff. Told him to apply for this security job. Said he'd let him know a bit more when he'd got it. Not a peep so far. But that woman was strange. Hadden was right: her eyes were scary. Crazy.

He thought about some of the men he'd known who'd gone crazy. Thought of that woman's body lying in the street, or what was left of her body after she'd stood on the landmine. He closed his eyes.

Shaking the memory from his head, he started to run back. It wasn't for him to question the doctor's analysis or treatment, but the look on Nurse Birch's face had puzzled him. In his experience nurses were either kind and jolly or severe and bossy. Nurse Birch was neither: somehow she was detached and disinterested.

After he'd had a shower, he went out for a curry. He got back about nine and re-read the notes. As he lay on his bed, Hadden's two words kept repeating themselves in his head: 'catastrophic' and 'terminal'.

\* \* \* \* \*

## Wednesday 24th June

In the moonlight, Cora ran along the edge of the sand. Her day had gone from bad to worse.

After the confrontation with Nellis and his gang, she'd decided that she really did need to carry out her threat to leave. She'd blanked out what had happened with Mrs Trencham. It was too terrible to think the teacher might be hurt and that she, Cora, had caused it. She clambered over some rocks as the tide lapped at them. Further on she knew she'd have to go quite near to a farm where there were dogs who might hear her, so she kept to the wet sand even though each footfall left a deep, water-filled hole. Eventually she passed it and headed for the little headland with the rock.

At the edge of the wood was the fisherman's hut. She'd been there many times with her father, so she knew where the key was hidden and that there were sleeping bags and some basic facilities. Once inside out of the cold, she found a bag and slid her shivering body into its soft interior. She knew she couldn't hide here for long. Although her mother had never been here, she knew about it. She'd be so angry when she realised that Cora had taken her stash of money from the box on top of the wardrobe. Cora had been surprised how much there was: over two hundred pounds. Where had she got that from?

In the morning she'd head through the woods and get the train from Cark. She knew one person in Manchester, a boy who'd left school last year. He'd written to her. She had an address.

From the silence of the hut she could hear owls hooting in the wood and the quiet sounds of the water rising as the estuary filled. Her mind was punctuated with images she didn't want to face, but eventually exhaustion overcame fear. She slept.

# CHAPTER 3

**Saturday June 20th**

Fletcher couldn't remember ever feeling so out of place and ridiculous. For a start the exorbitantly expensive suit he'd bought in Cannes had been secretly substituted – somehow, somewhere – with a replica two sizes smaller. It was either that or he'd put on two stones and grown three inches or, much more likely, the 'lovely young man in the shop' as Laura continued to tell everyone, had deliberately and maliciously convinced him that light grey with fine pink lines was perfect for him. Secondly, a pink tie. No further comment necessary. Thirdly, grey shoes. Ditto.

So what was the good news? OK? Picture clear?

Except of course Laura looked amazing: perfect in a frothy, mauve, full-length dress floating delightfully in the gentle Borders breeze, long sleeves, puffed up shoulders, tight at the waist, her hair a shimmer of tumbling, glossy brown curls.

Grace had gone for simple: a little purple dress. She'd turned into the tall, slim teenager, which Fletcher had always known would emerge from the dumpier, grumpier chrysalis. She wore her hair short, which served to emphasise her large hazel eyes. Her face was serious. Like Fletcher, she had never seen so much money in one space before. It was loud. It was extravagant. Both beauty and the beast all rolled together into a giant fashion show cum bear baiting – except there were far more bears than audience.

The happy couple had been married in a 'simple ceremony' at a tiny church – sorry, kirk – high above the Tweed. Fletcher's party and most of the rest of the guests had not attended. Now everyone was gathered at the husband's baronial mansion a few miles further downstream; although the distance from the kirk to the main gates was less than the length of the drive, which was packed with a veritable car showroom of every expensive vehicle imaginable. The bride had stepped out of one of her husband's collection of vintage cars.

Inevitably she'd chosen blue: the ultramarine dark blue of her eyes. Other than that, she looked liked she'd stepped off the set of *Dynasty*. She had abandoned the Lauren Bacall look for the centre-parting, flicked-back style favoured by the likes of Linda Evans. She caused a collective gasp of admiration as she sashayed across the courtyard and up the stone staircase to the main entrance.

Now, many hours later, she'd changed into a silver evening gown and was making her way through the assembled throng gathered in the enormous ballroom. A five-piece band was playing an assortment of jazz numbers, but Fletcher suspected the worst: that they were really waiting for the signal to launch into Scottish dancing music, at which point he would pretend to have a heart attack and spend the rest of the night in a quiet hospital bed. The only alternative was to figure out who his potential drinking companions might be and where they'd planned to slink off to when the dancing started. Unfortunately he'd not spotted a single person he knew since arriving. Louisa might have had specific reasons for inviting him, but he couldn't see any other members of the forces of law and order, although he suspected there might be a sprinkling of lawyers and even judges in the room. Of course, most of the people present were Scottish anyway; not that you'd think so, given the English public school accents all around them.

Just when he'd started to lose hope, he saw a face in the crowd. She wasn't looking his way and even as he caught a fleeting glimpse, she turned away. Other heads hid her from view. Fletcher stared in disbelief. He turned to speak to Laura but found she was deep in conversation with an older woman. Grace had disappeared. He'd last seen her in the company of a stand of tall young men. They obviously knew an alternative to swimming against the tide of the ancient rich.

He looked again towards where he'd seen the face. Without saying anything, he set off through the crowd. This wasn't as easy as he'd thought; although he didn't normally consider himself as being particularly short of stature, most of these people were taller than him so he found it difficult to keep heading in the direction he'd set off.

Soon he realised he'd gone way off course and pulled into a drinks stop to take stock. Having replenished his glass, he looked around the forest of drink-reddened faces. Then he realised he wasn't far from the band which was on a raised stage area far bigger than it needed. He made his way to the edge and stood on a step. Still not enough, so he sidled awkwardly onto the side of the stage. From here he could see the vastness of the room and the huge number of people crowded into it. He didn't think he'd met half as many people in his whole life as there were in this one space.

He scanned the room for that fleeting vision. He could see Louisa over to the other side, working her audience. Fortunately she had her back to him, so he didn't risk a sarcastic arched eyebrow. Laura was still talking to the same woman. And there she was, looking straight at him. Sadie Swift. She smiled. He waved. She shook her head. She pointed towards one of the many doorways off the ballroom. He nodded and jumped down from the stage.

It was only a few yards away but it took him more than five minutes to negotiate the distance. Sadie had disappeared. The door was shut, but opened to his touch. He closed it behind him: no-one in sight and a choice of three directions. Before he could make up his mind, a door opened along the corridor to his right and Sadie beckoned him on. He crossed to the doorway and entered the room.

It was a billiard room. There were three people present: Sadie pouring herself a drink; an older man standing, cue in hand, watching a younger man address the cue ball. The older man had his finger to his lips as he grinned at Fletcher. As the younger man drew back his cue, the older man waited until just the exact moment and sniffed. The intended side the player had meant to hit was not achieved. He did manage to hit the target, but it bounced harmlessly away from the pocket, missing by half an inch, the curve of the cushion sending it to a completely different part of the full-size table than was intended.

'Roger, you old fart. For God's sake grow up.'

The younger man stood up and glanced at the new arrival. 'Ah. Fletcher. Found us at last, eh?'

Fletcher sighed and accepted a large glass of wine from Sadie who, to her credit, was looking a little rueful.

'What an innocent I am,' murmured Fletcher.

'Um. Not really your scene is it. Out of your depth I imagine,' declared the man, now approaching him with his hand extended.

'Actually, I'd assumed that I'd been invited because the bride wanted to consummate her unbridled passion for me on her wedding night as the old laird looks like he wouldn't last half a session, never mind a honeymoon.'

Anthony Adversane laughed. 'In your wet dreams, dear boy, perhaps.'

Fletcher was making his way over to greet the older man, his friend Roger Aughton, ex-Home Office and bridge player.

'You could have warned me, Roger.'

'Didn't know, Michael, until I got here.'

Fletcher looked across at Sadie. 'And as for you, Inspector – had the loyalty instinct surgically removed, have you?'

Sadie's eyebrows gave him a look of mock outrage. 'My every move is D-noticed. Not a single breath unwatched,' she assured him. 'It's good to see you, sir.'

'I don't think we need out of date greetings here, Inspector. You're the same damn rank now and higher up the ladder, I would say,' added Adversane.

Fletcher stared at his one-time protégée. She met his gaze steadily. She'd reverted to the sculpted, glossy black bob cut she'd had when she first appeared in Rochdale. Even then she had been already working for Adversane, but was undercover, forbidden to explain her role to anyone. It hadn't stopped her and Fletcher joining forces to prevent a madman from destroying the whole of northern England and saving Adversane's skin, not that he would credit them with that. Her pale translucent eyes still held his. He wondered if she'd maintained her relationship with Geraldine O'Driscoll, the pathologist in Rochdale. Now was not the moment to ask. He needed to know what Adversane wanted.

'So what do I have to do to save the world this time?' he asked.

'Don't flatter yourself, Fletcher. As ever it's needs must. We don't have the manpower to cover all the potential disasters being inflicted upon us, especially just now by our friends from the Emerald Isle. You merely happen to be best placed and have acquired a working knowledge of how we operate. So I must remind you of your signature to certain documentation which remains in force until you die and beyond.'

Adversane was leaning on the edge of the billiard table as he said this, his eyes intently focussed on the red ball nestling on a side cushion. As he finished he looked up and stared at Fletcher.

Fletcher returned his gaze. 'As if I had a choice.'

'None of us do, dear boy,' said Adversane, as he spun the ball against the cushion and watched it spiral across and drop into the pocket opposite. He walked round the table and poured himself another drink. 'Barrow-in-Furness, Fletcher. It's not Cannes, but it is beside the sea. Ever been?'

Fletcher shook his head.

'Arsehole of the universe, but it's from there that Her Majesty's navy shit warships and submarines. Vicker's shipyard. Otherwise nothing. Longest cul-de-sac in the world, which is where you'd want the navy to have its babies, wouldn't you say?'

Fletcher shrugged and waited, a sense of foreboding growing in the pit of his stomach. He and Laura were beginning to feel at home in Penrith. Was this a sign he was getting old, wanting to stay in the same place rather than move on?

'Anyway,' Adversane continued, 'the Paddies have got it into their little green bobbins that they'd like to scuttle one of our new tubs at the same moment as one of our esteemed royals is bashing it with a bottle of bubbly, or so the pitiful few clues would have us believe. And given what happened to Mountbatten we wouldn't want to lose another one, would we?'

He took a sip from his drink, returned to the side table and looked at the bottle.

'Damn the little Scottie dog. Only put the bloody Montrachet in the billiard room. Sheer bloody arrogance of the man!'

He took another sip; his eyes closed, savouring the texture and the grapes. After due consideration, he came back to earth and stared at the three aliens in front of him.

'What? Ah yes. Fletcher, you've to go to Barrow. Immediately. I've squared it with Chief Constable Findlay and DCI Aske has been told. You're to replace an inspector who's suddenly gone on the sick, poor lamb. You're to pick up his case load, but actually you're following up the leads which we've come to hear about. DI Swift will fill you in on all the details. It won't take long mind, so enjoy it while it lasts.'

He smiled at Sadie. She gave him a disdainful look.

'Any questions, Inspector?'

Fletcher was still looking at Sadie. 'No,' he said.

'Good. So now we can all rejoin the festivities. I can't see that I'm going to succeed here if Roger is going to play dormitory rules.'

He turned towards the door, bethought himself and went back for the bottle. 'Wasted on the rest of you,' he announced.

'Just one thing, Adversane,' said Fletcher as the man held open the door.

He shut it again.

'Irene Garner. She's my sergeant. She's got to go as well.'

'What?'

'That's the deal.'

'Deal? Fletcher, I don't do deals. I give orders.'

'And I'm well known for not obeying orders.'

Adversane sighed. 'What on earth do you need to take a sidekick for? She's not exactly as highly qualified as your previous.'

He didn't look at Sadie and she didn't blush. She's hardened, thought Fletcher. Working with a bastard like Adversane must do that to you. She didn't give him a flicker of interest.

'I think she might be useful.'

'Why? Although from the little I know about the place, you'll need your wits about you. They don't like outsiders. The local chief inspector took a lot of convincing and I imagine his officers will be far less welcoming. I know you can deal with that, Fletcher, because you're always unwelcome, but how do you think your young arm-breaker's going to cope?'

'She's from Barrow.'

Adversane's eyes narrowed. He hated being outwitted; hated not knowing something another person knew. 'Ah. I take your point. I'll speak to Findlay.' He looked hard at Fletcher. 'Anything else?'

Fletcher shook his head. 'Enjoy the Scottie dog's wine.'

Adversane winced a smile and was gone.

The three remaining occupants of the room stood in the silence of his absence. Roger was the first to speak. He picked up his jacket and set off to the door. 'I'm off to find a very beautiful lady who is not getting married today and who will probably be wondering where her man has disappeared to.'

Fletcher and Sadie stood either side of the billiard table. Neither of them spoke for some time.

'How's Grace?' she asked.

'Much better. Happy. Doing well at school.'

'Laura.'

'As gorgeous as ever.'

He waited. She out waited him.

'Yourself?' he asked.

'I beat Yvonne. First time ever. But she's still national champion.'

He nodded. 'My favourite pathologist?' he asked.

She hesitated. 'We have an occasional night in.'

He grinned. 'Sounds a bit TV dinner.'

'More Mary Shelley.'

Fletcher's mind struggled with the implications of that.

'When do I get the details?' he asked.

'Same time as Chief Inspector Mancini: two thirty, next Tuesday morning in his office.'

'Mancini?'

'No ice-cream family jokes. No requests for tickets to his next concert. He's good. Italian family but he's local, born and bred. Cracked down hard on the drugs problem. Destined for higher things.'

'Like yourself, Inspector.'

She gave him a searching look. He spread his hands in surrender. 'Shall we go and rescue Grace from the clutches of the Border aristocracy's young bloods?'

She smiled. They returned to the ballroom. Fletcher knew before they opened the door that his suspicions about the band had proved true. The room was full of swirling and hooting dancers. The next few hours were not the best time he'd ever had.

Grace was thrilled to meet up with Sadie. Laura was cooler but polite. He didn't see Adversane again. Roger and Laura danced. Grace seemed to have acquired a new admirer.

Much later, Fletcher found a room with an open French window and was standing looking out towards the Tweed. He could just make out the water catching the light as it passed through John MacNeil Knox's estate.

He didn't hear her come in. No rustle of material. It was the perfume which told him she was there.

'Ah, Mrs Knox. Come to tell me you've changed your mind and want to drag me off to Gretna Green?'

She came level with him. 'I grew up eight miles further downstream, Michael. My father drank and gambled away all we had. I never thought I'd come back. Well, not to own a stretch of this river again, to be able to walk its banks in the moonlight, listening to the fish leaping from the water, the ducks scrabbling in the reeds. John has made that possible. I'm not going to lose it a second time.'

'Loud and clear, ma'am.'

She stepped towards the open windows. He followed her down towards her river. There was no moonlight. The party was still in full swing. Light poured out from every window along with laughter, singing and loud voices. All faded as they neared the riverbank.

The Tweed was wider than Fletcher had expected. He could see even in the dark that there was a strong current. It moved like a giant beast, unhurried but intent on its destination. They stood side by side, feeling its strength. She took his hand and led him downstream. A hundred yards or so and they came to a small hut. On the river side was a bench. She sat down. He sat next to her. They remained in silence for what seemed like a long time.

She got up and went to the water's edge and beckoned him to follow. There on the far side of the water were three swans, their white shapes luminous in the darkness. They stood and watched.

She turned to him and kissed him full on the lips. He was hesitant at first, before returning the kiss. It became a full embrace. He could feel her body through the thin material. He touched her hair. She pushed him gently away. He waited.

'Just remember, Michael.'

He nodded.

She turned and walked back to the house. He stood by the waterside for a long time. The swans swam strongly back against the current. Eventually he couldn't make out their shapes. He went back to find Laura. His head was filled with a clattering of questions, but he would always remember the three swans.

* * * * *

### Thursday 25th June

Cora woke with a start. It was pitch black. Not her bedroom. It all came flooding back.

After she struggled out of the bag, she could see a sliver of light between the shutters. She peeped out. It was daytime, but very foggy. She'd no watch, so had no idea what the time was. She knew it would be useless trying to find her way in the fog, so made a cup of tea. There was only powdered milk, but she didn't care.

She realised she was hungry. A quick look in the cupboard and she found a packet of soup. She lit the little stove again and waited patiently. There was no bread, so this would have to do. She would set off as soon as the fog cleared.

When she'd eaten the soup, she went outside. The only sound was the nearby lapping of the water. The tide was high. She could just make out the rock, completely surrounded by water. She sat on the bench and stared into the nothingness.

After she'd lost it with Mrs Trencham, she'd run out the back door of the school and legged it down town. She knew all the back alleys and was soon crossing the main road heading down to the bridge. She'd gone into her house briefly on the way, taken her mother's money and stuffed a few clothes into the rucksack her dad gave her for her last birthday. At the bridge she was wary. There was only one way across and she'd lived here all her life. Someone was sure to recognise her. She put up the hood on the anorak and hurried over. She didn't think she'd seen anyone she knew, but kept going until she reached the beach.

Along the path she could see the gang. What were they doing? As she got nearer she could see four of them running around laughing and throwing an old hat about. She stopped by the shelter. Naylor ran up shouting, 'She's coming! She's coming!' They all took up exaggerated positions and waited. Eventually old Mrs Jardine shuffled up, a bit bedraggled.

'You young thug! Give me back my hat this instant.'

'You young thugs! Give me back my hat this INSTANT !' mimicked Indie.

The old lady paused for breath.

'If my husband was here you wouldn't be laughing.'

'Well he isn't here is he?' said Hodge. 'You stupid old bat!'

'He's probably dead and buried' added Trev.

'Yeh – buried – under the ground,' laughed Ozzy.

'Worm's dinner,' said Naylor, wriggling.

'How dare you talk about my husband like that, you heartless thugs?'

Ozzy went up close. 'Look, lady, why don't you just push off, or we might have to kill yer.'

'Or worse!' laughed Trev.

'I'm not leaving here until you've returned my hat. It was a present from my granddaughter. Give it to me now.'

'Say please.'

'Just give me the hat. You should all be in school.'

'That's the trouble with old folk nowadays: they've no manners,' said Ozzy.

They went into a routine, using old lady voices, arms folded like Les Dawson.

'You give up watching the telly to go to school.'

'Hours of homework.'

'All that washing up.'

'Taking the dog for a walk.'

'And then they treat you like dogs.'

'Very funny. Just give me the hat. Please,' said Mrs Jardine, trying to be reasonable.

'Aw. Now it's too late trying to be nice to us after all that bad language and swearing,' declared Indie in his best teacher voice.

'I didn't swear at you!'

'Yeh you did!'

'When?'

'You said "you ought to be at sk . . ." Ooh I can't say it!'

'I said you ought to be in "Schoo-el"!' she repeated.

They all over-reacted as though she'd said something really terrible.

'There you are! You've said it again.'

'We're going to have to clean your mouth out with soap and water, old lady.'

'Take your hands off me, you hooligan!'

'Don't push me you old bag,' said Trev in disgust, pushing her towards Indie.

'Ugh! I don't want it. It smells!' He knocked her towards Ozzy.

'Urgh! You're right. What a smelly old pig,' pushing her to Hodge.

'Aw! What's this? She's just bones. A stinking coat full of bones. Dog's meat. Dog's breath. Here you are Nails. Catch!'

Naylor pretended to miss catching her. She fell heavily and lay gasping for breath.

'Aw, you missed her, Nails.'

'Butterfingers.'

'Hopeless.'

'Always said he was a useless goalie.'

They went up to her, started pushing her with their feet.

'Come on, old lady. Up you get.'

'Lying there won't get yer dinner cooked, will it?'

The old lady had obviously hurt her arm in the fall. 'Leave me alone, you bullies!'

'Now there's no need for that, old lady. We was just playing.'

Naylor kicked her hard. 'Now that's proper bullying. Kicking someone like that.'

He kicked her again. She cried out. 'HELP! HELP! Someone please help!'

'Sorry old lady, we can't hear you. You'll have to shout louder than that or else no one will hear you.'

Indie kicked her again.

Cora had come out from behind the shelter. 'Leave her alone, Indie, that's enough.'

They all turned to look at her, looked at each other and burst out laughing.

'Look who's here! It's superwoman flying to the rescue,' yelled Hodge.

They all pretended to see her whooshing about, spinning her around and staggering about as though they were dizzy, but really they were pushing and pulling her nearer and nearer to the old lady until eventually they pushed her on top of her.

'There you are old lady, the cavalry's arrived. Come to save you.'

'Hodge. Trev. Take this old lady to the bus stop. And don't drop her. Understand?'

Hodge and Trev reluctantly helped the woman up the steps and took her towards the bus stop.

Nellis sat on the wall and looked at Cora. She'd put the knife away. He looked at Grim, who produced a large plastic bag from his coat.

'There's the good news and the bad news. Which shall I tell them first, Grim?'

There was no reply. There never was.

'Well the good news is that Grim here has got in his rather large hands about six grand's worth, high grade, really good stuff.'

Hodge and Trev had returned at this point. They all looked at each other but said nothing.

'The bad news is that someone has told the filth that we've got it and they'll be turning us over any minute now. So it's like really inconvenient if any of you smack-heads get picked up for knocking an old lady about, because you're just as likely to grass us all up. You get my drift?'

They still had nothing to say.

'So has anyone got any clever ideas about what we're going to do with this stuff until the heat is off?'

They all looked at their feet and shuffled about.

'I thought not. So it's just as well that I know what we're going to do.'

He'd suddenly grabbed Cora, put her arm up her back, pulled out her knife and held it to her cheek. He was hurting her but she didn't cry out.

'You see, this little canary is going to look after our stash for us and she definitely won't sing. Do you know why? Because I know something about her father that would put him inside for

Cora got up with a kitchen knife in her hand. They backed off, surprised, but soon relaxed, looked at each other and started behaving cocky.

'Hey, Cora,' said Indie. 'Chill out, girl. We're just having a bit of fun here, OK?'

They spread out so as to surround her.

'Better put that knife away Cora. Accidents can happen.'

'Very nasty accidents,' sneered Hodge.

Naylor lunged at Cora, but she was too fast for him and cut him on the arm. It was just a scratch but it hurt and there was blood.

'Ayeeh!! Why, you bitch!'

'Hey, Cora. I said chill out, OK?' said Indie menacingly.

'You just leave her alone then,' she said, swishing the knife back and forth.

She hadn't seen Nellis and Grim as they arrived. They'd been standing watching the last few exchanges; the others hadn't noticed them either.

'Put the knife away, Cora,' said Nellis.

'Hey, Nellis,' laughed Indie.

'Shut it, you smack-head.'

'Hey, Nellis, you calling me a smack-head?'

'I am, Indie. Smack-head! You want to discuss it with me?'

Indie looked at the others, realised they weren't going to support him, so he kicked Mrs Jardine and stormed off.

'I said put the knife away, Cora.'

'Not unless they leave the old lady alone.'

'They're not going to hurt the old lady, Cora.'

He nodded to Grim who bent down and picked her up. Nell indicated the hat lying on the floor. Ozzy picked it up, took it ar put it on the old lady's head – just slightly too hard.

a very long time. So she's going to take the bag away and hide it somewhere safe and not tell anyone. Aren't you?'

He pushed her away, catching the side of her face with the blade. She crouched by the wall holding her cheek, blood seeping between her fingers. Nellis nodded to Grim, who came over to her, pulled her up and gave her the bag and backed off.

'You bastard!'

Nellis laughed. 'I've known about your dad for ages. I knew it would come in handy one day. Now it's time for you to pay back a little for what he did to my dad.'

Everyone stared at Nellis. 'And I know who my father is . . .'

The gang all looked at her.

'But you will do it. Won't you?'

She'd stared him out until a sob of frustration had made her look away.

'I'll take that as a "Yes" then.' He stood up. 'Come on smackheads. We've got deals to fix.' He smiled at Cora. 'Oh and by the way, that teacher you thumped is in hospital. Don't know whether she'll live or die.'

He laughed again. 'Oh, and another thing. Don't think that that wimp Robbie Grant is going to help you cos he's dropped you. He's going out with that tart Farah Rogers. We saw them at it last night down the alley behind the Black Horse.'

They'd all gone off laughing. God she hated him.

She stared into the fog. It hadn't shifted. She shivered. What did he mean: 'I know who my dad is'? She remembered another taunt when she was younger when she'd go berserk anytime someone said: 'Who's your dad? The milkman?'

She'd told him once when he'd found her crying in her bedroom. He'd laughed and said to take no notice, but she worried about it for some time. She was blonde and both her mum and dad were dark. In fact, before she started to go grey her mum had jet-black hair. And what had her dad done to get Nellis's dad put inside? He was out now and was one evil bastard. She didn't ever want to end up facing him.

She went back into the hut and found the drugs. She didn't want to get caught with them, but equally she didn't want to go back. No problem. She knew exactly where she was going to hide them. When she was safely in Manchester, she'd ring Nellis and tell him where they were. It was only a few hundred yards away; it would only take a few minutes.

\* \* \* \* \*

### Saturday June 20th

Luca sat in one of the bars of the Crown and Cushion. It was ten fifteen.

Crocus 10302006.

He'd struggled to choose what he would drink. He'd settled for a glass of white wine. It was undrinkable and he pushed it away. He checked the time again. The road outside was full of people, either travellers or tourists. He thought the locals probably went for their holidays at this time of year, but then reflected that it was the same as the Palio in Siena. You put up with the crowds because it mattered that you were there; partly from a respect for tradition and partly because it paid the bills.

Ten minutes to go.

He thought of his two dark angels. They were having a great time. They'd been instantly absorbed into the traveller community. After all, they were genuine Romany. He could speak and understand their language, but with other Romany present he stood out, would make them feel awkward. In any case, the cover was perfect. They'd already bought a horse each and had shown off their riding skills before a highly critical audience. The fact they'd spent their teenage years in the Camargue had given them these skills, and anyway they'd grown up with horses back in Croatia. They'd also made an impact among the young folk. They were both unashamedly promiscuous and had almost certainly broken a few hearts in the few days they'd been here.

Five minutes to go.

He thought of their last time together and shuddered at the visceral eroticism of the memory. They'd celebrated their last kill and the next day caught the plane to London. From there they'd made their way to Appleby in time for the horse fair and his rendezvous in this bar.

The door opened and a young woman entered. She was dark haired, with blue eyes. She looked at him and indicated the back door. He picked up his jacket and walked out into the back yard. An old Ford Granada waited, its engine shuddering intermittently. She followed him out and opened the passenger door. He hesitated, couldn't see the driver. She nudged him in the back. He bent down and looked inside. The young man was staring straight ahead.

'Either you get in or we'll get someone else,' he said. The Irish accent was muted but still there.

He got in. The girl was quickly in the back. The car set off at speed. They were out of town heading north fast.

Neither of them spoke throughout the journey, which lasted about fifteen minutes. After turning off the main road, the driver followed signs to a well-known public garden. In the car park the two of them stayed in the car. They told him to find the man with a tweed cap and brown shoes.

Luca paid the entrance fee and accepted the guide pamphlet. He found the man sitting on a bench looking over a large stone-walled pond. He nodded and sat on the other end of the bench.

'One of the main breeding places of the great-crested newt,' said the man.

'So I understand,' replied Luca, having glanced at the pamphlet.

They sat in silence for a few minutes as a noisy family took over the arena for a while.

'Decapitation and hand severing,' said the man.

Luca nodded.

'Positively medieval,' the man added.

'We try to make the punishment fit the crime as often as we can,' said Luca with a smile.

The man stood up and slowly made his way towards the outer wall. They passed through the gate and set off down towards the river. 'I'm afraid we don't have the luxury of such a close encounter for you this time.'

'Long range is possible.'

'We know that, otherwise you wouldn't be here.'

Luca was silent. He didn't take rebukes easily.

'However, the contract is complicated. One kill to cover another.'

Luca waited. They were strolling through the trees alongside the meandering stream.

'The date is fixed. First of July. We're not sure of the time, but imagine it will be early afternoon. *Trafalgar*. A suitably iconic name. The second target is a moveable feast. You choose the when and how it coincides with the more high profile target, who will have the highest level of security the British government is capable of providing. The secondary target is no easy hit either, which is why we are hiring you as a team. We suspect your two sexually excessive companions might be a great help in this second enterprise, but beware – he is utterly ruthless. We suggest you also enlist the help of the local criminal fraternity led by a nice wee chap called Eric Nellis.'

They'd come back up to the car park.

'My two companions will drive you back to Appleby. Goodbye.'

The man wandered off and disappeared round the corner. Before Luca could consider anything else, the woman appeared and guided him back to the car. Quarter of an hour later he was deposited by the bridge in town with an envelope in his inside pocket.

He walked into town, found his car and drove back to the hotel he'd selected in a smaller village not far from the garden he'd just visited. Back in his room, he ordered a small lunch and sat down. From his pocket he took the envelope. Inside were two photographs: a man talking to another man in a suit at what looked like a private view with lots of people, pictures on the walls. The other was at night-time: the same man with his arm round a much younger woman. Tall with a short, cropped hairstyle. On the back was his name. Thomas Hadden.

Luca's lunch arrived. Afterwards he sat and looked out of the window at the garden. He waited for the phone call. He was still there when dusk began to fall.

# CHAPTER 4

*Wednesday 24th June*

Roger was chasing a man in a flapping long coat, his hair like clinging wet straw, grey beard and big boots. They were running across sand: wet sand, sinking sand, his shoes were being sucked deeper with each step, whilst the man he was chasing was laughing at him from a grassy bank. The sand slowly dragged him down. A wave lapped against his knees. He fell forward, face down into the soft clinging ground.

He woke up to find himself face down in his pillow, suffocating, sweating, his heart beating like a ferret in a shoebox. He got up slowly, sat on the side of the bed and looked at his alarm clock. Six thirty: too early to get up, too late to risk going back to sleep again. He lay back. Miss Ridley's figure clacked into his mind. Was she sexy or not? He preferred girls with long hair. Couldn't think of any girl he'd ever been out with who had hair as short as she had.

Over breakfast, he re-read the doctor's notes. Was it possible to become so mentally ill because you'd lost a baby? He knew women who'd had miscarriages, babies born with terrible defects. He couldn't think of anyone he knew who'd gone mad. Who could he ask? Why was he suspicious?

In the car going up the west side of the estuary, he was pleased to see there was no fog this morning, although it was raining.

It was the starkness of Hadden's living quarters which unsettled him. Roger didn't know much about art or decoration. He only had a few photos and the odd print on the walls in his flat. Pictures of places he'd been or something he liked. He'd actually counted the number of mirrors he'd got on the walls: two in the living room, one in the bathroom and another in his little office. He didn't think he was a vain man, couldn't remember buying them or deciding where they should be, but no mirrors at all? Odd.

As he pulled up in the car park, he thought of Charlie. Yes, he'd ask Charlie what he thought. Charlie Conroy was in Cyprus with him. They'd both come back to Barrow. Not intentionally. Just saw each other in the street one day. It was Charlie who'd got him into the security business. Last year Charlie had set up his own private agency. Bit of security consultancy work and some private detective work. Charlie had always fancied himself as a detective, loved the old gangster movies: Bogart, Edward G Robinson – that sort of stuff.

Shirley was her usual cheery self. 'Miss Ridley wants to see you straight away!' she whispered.

Roger raised his eyebrows.

'I don't think it's you she's angry with,' she assured him. 'I think there was a bit of trouble upstairs last night, you know,' she winked and looked upwards.

Not sure what she meant, he made his way thoughtfully up to the office at the end of the corridor.

Today Miss Ridley was in green: a dark-green trouser suit with black heels. She was standing at the window. Maybe Hadden had suggested this as a ploy. Roger was careful to stand so that he could see her.

'I wouldn't waste your time chatting up Miss Thomas, Mr Skeldon. I understand her boyfriend plays rugby for Barrow, as a prop forward apparently. It sounds like a thick piece of wood, but nevertheless I should be careful.'

Before Skeldon could think of a response, she turned round and gave him a severe look. 'I dare say Shirley has also already told you that we had a minor problem last night; not your shift, of course, but just so you know and can be extra vigilant.'

Roger waited. He'd come to the conclusion that this lady wouldn't take kindly to interruptions. He tried not to stare at her haircut. Was it even shorter than yesterday?

'One of the nurses inadvertently provided Mrs Hadden with a weapon, which she tried to use against her husband. Fortunately he was able to dissuade her and she's now under sedation.'

He offered no thoughts on this either. Miss Ridley gave him a moment before continuing. 'The nurse concerned has, of course, been summarily dismissed. There can be no leeway as far as Mrs Hadden's safety is concerned.'

He gave her the briefest of nods. She narrowed her eyes at him.

'At some point this afternoon, you and a colleague will give Mrs Hadden's rooms a thorough search. It's possible that the nurse could have been more careless than we thought although she has assured us otherwise. Obviously, given the lapse in her vigilance, we can't take her word for that.'

At last, Roger thought he could safely say something. 'Of course, Miss Ridley.'

She continued to give him a penetrating stare. 'I'm glad you understand, Mr Skeldon.'

He waited. She picked up a file from her desk and offered it to him. 'This is a complete itemised inventory of every piece of furniture, object and decoration to be found in Mrs Hadden's suite. Anything not on this list or missing from it should be reported to me by six o'clock today. Is that clear?'

'Yes, Miss Ridley,' he replied, striving hard to resist the desire to salute and bring his boots together in a resounding click. Not possible anyway in a pair of soft leather shoes.

On the way downstairs, he met Shirley Thomas hurrying upwards. She looked scared. Didn't speak or make eye contact. What was going on?

He continued down to the ground floor and went in search of Sam White, the other security officer on duty. Sam was another local man, although being brought up in Millom didn't count as local with Barrow folk. He'd worked in the prison and had stood outside of most of the clubs in Furness. He was well known and most people, unless they were legless already, gave him no trouble at all. He was a big bear of a man, well over six feet, with fists like sledgehammers. Fortunately for most people he was slow to anger, given that a mild cuff from him was enough to send you into next week and therefore enough encouragement to not go upsetting him.

Roger was surprised to find him without his customary vacant smile. He was sitting in the small cupboard which counted as their office with a large mug of tea in his giant paw, staring at the wall.

'Hi, Sam. How you doing?'

Sam swivelled his cauliflower-eared head in Roger's direction. He had surprisingly soft brown eyes, but this morning they had acquired a harsher tone. He looked at Roger without recognition. Roger was momentarily disconcerted, unsure what to do or say. He wanted a cup of tea, but thought it best to wait.

'Not good,' was the eventual gruff reply.

'Oh,' said Roger. 'Anything I can do?'

Sam gave this some thought. 'No. I don't think so.'

Roger waited. The big man stood up and carefully placed his mug on the table. 'I don't think there's anything anyone can do,' he said, and left the room.

Puzzled, Roger helped himself to a brew and thought about the strange situation he'd got himself into. Suddenly he remembered he'd left the doctor's file in the car. He jumped up and set off for the car park. There was no one on reception as he went out, but on returning a few minutes later there was a different girl. She looked up and smiled. 'Can I help?' she asked.

Nonplussed, Roger approached the desk. 'Er . . . no . . . well. Where's Shirley?'

The girl smiled. 'I'm sorry? Mr. . . ?'

'Roger Skeldon. I'm a security officer here.'

'Oh, I'm sorry, sir. I'm new here this morning.' She looked down at her desk. 'Ah, yes. There you are. No photo yet. You must be fairly new yourself, I suppose.'

'Yes. I started yesterday. And Shirley?'

'I've no idea sir. I only arrived from the agency a few minutes ago. Was she the previous receptionist?'

'Uhuh,' he said, shaking his head.

He set off in search of Sam. He needed some answers. He found him in one of the workrooms, fumbling with a huge bundle of keys. He didn't look up as Roger entered.

'Sam? I need to talk to you.'

Sam grunted and continued to prise keys from the big ring and replace them with shiny new ones.

Roger was careful, but reached out and put his hand on Sam's left arm. Sam stopped and looked at the hand. Roger thought it best to remove it.

'Look, Sam. What's going on? Shirley's disappeared from reception. Sacked, for all I know. What happened last night? We can't do our jobs if we're kept in the dark and people keep leaving . . .' He ran out of steam.

Sam looked up at him.

'I've no answer for thee,' he said. 'Allus I knows, is that Miriam's been sacked. I don't know where she's gone. Her room were empty when I went to look this morning. Not a sign she'd ever been there. Madam upstairs won't speak to me; just walked straight past me this morning as though I didn't exist.'

'So what happened upstairs? Miss Ridley said a nurse had been dismissed because she'd let Mrs Hadden have a weapon, which she'd tried to use against Mr Hadden. Would that be Miriam?'

'Ay. We wus . . . you knaw . . . ,' he looked up at Roger with big wet eyes. Roger tried to picture the tiny Chinese girl brushing Mrs Hadden's hair yesterday afternoon in an embrace with this sad giant. He shook his head. It was too fairytale to be possible.

'Well, I'm sure she'll be alright. Maybe she wasn't given the chance to see you. Maybe they made her leave before you got here. I'm sure she'll be in touch.'

Sam shook his head. 'You might be right. I hope so,' he said.

Roger couldn't think of anything else to say. What could he do? He could hardly go and demand answers from Miss Ridley. Well, to be honest he didn't think he'd keep his job for long if he did. He'd still not heard from Marcus. He left Sam with his keys and went in search of Jim Birkby.

No luck. One of Birkby's fellow gamekeepers said he was out tracking poachers. Didn't know when he'd be back. He'd been out all night apparently. Hadn't been home.

Roger slowly made his way back to the house. As he rounded the corner, he saw a man get out of a car and head purposefully into the house. As Roger got up to the car he saw the 'doctor on call' sticker. He wondered what else might have happened, but the new girl, Mandy, said he'd come to see Mrs Hadden.

Roger made his way back to the office. He would call Charlie.

\* \* \* \* \*

### Wednesday June 24th

Adversane had not made an understatement when he said Fletcher would be unwelcome in Barrow. You could cut the atmosphere into nice little cubes and use it in your gin and tonics for weeks. Cold didn't come anywhere near. But the first night was something different.

He and Irene had driven down late afternoon. The plan was to book into a hotel for the duration, although Fletcher was hoping he could thrash back up the motorway a few times to sleep in his own bed. Laura was less than happy with the arrangement, especially when she heard that Irene was going with him. He didn't think she needed to know it was his idea. He needed someone who he could trust in 'the arsehole of the universe'.

Irene wasn't happy either. 'Why did you say that?'

'What d'you mean?'

'That I'm from Barrow!'

'You said you were!'

'Well that's to you. I'm actually from Askam.'

'Where's that?'

'It's three miles away.'

'Three miles? Good grief! That's less than Streatham High Street.'

'Yeh, well. You've not been to Barrow. I spent my childhood trying to escape the place and now you're dragging me back.'

She acted cross, but inside she was really chuffed. First that Fletcher had asked for her, but mainly because she could go back there as a detective sergeant. That'd show all those 'you'll be back' mongers.

So there they were sitting in the Edinburgh drinking Jennings. Irene had her back to the wall. She reckoned people she knew wouldn't recognise her, so she'd get first dig in. She'd had her hair cut Human League style: asymmetric, bleached, with heavy eye shadow and red lips.

And who walks through the door? Same hairstyle. Thin as a . . . as a . . . bloody biro. Only Alex 'skinny bitch' Henning!

First thing Fletcher knows is the two women are transformed into flailing banshees. Irene is up and over the table. Yes! Over the table! The darker banshee with the white stripe in her hair stands arm outstretched yelling 'Irene! Irene! Irene!' on and on! They meet, hug, start pushing and shoving.

'You fucking tart!'

'You sheep shagger!'

'You never phoned me, you slag.'

'So I did – 'spect you were out shagging penguins.'

'Penguins! Me? Fucking rhinoceroses!'

This went on for a good few minutes, the language and the insults and the bragging getting louder and worse.

Fletcher pretended he wasn't there. He noticed that the rest of the clientele were either indifferent or mildly amused. None of them were bothered. Eventually Irene remembered who she was with and what she'd promised herself she wouldn't do. She introduced Alex, who came and sat next to Fletcher and put her arm round him.

'Right that's me sorted. You fuck off and find a dog or sommat,' she said.

Fletcher looked at Irene.

'Actually, Alex you're the one needing a dog. You've got your arm round a detective inspector and his woman will cut your tits off if you don't back off right now.'

Alex laughed, looked from one to the other. Now the room was interested. 'You're taking the piss, Irene Garner. Never could hang on to a bloke.'

Irene gave her a triumphant glare. 'Detective Sergeant Garner to you, Alex Henning.'

Alex let this sink in. She took her arm from Fletcher's shoulder. 'You're kidding me, yeh?'

Irene reached into her bag and produced her warrant card.

'Fuck me. You're for real,' Alex whispered.

'You better believe it, and the sooner you let everyone else know the better.'

Alex gathered herself and stood up. She walked towards the bar. 'Does that mean you don't drink anymore?' she said turning to look at them.

'Does it fuck, you daft tart. It's your round.'

Such was Fletcher's introduction to Barrovian humour.

He did extremely well not to get totally paralytic that night. He'd had no idea what Irene could put away and still remain standing. They'd gone on a tour of various bars and clubs only getting back to their hotel after three in the morning. They'd an appointment with a DI Aston in the morning at nine o'clock. Fletcher didn't know how that would go, given that he was staggering about his room trying to find the telephone to book an early morning call. One thing for sure: it wasn't anything like banshee wailing. 'Still,' he thought as he rested his head on the pillow, 'there were no fights and a lot of laughter . . .'

\* \* \* \* \*

### Thursday June 25th

On first impression, DI Aston was one of those timeservers whom Fletcher hated more than anything else in the world: a man who'd been working out the date he was going to retire and how much his lump sum would be on day two of his working life. He'd a fair way to go and was not enjoying a single moment of it. Neither did he think anyone else he had to work with should, either.

They were early; hung-over definitely, but on time. Aston was late. He didn't offer them a coffee or a seat. He slouched into the office and sat behind his desk. Fletcher moved some files off a chair and sat down. Irene leant against an old filing cabinet so full of documents none of the doors would shut.

'Make yourself at home, why don't you? ' grumbled Aston.

'I will, squire, but I don't intend to stay long, so grin and bear it,' said Fletcher with a smile and a belch. Aston took this in and leaned back in the old chair. Fletcher crossed his fingers and prayed for it to break under the fat bastard's weight, which was considerable. Not a lot of pavement bashing on his recent agenda; more likely sitting in the corner of a pub waiting for snouts to bring the information to him.

'Good. Because we don't like off-comers poking their nose in our affairs. We know damn well there's nothing wrong with Frank. You're either spooks or internal investigation, so don't expect any help from us.'

'That'll be no coffee and no sugar then, Inspector?' said Fletcher.

'S'right. Unless you want it cold sprinkled with fag ash.'

'Good. So, welcome over, can we get down to business?' asked Fletcher.

Aston grinned. 'Frank's desk is next door. You can't miss it. It's the one with nothing on it.'

'That's the sort of desk we like, isn't it, Sergeant?' said Fletcher, getting up and knocking a pile of reports onto the floor. He didn't appear to notice, despite Aston rocking forward in disbelief.

'Just right,' said Irene, pushing herself away from the filing cabinet, which teetered towards Aston's desk. It would have fallen if he hadn't managed to get his shoulder under it in time.

'You bastards,' he yelled, as he struggled to set it upright again, but they'd gone.

'It's a good job you took me through the training course last night, Sergeant. Otherwise I might have thought that that was the rudest person I'd ever met.'

They made their way out of the station and down the road to a café which Irene had already told him about. Five minutes later they were tucking into their agreed solution to a heavy night's drinking. Irene had said it would be tough. She was not wrong. They decided they'd not bother with any more attempts to introduce themselves and would wait till the meeting with the ice-cream man that afternoon. That gave Irene chance to show Fletcher round town.

He couldn't say he was impressed, apart from the huge submarine sheds. They'd ended up on Walney beach for a blow before going to the King George for lunch.

As they sat having a quiet half later, Fletcher looked out of the window. 'That's the docks, right?'

Irene leant over so she could see where he was pointing. 'Yeh and that's the launch channel. Between them big cranes.'

'Um . . .' mused Fletcher, looking round the bar. Most of the lunch crowd had gone apart from an elderly couple and some young lads playing pool.

Irene followed his eyes. 'Ah. You think this would be a fine position for a pot-shot.'

Fletcher nodded. 'Yeh. I'm not a weapons expert, but I suspect it's within long-range distance. Besides, the other side is going to be crawling with security.'

'I suppose so, but surely they'd think the same as you. Give this side the treatment as well.'

'Yeh . . . well . . . unless . . .'

'What?'

'Suppose they're here already?'

'You mean the Walney Island IRA deep-sleeper division. Been here since 1917?'

Fletcher looked at the old couple, who smiled at him pleasantly. He smiled back. 'Well they can't be local, they smiled at us.'

To their surprise, the old fellow got up and came across to them, still smiling. 'Couldn't help but overhear you two,' he said. His eyes were actually twinkling. 'Younger people often make the mistake that us old 'uns can't hear properly. Just for your information, the *Trafalgar* will be coming down't slipway next Wednesday. We're invited, so I hope there won't be anyone taking a pot-shot as you put it.'

The two police officers looked at him dumbfounded. His wife gave them a big smile as well.

'An you'll be Tom Garner's young lass,' he said, looking at Irene. She stared at him in disbelief.

'I used to be stand-off to his scrum half. Hard little so-and-so he was, an' all. May have been small but he could use his fists. A right little scrapper.'

Out of the corner of his eye Fletcher could see that Irene Garner was actually blushing but seemed incapable of responding.

The old man sighed, turned to go then stopped and gave her a serious look. 'I miss him a lot . . . and your mum.'

Irene's face had turned into a frozen mask. 'Me too. Thank you,' she managed to whisper.

The man nodded and went back to his wife who stood up, and the two of them went out the door without another word.

A burst of loud invective came from the pool room. Fletcher arched his eyebrows at Irene. She gave him a panda-eyed look.

He stood up. 'I think it's time we went for a cornet.'

They made their way outside, which took them past the pool room. The game had finished and one of the lads was setting up the balls for the next. Despite her state of mind Irene caught a brief snatch of conversation as they went past.

'Nellis, you're a jammy bastard.'

'No, Nails, you're a crap player.'

Outside she followed Fletcher across the road to the car. He'd walked further along to where there was a coin-in-the-slot telescope. He tried to put a coin in but found it was jammed with a washer. Irene watched him struggle to extract it.

'Wasting your time, sir.'

'Why would you do that?' he said in frustration.

'That lot in there would do anything to upset the rest of the world. The short-arse with the Man United shirt, that's Eric Nellis's son. Don't know his first name, but if he's anything like his dad, he'll have taken the shirt off some other kid and broke both his arms if he'd not been happy about it.'

'Typical Barrovian, then,' said Fletcher getting into the car.

'No. He's real local. Walney Islander. If they had their way they'd blow the bridge up.'

'Well, I'll say one thing for this place,' he said as they crossed the bridge.

She waited.

'Tribal. That's the word I'd use,' he said.

'Bloody right,' she agreed.

She indicated for him to turn right at the roundabout and he drove through a canyon of red brick tenements and grey metal sheds.

'My mum got cancer and died five years ago. My dad lasted about six months. Nothing wrong with him . . . just couldn't . . .' She bit off the final words and turned to face the window.

Fletcher said nothing.

* * * * *

### Wednesday 24th June

Luca stood on the landing stage and studied the view up the lake. It reminded him of a night on Lago d'Iseo. The afternoon heat had made the air heavy; the sky was an inert, solid blue. The storm had come without much warning. It had been the wind which had alerted the waiter. He ran inside and told the *padrone* who came straight out and waved everyone indoors. Some people were already eating. Nevertheless, they were all ushered inside and the plates hurriedly carried in to the main dining room. Extra wine bottles appeared to placate the complainers. Not a moment too soon. The ferocity of the storm swept away the tables and chairs where they'd previously been sitting. The staff fought the terrified shutters, rattling on their hinges to be free until, job accomplished, they stood dripping wet to receive a relieved applause.

He didn't think such storms occurred in England, but the view had a shiny resonance. The mountains were softer and there wasn't a bijou castle on the island in the distance, but he could see why this was one of the most expensive hotels in the area. After the shabbiness of the one near Appleby, he thought he deserved it. Tsura and Marko were in the next room. They'd acquired a horse box for the two ponies they'd bought, although Tsura hadn't paid for the box or the car. The man had loaned them to her for a month in return for an evening he wouldn't forget in a hurry. Apparently he'd admitted to certain sexual preferences. He'd found the right person to administer both the pain and indulge the preferences.

She'd enjoyed sharing the tale with Luca and Marko, knowing it would arouse them both. She'd given them both a taste of what the man had asked for and they were both looking forward to further instalments. Tomorrow they needed to check out the killing ground, but tonight they could relax. He walked back into the hotel and went up to his room. There were a couple of hours before dinner. He listened at the connecting door then knocked softly. Tsura invited him in.

The scene he entered aroused him immediately.

Tsura was sitting facing a large mirror. She was totally naked, one leg crossed over the other. Her brown skin shone with oil. Her eyes were shut, her face immobile. Marko was also naked. He was standing close to her also facing the mirror. He looked at Luca in the reflection. His eyes were glazed with anticipation and amphetamine, his angel body glistening in the muted light. They'd been playing this game for some time. The painted fingernails of Tsura's right hand reached out. As Luca watched, her hand glided up and down, before sliding round to stroke Marko's sculpted hip, her fingers diving deftly into the gap between his thighs. He shuddered. She opened her eyes. A smile spread across her face: a smile of such malevolent dominance that Luca's legs trembled helplessly.

'*Buonasera, dottore.*'

Luca sank into a chair and watched, his hand descending to his own desire.

'*Vuoi guadare o vuoi giocare.*'

He wanted both.

They were late for dinner, the two men drained. But Tsura looked ravishing, her grandmother's heavy silver hoops catching the light.

* * * * *

### Thursday June 25th

The visit to the ice-cream parlour was far better than their first encounter with the Barrow police force. For a start, the room was two storeys higher up, full of seaside light and air. They were offered both a seat and a coffee. Mancini didn't say it was Italian, but they both knew it was. It was strong and slightly harsh. He offered them sugar. Irene had two, but needed three.

Mancini's desk wasn't clear, but it was neat and tidy, as was he. What Fletcher's sister would have called 'dapper': a well-cut suit and expensive shoes, black hair brushed firmly back from his forehead, watchful dark eyes and a thin moustache. Irene found herself fluttering her eyelashes and thought of Alex, which made her choke on her coffee. Mancini was gallant and brought her some water; Fletcher thought 'smooth bastard'.

When Irene recovered and Mancini was back in his seat, Fletcher was impatient to get on. 'We had a brief conversation with Inspector Aston this morning and . . .'

Mancini held up his hand. 'You don't need to tell me. He was rude, unhelpful and unwelcoming.'

Fletcher looked at Irene who was trying to control her grin.

'I'm afraid it passes for a joke here, Inspector. You'll find he's not like that when you get to know him.'

'Really?' said Fletcher.

'You'll find Inspector Coulton's case files on his desk. I've assigned two detective constables to do the legwork. They're waiting downstairs right now. They *will* be very helpful. They're both local, and know the town like the front of their hands.'

Fletcher waited, choosing to ignore the self-deprecating joke. There was more to come. Mancini leant back in his chair and looked from one to the other.

'I've talked to Chief Inspector Aske, Inspector. His word is good enough for me. We've met on a few courses. You will get all the support I can give.'

Fletcher nodded.

Mancini looked at Irene and smiled. 'You're a local girl I understand,' he said.

'Askam, sir,' she replied.

'Friendly with Alex Henning, I hear?'

Her face hardened. 'So? Sir?' she asked.

He smiled again. 'Despite its size Barrow is a small town, Sergeant. Word gets around quicker than the tide turns. As I'm sure you well remember.'

She continued to give him a stern look.

'Unfortunately, your friend hasn't managed to shake off her roots as comprehensively as you. She has acquired some unpleasant friends and we suspect she's involved in a variety of criminal activities . . .'

He'd chosen his words carefully. Irene's lips tightened, but she didn't speak. He waited a few moments.

'I'm sorry. I thought you ought to know.'

She looked at him fiercely. 'Thank you, sir.'

He stood up and accompanied them to the door. Neither of them spoke as they went downstairs. At the bottom Irene grabbed Fletcher's arm.

'I didn't know, honestly, sir,' she hissed.

Fletcher held her hand. 'I know that.'

She looked down at the floor. 'Stupid tart. Wait till I see her. Give her a good slap.'

'Not just yet, Irene. She might have some connections we could use. Let's save her soul later.'

She looked at him in surprise. 'D'you mean that?'

'Well we've not had much help so far, have we, and time's running out.'

He opened the door and walked into the office. The two young constables stood as they came in, looking a bit embarrassed. The desk they were standing next to had balloons tied to it, but it now also boasted a stack of files. The taller of the two constables introduced himself and his companion.

'I'm DC Holmes, sir and this is DC Watson.'

Fletcher looked at them venomously.

'No really, sir. They are our real names, honestly.'

Fletcher looked doubtful, but Irene was creased up with laughter. 'It's right, sir. I was at school with Sherlock. His real name's Ian.'

Holmes grinned at Irene. 'Hi, Irene. Sergeant, eh?'

'Yeh and don't forget it, Constable,' she said in a mock-stern voice.

Fletcher sighed. 'Can we get on, please? I hate reunions and I've had to endure far too many already in the last twelve hours.'

'Yes, sir,' they chorused.

'So what's on the go?' he asked indicating the files.

Watson seized the moment. 'Assault on a teacher by a girl who has subsequently absconded, sir, teacher still on critical list with head injury. We're bringing the father in for questioning. He has form. Local dealer found unconscious with stab wound undergoing surgery as we speak. Usual trouble Thursday through to the weekend outside nightclubs. Plus we're trying to crack down on drink-driving.' He paused and looked at Fletcher, who waited.

The two officers glanced at each other wondering if the rumours were true.

'Is that it?' asked Fletcher.

Again the two officers looked at each other. Holmes glanced at Irene as a puzzled frown began to take shape on his face. 'Yes sir,' he said.

'So what do you know about Alex Henning, Constable?'

Now it was Watson's turn to look puzzled, while Holmes glanced at Irene.

'She's probably on the game, sir. Not on the street. She hangs around with one of the local gangsters.'

'Would that be Mr Nellis, Constable?' asked Fletcher, thumbing through the top file. Again Holmes glanced at Irene. 'Yes, sir. Eric Nellis.'

'So what have we got on him?'

Watson picked out one of the files. 'This is his record, sir.'

Fletcher glanced quickly through it. 'Released three months ago.'

'Yes, sir. Time off for good behaviour I understand.'

'I'll bet,' murmured Fletcher. 'GBH, suspected murder, suspected rape, drugs, sex and rock n' roll.'

'Fraid so, sir.'

'And you've only managed to put him away for two years, less six months, for receiving a stolen television or three.'

'Yes, sir.'

'What about his son?'

'Chip off the old block, sir. Word is he's going to end up worse than his father.'

'So. Not only have you failed to catch them, but you can't stop them breeding either, is that it?'

The two constables shuffled their four large feet.

'We might have something on the young one, sir,' muttered Watson.

Fletcher waited.

'An old lady, sir. A Mrs Jardine, who says she was roughed up by a gang of youths down by the sea shelters. She thinks she recognises one of them, a Steven Hodgkins, known to be an associate of young Nellis, but . . .'

'But what, Constable?'

'I don't think she'll make a good witness, sir. Old lady. Glasses, which were damaged during the attack, sir and I think she'd be too frightened to stand up in court and identify them.'

'Well. It's time we upset the applecart, isn't it. We're not here for long and we've other things to do, haven't we, Sergeant? Let's go and find Nellis Junior, last seen cheating at pool in the King George. Come on.'

The three of them followed him out. This felt like war and he was carrying it to the enemy. The two local officers had heard the stories, but they shared a worried smile.

Fletcher and Irene had completely forgotten that Sadie Swift had said she'd be at the meeting.

\* \* \* \* \*

*Wednesday 24th June. Evening.*

Roger had had a very frustrating and worrying day. He'd not been able to get any answers to his questions. He and Sam had spent the afternoon searching the suite and filling in the inventory. Nothing missing. Nothing additional. Four hours work. And after all that, Miss Ridley had met them at the door to her office, taken their report and said goodnight. No 'thank you'. No 'well done'. Dismissed. Her hair was definitely shorter, thought Roger, as she turned away. And no, he didn't fancy her at all.

He followed Sam downstairs. The big man's shoulders drooped. Sam walked straight out the main door and went to get his car. No goodnight there, either. Roger sighed and got in his own car. He could see Sam's rear lights heading along the road until he turned right along the main road. He lived in Grange.

Roger turned left and drove slowly along towards Barrow. The fog had reappeared a couple of hours ago. He was trying to make sense of the day's events. Suddenly, as he came round a bend, his headlights picked out a figure staggering along beside the road. Quickly, it tried to escape the light by running into the wood, but tumbled blindly into the ditch. As Roger pulled up he could see the struggling body as it tried to extract itself from the briars. He got out of the car and shouted.

'It's OK, I'm coming.'

The figure increased its efforts and Roger saw the terrified face of a young woman. It was the nurse, Miriam.

'Hey, Miriam. It's me. Roger. Just wait. I'll help you.'

It took him a good few minutes to get her out of the ditch, by which time she was covered in dirt and scratches. He helped her into the car. She sat, shivering and sobbing. He couldn't get a word out of her.

'Look. Is there someone or somewhere I can take you to?'

She shivered again. He didn't know what else to do, so he drove home.

By the time he'd got to Barrow she'd quietened down. She started to look out of the window but showed no sign of recognition. He pulled up outside his tenement and turned to look at her. She was peering out at the tall buildings.

'You live here?' she said.

'Yeh. It's OK. Better inside than out. You want to come up? I've got a spare room.'

She gave him a doubtful look.

'Or I can find you a hotel,' he suggested quickly.

She shook her head.

'Or there are a couple of girlfriends I could ring,' he said lamely, knowing he couldn't think of anyone who'd agree to take her.

She waited. He got out of the car. She followed him up the stairs. She sat in his living room and looked at his photos.

'You in army?' she asked.

He nodded. 'You want a cup of tea or something?' he asked.

She shook her head. He felt awkward.

'How about we go for a Chinese?' he said.

She checked he wasn't joking, then nodded. He showed her the bathroom and waited while she washed and cleaned her wounds.

Half an hour later they were in his favourite Chinese restaurant. She had bowed and smiled at the young woman who showed them to their table. It was early. Empty. They ordered. The food came. Miriam ate hers rapidly.

'You've not eaten today?' he asked.

She shook her head, finished his off as well. It was like watching a hungry stray dog.

When they'd finished, Roger wasn't sure what to do. Miriam was watching the older woman who Roger thought might be the owner. Before he could make any suggestions, Miriam made up her own mind. She went over to the counter and spoke to the woman. The conversation was harsh and sounded argumentative to Roger. He began to worry that she was going to cause a scene, but saw the glimmer of a smile on the older woman's face. She looked across at Roger and nodded. They continued their conversation. The older woman shook her head and indicated Roger. Miriam shook her head. Her voice became louder and more animated. The woman left her standing there and went through a door at the back of the restaurant. She was only gone for a few moments. Miriam had looked across at him and given him a funny look. The older woman returned and gave Miriam a small card and an envelope.

The two of them came over to Roger. He stood up, but the older woman motioned for him to sit down. She and Miriam sat opposite. He had no idea what they were going to say.

'Your friend has been badly treated, Mr Skeldon.'

His eyes widened, as much because she knew his name as anything else.

'She has asked me to help her. I have given her a name and address in Manchester. She will go tomorrow. She has no money, so I have given her some. She has asked me to say she is very grateful to you, but cannot repay you for your kindness and hospitality.'

Roger was about to say it didn't matter, but the woman put up her hand.

'She does not want to go to the police, because...' She hesitated, her eyes on Roger. He thought he understood and nodded.

'She says she would be happy to stay with you tonight, but . . .' Again he nodded and looked at Miriam, who was looking down at the table.

'Miriam,' he said. 'I'm very happy for you to stay tonight and I'll get you onto a train tomorrow morning.'

She looked up, her eyes dry but wary. She spoke very quickly to the other woman, who smiled.

'She asked me to tell you that you are a very kind man.'

Roger blushed. He paid for the meals and they went back to his flat. He showed her the spare room and asked if she wanted anything. She came close to him and said: 'You want sleep with me?'

He backed away and blustered. 'No. No. You don't need to do that,' he said.

She hung her head. 'I insult you?' she said.

'No. No . . . but . . . in any case, I know about you and Sam.'

She looked away. 'Better he not know,' she said eventually.

Roger nodded, not sure he could do that. They stood looking at each other. Roger backed away.

'Goodnight Miriam,' he said and walked back into the living room, where he took a deep breath and went to make himself a cup of tea.

He was staring at the kettle when she slipped into the room. He poured the hot water into his cup. She stood in the doorway and began to take off her blouse.

'No. No!' said Roger urgently, but gasped as he saw the bruises on her arms. 'Who did that to you?'

'Nurse Birch and Miss Ridley.'

'What?' he said in disbelief. 'Why?'

'They think I help Mrs Hadden. They think I give her knife.'

Roger looked at her. She shook her head. He waited.

'Mrs Hadden not mad. She prisoner,' she said, giving him a stern look.

He shook his head again. She nodded, her eyes glared.

'But why?'

'I not know, but I work as nurse with mentally ill. She not ill. She given drugs. Bad drugs.'

Roger waited.

'She need help. Mr Hadden very bad man. Nurse Birch and Miss Ridley bad people. He . . .' she hesitated. 'He force her. Fuck her. All bad people.'

She put her blouse back on and sobbed. The next moment she was in his arms. He held her until she stopped shuddering. He couldn't help but think of what Sam would do if he found out what they'd done to her.

She withdrew from his embrace and stepped back. 'Thank you, Roger Skeldon. You good man. One day I repay you.'

Before he could argue, she slipped away. He sat in his armchair for a long time. Eventually he went to bed. He kept seeing the man in a long black coat running towards him.

In the morning she was waiting for him when he got up. He took her to the station and bought her ticket. The last he saw of her was through the window of the train as it pulled out of the station. The last thing she said was to tell him her real name: Mai Zhu.

He was late for work. He spent the drive thinking of what excuse he was going to give and how he might help Mrs Hadden escape. Neither was much help as there was a letter waiting for him at reception. He was no longer required and would he kindly leave any keys with the receptionist. He asked her if he could see Miss Ridley or Mr Hadden only to be told that neither of them was available. Two men in suits exactly like his smiled at him.

He left.

# CHAPTER 5

*Thursday 25th June*

The King George was empty when they got there. Their questions only provoked grunts and whistles as though they were asking the whereabouts of the Great Train robbers.

They'd taken two cars: little pandas to catch hyenas. They found them down by the school. Well, three corners away. Watson had stopped a kid in the street scuttling his way home; Fletcher saw the twenty-something-year-old officer offer the lad a fag. Anyway, the informant was correct, although from his point of view it was no secret.

Nellis was leaning against the red and white car; there was someone in the driving seat, arm dangling a fag, and a much bigger lad leaning against the wall. Five girls, half-dressed in school uniform, half dressed in the sense that some of it wasn't school uniform and most of it was too short: skirts three inches long, blouses tied in a knot halfway up their midriffs, hair uniformly straggly, hanging down over pinched faces with sooty eyes like they were all Culture Club groupies. Fletcher only knew about this from the derisory comments Grace made about them. One of them was leaning next to Nellis, her arm tentatively round his hunched shoulders. He was rolling a ridiculously fat joint. One of the other girls was sitting on the bonnet, skirt even higher, legs crossed.

The two police cars rolled to a stop either side of this idyllic scene. Fletcher drank it in.

Watson got out of the car and waited. Irene stood half out, leaning on the open door, Holmes still with the engine on. If it were a film, it was a spaghetti western, thought Fletcher. He eased his way out, almost checking his holster to see if he'd remembered to strap it on, image of himself leaning down to adjust the string attaching it to his thigh, cheroot sticking out the side of his mouth, not taking his eyes off the man in black, except it was the 'acne kid' in red, who had continued to roll the joint as if it were the most ordinary thing in the world. Now he licked his lips and smeared the gum on the paper. Reaching to his left, he took the dangling ciggie from the driver's hand and began to make exaggerated smoke signals with the wadge of tobacco paper hanging from his puckered mouth.

All the time, Nellis watched Fletcher. Not the others. Two of them he knew. He'd heard about Irene Garner. He'd give her one anytime. But this was the guy in the funny leather coat. Orange? From London? What a twat. An orange leather twat.

'Mr Fletcher. I presume,' he announced in a ridiculous squeaky voice. Fletcher almost laughed out loud.

'Steven Nellis,' responded Fletcher, a twinkle in his eye, but only in his head. In the real world he said nothing. And his eyes didn't twinkle, they glowered. He felt like the movie had just shifted into a Dickens' novel with him as the new headmaster, doomed to failure and disgrace. He shook this off and wandered over. Irene was still leaning against the car, arms folded with a mischievous smile on her lips that she was trying to hide. Watson was a big boot step behind Fletcher. They'd agreed the young detective would do the talking: he spoke the language and he was young enough to have siblings still at the school round the corner.

Watson stood in front of Nellis.

'Is this your car, lad?'

Nellis ignored the plod and his old-fashioned phrase, merely raised his eyebrows at Fletcher. Watson made a show of walking round the battered vehicle. Although it sprouted a drainpipe-size exhaust, it was monogrammed with a history of dents and scrapes, some of which had been repainted, but most left rusting to inform bystanders that one of the car's functions was to be a weapon. He leant down to speak to the arm dangler.

'Can I see your licence, young man?'

Another acned face appeared above the arm: short green Mohican, blue eyes and regulation Stanley knife scar down left cheek.

'Fuck off, you fucking plonker.' Quietly spoken, fleshy lips. Fletcher was reminded of one of his teenage mates. Streatham Locarno? He'd forgotten his name?

Wind whispered from the sea. Ash fell from the end of Nellis's joint.

As it hit the floor, Fletcher reached out and grabbed the driver's wrist and yanked it hard. The door was shut. The rest of his scrawny body couldn't follow. He yelped as his ribs crunched against the internal door handle and the top of his head scraped against the rough metal of the top of the doorframe. With his free hand, Fletcher opened the door and gave the arm another yank. The driver tumbled out onto the road like a rag doll, blood streaming from his scraped head. Tartan skirt! The film set tightened like the air had been sucked out of it.

Gradually, the other characters reacted. The girl with her arm round Nellis recoiled like a retreating python towards the other girls. The girl on the bonnet stood up. Her skirt stayed rucked up, but she didn't pull it down. Watson backed off. Plod. Irene unfolded her arms and zipped up her jacket. Not plod. The figure against the wall had manufactured a baseball bat into his left hand. Holmes watched the whole scene unfold from pause to slow-motion like a fire starting. Fletcher let go of the Mohican's wrist. He staggered to his feet, blood dribbling down his cheek and spreading all over his pink and black t-shirt. His hand unsheathed a cylinder of grey metal, his finger sliding the blade out.

'You fucking twat. You're fucking dead.' He crouched, ready to launch himself at Fletcher, paying no attention to the blood now covering half his face. Watson faltered first, glanced at Fletcher, who was grinning. Holmes was out of the car, radio to his ear, its coiled wire stretching back through the window. Irene waited, her eyes on the baseball bat.

Fletcher looked at Nellis, who raised his eyes to meet the policeman's eyes. One green. One blue. Nellis took a long drag on his joint and blew the smoke in Fletcher's direction. The wind took it away. He closed his eyes. The girls were all edging step by step from the arena.

'Cool it, Indie,' said the squeaky voice, both soft and cold. 'You're the twat. You're the one covered in blood. You only got eight pints. Two of 'em 'ave soaked into yer fucking shirt already. Fuck off and bleed somewhere else.'

The Mohican wiped his hand over his face, covering his arm with blood. One of the girls turned away and threw up.

'I'm gonna 'ave him, Nellis.'

'Naw. You're not. Not yet. Later. Grim, take the daft bastard away.'

Baseball Bat took Mohican's arm and held onto it as it wriggled in his grasp. The knife came up. Another hand knocked it from the bloody fingers. Watson bent and picked it up. Holmes was speaking into the radio.

Nellis strolled over to Fletcher and looked up into his face. 'Is there sommat I can do for you, copper?' he squeaked.

Fletcher grabbed him by his shirt and lifted him off the ground.

'You can get in the police car quietly or I'll stuff you in the boot. Your choice.'

The shirt began to tear. The joint had slipped from Nellis's fingers. He squirmed in Fletcher's grip, tried to kick him with his dangling legs, but Fletcher was holding him too close. The boy's face turned red as he fought for breath. Fletcher dropped him in a heap on the floor. He lay gasping. Fletcher silenced the gasp with a deliberate kick in the ribs. He grabbed him by the back of his now ragged shirt and half dragged, half pushed him into the car. A police siren sounded in the distance. The kids melted away.

A stone bounced off Holmes's car. There was no-one in sight. A few curtains twitched. Faces disappeared behind closing doors. Nellis's red face was squashed up against the window. Two other police cars slewed to a halt and emptied six extra officers onto the street. One of them stared at the pool of blood on the ground and the bloody footprints fading away across the pavement. The remains of the joint smouldered, crushed beyond repair. Another officer bent to pick it up, burned his fingers and cursed. They all looked at Fletcher, sitting like a smug funeral director in the front seat of the car. Irene and Watson got back in their car. The convoy set off back across the bridge.

'Don't ask,' Irene said, as Watson exhaled, as though he'd been holding his breath throughout the entire event. They drove in silence, Watson's head churning with consequences, desperate to tell someone, knowing that he couldn't.

\* \* \* \* \*

### Thursday June 25th

Although Luca had Romany blood in his otherwise refined veins, he had to confess to disliking horses. To be honest, he was frightened of them – and they knew it. It amused Marko and Tsura, who could sleep with horses, eat with them, talk to them and would probably have sex with them if it were feasible. Was it feasible? He shuddered. He'd also seen horses in pain and disliked that even more. He'd been only a few feet from the one which fell during the Palio three years ago. Its screaming had filled his nightmares for months; the frothing mouth and the bulging eyes and the mixture of fear and morbid curiosity on the faces of the crowd, not wanting to look, but unable to get away.

So Eric Nellis's choice of venue was far from appealing, although Luca could see from the other man's point of view that it was a chance to show off his status: somewhere they were unlikely to be interrupted by strangers or other members of the Barrow criminal community.

Luca had borrowed the 4x4 which Tsura had on loan from the man in Appleby, so at least he arrived in an appropriate vehicle. The stud farm was outside Cartmel on a large wooded estate with extensive parkland grazing. The stables were some way from the large manor house standing on the nearby hillside.

Nellis was already there, chatting with the stud owner. A couple of his men stood nearby looking and feeling uncomfortable in their black-and-white shell-suits, worrying that they might have to walk through horse shit in their Nike trainers. Another younger man was leaning against Nellis's dark-green Range Rover. He gave Luca a mean look, but received a dazzling smile in return. Luca might not appreciate the finer points of a horse, but he could recognise a well-hung stallion when he saw one and this one had the semblance of fashion sense: dark-grey Armani suit. The man looked away, but Luca didn't miss the way his hand pushed its way through his thick blond hair.

Introductions over, Luca went for a stroll with Nellis. They stood by a high fence and watched a young woman riding a frisky white horse round the paddock. She was attractive in a horsey sort of way, although Luca could see from the leering mouth that Nellis had a preference for younger women.

'Not a bad looking young filly, eh?' nodded Nellis, predictably.

'Pedigree is all, I understand,' said Luca.

Nellis squinted at his contact to see if the smooth bastard was taking the piss, but he was watching the girl with some interest. Nellis wasn't sure he wanted to get involved with these nutters, but the bait was too attractive to resist. As well as the money, the chance to get one over on Hadden was not to be sneered at. Besides, what could an old gimmer do to him? This one had escaped from a fashion show.

He'd had him watched since he'd arrived at the lakeside hotel. Now he was standing next to him, he was having doubts. And what was that smell? Bloody perfume! The guy was wearing perfume! Bloody poofter. He straightened up and realised the fairy was talking – quiet voice, slight accent – bloody foreigners!

Luca knew he'd been assessed and found wanting. Nevertheless he continued. 'We require some information, Eric.'

Bloody cheek. No-one called him Eric, apart from Doreen,

and then only when she wanted to wind him up. He tuned in again.

'. . . young couple, new to the area, in a house facing the launch site, as near to the bridge as you can get. Also where the woman works, preferably in Barrow.'

What kind of rubbish idea was that? The security would be over the top. Last time they'd yanked up all the manhole covers for Chrissake and put men down them!

'. . . good idea for you to have a bit of a commotion in the nearest pub at the same time.'

'Commotion' in a pub on launch day? Try and stop the buggers. Piece of piss.

'No problem, Mister Luca,' Nellis said. 'Anything else?'

'No,' said Luca, but put his hand on the arm on Nellis's new tweed jacket. Nellis looked at the hand. It was manicured. Nail varnish. The hand rested gently. Didn't move.

'But may I remind you who we're working for. They don't like their little secrets to get out. Tend to get rather tetchy. Knees and ankles. None of us are a lot of use without them, eh?'

Nellis wanted to show he understood, but also that he wasn't scared of bloody daft Paddies.

'I'm sure they've asked us because they know we're good at our jobs, Mr Luca. No worries on our part.' Bloody patronising poofter.

Luca nodded and offered his hand. Nellis hesitated for a millisecond, but then forced himself to take it. Soft, but firm. Twat.

'Oh,' Luca paused and looked at the blond man. 'One other thing: there's no need to follow me about, Eric. As you say, we must be good at our jobs. I'm afraid some of your team are in need of some extra training, which I think you'll find has recently been provided. No charge, Eric. I'll be in touch.'

Luca turned and walked towards his car, conscious that two pairs of eyes followed him. He coughed up his disgust as he drove towards the main road. Doing business with scum like Nellis was the worst part of what he did, but it would have its compensations. He smiled at one of the more likely outcomes. He watched Marko pull out and follow him. He'd tell him about the young man. Later. He wasn't averse to sharing.

He passed the shattered remains of a Range Rover welded head first into a telegraph pole. One man was struggling to release himself from the ropes tying him to a nearby tree, whilst another seemed to have given up trying to prise himself from the window frame tightly shut round his chest. Both men's shell-suit trousers fluttered around their ankles. Pink bottoms in the afternoon. Tsura's idea. No doubt.

Even as the Land Rover disappeared from sight, the phone in Eric Nellis's car rang. He took it from the driver's hand. He listened.

'What?'

He held the phone away from his ear. A tinny voice was yelling at him.

'I'm on my way, Doreen.'

He handed the phone back. 'Bloody hell, got her knickers in a twist. Bloody little shit got himself arrested.'

The four men got in the car and set off in a cloud of dust. Bloody horseshit. They didn't pass the pink bottoms. That was for later.

\* \* \* \* \*

Eric Nellis had a bad reputation, in Barrow at least, but Doreen Featherstone had earned hers in Glasgow. So she'd no time for Sassenach polis throwing their weight about, especially if it was family. Alright her son was an evil little bugger, but he was her flesh and blood.

She'd arrived at the police station about an hour after him and had caused such a commotion in the outer office that she was shown into an interview room. That didn't work. She'd upended the table and thrown the chairs at the windows, making a nice new carpet of broken glass. Sergeant Barlow had been sent for. Apart from anything else, he was big and loud. He and Doreen had a shouting match. He wasn't winning, but she was getting hoarse. Fifty a day wasn't good for sustaining a long shout.

Suddenly she stopped in mid-yell. There in the doorway stood a plain clothes policeman she didn't know. But it wasn't his lack of identity which stopped her; it was the red shirt hanging in tatters from his left hand that took her breath away. Fletcher took the opportunity to say a few words.

'If you don't shut up, madam, and calm down I'm going to have you forcibly removed to a cell and strip-searched to make sure you're not carrying any dangerous weapons.'

She gasped. Burst out laughing. 'You widna dare!' she bellowed.

Fletcher sighed. Six officers came into the room, two women and four men. They walked towards her. She backed against the wall.

'I'll have your balls for this, you wee Sassenach bastard!'

'I can add verbal abuse to the charges of assaulting police officers, wrecking a police station, resisting arrest, if you want?' said Fletcher.

She cackled. 'You widna unnerstand it, yer shitebag!'

'Take her down,' he said.

She put up her hands. 'OK! You fucking wee cowardy bastards. We'll wait till the fucking solicitor arrives.'

Fletcher came through the crowd and went up close. 'You might frighten the local scum, Doreen, but I think you can tell I'm not from hereabouts and I don't play by anyone's house rules. So we'll see about your fucking solicitor, if and when he arrives. Until then you'll behave or I'll rip the bloody clothes off your fat tits myself.'

By the time he finished, his face was inches from hers. She'd nowhere to go. No-one had spoken to her like that since she was a kid. No-one had ever mentioned her tits. He waited till her eyes showed the first hint of uncertainty, then grinned in her face. She was minded to spit at him, but instinct told her to bide her time. He wouldn't always be surrounded by his mates. He'd have a little wifey somewhere. She would get her revenge in good time. She glared at him and cleared her throat.

Fletcher left the room. The tension subsided like water draining from a sink. Everyone but the two women officers also left. They stood near the door and watched her. She spat on the floor, picked up a chair and sat down.

Fletcher walked back along the corridor and up the stairs. At the top stood Sadie Swift. In this seedy environment she looked like she'd come from outer space. The black hair like a metal helmet, shiny grey suit, white blouse, grey shoes, grey leather gloves, pale blue eyes drilling into him. He indicated the way. She followed without a word.

He took her to the office Mancini had provided. Irene was sitting on the edge of the desk looking out of the window. She looked up as the two others came in.

Sadie looked at her. 'Go away, Sergeant,' she hissed.

Irene looked at Fletcher. He nodded his head in the direction of the door. Irene thought of flouncing, but the other woman's eyes told her it would be a waste of time. She went without a word.

'What the fuck are you doing?'

'What I always do.'

'Mancini's steaming.'

Fletcher smiled; thought of a vicious racist comment; deleted it.

'You'll have to let them go.'

'In time, yeh.'

'You've nothing.'

'Resisting arrest, carrying weapons with intent, possession, a string of vehicle infringements, causing an affray, trashing a police cell, abusive language . . .'

'And any half-decent solicitor will rip it all to shreds. Assaulting his clients, violent conduct, lack of evidence, an army of witnesses prepared to send you to the high court . . .'

Fletcher slammed his hands down on the table. 'Look Sadie Special! You know how I operate. So does Adversane. That's why I'm here. To do the dirty work you lot don't want to be seen doing. Fucking witnesses! Who are you kidding? The only person who matters here hasn't even arrived yet. It's Eric Nellis I'm after. Who else is going to know what's going on? The men in green aren't going to come skipping along to the launch ceremony with a fiddle and drum, are they? Not after what's happened in the last few years. Your lot are all over them. That's why they're using someone else. But strangers can't come here – some east European gangsters. They don't even speak English in "Barra" and they'd smell an outsider from a thousand yards. So. Applecart all over road; Mr Nellis on his way in to rescue his wayward brood. Not in a good mood. Not thinking straight. Chink in the armour. Knife through the curtain. Bloody hell, Sadie, did you learn nothing from me?'

She stared at him, her eyes shimmering with anger. The air zinged with electricity. She walked to the other side of the table. He watched as she stroked the sleekness of her hair and cupped it carefully at the nape of her neck.

'Alright, I'll buy you two hours from when he gets here.' She went to the door. 'I'd rather you didn't yell at me like that. It makes me inclined to break your neck.'

She was gone. He sighed in exasperation. What was he like? Why must he always do this? He heard the door open. Irene sidled into the room.

'That told her, eh.'

He swung round at her. She backed away from the seething anger in his face.

'Sorry, sir. Out of order,' she offered.

He deflated, sat down. 'We've got two hours with Eric Nellis. Otherwise we're going to be eating a submarine full of humble pie. Have you seen Mancini?'

'Heard him. Speaking in tongues. Angry doesn't get anywhere near.'

'Where is he?'

'Is that . . . a good . . . I'll go and see . . . if you . . .'

She followed him out of the room. Assistant or carer? She wasn't sure.

They walked down the corridor. People stepped aside, flattened themselves against walls. They stood outside the door.

Fletcher knocked and went in. Shut the door behind him. Irene stood guard. The corridor emptied

He reappeared two minutes later, shut the door quietly behind him, leaned against the opposite wall and looked at the ceiling. She waited. He let out his breath and looked at her. A smile spread across his crumpled face. He motioned to her to lead on.

Down in the canteen he gulped at a coffee, asked for another. 'And a bacon sandwich. And some cake.'

Feast assembled, he attacked, stuffing food in, batting away memories of his sister's admonitions. Irene watched and waited.

'Don't ask,' he said through a mouthful of food. 'But don't expect an invite for two, palazzo in Naples, when this is all over. Or ever.'

She allowed a smile to creep onto her face. 'I'm not that keen on ice-cream anyway.'

'And I shouldn't bother applying for promotion here.'

'Never on my list. I'm only here because you dragged me kicking and screaming . . . sir.'

He burped loudly. 'Is his nibs here?'

'Don't know; too busy keeping up with you, sir.'

'Well go and find out, Sergeant. The only thing I'm going to attack in here is another bacon sandwich.'

Irene left as he approached the counter. The woman switched the cooker back on and reached into the fridge. She couldn't keep the smile off her face.

DI Sadie Swift, on the other hand, was beyond angry – mainly with herself. OK, the accident on the A590 didn't help. Some idiot running across one of the few fast bits, overtaking car braked hard, swinging into oncoming traffic. Carnage. No alternative routes for non-locals. Eventually she tailed a likely looking company car, followed him on a switchback until she had to use the blue flasher. He was a Vickers' engineer relieved he wasn't being done for speeding again, who enjoyed every second of the legitimised high-speed chase through the back lanes, which Sadie knew even she wouldn't remember, although she wouldn't forget flashing through a five house hamlet proud to declare itself Paradise. If that meant grey fog folding green hillsides, a lot of God-fearing folk were going to be seriously disappointed.

Arriving flustered and embarrassed to meet a volcanic Chief Inspector Mancini — all trace of Italian charm evaporated in a cloud of Neapolitan steam. Having to listen to the ritualistic list of convention and legal flouting considered by Fletcher and his Valkyrie to be proper police procedure. Having to ring Adversane and persuade him to speak to the Italian job. None of this is how she had wanted her first solo op to go. Damn you Fletcher! Fuck you, Adversane! Go to hell, Chief Inspector Man-fucking-cini! Men! All of you!

She'd taken herself off to a local gym and done forty lengths before the adrenaline started to dissipate. Ten minutes whipping the arse of some half-baked Karate fifth Dan — who was he kidding? — before she got some self-esteem pumping back through her chest. Him backing off, grinning with undisguised fear as he tried to roll blows which were hurting, and turning nowhere jabs into feints.

OK. Back to the station. To find Nellis had been and gone. Fletcher had spent just ten minutes interviewing him before escorting him off the premises with the rest of his family. Mancini gave a growl of impotent disbelief.

'After all that! Ten minutes! Not even ten minutes,' he told her. His suit was crumpled, his hair was a mess, face blotchy and hands shaking.

'So what did the inspector tell you he'd achieved?' she asked as calm as she could.

'You'll have to ask him yourself,' he bristled. 'Didn't deign to report to me. The man makes me look a complete fool. The officers I assigned to help him are either enthralled or terrified – probably both. They've gone. I think they're following up another lead . . . schoolgirl on the run. I can't see how that's connected, but then . . .'

She genuinely sympathised with the man. She'd had her share of running with the wild dog which seemed to inhabit Fletcher's otherwise charming persona.

'What can I say, Chief Inspector? The thing is, he gets results. I can't approve of his methods either, but the schedule is tight and the stakes are high. I'm afraid the rollercoaster is running and we're all in the mix. I dare say we'll be spat out at some point when it's all over. All we can do is hope we're not holding the tickets when the debts are added up.'

Mancini gave her a glum look and shook his head. 'It was going so well for me here.'

'Believe me. I know exactly how you feel.'

She stood up and went to the door. 'Can you tell me where I'm likely to find him, sir?'

Mancini gazed at the wall.

'Sir?' she repeated softly.

'Ask the communications room. He's out with a PC called Holmes.'

She couldn't prevent her eyebrow rising.

He nodded. 'I know. Before today it just seemed like a slightly lame joke. Now it's pure Commedia without a script.'

She wasn't sure of the exact reference, but knew well enough the part Fletcher was playing – always played. But she'd no intention of being his Judy. She set off downstairs.

Armed with the girl's mother's address and some directions from a young woman police officer she set off in pursuit, although horses and closed barn doors came to mind. And she'd not even managed to tell him the scraps of information she'd been provided by Adversane. In any case, he'd sussed one lead for himself.

* * * * *

### Thursday 25th June

The girl was in the fog. The bag was in her hand. She made her way cautiously to the hiding place. She knew it was about a hundred yards into the wood. Fortunately there were guide posts along the way. Up the track. Through the gate – turn right. Stay on the forest track. Hundred yards on the left. It was her favourite distance. One of the few things she excelled at. She'd won every year since she arrived at secondary school. Junior champion for three years. Senior champion last year. No chance of her losing it – except she wouldn't be there.

She stopped. Probably twenty yards gone – just getting into her stride. It was the first time she'd thought of what she was going to miss. She carried on. Shut that voice up. She reached the building. It loomed up on her right. In clear light she knew she'd have seen it earlier. White stone ghosting into view. Three high walls. No roof. The front wall collapsed in on itself, filling the inside with a humpy mass of rubble. Wooden beams from the roof sticking up like dislocated arms and legs.

She scrambled over to the far back right corner. The cellar entrance remained hidden under a sheet of corrugated iron roofing. Impossible to move quietly. She stood and listened. Nothing. Not even the estuary, although she knew it was only a hundred yards below her. She pulled the sheet of iron to one side, the metal scraping on stone. Beneath was the dark hole, steps descending towards a small doorway.

What was that?

Nothing.

She went down a step at a time. They were wet and uneven, but she knew the cellar would be dry. Some freak of geology she didn't understand or even consider. It was as it always was.

Her father had shown her years ago. He'd taken her there one night in the dark, frightened her to death. Told her ghost stories – watched her tremble as he descended. But he'd had a torch and shone it under his chin as she followed him down. She'd gulped her scream. He'd laughed. A pantomime laugh.

She didn't have a torch and she wasn't frightened.

Not frightened.

She pushed at the door. It swung open on its well hung hinges. Don't make things like this any more. People not interested in craftsmanship nowadays.

Shut up, Dad.

She stepped into the cool dark space. Felt her way towards the table on the right; put the bag underneath – plastic – wouldn't let the damp in. She gave it a soft pat. You'll be alright here, little bag.

Silly.

She turned, left hand against the wall. Faint outline of the doorway . . . three strides . . . four steps.

As she reached the top, she saw the trees. The fog was lifting. She'd be gone within the hour. She put the cover back and scrambled over the rubble.

What was that? Shadow in the mist? A deer?

She listened. She knew they could move without a sound.

Nothing.

Back on the track.

She reversed the route to the gate. Turned and looked.

Something there.

Following her. No! Can't be.

A deer . . .

She hurried down the track. The hut came out of the fog. She could see the rock beyond. Hear the slurping of the retreating water gurgling its way down the channels.

She reached the door, looked back. Was that a shape? Quick! Inside! She felt the knife in her jacket.

Shut the door!

But she knew.

Someone was there. Moving fast. Too fast. A big shape. Getting bigger, darker. Big cloak. Hair. Face. Man!

An arm flung out. Pushed her through the doorway. Followed by the rest of him.

Pushed her to the ground. A scream died in her throat — came out as a gasp. Stopped by a rough heavy hand. Face up close. Stinking breath. Big eyes. What big eyes you've got, Grandad! Knife in hand. Got it out. Another hand grabbed her wrist. Twisted. Pain. Knife clattered on the floor. His weight on her.

Pantomime laugh?

Dad?

Black.

Nothing.

# CHAPTER 6

***Thursday 25th June***

Fletcher and Garner had moved fast. Corners were scraped, but they were getting answers. They were helped by a laconic detective sergeant called Eddie Sykes, who was Fletcher's favourite type of copper: knew everyone and where to find them, said little, not full of bright ideas, but dogged. He was from Barrow Island – which Fletcher couldn't understand as it looked very much part of the mainland – but with a dry sense of humour once you cottoned on.

The session with Eric Nellis had served its purpose. Fletcher had let him rant on until he ran out of breath. He sat at the interview table with his arms folded, while Irene was leaning against the wall filing her nails, until it eventually dawned on him that his ranting was falling on deaf ears. He approached the table and, leaning on it with both hands, yelled at Fletcher. 'Are you listening to me?'

Fletcher shook his head. 'Were you listening, Sergeant?'

'Nah,' she said, blowing a huge bubble and swallowing it back into her mouth.

Nellis looked from one to the other in disbelief.

Fletcher leaned forward. 'If you would like to take a seat, Mr Nellis,' he said.

Nellis huffed and puffed, but eventually snatched at the chair, sat down and folded his arms.

'We're glad you came in. We wanted to give you some advice.'

'Advice?' he sneered, but his eyes went small and beady.

'Um,' said Fletcher.

'What makes you think you can give me any advice, copper?'

'Well. For a start, you need to get a grip on that son of yours or else your little empire will disappear in the wink of an eye. He's ruffling some very big feathers.'

Nellis laughed. 'Bollocks. What d'you mean, empire?'

'Secondly, your wife . . . well . . . I can understand why you'd prefer a younger model.'

Nellis was back on his feet, leaning across the table his face bulging with blood and fury. 'You cheeky Cockney bastard! Try saying that outside these four walls!'

Fletcher smiled at him. 'If you're going to hit me Mr Nellis, you'd better make sure it's fatal.'

Nellis laughed and with one final sneer set off towards the door. Irene barred his way.

'The last villain she didn't like ended up with two broken arms,' Fletcher said.

Nellis looked at the slim figure standing in front of him. 'Why? Was he a cripple?'

'No, but you will be if you're not careful. You're playing with the really bad lads from across the water, aren't you Eric? I should be very, very careful, if I was you.'

Nellis turned to look at Fletcher, the smirk fading for a few seconds. He walked back across the room. 'No. It's you who ought to be careful, copper. This is Barrow. My patch. You'd better watch your back or fuck off back to where you came from.'

They stood face to face. Neither flinched. Nellis turned to find the door was open. Irene had moved to one side. He walked.

As he reached the door, Fletcher called after him. 'We're going to need to question your son again regarding the recent stabbing of a drug dealer near one of your clubs, Mr Nellis.'

Nellis stopped, gave him shrewd look and shook his head. He was gone.

Before Irene could say a word, Fletcher had hustled her out of the building and found DC Holmes getting out of a car. Seconds later they were heading across town.

'Where are we going, sir?'

'First decent pub we come to.'

Holmes looked at Irene sitting next to him. She was looking straight ahead. 'The Roxy?' he said. She nodded.

'I hope that's not a bloody cinema,' said Fletcher.

'No, sir. Roxburghe Arms. Jennings house, sir.'

Fletcher grunted.

It was after the first pint that Fletcher described the person he needed. Holmes called the station. DS Sykes was there in twenty minutes.

'So, Sergeant. What do you know about the stabbing?'

'Not a lot. My money's on one of Nellis's men, but that's the obvious choice. An outside bet might be one of the young lad's gang. A nasty piece of work called Ian Dyer, known as Indie, green Mohican haircut. I believe you've met, sir.'

Fletcher nodded at the memory. Ugly.

'Do we know why?'

'Working for a rival dealer, I should think. We've seen some higher grade stuff about during the last few weeks. The chief inspector is pretty certain it's Manchester villains wanting to get a foothold.

Nellis would have to respond.'

'Why here?' asked Fletcher, looking at Irene.

Sykes took a drink from his orange juice. 'First off, don't get the wrong idea about this place. Barrow is my town. Most of the people who live here are law-abiding, friendly and loyal. Strong family relationships and, above all, proud. They may slag each other off from one minute to the next, but don't be fooled. You say a word against them or this town, they'll put you straight and you'll make a lot of enemies very fast.'

Fletcher looked him in the eye and smiled. 'Message received, Sergeant. Not to worry, I'm used to being unpopular.'

Sykes looked at the other three, who were trying hard not to grin: 'That's told him' they were thinking.

'So. Why here?' Fletcher repeated in a quieter, but more determined voice.

Sykes leaned forward and spoke quietly too. 'Two things. One: an easy market. There are some parts of Barrow off limits for most people at night. As I said, strong family ties. Don't like the police. Lots of gangs. The drug scene is just taking off. Secondly, the trains come straight from Piccadilly. There's three or four local stations the stuff can change hands at, plus the motorway . . . difficult to catch them at it.'

Fletcher was silent for a moment. 'What else?'

'I think there might be a connection between the girl who's on the run after hitting the teacher and young Nellis's gang. The teacher's recovering: turns out to be only concussion. Probably be out tomorrow. When I spoke to her, she told me that the girl's boyfriend had said she was seeing someone in the Nellis gang.'

'As in "seeing someone"?' asked Irene.

'I think that's what the lad meant.'

Sykes hesitated.

'Spit it out, sergeant. We don't have for ever,' said Fletcher softly.

'Well, sir. This may just be a coincidence but the girl – she's called Cora Beck – her father used to work for Nellis.'

'Doing what?'

'He was running the bar in one of his clubs. A members' only den called The Sub.'

'Imaginative,' said Fletcher.

'Anyway, the rumour is that they fell out. Beck did a runner. He's not been seen since.'

'Was this before Nellis got put away?'

Sykes nodded, looked across at Holmes.

'Come on. No secrets, eh,' said Fletcher, sniffing the air like a dog.

The two officers looked at their hands. Holmes let out a sigh. Sykes shook his head.

Fletcher glared at them.

'You didn't get it from me, sir.'

'What?' demanded Fletcher.

'I'm not sure, but I think Beck might have tipped someone off about the TV scam, which got Nellis put away.'

Fletcher looked from one to the other. 'DI Aston?'

They both looked away.

'So where do you think this Beck character's gone.'

They both shook their heads.

'So who would know?'

Sykes looked doubtful.

'His wife?' said Holmes.

Fletcher looked at Sykes, who was shaking his head.

'Left her some time ago.'

'So who?'

Silence.

'Alex will know,' whispered Irene.

They all looked at her.

* * * * *

Roger Skeldon hadn't been idle either. He'd left a brief message on the number Marcus Pole had told him to use. He'd not heard anything so far. But he'd already made a plan himself.

He'd found Charlie Conroy on the golf course. Or rather he'd had to wait an hour in the bar until he'd finished. Roger didn't understand the attraction of golf but knew that Charlie regarded it as a great place to do business and make lots of connections. Especially as a lot of his clients were the sort of husbands and wives who played away and wanted to know who was playing with whom; in short a lucrative talk-shop which played nicely into Charlie's pocket.

After his client had disappeared, Charlie came across to where Roger was sitting and plonked himself down. A young girl arrived with whisky and a jug of water. Charlie watched her wiggle back to the bar, before turning his attention to the much less enticing friend sitting patiently looking out at the sea.

'So what's the crack, Skelly?' he began.

Roger told him. At first Charlie was less than interested, but the mention of Thomas Hadden's name brought him to the edge of his seat. He looked round, checking the nearby members: deaf, asleep, laughing – safe.

'Do you mean the guy who owns the electronics company? Has a big house other side of the estuary?'

'That's what I was telling you,' replied Roger.

'Sorry. Go on. I'm all ears.'

Roger knew Charlie thought he was a bit slow, but he carried on.

Ten minutes later, Charlie took a big gulp of whisky, leaned back in his chair and closed his eyes. Roger looked around the bar. Most people had gone, apart from a couple of Pringles at the bar. Pink and yellow? What was that about?

'So,' said Charlie, opening his eyes. 'Let me get this straight.'

Roger leant forward.

'You want to mount an operation in which the two of us . . .'

'Three,' said Roger. 'There's Sam as well.'

Charlie looked doubtful. 'OK, the three of us are going to bust this man's wife out of his own house, from the second floor . . .'

Roger nodded.

' . . . from the second floor of a modern house with state-of-the-art security owned by a guy whose firm makes electronic systems for nuclear submarines and take this wife to a reputable mental institution and have her checked out?'

Roger nodded, fearing the worst.

Charlie closed his eyes again. He began to laugh. 'You're mad. Absolutely barking, Skelly. You've no chance.'

Roger waited. He'd thought long and hard about this. He couldn't do it on his own but he wasn't going to tell Charlie about Pole. But this is what they'd trained for. Undercover ops. Go in hard and fast. Seize the suspect. Out and away. They'd done it loads of times. Nobody got hurt. Well – apart from the bad guys.

'Listen Charlie. We can do this. Sam has still got his keys. He knows the systems. We know the guards' routines. There's no dogs, only electronics. We can turn them off. They won't be expecting us. He's an arrogant bastard. No way will he think this is going to happen.'

Charlie looked at him and shook his head. 'What if you're wrong? What if she is ill? What then?'

'I've seen her, Charlie. She's drugged. And I believe Miriam. Why would she lie?'

Charlie rubbed his chin. 'So what do we get out of it? Where's the profit?'

Roger leaned forward and put his hand on Charlie's shoulder. 'When did we ever do it for profit, Charlie?'

'Yeh. But we were soldiers. It was our job. We got paid.'

'Is that all you remember? Getting paid? Shit! We'd drunk or fucked most of it away the first two nights on leave.'

Charlie's eyes shone at the memory of it.

'We didn't do it for the money – or to please the fucking brass. We did it for the buzz, Charlie. You more than anyone taught me that.'

Charlie got up and walked to the big window looking out towards the setting sun. Roger held his breath. A foursome of Pringles came laughing into the bar. More pink and yellow. He looked back at Charlie, who turned at the sound. One of the Pringles waved at him. He waved back. He looked at Roger.

'OK, Roger. I'm in. But I need to meet this other guy, Sam.'

'No problem. Later tonight. The Swan in Ulverston.'

'You've got it all worked out haven't you, Skelly?'

'Just like we used to do it.'

The man who'd waved at Charlie was on his way over. Roger looked Charlie in the eyes. 'Thanks,' he said and sidled away.

In the car he was nearly sick with fear and excitement. He hadn't realised how much he'd missed it. He thought of the woman. Her startling eyes. They were going to do it.

He drove off into the night, the last rays of the sun flashing green on the horizon. A sign? Go!

**\* \* \* \* \***

*Thursday 25th June. Evening.*

Alex was easy to find. Early evening on a Thursday, Irene knew exactly where she'd be. She waited outside the hairdresser's for only five minutes until Alex hit the street. Hair, make-up, new dress, new shoes – next stop the new wine bar across the road. She didn't even see Irene as she tottered between the rush hour cars and bikes. Irene followed her, checked out the opposition and pushed open the heavy glass door. Alex had disappeared. Irene made straight to the loo and found Alex preening herself in the big mirror.

'You look gorgeous. I'd fuck you myself, but I'm not rough enough for you any more,' she said, standing behind her.

Alex froze for a second or two before she smirked and looked in the mirror at the friend who'd turned into a cop.

'You can fuck me anytime, Irene. Especially if you put your uniform on and bring your truncheon.'

They both laughed. In the old days they'd have hugged and kissed, but not now.

Alex continued to fiddle with her hair. Irene stood beside her and found her own hairbrush.

They were quiet for a moment. Another woman came in, used the loo and slid back out. Irene put the handle of her brush under the door. Alex watched. Her face was well made up, but it couldn't disguise the fear.

Irene leant against the door, arms folded.

'Do you remember when the two of us got that lad – what was his name – Danny Hargreaves? We took him upstairs at your house and got his cock out. Poor lamb. How old were we then? Thirteen? Fourteen?'

Alex wasn't stupid. She knew this was only foreplay. She took her new lipstick out of her bag and put it to her lips.

'But the best bit was when he'd gone. Do you remember?'

Alex put the lipstick away and turned to face her. 'What do you want, Irene?'

Irene took a step towards her and with a careful finger tip wiped the excess lipstick off Alex's cheek.

'Well. For now, only an address.'

Alex waited, dreading any number of possibilities.

'Jimmy Beck.'

Alex nearly smiled. The relief flooded her body. 'I haven't a clue.' She went to go past Irene, who didn't move.

Irene's face hardened. She took hold of Alex's arm and pushed back her sleeve to reveal the marks. She pulled Alex towards her. Faces close together. She could smell the same perfume Alex had always worn, since she was sixteen, for God's sake. Their eyes met. Alex was defiant.

'But you could ask Julie Carter,' she whispered as the hand twisted her wrist.

Irene let her arm hang loose, reached up to finger a stray lacquered hair back into place. 'Like I said. You look gorgeous and now I know how to fuck you real good. But I'll wait till you've got yourself out of this mess. You need to get away, Alex . Before it's too late.'

Their eyes met again – the same defiance from Alex. She pushed past Irene and kicked away the hairbrush. Irene let her go.

Out in the bar, Alex was standing facing a young man with thick blond hair. He had his back to the loo. Irene walked straight out the door into the bright town centre lights without a second glance.

She found Fletcher and Sykes in the car park. 'Julie Carter. Could be anywhere at this time of night, but later I think I've got a good idea where she might turn up. Time for a couple of drinks, if you two gentlemen would like to join me.'

Sykes looked at Fletcher who shrugged his shoulders.

'She's the boss, Eddie. Do as you're told.'

\* \* \* \* \*

'Who was that?'

Alex looked away.

The man's hand rested lightly on her shoulder. She turned and reached out for her drink. She looked him straight in the eye. 'An old friend. We were at school together. She's just back in town.'

'Good looking woman,' he said with a smile.

Alex sighed. 'Not your type,' she said.

He raised his eyebrows.

'More "arresting" than attractive actually and she's got a foul mouth on her.'

He looked out through the window. 'Ah, I see,' he said.

Later in his hotel room. It wasn't the first time. No need for excess. Despite their very different lives and the huge risks they were taking, they'd been attracted from the start.

Alex wasn't accustomed to such gentleness. She was more used to the back alley or back of the car encounter. He did things she'd only read about. But she knew it wasn't love. More like two wounded animals finding affection to escape their troubled lives.

She'd told him far more about her descent into the inescapable hell she currently inhabited than he'd given away, but she knew from the few things he'd said that he was locked in a similar prison of his own making.

The one thing they were agreed on was that their two very different relationships with Eric Nellis were the worst that had happened to them, although she knew his was for more deliberate reasons than hers.

As she lay in his arms, she could hear him thinking, could feel the tension in his body which normally drained away as they made love. She waited.

She was aware of his other hand performing the habitual pushing back of his hair from his forehead.

'Your friend?'

'Irene?'

'Not in the local police force?'

'No. Some kind of transfer. She's with an inspector called Fletcher. She wouldn't talk about it.'

'And this evening in the loo?'

Alex considered her options. Julie Carter was no friend of hers, but . . .

'Why do you want to know?'

'Just curious.'

'She was asking if I knew Julie Carter.'

'And you told her?'

'It's hardly a secret.'

There was a long pause. She'd no idea what he was thinking.

He untangled himself and reached for his cigarettes, lit one and offered it to her. When she passed it back, he got up and walked to the window. The room was in darkness, but through the gap in the curtains the fading light lit up one side of his lean face and body.

Alex watched him. Her insides told her it was lust, but her head wanted something else, something more sustaining.

When he spoke she listened. 'I had a brother once. He's dead now.'

She waited.

'He was an arrogant bully. No-one deserved to die more than him. But only I know what he was really like. Everyone else thinks he was a hero. Gave his life for Queen and country. Killed in an ambush in Northern Ireland. They gave our mother the medals. No-one loved him more than her and no-one is as blind to the truth about him.'

Alex couldn't think of anything to say. She wanted to hold him in her arms, but was afraid to interrupt the flow of words. She waited.

He turned towards her. His face in the shadow, silhouetted against the orange streetlight. 'He was called Richard. After Richard the Lionheart.'

She nodded, thinking of Robin Hood and all that stuff her brother liked reading when he was a kid.

He turned back to the window. 'And like him, he was a sadistic, homosexual, vicious bastard.'

She stared at him. He didn't move. Just stood there, his hand holding the cigarette dangling by his leg, the ash slowly fluttering onto the carpet.

There were no more words.

Eventually he came back to bed and they lay in the darkness. When Alex came awake he'd gone. She cried.

* * * * *

## Thursday 25th June Late evening

Charlie was late.

Sam was looking dejected; he'd only drunk half of his pint. It was going flat. Few words had passed between them. Roger looked at his watch for the fourth time.

The door opened and Charlie looked round the gloomy bar. No-one paid much attention, even though he was wearing a suit none of them would have allowed their wives to buy them, never mind actually wear.

'Bloody hell, Skelly,' he muttered as he sat down. 'Worse than a Turkish bar without the sound effects.'

Roger got him a drink and they huddled round the table in the side room.

Introductions over, Roger outlined the plan. Sam would arrive for his usual shift tomorrow night; Charlie and Roger would leave their car down the drive and arrive on foot. Sam would disengage the alarm systems and stay downstairs while the other two went up to the second floor. The next bit was the main problem. Roger and Sam were sure no-one would open the door or provide a key, but it was still the quickest way in and out. Charlie had talked to an old contact who would provide them with the semtex and the detonator. He'd also already got a supply of weapons from previous escapades. Roger and Sam weren't too happy with the idea, but as Charlie explained: 'We won't have to shoot anyone, will we? A quick round or two in the ceiling will be enough to terrify anyone. People aren't used to it. They'll either faint or hit the deck or freeze. Whatever, I'll cover you while you get the woman, Skelly. Down the stairs and out.'

He didn't mention what he and Roger had agreed: that they would demobilise any attempt to pursue them by putting a screwdriver through the tyres of the cars outside. Sam's car would be their first getaway vehicle. They'd swop cars further down the drive. Straight to Lancaster General; Roger to stay with the woman until the police arrived, the other two to disappear. Charlie had a safe house in Preston that he'd had to use a few times when keeping out of the way of angry husbands.

'I don't like guns,' mumbled Sam.

'It's OK, Sam. We've slept with the buggers. Take 'em apart, put 'em back together in our sleep or dead drunk. Just like another arm, mate,' laughed Charlie.

Sam looked from one to the other. 'No shooting anyone? OK?'

'No body count,' said Charlie, hands in the air.

Roger nodded. Part of him was remembering the time Charlie completely lost it and sprayed an entire room full of people: blokes playing cards and drinking coffee – except one of them drew a gun. Well, it turned out to be a wallet. Huge cover-up required; Charlie back to Germany next day. Straight into the cooler was the story. They didn't see him again for months until he turned up one day when they'd come back from a tour, sitting there as though nothing had ever happened. They'd never talked about it, but he needed to talk about it before they went out tomorrow.

He waited till Sam left. They'd shaken hands. Sam had given him a sad look. 'I hope we're doing the right thing, Roger.'

Charlie insisted on going to another pub as soon as the big guy had left. 'You could get terminal depression sitting in there, Skelly. Jesus!'

They walked into town. Charlie chose the pub with most lights on. A rock band had just finished their first set. The place was heaving.

'This is more like it, eh, Skelly?' Charlie looked round. 'Plenty of totty as well.'

Roger sighed. He'd forgotten what Charlie was like the night before an operation. The adrenaline rush started early and went on, generally fuelled by considerable amounts of alcohol and sex. He started having a bad feeling about the whole thing, but before he could say anything Charlie was pushing his way through the crowd.

The rest was predictable. Two or three different women chatted up. An argument with a younger man. Out the back. Charlie coming back in with a huge grin on his face. The other man didn't reappear. A blonde woman with her arm around his neck. A wave goodbye. He'd gone.

Roger stared into his empty glass. The band had finished and started packing away. People were saying goodnight and leaving. He zipped up his jacket and headed for the loo. It was down some steps and through another smaller room. He was halfway through when a voice stopped him in his tracks. He turned: long dark hair down one side of her face, red-lipped smile. Shirley Thomas. He smiled back.

'Hi, how are you,' he said, clocking the two glasses in front of her.

'Better now I'm not working in the prison shed,' she replied.

'Aye. Me as well.'

She laughed. 'You didn't last long. I'd been there a couple of months.'

'Well. Not sure what I did wrong either, but there you go.'

'I know what you mean. Although I know who I upset.'

He paused. Her eyes were dark. Pupils enlarged. She'd had a few.

'Miss Ridley?'

'Riddly-raddly. Stuck-up bitch,' said Shirley venomously.

Roger was at a loss. He knew this was an opportunity, but also knew he was hopeless at saying the right things. She came to his rescue. 'On your own are you?'

'Yeh.'

'Me too. Scrawny cow has copped off, left me all alone.' She tapped the seat beside her. 'Why don't you join me?'

He couldn't believe it, but it went from better to unbelievable.

After a last drink as the chairs were stacked around them, she took him to a nightclub he'd only heard about. It was full of people he'd seen in the pub. No-one he knew. Most of them were at that stage of drunkenness where they'd forgotten they couldn't dance and were strutting their stuff like demented chickens. Drinks were three times the price in the pub and that was after he'd paid the ridiculous entrance fee. Shirley got in for free. They danced. Well, she danced. Outside, she kissed him and asked him where he lived. They got a taxi to her place instead.

Later, as he lay next to her hot body listening to her excessive snoring, he wondered how he'd arrived at this moment. Tonight he'd been shagged three times. He couldn't say he'd been the dominant partner. She knew what she wanted and she was insatiable. In less than twenty-four hours he was going to make an armed entry into someone's house and abduct his wife. What was happening to him? He stood at the window and stared down at the road. The snoring stopped. A hand wound its way round his thigh. He was pulled back. He groaned and fell into the darkness.

*****

### Friday 26th June. Dawn

It was dark when Cora opened her eyes. Was it a dream? She sat up and stared at the fire. Fire? There wasn't a fire in the hut? She tried to push up against the wall but found it was made of rough stone. Where was she?

As her eyes accustomed to the dancing light, she realised she was in a larger room than the hut. The fire was on the floor like when she'd been camping with her dad in the woods. A circle of stones to keep it in. It wasn't big but she could feel the warmth. The flickering lit up the other walls. Also stone. She looked up. She could see the stars, but the walls were high. Dark spaces higher up and a large window space at first-floor level. She'd no idea where she was. How had she got here? She shuddered as she remembered her dream – a big man in a long coat running after her.

She brushed her hand through her hair. It felt awful. She needed a bath. She remembered the stench of the man's breath in her dream. Was that normal? Remembering a smell from a dream? She stood up and felt her way round the wall. She could make out a door-sized space opposite, but could also feel a draught coming from her right. It got stronger until she could see it was a window space. No window. No frame. Wide ledge. She looked out.

To her right she could see the estuary. The restless water glittered in the moonlight. The tide was high and full. She could make out the current flowing powerfully upstream. Over to the left was a huge building with lots of lights.

There was a sound behind her. She turned. It had been no dream.

In the doorway, lit by the dying fire, stood the running man. She wondered if she could climb out of the window, but she couldn't move. He stepped forward further into the light. His long coat nearly touched the floor. It was heavy and full. As she stood transfixed, he moved further into the room towards the fire. A dead rabbit hung from his hand. She'd seen one before, of course, but she still stared.

As he looked at her, she saw the glint in his dark eyes. He took off his large hat. His hair was long and matted, hanging onto his shoulders and the collar of his coat. He placed the rabbit on a stone near the fire.

'Have you slept well, my pretty?' he asked.

His voice startled her. It was odd, deep, but it was the accent which confused her. Where had she heard that before? He wasn't local, that was for sure. And what did he mean by 'my pretty'?

'I've a fine morsel for thee, here, my pretty,' he said, holding up the rabbit.

She didn't move. She was no-one's 'pretty'. Terrible thoughts flashed through her head. Her chin jutted out. She'd fight if he touched her.

He kept looking at her, knelt down. Taking a knife from his waistband, he began to skin the rabbit. She'd seen that done before as well, but not with such dexterity and speed. It only took a few seconds, before he was forcing a stick through its innards and out through its mouth. The skin lay rumpled where he'd dropped it, like an old scarf.

He made a quick arrangement with some other sticks to hold it across the fire and added more sticks to the flames. He blew them into action and held the end of the stick through the rabbit for a few seconds and turned it slowly. Throughout this he hardly took his eyes off her. She was still as a deer.

'Thee can speak, can't thee?' he asked. 'I'll not hurt thee.'

For some reason her brain decided that this was the moment to inform her where she'd heard the accent before: Butlins, Minehead, in a pub with her father outside the camp. He'd said he'd had enough of redcoats and all that silliness; needed some real world, men in the bar. 'Zummerzet' they'd said and laughed.

127

'How did I get here?' she blurted out.

He stared at her. 'I carried thee.'

'Why did you bring me here?'

He shrugged. 'It's warmer by the fire.'

'Where are we?'

He looked round. 'Why it be different than I 'member it, but it t'were a fine house afore they were sent to the Tower.'

She didn't really understand that.

'We're a bit further down the estuary aren't we?' she asked.

'Ay, pretty. Thee has good eyes.'

She took a step towards one side. He looked at her. She stopped.

'Thee needs to eat, my pretty. Thee's thinner than a least weasel.'

He reached forward and tore a strip from the rabbit's flesh. His fingers twitched in and out of the flames. He didn't wince, just gave a couple of quiet grunts. He offered it towards her. Again this wasn't new to her. She remembered the first time. Her father smiling at her as he watched her tentatively put the dark meat into her mouth. It didn't taste anything like any meat she'd had before and she was surprised by its texture, but she'd liked it.

She took a few steps towards the man. He continued to hold out the smoking flesh. She took it gingerly from his greasy fingers. Even by the fitful light of the fire she could see his hands were filthy, the nails broken and black, his knuckles covered in scars. She hesitated. He caught her eye and grinned. His beard had hidden the ugliness of his mouth. But now her mouth twisted with disgust. The lips were blackened and covered in sores. Inside was worse – a few brown stumps – fangs in a dark hole. She looked away.

His hand touched hers. She recoiled. He held her firmly, put the hot meat in her other hand. She nearly dropped it. The soft texture and the heat. But she hung on. He released his grip. She backed away, back to the wall. Sat down and briefly closed her eyes. She was shaking. She opened her eyes like a startled cat. He was still there. Hand to his mouth, chewing, tearing at the flesh with his remaining teeth with a slight smile adding ever more folds to the creases of his face. He nodded at the flesh she held in her own hand. She put it her mouth. It smelt and tasted of smoke. She bit off a small sliver and chewed it. It was still quite rubbery, but not unpleasant. She remembered she'd not eaten since the previous evening. How long ago was that? What time was it now? What day was it?

She accepted three more pieces, which he brought over to her. He stank: unwashed, dirty, like food that had gone off.

She needed a drink. The rabbit was heavy in her throat. She gagged, choked up the last piece. He appeared in front of her and held out a soft bag. She looked at it suspiciously.

''Tis only mead, my pretty.'

She took hold of the bag. It felt like her grandma's water bottle. Leathery. At the top there was an opening. He held the stopper in his fingers. She took a sip. It was revolting and she spat it out. Like the worst medicine she'd ever had to take. He grunted a deep laugh. Her throat cried out for it, whilst her nose wrinkled. She tried again. It was thick; dribbled down inside her, sweet. Was it honey? She took some more. He grinned, his teeth catching the light – like a wolf. She handed it back.

He squatted by the fire and stared into its glow. She looked up. The sky wasn't quite so dark. The stars had faded. They sat there in the breathless twilight, neither speaking, him looking into the fire, her watching him.

'What's your name?' she whispered.

He looked up as though surprised to see her there. He stared at her. She could see anger in his eyes, but knew he wasn't stupid like Hodge or Ozzy. He had the same look as Indie: a mixture of mischief and cleverness, weighing you up, often followed by a sly or nasty comment.

'And who be thee, my pretty? To be asking such a question of a gennelman?'

Gentleman didn't seem like the right word to Cora. More like tramp. But she answered him nevertheless. 'My name is Cora. Cora Ellen Beck,' she said.

His eyes went wide. He considered what she'd said. 'Well. Cora Ellen Beck. I be pleased to meet thee. Maliverny Catlin be my name. And many are those who fear it.'

It was her turn to look surprised and consider.

'Why?' She heard herself utter the word unbidden.

He frowned but it was quickly transformed into a guilty grin. 'Ah. There's many a reason for that. But, in truth, it be my master people fear the most.'

She puzzled at this too.

'Thee must have heard of him, my pretty, even this far from the world.'

She couldn't think who he might mean or which world he thought they were far from.

'The Lord Walsingham, whom the Queen doth call "her moor".'

Now she was completely lost. Was the man mad? His eyes were gleaming like a mad man. She put her arms round her body and shivered. The fire's warmth had gone.

He watched her, waiting for her next question.

'I'm sorry. I've never heard of this Lord "Walseyman". Do you mean the real Queen?'

He caught his breath at such outlandish treason. 'Thee better guard thy tongue, wench, or thee will lose it.'

She nearly laughed at that. It sounded like her mother's threats, but then saw that he was serious.

'You do mean Queen Elizabeth, don't you?' she asked. Her confidence was coming with the dawn. The man had shrunk in the daylight.

'Ay lass, and thee must take care. Words spoken in jest can lead to a rope round thy pretty neck.'

This time she couldn't help but giggle.

He stood up, loomed big again. She cowered away from him. Her hand scrabbled the floor searching for a stone – anything. He crouched down in front of her, his face close, eyes burning. The stench filled her nostrils. She willed the rabbit to stay where it was.

He glared at her for a while but then his eyes lost their strength. He stood up and went to the window. She waited. Started to judge the distance between where she leant against the wall and the doorway, figured it to be too far, especially as she would have to start from a sitting position. He turned and walked towards the doorway himself.

'Come with me, Cora Beck. I'll show thee a secret.'

She frowned, but pushed herself up onto her feet. Her knees rebelled and cracked. She staggered the first few steps before she found her footing on the uneven floor. He waited until she got up to him, turned and walked through the dark doorway. She followed, leaving the dawning light behind her as she stepped down the steps behind him, the only light coming from the burning torch he'd thrust into the dying embers. The smell of tar in her nostrils, fear and excitement fighting in her guts. She could hear his boots clanging their metal heels on the stone. Shadows leapt up from his descending silhouette. She felt her way, her hand on the rough wall.

At the bottom he turned to face her, his face a mask. His coat flipped to one side to reveal a long thin sword against his leg. She gasped. He set off along a low-roofed corridor, stooping beneath the uneven stones of the ceiling. She took one glance back at the faint light at the top of the steps, before following his disappearing figure into the darkness – her heart fighting the screaming of her brain.

# CHAPTER 7

**Thursday 25th June. Afternoon**

Everyone seemed to have forgotten about Sadie – which was fine with her. She'd failed to catch up with Fletcher at any point the afternoon she arrived, and he hadn't made any attempt to contact her. She still hadn't told him about Thomas Hadden. She'd gone looking for the girl's mother. She wasn't in, but as Sadie stood uncertainly outside the house, Cora's mother arrived carrying two heavy bags of shopping. She didn't seem surprised to find a police officer waiting for her, refused the offer of help and told her to go away – at which point one of the bags split open and emptied its entire contents into the gutter.

Maggie Beck stared at the spoil heap. A malevolent apple escaped its paper bag and jumped into the nearest dirt-filled pool, where it sat and grinned at her. She took one step forward and kicked it as hard as she could. It was a wonderfully executed free kick: sailing across the road and splicing the insolent apple through the intricate design of the garden gate opposite.

Sadie's mouth fell open, in itself a unique event. She looked from the centre forward back to the ball nestling in shreds against the back of the goal.

The centre forward reverted to her original form and swore in a totally deadpan voice. 'Fucking great!'

Sadie was caught between wanting to be somewhere else and giving the woman a resounding cheer. She was saved by the woman herself.

'Well. If you've nothing better to do, you can help me pick up this lot and I'll make you a cup of tea.'

Five minutes later they were standing in Maggie's kitchen looking at each other over the tops of their cups as they sipped the hot tea.

'I've no idea where the thieving little cow is, so don't ask me,' she said.

Sadie said nothing.

'We had an argument at breakfast time. Again. That was the last time I saw her.'

Sadie considered this. 'You've heard about the incident with teacher?'

'Yeh, they phoned me, wanted me to leave work and go in. Bloody teachers. They've no idea. I can't just walk out of work.'

'She was badly hurt. They were quite worried for a while at the hospital.'

'Yeh. Well. She's always been a stuck-up cow. Can't keep her nose out of other people's business. She were like that at school.'

'You mean Mrs Trencham?'

'Mrs Trencham! She'll always be Betty Wilks to me. She's not even married. Well, not anymore. He soon realised his mistake. Long gone.'

Sadie paused. 'Do you know what happened?'

'How could I? I wasn't there, was I?'

'But Cora's been in trouble with this teacher before?'

'Ay, like I said. She's a bossy cow. Just cos she's been to college she thinks she's better than anyone else.'

Sadie felt like she was going nowhere.

Maggie poured herself another cup of tea and held out the pot toward Sadie, who declined.

She walked to the window. 'If you want to find Cora, you need to look for her dad.'

Sadie was about to ask the obvious question.

'Don't ask me. He's gone to ground somewhere. He's upset Eric Nellis. He'll be lucky to escape with just a beating, daft bastard.'

Sadie wondered whether she'd get away with pretending she hadn't heard the man's name, but thought better of it. She put her cup on the table and looked around the room. It wasn't the worst she'd ever been in. Things were clean and tidy. The rescued shopping sat in orderly fashion on the kitchen table. It wasn't the poorest collection of items. The woman must earn enough to keep herself and her daughter. It was, however, unbearably sad. Sadie could see that she'd bought the sort of stuff teenagers ate: three lots of cereals, crisps, burgers. The woman was hiding it well, but she wanted the runaway back. Sadie thought of her own mum: the way she embarrassed her on the few occasions she went back. How she bought stuff which she hadn't eaten since she left home.

She picked up her bag and went to the door. 'Well. Thanks for the cup of tea. I'll see myself out.'

Maggie didn't turn when she spoke. 'When you find her . . .' She swallowed the rest of the sentence.

Sadie couldn't find any words which wouldn't sound trite, so quietly opened the front door and went. Back on the street she looked across at the apple. Not laughing now. Bottom corner. Forgotten.

She walked back to the car and drove to the school. She'd made an appointment to meet one of the teachers, a Miss Prescott. The school was on the way out of town, down a side street, along a drive, playing fields on the right – fifteen or so boys playing football. Well, most of them were standing about. She pulled up where there were other cars parked and walked up the steps to the main door.

She sat in the entrance hall while she waited for the teacher to arrive. She'd attended a similar school: red-brick building, old-style quadrangles. She hadn't enjoyed school much. Not after the fourth year.

A door opened. A woman with short blonde spiky hair came towards her. 'Hi. I'm Sally Prescott.'

Sadie introduced herself and followed her to a large room. There were only a few chairs gathered in clumps in three of the corners, otherwise it was largely empty. The teacher led Sadie to the furthest corner and invited her to sit down. Sadie came straight to the point.

'I understand you might have some clue about the whereabouts of Cora Beck?'

The woman smiled, but shook her head. 'Well. No. Not really.'

'Oh, I thought . . .'

'No. Other than anywhere she might have been with her father. She . . . er . . . rather idolises him.'

'I see.'

'Not uncommon for teenage girls,' added the teacher.

Sadie declined to explain her own completely different opinion about this.

'No. I just wanted you to know she's not all bad – a bit outspoken maybe. Well more than that, which is why she's always in trouble with lots of the other teachers.'

Sadie waited.

'Although I think you ought to know that she has been mixing with some much worse people.'

'Such as?'

'Steven Nellis. He didn't come to this school, thank goodness. But some of his gang did. In fact one of them was finally expelled about six months ago. Not a very nice lad at all. We got on fine for the first two years, but . . . well . . . his stepfather lost his job, ended up in prison. His mother died from an overdose, the young lad went off the rails. I tried my best, but some of the older staff . . .'

'So what's his name?'

'Ian Dyer.'

'What was he expelled for exactly?'

Sally shook her head. 'Threatening a teacher with a knife.'

Sadie gave her a questioning look.

'A Stanley knife.'

'But technically he should still be in school.'

'Yeh. But no-one will have him.'

'Is that allowed?'

Sally shrugged her shoulders. 'Not really, but . . .'

Sadie paused, then asked, 'Is there anything else you can tell me?'

'No. I don't think so. I just wanted someone to know she . . . she's . . .' Words failed her. She looked away.

Sally showed Sadie to the front door. They said goodbye and Sadie went back down the steps and towards the car. The footballers had gone, but across the field stood a group of lads leaning against a red and white car. She tried hard not to stare, but felt their eyes on her. She reached her own car. It took her some time to register what the letters said.

She turned and looked across the field. The gang was laughing. Their car revved its engine and roared across the grass towards her, leaving deep tyre marks across the playing pitches. It reached the school drive and swerved onto the tarmac, showering her with grit.

Someone leered out from the driving seat: short blond hair, spotty face and a red T-shirt. She could make out that there were four other people crammed in the car: two of them were girls. All of them were laughing and giggling hysterically.

'Nice car,' grinned the fleshy mouth. 'Shame about the paint job.'

Sadie smiled at him. His face turned into a grimace of hate.

'Fuck off, bitch. Fuck off out of our town.'

The engine raced. The gravel spurted and he careered out through the gates and sped off towards the main road.

Sadie was calm. She'd faced worse than this. She got in her car and drove it to a garage she'd seen on the main road, walked into the office and asked them to remove or cover up the graffiti as soon as possible. The mechanic was about to give her the 'you've got to be joking' line until she showed him her warrant card and pointed to the car. The combination of card, words and the look on her face was enough.

'No problem, officer. A couple of hours? OK?'

She nodded, turned on her heel, left the garage and set off towards town. The mechanic made sure she was well away before calling his mates to have a look. They'd seen stuff like this before, but not this particular combination of words. They looked at him. He shrugged his shoulders.

'She's a copper.'

They nodded their understanding – although it still seemed disproportionate to him:

'FUCK OFF LEZZA.'

****

### Thursday June 25th Late evening

Irene found Julie standing on a corner near a brightly lit nightclub. Some of the young lads eyed her furtively, but none had the courage to approach . . . yet. Come chucking out time or earlier, when they'd had a few and failed to impress or persuade any of the noisy girls laughing and giggling beside them in the queues . . . then maybe she would still be there.

She saw Irene coming. She'd heard the rumour. She slipped back into the shadows, hoping she'd not seen her. She couldn't run in these shoes! And in any case she knew she'd lose what little balance she was managing to maintain. She flattened herself against the wall and held her breath. Just when she thought she'd got away with it, a slim figure came round the corner and came up beside her.

'Hi Julie,' said Irene. 'Long time no see.'

'Fuck off, Irene. I'm telling you nuthin'.'

Irene turned towards her and smiled. 'I haven't asked you owt yet. Do you want a fag?'

Julie took the proffered cigarette and leaned forward towards the lighter. Irene was sickened by the smell. Cheap perfume didn't hide the bad breath and unwashed body. She shivered. She remembered Julie at school. She was five years older than Irene. Julie had been a clever girl, popular with the teachers. Good at netball and hockey, well-turned out. Now look at her.

They stood leaning against the wall in silence, blowing smoke into the clammy darkness, the blare of neon and laughter filtering round the corner.

'Are you working for Eric Nellis?'

'As if I'd tell you.'

'He's going down, Julie. You've a chance to help us do that.'

Julie sighed. 'Yeh, right. Two years and out in half the time. That your best effort?'

'Not this time. He'll be there till he gets his pension.'

Julie gave a weary laugh. 'And you think anything I tell you will make a difference? I know less than nowt.'

Irene waited. She could hear a police siren in the distance. 'Jimmy Beck.'

'What about him?'

'We need to talk to him.'

'Ask his wife.'

Irene laughed. 'Come on, Julie. Everyone knows.'

'Do they? Well ask them, then.'

'I'm asking you. Here. No-one's listening. Otherwise it'll be down the cop shop. And then everyone will know you've been talking to the police about us being after Jimmy Beck.'

Irene turned to look a Julie. Her once good looks had long gone. The skin was tight over her cheekbones; less fashion model than scarecrow. Her eyes were shut. The tension drained from her body. The thin dress and tatty fur jacket provided little protection from the wind playing with the litter and cans in the alley. Without the adrenaline, her body contracted into a shivering whippet-tremble. Tears trickled through the thick make-up.

'You fucking bitch. You always were a sly one.'

Irene wanted to put her arm round her, but knew it wouldn't work. She waited, although she knew Fletcher's patience wouldn't last very long.

'What's in it for me?' Julie asked.

Irene wished she had something better to offer, but knew Julie would laugh in her face. She reached inside her bag. 'Doesn't your brother live in Newcastle now?'

'You're a nosey cow. He wouldn't have me anyway. He's got a good job, wife and kids.'

'You're still his sister.'

'Not any more.'

Irene offered the money. She knew Fletcher would disapprove – to say the least. Julie looked at it and looked up at Irene.

'Are you for real?'

Irene held out the money.

'How far do you think that'll get me?'

'Manchester. I can give you an address. People who would help you.'

Julie stared at the money. 'What makes you think I won't just blow it tonight?'

Irene went to put it back in her bag. 'Your funeral.'

Julie's hand closed on hers. 'OK.'

Irene kept her fist firmly round the wad of notes. 'Jimmy?'

Julie threw the unfinished fag onto the floor. 'Caravan at West Shore. It's got a seahorse painted on the side. Belonged to my dad.'

Irene hesitated. Julie looked her in the eyes. The tears had gone.

'You'll do what I said, yeh?'

Julie nodded. Irene gave her the money and a card. Julie shoved them both in her jacket pocket and glanced towards the street end. 'You'd better go. Just being seen talking to you is bad enough,' she said.

Irene nodded and took two steps to the end of the alley, her body dark against the red and yellow light. She thought of saying something else, but Fletcher's eyes killed it in her head. She turned away. She heard the word: 'Thanks.' She looked back. Julie had disappeared into the emptiness of the alley.

Irene made her way across the road to the parked car, seeing Fletcher's stony face looking through the windscreen as she approached. She opened the car door and got in.

'Where to?' he asked.

'West Shore caravan site.'

Sykes started the car. They drove away quietly.

\* \* \* \* \*

Back in the alley, Julie stumbled over beer cans and discarded fish and chips. She'd only got about ten yards when a hand came out from a doorway and fastened round her wrist. Her heart stopped. A face appeared: glistening eyes, a furry strip on a shaven head, the thin line bisecting the left cheek.

'Aunty Joolie,' he whispered in a sing-song voice.

She tried to pull away. Her heel broke. He pushed her against the wall. A blade glinted next to her right eye. She tried to scream but a fist punched the breath out of her. She slithered down the wall. He followed her down, the Stanley against her cheek. His hand ferreted through her pockets and found the money. His eyes met hers.

'What did she want to know?' he asked.

She shook her head. She felt the point of the blade puncture her cheek, blood filling her mouth. He punched her in the face. She fell to one side.

He was standing now. She could see his heavy boots and knew what would happen next.

'Jimmy . . .' she whispered.

He crouched down, his face close to hers. 'What?'

'Jimmy. I told her where . . .' She spat out the blood which was clogging her mouth.

Another pair of legs appeared by the side of the crouching figure, who stood up. She knew who it was. No-one else wore shoes like that. Polished so well she could see her face in them. Her eyes closed. She heard the words, but made no effort to get away. She felt them drag her to her feet. The other face appeared in front of her.

'That was very stupid, Julie. Very stupid.'

Ridiculously she tried to smile, wanted to say she was sorry. Thought of her dad offering her a half crown he said he'd found in the park. She sobbed.

She didn't see it coming; even though she knew it was going to happen. She felt the thump in her chest. A searing pain shot down through her legs. She crumpled to the ground. Her face crunched up against a broken bottle. She watched as the two figures, distorted by the glass, blurred towards the lights. Her eyes became the same.

Glass.

Fletcher and Sykes had been watching the fun and games outside the clubs from a nearby car park. Sykes had parked in the shadow of the Town Hall, so there was little light shining into their car. Apart from the crowds writhing round the entrance doors, they could make out the women standing in twos and threes: short skirts, shiny jackets, big hair. They'd lost Irene as soon as she merged into the club crowds. Fletcher knew this was something he couldn't do. They'd have just stared at him. Copper!

They didn't see where she went. But in any case there was other entertainment. Sykes saw it first, nudged Fletcher and nodded in the direction of the women. Another girl had arrived, who they didn't seem too pleased to see. Two or three of the smaller groups had come together. Out of this clump came one of the smaller girls. Small, but well built like a scrum-half.

'Tina Goodnight,' muttered Sykes.

'Is she?' asked Fletcher.

'Only if you can afford it and you don't give her any aggro. She's put at least two blokes in hospital to my knowledge.'

'Nice.'

As they watched she approached the new girl. It was beginning to look feisty. The car door opened and Irene got in.

Fletcher and Sykes didn't stay to see the action but went in search of Jimmy Beck.

\* \* \* \* \*

Tina asked the girl what she was doing.

'Why? What's it to you?' said the dark-skinned girl with the slicked-back ponytail.

'This is our patch. Go find somewhere else before you get hurt.'

'Your "patch"? Do you own it or something?'

'Not us. Someone you don't want to cross.'

'Like you?'

'No. Worse than me.'

'You mean uglier or bigger.'

Whatever patience Tina had been using up snapped. She pushed the girl away, trying to catch her heel as she lost balance. Except it didn't quite work like that.

As her hand reached the girl's chest, it was clasped by a strong grip. The intended trip meant that her leg was stretched forward. The dark-haired girl leaned back, using Tina's weight before yanking hard. The diminutive figure sailed over the new girl's shoulder and landed on her back in the nearby bushes.

The astonished girl pack recovered from the shock and launched themselves at the new girl in a frenzied phalanx of screaming harpies, but the girl was too quick. She dodged the first two or three, put another two down as she zigzagged off to the left and disappeared behind some parked cars. Flummoxed, the remaining cohort floundered in disarray. Some of them picked up the fallen and two of them went to help a dazed Tina out of the bushes. By this time the new girl had disappeared, but not before the display had been observed by two figures standing at the entrance of a dark alley.

'Who's that?'

'Dunno.'

'Find out.'

The other nodded and made his way through the crowds. Those who saw him coming got out of the way. Those who didn't wished they had. He drove a straight line, like the mark on his face. He grabbed one of the girls on the edge of the crowd.

'Where's she gone?'

The terrified girl looked at him, at his bony hand gripping her arm. 'I dunno, Indie. Honest. Don't know who she is. She just turned up tonight.'

He put a hand in his jacket pocket, brought out a wad of notes.

'There's fifty for the first person to tell me, OK? Spread the word.'

He pushed her towards the girls who were still tending to the fallen and the shaken. She grabbed another girl and gestured at the figure standing watching. The red and orange neon was backlighting him, but they all knew who it was. The short Mohican, black against the red, his bare tattooed arms hanging by his side. The tartan skirt over the knee-shredded jeans. The unlaced Doc Martens. They clucked like hens and spread out in every direction. He grinned and spat high into the night air.

Tsura had to admire the chutzpah of the little man. She also knew he carried a knife and was more than happy to use it. But she was more interested in the other man she'd seen – the one that Luca had told her about. She ran round the Town Hall and spotted his languid form as he strolled towards a silver sports car. He hesitated as he took out the keys and looked in her direction. She stepped forward from the side of the building and walked towards him. He stopped and watched her approach.

'You going my way?' she said.

'Depends where you're going,' he replied, with a faint trace of a public school accent.

'Depends whether it's interesting enough.'

'Oh, it will be interesting: if you like a drive along a lake in the moonlight and an expensive restaurant.'

'Sounds like a good start.'

'Perhaps we can choose dessert later.'

He opened the passenger door. She got in. As he went back round to the driver's side, he saw one of the girls watching him, hands on hips. He waved at her and got in the car. He didn't disappoint her or any other watching bystander. The car could do nought to sixty from where it was to the nearest roundabout. It did. It could still be heard as it shot through a red light up Abbey Road, travelling at double the speed limit.

\* \* \* \* \*

When his dog growled a low warning, Jimmy Beck came abruptly awake. He slipped out of bed and peered through the curtain. He couldn't see anyone, but he trusted the dog. He dressed quickly, grabbed his bag and pulled back the loose carpet. By the time they crept round the side of the nearest caravans, he'd gone.

West Shore site was a desolate place in the winter, but at this time of year there were plenty of people around. The little community room was busy and all heads turned to see the newcomers. Their conversation dissolved into muttering when they realised it was the police.

Sykes knew some of them and spent a few minutes talking to an older man, a big fellow with huge hands who looked across at Irene. It was obvious what he thought of her. Fletcher had wisely stayed outside. He'd walked down to the end of the road and was looking out at the sea, except it was so far away he could only make out the occasional crumbling line of white in the distance. There was a slight breeze, but the night was clear. To his right he could see lights further up the coast. Above him the Milky Way was spread like a giant shawl. He heard the crunch of shoes on the gravel behind him. The other two came to stand beside him. All three of them stared at the stars.

'It's at the front,' said Sykes, 'about eleventh or twelfth along.'

'So what's the plan?' asked Fletcher.

Sykes hesitated, uncomfortable with the responsibility. 'Well, if we take the path, he'll hear us on the gravel. So I suggest you two approach through the site, keeping to the grass, while I go down the slipway, along the sand and get up as near as I can that way.'

'Sounds good to me,' said Fletcher. 'Come on, Irene.'

Sykes watched them saunter back to the main gate. He'd not met Irene before, but he'd heard a lot about her. Always in trouble at school, but clever enough to pass her exams and get away. Fletcher was a different animal altogether – with the emphasis on animal. Watson's account of his encounter with young Nellis and his gang was unbelievable. But the young villain would respond. Sykes feared a lot of violence would be unleashed as a result. He sighed and set off down the slipway.

They were reunited in the caravan with the painted seahorse. Sykes had known Stan Carter. As a lad he'd been out fishing with him from this beach. He knew how much he'd loved his little hideaway. He'd painted the seahorse and he'd died on the bed now lying empty. He also knew Stan would have been upset and angry to see the state it was in. Unwashed crockery and pans in the little sink, clothes on the floor, the smell of cigarettes. A corporation bin stood in the corner full of cans and discarded food containers. It all said 'Male occupant. Bed all day'.

On the side table was a transistor radio. Next to it was a photo in a small frame. Irene picked it up and showed it to Sykes. 'Is this the girl who's on the run? His daughter?'

Sykes took it. It wasn't recent. She looked about ten, squinting at the camera, hair blowing across her face, a stick in her hand. Behind her were trees and the corner of a wooden hut. It looked familiar, but he couldn't place it.

'I expect so, although I've never met her. I'll take it to the school in the morning.'

Fletcher was looking at the carpet. It was slightly wrinkled at one end. He bent down and pulled it to one side, revealing a trapdoor. He took the little ring and pulled it up. The night air seeped in.

'Mole down a hole,' he said.

'Not that long ago,' said Irene, feeling the bedclothes.

They went back outside. The stars looked down. They could hear the faint sounds of music and voices from the community block – otherwise nothing.

'Do you think he's got a car?' asked Fletcher.

Sykes shrugged his shoulders. 'Whether he has or not, he'd have no trouble getting one. Walney folk often leave their cars unlocked and anyway, he's from Barrow Island. He'd have learned how to hotwire before he went to school.'

'So. End of trail,' sighed Fletcher. He was getting fed up with this, plus the previous night's exertions were catching up with him.

'Let's go,' he said. 'We'll meet you at the school tomorrow. Maybe the teachers might have some bright ideas.'

The other two looked doubtful – they'd both attended Barrow schools – but they trudged after him as he jumped down onto the path and walked back to the slipway, looking out at the faraway grumbling of the waves shuffling the shingle like a restless insomniac.

They drove back to the mainland. Fletcher and Irene had no trouble sleeping that night, but Sykes tossed and turned, the picture of Cora Beck digging into his subconscious. The wooden hut? Gurgling water?

\* \* \* \* \*

Jimmy Beck could have seen their car crossing the Jubilee Bridge, but he was busy concentrating on not falling into the mud as he crossed by the Middle Steps to Ormsgill. Once there he quickly found an unlocked car, fired it up and drove to Ulverston. He parked it in a side street and nipped into the Cattle Market for a quick pint. No-one knew him there, but he kept his hat on nevertheless. Later, after a bag of fish and chips, he set off through the lanes until he came out at Arrad Foot. From there he followed the main road until he came to the old railway bridge. Half an hour later, he was round the small headland and set off across the gleaming sands towards the hut. It was a full moon. The stars filled the sky.

If only this was his life. Free to roam the sands and the woods. Fishing and catching rabbits.

He was pretty certain Cora would be there. His heart lifted. He sniffed the air. The tide was turning. His dog came back from investigating the rock pools. He was happy too. They both ran along the sand.

* * * * *

The silver car sped along the switchback road with the silver lake blinking through the trees.

They hadn't said much since their escape from Barrow. He hadn't said where they were going and she hadn't asked. Except, about halfway along the main road, he had said his name.

'Philip, but most people call me Keane.'

Tsura grinned.

'But I'm not,' he added. 'Well, neither eager nor given to uttering wailing noises.'

'How about like a knife edge?' she asked.

He smiled and accelerated past a slower car. 'What's yours?'

'Tsura.'

He glanced at her as he looked in the mirror. He turned left up the lakeside road.

'Sura?'

'No T – sura. Try to say the T and the S at the same time.'

'Tut-sura.'

She smiled. 'It's Croatian. It means "light of dawn".'

He drove on. About halfway up the lake she spoke again. 'You know what I like about sports cars?'

He looked at her and shook his head. 'The speed?'

'No. This.'

She reached out with her right hand and put her hand on his crotch. He flinched in surprise.

'You watch the road,' she said. 'I'm checking the equipment.'

He relaxed, felt his cock grow hard as her strong fingers alternately gripped and stroked it awake. He wriggled uncomfortably as it became constricted in his pants. She took her hand away. He gave her a quick look. She was grinning.

'Well?' he asked.

'Not as thick as I prefer, but long. I like long. You need to get rid of the pants though. Otherwise it'll end up tied in knots.'

He laughed. 'You don't hold back, do you?'

'I take what I want – when I want.'

She looked out at the flashing lake. He thought of other things to say, but kept them to himself.

He drove quickly through Windermere and out the other side, still with the lake on their left. Just as it started to veer away, he turned abruptly into a gravelled drive. It dropped down back to the lake. He swerved to a halt with a wave of pebbles, in front of a brightly-lit hotel. She got out of the car and walked towards the lake. He followed her. A boat full of lights broke the stillness of the water, sending out a wash which sloshed onto the beach below.

She reached into her bag and produced a pair of earrings and threaded them into her ears. They were clusters of diamonds, which glittered in the moonlight. She turned to him and smiled.

'I'm very hungry,' she said.

She turned and walked across the gravel. He followed her, watching the sway of her hips, the muscles in her calves and the light shining off her gleaming hair. He smiled to himself.

They were late, but the waiter showed them to a window table with a view of the lake. She chose lobster and venison without hesitation. He agreed and picked the most expensive wine on the list. After the lobster, he excused himself and visited the men's cloakroom. When he returned, the room was nearly empty. The large party had left, so there were only two other couples to be seen and they were some distance away. The venison came. She finished hers quickly, pointedly leaving what she regarded as inedible potatoes. She stood up glass in hand to look out of the window at the mountains he had pointed out to her. He finished his meal.

She was standing in profile framed by the window. She wasn't classically beautiful like some of the girls he'd taken to hunt balls in his youth. She had the hooked nose and full lips of some of his Jewish girlfriends. He knew that her eyes were dark, but not as black as her lustrous hair. No affectation there: straight, pulled back into a loose ponytail hanging at shoulder height. Her body was muscular rather than elegant. The short dark blue dress caught the shape of her breasts and the swell of her thighs. Maybe not beautiful, but the most erotic creature he'd come across in this Godforsaken backwater.

She caught him staring at her and smirked. She came back to the table, moving her chair a little closer. 'Do you like what you see?' she asked.

He nodded, as he felt her hand feeling its way along his leg. He angled it her way. The waiter appeared at his elbow.

'Dessert, sir?' He proffered the menu.

Tsura continued her fondling, whilst smiling at the waiter. 'Not for me,' she said, giving her victim a savage grip.

Keane managed to shake his head through the grimace.

'Coffee?' asked the waiter.

The dark eyes smiled at him. They both nodded. The waiter glided away.

She looked straight at him, the smirk crinkling her lips. But after a while she looked across the room at a couple on the other side of the room.

Keane had noticed with satisfaction that most of the men had stared at her as she'd crossed the room when they arrived. That included the man at the table opposite. His wife was talking to him diffidently, but he'd been caught by the eyes from the window table. Tsura's eyebrow rose in his direction, whilst her hand kept up with its deliberate and increasingly forceful movement under the table. The man's eyes widened. His wife realised she'd lost her audience and followed his gaze. Whether she realised what was going on, she stood up and stalked out of the room. Her husband had little choice but to follow her – with one last glance over his shoulder. Tsura capped it all with a little wave with her free hand. He fled.

The waiter arrived. The movement ceased, but her hand still gripped him hard. As the waiter placed the cups on the table, she squeezed harder and harder. The waiter retreated. She removed her hand and took a sip of her coffee. Keane didn't know whether to be relieved or cheated. He looked at her smile. Her eyes closed and he could swear she was purring.

'Do you bring lots of women here?' she asked as her eyes opened and drilled into him.

'No,' he replied.

Her eyebrows arched in disbelief. He shook his head. He leaned back in his chair and looked out at the trees and the lake beyond. When he looked back her she was still watching him, still smiling.

'What are you doing here?'

'A man in a silver car invited me,' she replied.

'I mean in Barrow,' he said, ignoring the smile.

'We're here on business.'

'We?'

'My uncle. He provides solutions.'

'Solutions?'

'Permanent ones.'

'Permanent?'

She nodded.

'And you?' he asked.

'I prefer more temporary arrangements,' she said, her fingers turning the spoon over and over.

The room was silent. Only the distant sounds of kitchen staff like an orchestra tuning up.

'Do you play?' he asked.

'I like to ride.'

'Horses?'

She shifted in her seat. 'In the moonlight on a beach.'

He nodded. She stood up and headed for the ladies' room.

He beckoned the waiter and ordered the bill. He told the waiter to tell her he'd gone outside for some air. He leant against the car and drew breath. Eventually she came down the steps and towards the car. She kissed him full on the lips.

He knew just the place. He drove as fast as he dare through the dark lanes leading over to Coniston. Halfway down the lake he pulled in. They got out. They walked a few yards to the edge. Three beech trees stood near the lapping water, their roots exposed by the constant washing away of soil. She walked up to one of them and leaned against it looking out at the dappling water. He walked up to her, reached out and stroked her hair back from her forehead. She rested her head on the bark and closed her eyes. She didn't flinch as his hand followed the line of her cheek to her lips, her chin – down to her neck. After a slight hesitation he continued, feeling the firm shape of her breast through the soft material, and fingered the hard nipple. He leaned forward and kissed her neck. She pushed him away and turned to face the tree. With one hand on the trunk she pulled up her skirt. She was naked. She widened her stance and swayed her hips from side to side.

He reached forward and gripped her ponytail, wound it round his wrist and pulled her head back. She gasped. He put his other hand on her hip and thrust himself inside her. Five or six deep thrusts were all he could manage. She snarled as he erupted inside her: shook his hands from her hair, pushed him away and walked back to the car. She said nothing until they were back on the main road.

'I'm assuming you have somewhere I can have a shower and a bed for the night?' she asked.

He nodded. He did. It wasn't anywhere near the best hotel he'd stayed in but it was the best Barrow had to offer.

An hour later she lay on the bed, her back to him, her breathing regular. He wanted to trace his fingers down the knots of her spine. He watched her for a long time before sleep overcame him.

* * * * *

Sadie had made a list. She ruled out Fletcher straightaway: even dead drunk she trusted him, and with some reticence, Irene. She'd even considered Laura. She made their cases, but they didn't hold water. She'd considered people in Rochdale and West Yorkshire. The most likely vengeful person, DI Sutton, had more reason to attack Fletcher than her. She knew it wasn't Geraldine. So . . . she'd run out of suspects. She went through them again. Her pen hovered over the line through Irene's name. OK . . . but no.

And then it came to her. It was the way he'd looked at her the first time in the office. They'd been introduced. She hadn't realised what the look meant at the time, but now . . .

So how did he know? Why would he tell *his* local villains? Precisely. His local villains! She didn't know how she would prove it or how to even prove it to herself, but she was sure.

She didn't sleep much, not least because the most disturbing thought was that Adversane might know but hadn't said anything. Did that mean he was protecting him – or what? In her dreams she was back in the dark shadows of that church on a hill, each sound amplified and transformed into shapes that shifted and whispered meaningless but menacing sounds.

# CHAPTER 8

*Friday June 26th*

They didn't get to the school in the morning. Fletcher awoke with a start as the bedside phone interrupted his dream. He was swimming in a purple sea. Laura's face was coming out of the water in front of him, her hair like seaweed streaming down her body. . .

He scrabbled for the phone and put it to his ear. At first he couldn't work out who he was listening to, couldn't make sense of the accent or the words.

'. . . down an alley . . . around about ten last night . . . think it's . . .'

Fletcher sat up. It was DI Aston. He recognised the sneer.

'And good morning to you, Inspector,' said Fletcher.

The voice stopped.

'You'll need to say that all again, young man. I was swimming in the Mediterranean with a beautiful mermaid.'

He could hear the other man breathing. It morphed into a hacking cough, which made Fletcher think perhaps he wouldn't make it to his pension.

'It's not a pretty sight, Fletcher. The chief inspector's on his way. The scene of crime officers have just arrived. Get your arse down here.'

'There's no way you're ever going to see my arse, Aston. Where's here?'

'Behind the Town Hall. The Majestic.'

The phone went dead.

Fletcher lay back on his bed. The sun was pouring in through the gap in the curtains.

Majestic? He could see a big red and yellow neon sign. Ten o'clock? They'd been there. He found the phone again.

'Yeh,' said a nicotine morning voice.

'Your Miss Julie has come to a sticky end, I think.'

There was a sharp intake of breath.

'Can't have been long after you spoke to her.'

'Where?'

'Alley by the Majestic club. Ten o'clock.'

The phone was silent.

'Are you there?' He thought he caught a suppressed cough. 'Are you OK?'

'Yeh. I'll see you downstairs in ten.'

The phone went dead again. He looked at it, put it down and sighed. He went to the window and opened the curtains. It was going to be a beautiful day. Except he knew it wouldn't be.

Twenty minutes later Fletcher and Irene were walking side by side across the road towards the alley. There were four of five police vehicles blocking the way and lots of uniform standing around. Down the alley they could see one of the small white tents which would have been erected over the body first thing. One of the car doors opened and Chief Inspector Mancini got out. He waited until they approached. His face was blank.

'Inspector,' Mancini said, and turned on his heel to walk towards the tent. Fletcher gave Irene a rueful look and followed the senior officer.

As she got level, Fletcher spoke to her. 'You know, you don't . . .'
The glare of anger sealed his mouth shut.

They continued to follow the chief inspector.

In any other circumstances Mancini would have changed his shoes. The detritus and ordure between the street and the tent was going to ruin them. The trouser legs as well, meaning the whole ensemble would have to be replaced. Nevertheless, he made no effort to avoid anything as he waded onwards, clearing a path for the less expensive footwear of his inferior officers. The scene of crime officers were in short wellingtons. One of them pulled up the side of the tent for them to see the body.

Julie Carter had once been May Queen, but this June she was a half-eaten corpse. The flies buzzed angrily, a huge chorus landing on the inviting carcass as often as they could. Irene made herself look. She knew she was almost certainly the last person to see Julie before she met her killer. Her eyes filled with tears. She wiped them away viciously. She'd seen enough.

Irene forced her way back out of the tent, nearly ripping it apart in her fury. She strode back towards the street, barging into one of the uniforms and knocking him against the wall. The blow was such a surprise that he was unable to stop himself from collapsing in a heap with both hands in the shit.

'Hey,' he yelled, only to be silenced by Fletcher's fierce look. A colleague helped the uniform up and the two of them walked away.

'Will she be alright?' asked Mancini.

'I doubt it,' said Fletcher. 'She was speaking to this woman only moments before . . .'

Mancini sighed and went back into the tent. Fletcher followed him. A tall angular man Fletcher hadn't noticed until now stood up from where he'd been kneeling next to the body.

'Inspector, this is John Fox. Pathologist.'

The man straightened his back and winced. 'You'll be DI Fletcher. "*Sturm und drang*" a speciality, I hear.'

Fletcher had heard the words before, but had forgotten the exact translation. 'I'd like to think I am the cure rather than the cause, Doctor,' he said, offering his hand.

The doctor extended an arm like a desk lamp. Thin and bony like the rest of him. Fletcher was reminded of the teacher from the *Beano*. Except this man's accent was more Biggles and Ginger.

'I can't be very definite at this point. You can see that unless our killer is also a cannibal, the victim has been attacked by other feral beasts. Dogs, cats, rats, foxes, seagulls.'

He looked up as three or four of the latter wheeled about above them, squawking and screaming with frustration. 'Take your pick.'

Mancini forced himself to ignore the white deposit which had landed on his coat. 'Time?'

Fox shrugged, his shoulders looking as though they were going to pop out of their sockets. 'I'd say last night given the amount of damage. But the cause of death is almost certainly the hole in her chest, which would have been just the encouragement the creatures of the night would need. As to the weapon, the subsequent attacks are so extensive I doubt whether I'll be able to tell for certain.' He swotted away a large bluebottle which had the temerity to land on his face. 'Most importantly, I need to get what's left to the lab as soon as possible.'

Mancini beckoned to one of the grim-faced officers, who nodded and departed with great relief. 'There's nothing else we can do here, Inspector. Better let the experts do their jobs.'

Fletcher looked down the alley. It went down to a brick wall, but he could see that there was a gap to the left which presumably led to a way out. This was confirmed by Sykes who had arrived a few minutes ago. He followed the chief inspector to his car.

Mancini was looking across at the Town Hall. 'They're not going to be pleased about this,' he said.

Fletcher nodded. He'd little time for men in suits puffed up with their 'little brief authority'. 'Maybe, sir. But we need to find out who is pleased about it.'

Mancini gave him a sad look. 'I think we all know who that might be. The problem will be proving it.'

'Yes, sir,' replied Fletcher, looking across at Irene who was leaning against their car smoking a cigarette and staring into a very dark place. Mancini followed his gaze.

'I need to report to the chief constable, Inspector, and arrange a press conference. It would be helpful if we can have some positive news by then. They want it by four o'clock this evening and by that time the nationals will be here . . . and the television crews.'

Fletcher continued to stare at Irene. He nodded. Mancini gave him one last look and got into his car.

By now there was quite a crowd gathering. More uniformed officers had been drafted in to hold the line. The crowd went silent as a mortuary van made its way through to the end of the alley. Fletcher walked over to Irene. He didn't say anything. Sykes had followed him.

'I'm taking Sergeant Garner for a walk, Sergeant. We'll see you at the school in half an hour. Alright?'

He got in the car and started the engine. Irene didn't move. He stared through the windscreen and waited. Eventually she threw the cigarette away and got in next to him. Fletcher drove slowly out of the square and headed for the beach.

Five minutes later, they were sitting in the car staring out at the sea. He'd driven to where the road ended near the caravan site. He turned the engine off and waited. Irene opened the car door and got out. He followed. She walked down the slipway and went a few yards along the little bit of sand which hadn't been covered by the high tide. Fletcher sat on the sea wall and watched the breakers. Further out he could see five or six little boats bobbing in the swell. He could make out a figure on the nearest boat pulling in a line from the water until he was able to retrieve a large basket.

Irene appeared by his side and sat next to him. He didn't speak.

'Can't have been Jimmy, can it?' she said.

Fletcher shrugged. 'Not unless it was someone else keeping his bed warm.'

'Not his style anyway,' she added.

Fletcher gave another shrug. He didn't know the man, but it seemed unlikely.

'I gave her a hundred pounds,' she said. Her voice was flat.

He said nothing; didn't look at her, continued to watch the man on the boat.

'And an address in Manchester. . .'

He nodded.

'We've got to . . .' she bit her lip and wiped her eyes.

'We will, Irene.'

They stayed there for another ten minutes or so. Neither spoke any more. He waited until she looked him in the eye.

'I'm ready. Let's go.'

They drove back across the island and went to the girl's school. Sykes was waiting for them. They pulled up level. He looked at Irene who stared resolutely ahead.

'I think I've got a lead. Not from them in there. No bloody use. It's the photo. I know where it was taken. I've talked to her mother. She confirmed it. It's a fishing hut up on the estuary beyond Ulverston.'

Fletcher nodded.

'Also, I phoned into the station a few minutes ago. A car was reported stolen from Ormsgill last night. They found it in Ulverston this morning.'

'OK, Sergeant, let's go.'

Fletcher followed Sykes along the coast road. He'd not been aware how big the estuary was until now. As the tide was in he could see the vast expanse of glittering water stretching into the distance as far as a small rectangular block on the far horizon.

'What's that?' he asked.

Irene looked where he'd pointed. 'Heysham power station,' she said.

They continued along the road.

'Used to come out here with this lad, when I was jigging it from school,' she said quietly. 'We used to stop along here and go down on the beach to smoke pot.'

Fletcher kept his mouth shut.

'I thought he loved me and that we'd have babies together.'

'So what happened?'

'He was killed in a car crash about a mile back.'

Fletcher glanced at her.

'He was with another girl. End of story.'

He couldn't add anything to such a declaration. They reached Ulverston, followed Sykes onto the main road and drove out of town. Ten minutes later they were standing on the disused railway bridge looking down into the water rushing upstream.

Sykes pointed at the water lapping the side of the fields. 'We'll have to wait, if we want to get round by the edge of the water . . . or we can go through the woods.'

'Lead on,' said Fletcher.

'I've got some walking boots in the car. You'll not get far in them,' said Sykes, looking at Fletcher's shoes.

Fletcher wished he'd got his own boots. Sykes' spares were a bit big, but Irene looked fine in his wife's wellies. They set off back across the bridge and followed the track through the fields. Like Cora, but with a more confident authority, they'd ignored the sign telling them that the bridge was dangerous and access was forbidden.

From the road, their figures dwindled into the distance and were soon lost in the trees. The rush of water in the channel reached a peak, swirling back on itself. The sun was occluded by the fog which came without warning. Within seconds anyone standing there could see nothing beyond the end of the bridge. The estuary, the fields and the woods all disappeared. Only the sounds remained, deadened and difficult to judge.

A woman stopped with her dog and changed her mind, even though she regularly ignored the sign. She knew only too well how unwise it would be to continue, no matter how well she knew the paths. She glanced at her watch. Six hours. Low tide would be half four. By then it might be clear. She pulled at the dog's lead and they went back inland.

### Friday 26th June

Cora had assumed that descending into the darkness meant they were going underground but as she followed the spluttering torch in Catlin's greasy hand, she saw the encroaching light.

He doused the torch on the floor and they came out onto the side of a courtyard. On their side there was roof above them, supported every few yards by round pillars. To the left she could see the remains of what must have been a quadrangle like at her school, although most of it was now lying in ruins. The courtyard itself was a mass of tangled brambles crawling all over the tumble of stones.

Catlin headed on steadfastly, paying no attention, even though the morning sun was coming over the hill and catching the high wall behind them, making it glow. She figured that the window space high above where they'd come out must be at the level they'd come from. He'd nearly disappeared, so she ran after him.

He was beyond the building heading for the nearby trees. She jumped the long grass, trying to keep up with him. In the trees it was dark. The sun hadn't reached here yet. She followed the trodden-down undergrowth in time to see him reach another smaller ruin like a little church. It was completely overgrown with ivy and surrounded by those dark trees you saw in churchyards. She couldn't think of their name. Her father had told her. There was a wooden door with huge studs in it. It was slightly ajar. She crept up and peered inside.

It took some time for her eyes to get used to the cobwebbed gloom. There was a window, although the foliage outside was obscuring most of the light. She didn't realise where Catlin was until the solid mass of his body moved with a grunt of effort. She stumbled on roots and stones underfoot as she came up beside him.

He seemed to be trying to lift a huge flat stone lid away from its base which looked like . . . a coffin! She shrank back.

'What are you doing?' she hissed.

He gave a final heave and the stone moved. A dark triangle in the corner revealed a hollow depth inside. She was transfixed: all the horror stories she'd seen or read merged into one giant Dracula-ghost-werewolf-monster waiting to leap out. But there was only the smell of dry dust.

Catlin leant against the stone and breathed heavily. 'Thee could give me a hand, my pretty,' he gasped.

She hesitated, before approaching and feeling the cold rough stone of the lid. The two of them pushed with all their strength until she thought her arms would break. The lid shifted with an irritable scrunch. Catlin cried out and leapt back, rubbing his hand furiously. It had shifted over to one side, but she couldn't see anything and didn't want to get any closer.

Catlin stopped dancing about and cursing, shook his hand a few times and came over to look.

'There she be, my pretty,' he said.

'What?' asked Cora, her thoughts going back to ghosts and skeletons. But she could see nothing.

He reached inside and felt about for a bit, before withdrawing his big hand holding a clutch of chinking metal. Even in this minimal light, Cora could see that it glinted and sparkled. Treasure? He held it up so that the increasing light caught it, flashing into the dark corners of the room.

'What dost thee think o' that, my pretty?' he asked, his own eyes glinting in its reflection.

'Is it treasure?' she asked, immediately aware of the childishness of the question.

'Ay. But it be cursed. So we can look but we mussent take!'

Cora laughed. It seemed like she was in some bad kid's film, but she wasn't. Her laughter died, echoing in the emptiness of the room and its ancient walls.

He put the handful back in the hole and rustled about a bit more. This time he brought out a bag bulging with what looked like small stones. He beckoned to her and she followed him out into the daylight. In the alcove of the doorway was a stone bench. He sat down leaving space for her and undid the string on the neck of the bag. Carefully he let the contents tumble out onto the ledge.

They were stubby, dirty, white statues about four inches long. He held one up for her to see. It was a squat figure, sitting down. It was wearing a crown and had staring round eyes. He handed it to her. It was cool and smooth to her touch. He handed her another. This one was bigger. A similar face but he seemed to be biting the top of the big shield in front of him. Another one also had a crown, but with a hand up to its face.

'That be a Queen, my pretty. The other two be a king and a warder. Here be a bishop. He be fat like all men o' the church.'

'They're chessmen,' said Cora softly.

'Ay. There be a lot more in there. Four or five bags.'

'What are they made of?' she asked, turning the fat bishop round in her fingers.

'They be the bones arv sea monsters, pretty. Sea dragons.'

She looked at him. 'Like walruses?'

'I know not of their names, pretty. Only terrible stories told by drunken sailors in the Bristol docks.'

He started to put them back. She handed them over, but was careful to use the trick her father had taught her, palming one of the pieces into her sleeve.

After he'd put the bag back, he put his shoulder to the lid and scraped it closed.

'Time for sleep, my pretty. I be travelling a long road tomorrow.'

She followed him thoughtfully back to the main building. He seemed uncaring as to whether she followed or not and was muttering to himself as though she wasn't there.

When they got back to the higher level, he sank against the wall and held his hand. She went over to look. His fingers were covered in blood. She winced, but took it gently in her own hand to see.

'You need to clean that, Maliverny, or it'll go bad.'

'Ay, my pretty, but the sickness comes upon me. I must sleep.'

She left him there and went to find some water.

Outside, the sun was bursting though the trees. Birds twittered and called cheerily as she made her way in the direction of the hut where she knew there was a small freshwater stream, but she was disorientated. She came to a fence which she didn't recognise and followed it along to a gate. Over it, she saw a much larger, more modern hut. She went to the door. It opened with a bit of a squeak. She stopped and listened. Not a sound – which her father had always said was a warning sign. She looked around fearfully. No-one in sight.

She darted into the shed. There, right in front of her, was a box with a red cross on it. She took it off the shelf and saw a shadow pass the window. She slipped behind the door. A man stepped into the room and stood still. She held her breath. He turned round and stepped back outside.

'George?' he called out, making her jump.

'Over here,' came an answering voice some distance away.

'Do you want a brew?'

'Five minutes,' came the response.

The man came back in and clattered about for a bit. She heard water being poured and a gas flame popping. The man was whistling under his breath. After a few moments he went back outside and she heard his whistling fading into the distance.

She came out from her hiding place, snatched up the kettle and after peeping out of the door, crept out and made her way back to the gate. Once through, she quickened her pace and headed back to the ruin.

Twenty minutes later she was back in the room. She'd thought he might not be there – just a trick of her mind. But he was lying where she'd left him, snoring fitfully. She knelt down beside him and spoke his name. He grunted. She shook his shoulder and his eyes opened abruptly. They gleamed fiercely, but softened when he saw who it was.

'My pretty,' he murmured.

'I'm going to clean your hand and bandage it,' she said.

His eyes closed. He grunted a few times and winced, but she managed to wash his hand and clean the wound. It was what her dad called a blood blister, but fortunately it had burst so she knew it would be less painful. She tried to wash the other hand, but ran out of water.

Afterwards, she sat and watched him sleep. The sun was coming round and creeping in through the window. She stood and looked out at the estuary. What was she going to do? She thought of Mrs Trencham and gritted her teeth. If only her father were here. He'd sort it out.

She thought of her mother. She remembered her when she was pretty. Well not pretty; but attractive and full of fun. Now she'd got old and crotchety.

She looked back at the big man. He had shrunk into his coat. Who was he? When she looked back out again, she saw the fog coming towards her like a wall of white. She shivered as the sun was hidden. She retreated to the wall beside him. Tiredness crept over her like the fog: a soft encompassing blanket. Her head lolled to one side and she slowly slid down until she nestled at his feet, their putrid smell not keeping her awake.

* * * * *

### Friday 26th June

Roger was in the Turkish café again. People jiggled about like deranged puppets, until their strings broke and they all fell down.

He struggled to the surface fighting his way through their screaming and jolted awake.

A stream of sunlight lit up the mirror on the dressing table, sending reflections all over the room like a glitter ball. But he didn't have a dressing table. And the sun didn't get into his bedroom until the evening. Where was he? His eyes focussed on a green skirt on the back of a chair. Shirley Thomas!

He sat up with a start. It couldn't be true. He flung back the bedclothes. No pyjamas! He saw his jacket hanging behind the door. A scrambled version of the previous night seeped into his head: Charlie grinning at him as he waved from the door, the blonde pulling at his shoulder, Sam staring into his beer, Shirley patting the seat next to her and her bouncing tits as she jumped up and down on top of him.

'My God,' he breathed.

He listened intently. The door was shut. He'd no recollection of the rest of the house or where it was or how they'd got there. An image of dislocated bodies whirling amongst flashing lights arrived, accompanied by a thumping headache. He saw a glass of water on the bedside table and gulped it down, only to retch it straight back up again. It was neat vodka. He held his mouth shut and stumbled across the room, wrenched open the door and quickly decided which door was the toilet. Fortunately he was right. He threw up violently three times and sank to the floor.

He must have dropped off again for a few moments. Slowly his eyes opened and took in his surroundings. It was true: he must be in Shirley's house. The bath was clean; lots of bottles and plastic containers on a shelf. He levered himself up. His head swam. He leaned on the sink and put his head under the tap, before using his hand to fill his mouth with water, drinking greedily.

It was much later, after he'd managed to find his clothes and quietly go down the pink carpeted stairs, that he found the kitchen and the note on the table. Beside it were a mug, a plate, knife, spoon and a bowl. In the middle of the table were three boxes of assorted cereals.

He picked up the note and read it. His eyes opened wider as he mouthed the words. He looked across to see the toaster on the side and then went back to the note. He finished it and let it fall onto the table. 'Lewd' was the word that came into his head. A word his mother had often used to describe any kind of sexual content in a newspaper, on the television or when she was peering through the chink in the net curtains.

The words were graphic and clearly reminded him of last night's bedtime activities, but more worrying was the very explicit promise of 'to be continued' tonight. He had to go back to the beginning to find that she'd left for work at eight thirty. He looked at his watch. It wasn't there. The clock on the kitchen wall said twenty to ten. He rubbed his face – he needed a shave. He went back upstairs, found his watch and a man's plastic shaver still in its wrapping.

He forced down some toast and made himself a cup of tea. Everything was clean and neat and tidy. He sat at the table and contemplated his situation.

It didn't seem real.

He'd been with plenty of women before – but mostly ones he'd paid for or Charlie's seconds. He couldn't remember ever meeting a girl and ending up in bed with her the same night. The desperate travails of his youth were best forgotten. He sighed, looked at his watch and shifted in his seat.

What should he do? Just sit here and wait? The note didn't say when she'd be back. He got up and wandered round the house, looking at her books and the photographs on the walls. There were pictures of her with other girls, a smiling older couple who might be her parents. He peered out of the window. There was a small front garden which looked out onto a terrace of houses opposite. He vaguely remembered coming up a hill from the town centre, but he didn't really know Ulverston, apart from three or four pubs.

Roger stepped back from the window. He had an image of Sam staring morosely into his pint. He slapped his forehead in horror as the plan for this evening came surging back in all its ludicrous stupidity.

He looked round the room in desperation. Where was the phone? He went out into the small hall and found it on a table near the door. As he picked it up and looked at the numbers, his brain shut down. He sat on the stairs, saw the phone book. He fumbled and dropped it twice, before finding Charlie's number in the Yellow Pages.

The phone rang and rang. No answer. He slammed it down, knocking it off the table. As he picked it up and reassembled the phone, book and table – and vase – his mind raced. Where would Charlie be? Roger remembered the blonde. He sighed. He sat back down on the stairs. What was he going to do?

They'd agreed to meet at eight in the lay-by on the way to Haverthwaite. Sam was to go to work for six o'clock as usual. He couldn't think of his surname. A memory of Shirley's long hair falling across his face distracted him for a moment. He allowed himself a boyish grin – which disappeared the moment he thought of Miriam brushing Mrs Hadden's long blonde hair.

He got up and prowled about the house. He found himself in what appeared to be a spare room. There were the usual piles of boxes and spare bedding, but there on the side table was a photo album. He picked it up. A few flicks of the pages told him he shouldn't have looked: Shirley in a wedding dress smiling at the camera next to a good-looking young man in a soldier's dress uniform. He closed it and put it back on the side.

'White!' He went back into the hall and flicked through the telephone book. Only one S. White listed. He rang the number. No answer.

He stared into the dust motes writhing about in the sunlit air as they fought to regain some equanimity after his rushing about. Just as they were achieving some level of stillness, the phone rang. Its deafening noise buffeted Roger's head which was lolling against the banister rail. He looked about himself, trying to grasp what was happening, stared at the phone for two more rings and grabbed it.

It was Shirley. 'How are you, lover boy?' she whispered.

'Er . . . fine . . . Shirley?'

'Oh! Just fine is it? You wait till I get home,' she giggled.

'No . . . no. I'm more than fine. I'm . . . I'm . . . shagged out, actually,' he managed to say with a grin.

There was more giggling on the other end of the phone. 'That's terrible. But I can't promise anything other than more of the same.'

He laughed. 'Er . . . Shirley. What time will you be back?'

'Oh. Listen at you. Can't wait, eh?'

'No . . . I mean, yes!' he replied. 'But it's just I've got a job to do tonight.'

'A job?' she asked.

'Yeh, it's a sort of a one-off security . . . thing, escorting some woman or other. My mate Charlie has fixed it up, needed some extra help.'

'Oh. Like extra muscle, you mean,' she breathed huskily.

'Yeh. Sort of, but it's not till late. Don't have to be there till half seven.'

'Oh.' There was no disguising the disappointment in her voice. 'So when will you be finished?'

'Not sure, maybe not until late tomorrow morning.'

'I see,' she said.

'It's just a one-off. After that I'm all yours!' He tried to sound cocky.

'You better believe it,' she replied.

There was an awkward pause.

'Well, I'll be home by five thirty,' she said.

'Is there anything I can get you?' he asked.

'How about fish and chips?'

'OK.'

'Before or after?'

'Sorry?'

She giggled.

'Oh! Best be after. Work up an appetite.'

'There's nothing wrong with my appetite.'

'I know, Shirley. I know.'

'Good. See you later, alligator.'

Without being able to stop himself, he replied: 'In a while, crocodile.'

'Snap!' she said and put the phone down.

He smiled to himself and then put his head in his hands. What had he done?

I'll tell you what you've done, Skeldon. You've done a Charlie. You've set yourself up to have rampant sex a few hours before going out on a special operation, which could go horribly wrong and during which people could get killed. He stared at himself in the mirror. He needed to find his car, go back to his flat, get all his gear together and go round to Charlie's place. He looked at the hall table, picked up the key and checked it fitted the front door.

Moments later, he was marching down the lane into town. There was briskness in his step that reminded him of his days in Nicosia. People looked away. They were scared to make eye contact. He felt the power of those action-filled days filling his body with confidence. The sun was shining. The sky was a Mediterranean blue. He began to whistle. He'd forgotten all about Marcus Pole.

*****

### Friday June 26th

Jimmy Beck opened his eyes and checked his watch. Nine forty. He huddled into his sleeping bag and blinked at the light filtering through the cracks in the shutters. His dog lifted his head from his paws and gave him an appealing look. Jimmy agreed. They both went outside for a pee. The morning sun lit up the clear beauty of the estuary and the surrounding landscape. Jimmy stood and gazed. The dog came back from his explorations and rubbed against his legs.

Jimmy went back into the hut, rummaged in the cupboard and found some old dog biscuits which he knew he'd put there. The stove had been left on the hearth by whoever had used it last. Not good. He went to get some water and made himself a brew, found a tin of baked beans and put them in the pan.

When they were hot, he took them outside and sat on the rock at the edge of the waterline. There wasn't a breath of air. The tide was probably on its way in. He could hear the gentle sucking of the first trickles seeping up through the sand. Across to his right he could see the cars on the main road. He couldn't stay long. He'd hoped Cora would be here, but she must have gone elsewhere. She wouldn't have left the stove out like that. What had he done to her? Making her turn out like him? In trouble at school? Violent? On the run?

He took the tin back in and put it in the rubbish bag. He cleaned up, put his bag back in his rucksack, the stove on its shelf, quick look round. What was that? He knelt down by the cupboard and pulled out a pair of walking socks. They were Cora's! She *had* been here. Where was she? What had happened to her?

He went outside. Fought with the idea for a few minutes, first rejecting it as pointless and secondly as dangerous, but couldn't stop a more primeval urge. He cupped his hands round his mouth and yelled: 'Cora!'

His voice carried across the sand and into the trees. Crows fluttered up from their perches and cawed away downstream. A heron launched itself in elegant haughtiness and flapped its way across the main channel. Stillness returned. The incoming tide was beginning to rise in the channels. He knew she would never dare to cross the sand against an oncoming tide. He'd frightened her too much with tales of grown men drowning, their whitened, half-chewed bodies washing up on the beaches down the bay. He called again. 'Cora!!!'

The dog growled at him. He stared at it, went back in the hut and found Cora's socks. He thrust them into the dog's face. It sniffed and grumbled, sniffed round the hut and gave a little bark, then went out of the door and up the path. Jimmy followed it, knowing full well where it was going. His guts filled with dread.

The dog turned right at the gate and headed for the ruin,

straight to the hidden cellar. It stood whining and scratching in the corner, waiting. Jimmy caught up, pushed aside the weeds and lifted the corrugated iron sheet. He'd brought his torch and feared the worst. Down the steps, into the underground smell. The dog rushed forward under the table dragging out a bag.

'Drop!' said Jimmy.

The dog reluctantly gave up its prize, pushed it with its nose at Jimmy. He picked it up and undid the knot. Took one look inside and sighed. He'd known all along. He hesitated. What to do?

Leave it where it was? Least harm? No, it might be useful. You never knew when you might need something to barter with. He stuffed it in his jacket, went back up the old steps. Back to the hut where he gathered his things. He was about to set off but found himself staring at the stove, something nagging him.

His brow cleared. He took a couple of steps and opened the wall cupboard, reached up and felt along the surface of the shelf covering. At the very back he felt the thin shape underneath, pulled back the covering and plucked out the slip of paper.

He opened it and read the message. Date, time and her secret name: Eleanor.

The message was brief. His secret name: Kelso. 'Crak' meaning Cark. Big 'M' for Manchester and a phone number without the giveaway code. She'd gone. Not exactly safe, but at least away. He could find her.

But first he had a little job to do. Something he should have done a long time ago. He set off back past the ruin and headed towards the house. He'd worked these woods for a long time, first as gamekeeper and later as poacher. He knew the way in his sleep, which was just as well as the fog began to seep into the trees. It would cover his approach and hinder any pursuers.

The dog stayed close as they both loped along together, disappearing like wraiths into the thickening silence.

*****

*Friday 26th June. Morning*
Tsura had woken him earlier with her mouth softly enveloping him. He allowed himself to be manoeuvred onto his back. She climbed astride him, moving slowly at first, until she'd established a rhythm. She began to croon, a strange ululating sound that gradually deepened into a low purring. He lost sense of time, drifted in and out of sleep, until he felt a stronger urgency which became a mauling and savaging. He gave himself up to it. She pawed him, slapped him, strangled him and bit him. He surrendered to it all. It finished. She collapsed on top of him, her hair drenched in musky sweat on his face.

Time passed. She dragged herself away. He heard the shower running and lapsed into a deeper sleep.

Later they had breakfast in the bedroom. Keane suspected that at eleven thirty they were pushing their luck, but he tipped well. He ate everything. She picked at the bacon, tried some, spat it out. Tasted the coffee and pulled a face, ate some toast, left the crusts. Drank three glasses of orange juice and demanded more. No words were spoken, only occasional eye contact. He smiled; she glared or looked away.

'I need to get my clothes' she said.
'Where are they?'
'In my car.'
'Which is?'
'In the town. Somewhere. Outside a hotel.'

'Name?'

'I forget. You drive. I tell you directions.'

They found the car. She took a case into the hotel, went upstairs and changed; came down, paid her bill and got back into his car. He sighed and put her bag in his boot. She was wearing a black leather jacket over a crisp white blouse and short black skirt, black boots and hair tied back as usual. He got back in the car.

'I have to see someone,' he said, gunning the engine.

She looked out of the window.

He drove into town, crossed over a bridge and along a road beside the water. He pulled up in front of a large pub. 'Are you coming in with me? If you are, you neither speak nor understand English, OK. Better for both of us? Yeh?'

Her dark eyes held his for a second. She got out of the car and walked across the road. He watched her as she stared at the shipyard. He followed her over.

'Not very pretty, is it?' he said.

She looked over to the castle. '*Sporca cittadina.*'

She turned and looked at the pub. '*Genti orrible.*'

He smiled and set off back across the road. As he reached the door, she began to follow him. He waited, holding the door open for her. She entered and he followed. The bar went quiet.

He indicated a seat near the window. She weaved over, ignoring the men who looked her way. None of them could hold her gaze, but most heads turned to follow her. She sat on one of the window seats and crossed her legs. Her skirt rode up. From her bag she took a packet of cigarettes and a black lighter, lit the cigarette and put the lighter on the table. She put her head back and smoothed her hair. Her dark eyes surveyed the room.

Keane half-watched this performance as he made his way to the far corner of the room. On a chair with his back to the wall sat Eric Nellis. He'd watched their entrance like all the other men in the room, but his smooth face showed no emotion. There were three other men at his table, all considerably older than him. Dominoes lay in an angular 'S' shape in front of them, whilst others clicked and chipped the polished hardwood surface. One of the older men had to twist round awkwardly to see what they were all looking at. He looked across at Keane and back at Nellis. The man to the left of Nellis coughed and placed a domino at one end of the line. Nellis didn't look, even though it was his turn. Without taking his eyes off the woman by the window, he selected a domino and played, all with the deft manipulation of one hand; the other was beneath the table.

Gradually the tension left the room. Someone got up and went to the bar. People coughed, resumed their conversations. Keane came over to the table where Nellis was sitting and pulled up a chair so he could sit at the edge of the domino players. The young woman behind the bar carried a glass of white wine to the woman by the window. Those near enough might have heard her speak.

'*Grazie.*'

She continued to smoke, blowing blue-white clouds into the air above her. Her fingers played with an earring or the large green stone on the first finger of her right hand.

Keane studied the game and watched as the man on the right of Nellis placed his last domino. Coins clattered across the table as he drew them towards his stash. It was the biggest. The man with his back to the room gathered all the dominoes together and swirled them around. Each man took his share and they recommenced playing.

It was only at the end of the next game that Nellis made any show of acknowledging Keane, who knew this was his way of expressing his disapproval. He wasn't bothered, but knew he'd cause more trouble by not deferring to the man. In any case, it allowed him time to play eye-tennis with the woman sitting on the bench to the left of Nellis.

Alex Henning was one of the few people in the room not to have enjoyed the woman's entrance. She could spot competition when she saw it demonstrated so blatantly. She was the one who normally turned heads. But this woman was different. She knew immediately that she was the woman who'd upended Tina last night and then driven off with Keane. Bitch! And now they were teamed up: more than, if her brief encounters with Keane were anything to go by. No-one else would have dared to make a pass at her, never mind track her down and take her to his hotel room. It made a refreshing change from jacking old man Nellis off or pretending to enjoy his premature ejaculatory efforts. Now Keane had got a new tart. Well good luck to you girl. You'll need it. She pulled a face at him and flounced off to the toilet.

'I think your latest fancy has got up the young lady's nose, Mr Keane.'

The players picked up their next set of dominoes. Keane smiled slightly, but offered no response. A couple of rounds went by.

'I'm not happy, Mr Keane.'

Again Keane gave no response.

'A terrible thing, dying in an alley outside one of my clubs.'

'Death is final wherever it occurs, Mr Nellis. The dead don't care where they lie.'

One of the old men chipped the table. Nellis raised his eyebrows.

'No fives, Ernest?' He looked across at one of the other players who gave a gentle shrug. 'You old villain, George.'

Nellis chipped as well.

The game finished. The man with the big stash was running out of space.

Nellis finally looked at Keane and spoke very quietly. 'I think you need a break, Philip. I suggest you go away for the weekend. Give me time to sort out some little runt who is trying to play rough in the scrum. Needs a wee lesson, as Doreen would say.'

Keane nodded and stood up. He looked across at Tsura, who'd not touched her drink. She got to her feet, straightened her skirt and walked towards the door. At the door, she turned and smiled at Nellis.

'*Avere una buona serata, capo,*' she said and winked at him.

He couldn't stop his eyebrows from shooting up. The wink made him smile. He nodded to her. She went through the door, followed by Keane.

Alex stood in the doorway and glowered. Nellis looked across at her and grinned. Her heart sank.

# CHAPTER 9

*Friday 26th June*

'Smart,' said Keane.

She stared out of the window.

'Don't think Alex liked the wink though,' he said with a grimace.

She ignored this. 'Where to now?'

'Somewhere more refined.'

'*Non e difficile.*' She sighed and let her head rest against the back of the seat.

He looked at her, wanting to meet her dark eyes, but she turned her face away. He started the car and set off. He felt as much contempt and lack of trust in the man they were going to see as in the one they'd just left, but at least this one would provide something she might drink.

She showed little interest in the scenery and remained silent throughout the journey. The estuary was a plate of shimmering glass. The trees enveloped the road beyond Haverthwaite like a green velvet tunnel. He turned right at the lane and swept past the Hadden estate sign and down to the house. After a few moments he got out of the car and went round to open her door. She stepped out and gave the building a cold stare. '*Mostrouoso.*'

The door opened and a tall thin woman with very short hair came down the steps to greet them. 'Philip. Good to see you.' They kissed on both cheeks. She turned to look at the gypsy wrestler he'd brought with him, trying hard not to wrinkle her nose.

'Susannah, this is Tsura.'

'Hello,' she said in her most neutral Sloane voice.

'*Buongiorno*,' replied Tsura in her best husky Italian voice.

'Ah,' said Miss Ridley, wishing she'd paid more attention at the finishing school and deciding to ignore the opportunity to expose her linguistic ignorance.

She led them into the 'monstrosity' and along to the right of a hotel reception area to a small dining room where a table for four was laid out for lunch. Their host appeared from another door, shook hands with Keane and kissed Tsura's proffered fingers, giving her an inquisitive smile.

Tsura ignored the men's opening conversation and, slipping out of her jacket, placed it on a chair to one side. She went to the large window and looked out at the fog foreshortening the view to a few trees and the indeterminate edge of the water. Hadden came to stand beside her with a glass in his hand.

'I won't apologise for the lack of a view, *signorina*. In an hour or so we will be rewarded for our patience. In the meantime, perhaps this Prosecco may appeal to your other senses.'

She turned and looked at the man with her liquid eyes. She saw self-assurance written across his handsome face and sensed the raw power contained in the expensively-fitted suit. She gave him an enigmatic smile and a raised eyebrow.

'My wife will be joining us shortly, although I must warn you that she finds company a little difficult. She has been unwell and I may need to rescue her if she becomes overexcited or disturbed.'

Before either of them could offer any response, the door opened and the lady in question entered.

Keane had heard about her beauty, but found it difficult to hide his surprise. She must have been about twelve the last time he saw her. Her hair was pulled back from her temples to a silver clasp at the back of her head, with blonde curtains falling straight to her bare shoulders. Her dress was white silk and full, hiding the skeletal figure beneath, but it was her eyes which shocked him. Not as dark as Tsura's, and too close together, or was it the intensity of the dilated pupils and the look of such desperate fear and penetrating need that he couldn't meet for more than a few seconds? There was no sign of recognition. Her gaze turned to Tsura, who took one glance and looked away. She'd seen the same look in Marko's eyes, when he talked or thought about his childhood.

Hadden asked them to take their seats. Susannah Ridley left the room. He went over to his wife, who hadn't moved after she'd come in. She seemed uncertain of what to do or where to go. He took her elbow and guided her to the nearest chair. She sat down with a slight stumble. Keane glanced at Tsura who was already looking at him. They took their places. Hadden offered them more wine.

The rest of the meal passed in a haze for Tsura. At one point she thought that the wine had been spiked, but as it didn't get any worse she just assumed it was the unreality of the whole event. Not that she wasn't used to unreality. In some ways it resembled her experience of watching football, a game which bored her beyond measure. Once it had been necessary as part of a sting set up by Luca. The away team, herself and Keane, were out of touch. Neither of them spoke to each other or passed a spoon or plate.

No eye contact was made. It was as if they were playing in separate games, which, of course, they were.

Their hosts were even more dysfunctional. Her eyes met his, only to flutter away to some distant point way beyond the room. Hadden did most of the talking, although Tsura would be hard pressed to recall any of it. However, she was surprised by the sudden departure of Hadden's wife, who suddenly stifled a cry and ran from the room, out through the door and into the waiting arms of the white-coated medical staff.

They finished their meal without further comment and retired to the balcony where indeed the view had improved.

Hadden invited Tsura to descend and follow the path to the water's edge, whilst he and Keane discussed a brief but important business matter. Tsura performed the 'lonely figure silhouetted against a hazy bright shoreline' pose, thinking mischievously that one of her collection of gauzy *chalwars* would make a more fitting addition to the scene. She undid the band which held her hair and shook her head to release the thick black mane. It was only as she glanced briefly at the two men to see if they were watching that she noticed the face at the window two floors above: a snow-white face with black pissholes for eyes, her mouth a Munch-like silent scream. Tsura froze. She could feel the intensity of that gaze even at this distance. She stopped playing and headed back towards the men. She'd had enough of this game.

They were a little discomfited by her sudden return but were even more surprised when she collected her discarded jacket, completely ignored them and walked straight through the dining room and entrance hall and out of the house. She didn't stop until she was at the end of the long drive, by which time Keane had caught up with her. He stopped the car. 'Are you going my way?'

She got in. He drove on.

Later he lay on the bed watching her dress. 'Will I see you again?'

'Yes,' she said.

'Can I ask you a question?'

She didn't reply.

'Why would a beautiful woman have extravagant sex with a man she doesn't know and doesn't trust . . .' he hesitated, 'for no apparent reward?'

She looked at herself in the mirror. '*Un cena ultima per il condannato*,' she whispered.

He didn't really hear it but his Italian was good enough; so was he the condemned man or the final meal.

'Is that the only reason?' he asked.

She hesitated at the door. 'What else is there?' she asked and was gone.

He lay back and contemplated what she'd said. He wasn't surprised that she was Italian. He knew the IRA had strong links with both the Mafia and various revolutionary groups. So he suspected she'd been sent to check up on him. Still, he'd not revealed anything of his real intentions. But there was no doubt that things were getting tricky, to say the least, although 'what else is there?' seemed the only answer to him as well.

### Friday 26th June

'I'm surprised he didn't kill us both in the fog,' said Irene.

'It was my fault. I've never been lost there before,' replied Sykes. 'We did find the hut though, even if it was empty.'

'No worries, Eddie. You can take all the blame.'

They were waiting in the canteen for Fletcher to come back from a meeting with Mancini. They'd already gathered the size of the operation the chief inspector had set in motion while they were going round in circles in Roudsea Wood. The station was full of people being interviewed, or sitting waiting to be interviewed, or waiting to see if they could go home. There was laughter, glum faces, people looking at their watches and lots of arguments.

'A bit like Cartmel Races, eh?' said Sykes.

'Ay and I'll bet there's some money changing hands as we speak.'

They shuffled up to let a couple of uniforms get a seat at their table. They didn't recognise them.

'Where are you two from?' asked Sykes.

'Grange,' said the Stan Laurel member of the partnership.

'More action since we got here than you see in Grange in a month,' added the Oliver Hardy.

'Well, I dare say our villains might be a bit quicker on their feet than yours,' laughed Sykes.

'Aye, but most of them aren't pretending to be deaf or gaga,' replied a po-faced Ollie.

Irene beckoned Sykes to the doorway where an amused-looking Fletcher was standing. He saw them and waved them over.

'Let's get out of here,' he said. 'I hate crowds.'

They followed him out and down the road to the pub, only to come straight back out again. It was even busier than the station with both police officers and dismissed interviewees. Fletcher suggested the King George. Sykes gave him a doubtful look, but went back for the car.

It was the right decision. The pub was empty. There wasn't even anyone behind the bar. Sykes shouted hello and after a few moments they heard someone running down the stairs. The young barmaid steadied herself and straightened her hair before coming through the door. Unfortunately the smeared lipstick was a bit of a giveaway and her activities upstairs were confirmed when she turned to put a glass up to the optics. She'd caught her blouse in the zip of her skirt. Irene grinned at Fletcher but he didn't seem to have noticed.

Sykes arrived with the tray of drinks and sat down. 'Listen, Inspector.'

Fletcher interrupted him. 'Rule number six, Sergeant. If you're working with me, never apologise.'

Sykes was wondering what the first five were, but Fletcher was musing aloud. 'Interesting approach the ice cream man's taking.'

'Why so?' asked Irene.

'It's quite clever, actually,' he continued.

They waited. He took a sip of whisky and followed it with a gulp of his half.

'Well, you can see he's brought in half of the town's population for questioning, including, if I'm not mistaken, most men and boys of drinking age from this island.' He gestured with a theatrical sweep of his arm at the empty room. He checked his watch.

'Half past four on a Friday evening. This place should be packed; most of them halfway through their pay packets from across the water.'

Sykes nodded in agreement. The girl at the bar had slipped back out.

'But the clever bit is that no member of the Nellis family has been invited for questioning. Lots of known gang members, muscle, night-club staff, drivers, street girls, people who were at the Majestic last night and others who were named by them.

I imagine there are a fair number of relationships falling apart in there. "You said . . ." and "I was just passing by . . ." etcetera. A few fights by the end of it; a few more homeless than before and a few in hospital. But no Nellises. Neat.'

Irene and Sykes gave this some thought.

'I can't imagine they'll get much from anybody,' said Irene.

'Ah. But that's the clever bit, isn't it?' said Fletcher, leaning forward. 'With so many of his people in there, he can't be sure there won't be a slip here or a wrong time there, can he? The hard work will start when all the statements are collated. It's the inconsistencies which will chip away at the truth.'

Sykes and Irene exchanged a look.

'Anyway, as I explained to him, not my strength, so I'll love you and leave you.' He got up and walked towards the door. 'See you in the morning: bright and early at the pathology lab to hear the findings from the quick brown Fox.'

Irene looked at the Fletcher-sized space he'd vacated at the doorway and turned to Sykes. 'Me neither, Eddie. Mine's a pint.'

Sykes got up and went to the bar, just in time to see a red shirt sidling out of the back door. He had to fight hard to stop himself chasing after the little git, but realised that wasn't the game they were playing.

The girl reappeared. One look told him what had happened. Her mascara had run and, even though she turned away from him, he saw the red mark on her cheek. He ordered their drinks and took them back to Irene. He didn't need to tell her. The girl disappeared into the toilets. Irene took one sip of her pint and went after her.

This was getting to be a regular occurrence: following other women into toilets to get information about men. As it always had been, Irene reflected. The girl was washing her face, but it wasn't doing much good as she was crying too much. Irene leaned against the wall and gave her some time. Eventually she turned off the tap and turned to face the woman she knew to be a police officer.

'I'm not telling you anything,' she blurted out.

'Your choice,' said Irene. She could do hard bitch if she wanted.

The girl waited, sensing a trap.

Irene walked up to the mirror and fumbled in her bag. 'The thing is, I really did think having a baby was the best thing that could happen to me. The only thing that changed my mind was going to its father's funeral.'

The girl gave her puzzled look.

'He didn't even know I was pregnant. I were going to tell him, but he went and got himself killed, didn't he. So that was that. I got rid of it.'

The girl gasped.

'What's the matter? You not heard of having an abortion? Having some old granny fiddle about up your fanny with a knitting needle. Half a pound of bloody octopus dribbling down your leg in the back alley outside.'

Irene wasn't looking at her. She was carefully applying a considerable amount of dark blue eye shadow. When she did look at her through the mirror, the girl had gone white.

'Anyway, you make your own choices in this world, don't you?'

The girl didn't speak. Irene started on her other eye. 'You appear to have signed up for Man United. Is that right, Jenny?'

'How do you know my name?' demanded the girl, getting some of her confidence back.

'I heard someone call you that the other day, plus you're Amy Dobson's baby sister, yeh?'

'So?'

'So? Nothing. With a scrubber like that for a role model, you've no chance.'

'What d'you mean?' said the girl, anger and family loyalty rising in her voice.

'Well, darling. Where do you think she is right now?'

'I've no idea,' said Jenny.

'Not your sister's keeper, eh? But we both know who is, don't we?'

'What?'

'She's where the rest of this pub crowd's spending their Friday night. In the cop shop answering the same questions again and again.'

'She hasn't done nothing.'

Irene had finished her eyes and was now doing her lips.

'Course not. I expect she was stood outside the Majestic last night waiting for a knight in shining armour on a bloody white whale to show up.'

'Maybe she was in the queue to get in. She likes a bit of clubbing, does Amy.'

Irene finished her lips and brushed her hair, giving it a severe spraying and spiking to achieve the look she wanted. Jenny watched. Irene turned to face her. 'Except she wasn't in the queue, was she Jenny? She was hanging her washing out with Tina Goodnight, looking for a bargain hunter. She's not the pretty young thing she was at school any more. I wouldn't fuck her if you paid me.'

Jenny went to go, her anger boiling up. Irene caught her by the wrist and pulled her up close. 'You can get out of all this, you know. I did. But you don't have to get pregnant and have an abortion to escape. You or your sister ever want to get out, just come and talk to me. I can make it happen.'

She let go of the girl's wrist. Jenny stared at her. Irene raised her eyebrow at her. 'You like what you see?'

The girl shook her head fiercely.

'Finally, for God's sake, Jenny. Please. Anyone but that disgusting little gobshite. Not only is he the most evil little shit, but how can even you touch. . . ! Ugh! Enough to make me sick.'

She made for the door. 'I'm easy to find. Think about what I said.'

Sykes was glad she'd come back out. He was beginning to get worried. Not so much for Irene – he wasn't that naïve – but the girl. The bar was filling up and he was beginning to feel uncomfortable.

Irene took in the gathering surly crowd, gulped her whisky and headed for the door. Sykes followed her out. Two minutes later they were heading back across the bridge. Sykes didn't ask. She didn't share. They parted in the middle of town. Sykes headed home to his wife and three kids. Irene found a taxi and headed for somewhere she wasn't known. She envied Fletcher who she reckoned was probably going over Shap by now, singing at the top of his voice. Four Tops or The Temptations. Old git.

As the taxi sped through Ulverston she shook her head at herself. 'Listen at you, Irene Garner. You're nothing but a lonely old tart, out on the prowl. Sad or what?'

The driver glanced at her in the mirror.

'Not that sad,' she said, meeting his enquiring grin

'Charming!'

'No offence, Matty, and I know your wife, so behave.'

'Where to?'

'Posh hotel in Lancaster. One with a conference going on.'

'Any preferences?'

'I do. But I may waive them tonight.'

\* \* \* \* \*

There were only two people who escaped Mancini's widely thrown net. The first was hiding out in a squat in Lancaster. He'd divested himself of the trademark tartan skirt and had his head shaved by one of the women in the house. There was nothing he could do about his scar but he acquired an old anorak with a hood which allowed him to get about in the dark at least. As he didn't normally frequent daylight hours, this wasn't much of a handicap. He was able to pay his way with some drugs he'd had stashed away for such an eventuality, but they wouldn't last forever.

Despite his appearance and reputation, Dyer was an intelligent young man. Ally that with a natural cunning and propensity to extreme violence, and he was a potent weapon for those who were tough enough or desperate enough to employ him. He knew all this. It made him smile, which wasn't a pretty sight as the crinkles round his mouth crossed with the indelible vertical mark of a not-too-recent encounter. The person who'd done this was still alive and thriving, but Dyer knew he would return the compliment one day – with dividends.

The people in the squat asked no questions. He ate with them and shared their drink. A small stray dog attached itself to him on the second night. He fed it scraps. It slept at his elbow.

He made a phone call the same time every day. The conversation was short.

'When?'

'Not yet.'

The one quality he did lack was patience. He needed action. He went looking for it.

\* \* \* \* \*

Keane had also received a phone call that evening.

'Time to visit your cousins. Be in touch.'

He'd already packed a few clothes. It seemed no-one wanted him around. He didn't like it, but he was playing a long game. He could wait.

Leaving his car in a lock-up in Kendal, he got a taxi to the mainline station and bought a ticket to Preston. Got off there and paid cash for the last train to Edinburgh.

He arrived at the flat in Morningside in the early hours of the morning. The woman was waiting for him; he'd phoned her from Preston station.

She wasn't any cousin of his.

His real cousin was a spectre. Her eyes haunted him. If nothing else, he would end her suffering before he died.

The plan was becoming ever more exquisitely perfect. He reckoned that after the royal, Hadden would be a close second, although he intended to reach double figures if he could. His brother's heroic reputation would be outgunned and the family's name tarnished beyond recovery.

\* \* \* \* \*

'Change of plan, Philip.'

'Always happy to adapt.'

'Chaos on the board I'm afraid. The Queen's knight isn't playing by the rules.'

'Makes the game more interesting, don't you think?'

'I prefer to be the one breaking the rules, Philip.'

'Do you want me to remove him from the board?'

'Not just yet. I'm inclined to withdraw, defend, wait.'

'Your call: not my sort of game plan.'

'Which is why I want you to disappear for a while.'

'Who's going to watch the King?'

'I've spoken to our friendly warder and he's got a neat plan.'

'He's a neat man. A veritable Poirot.'

There was a pause.

'I've also removed a rather ugly little pawn, but he could easily be replaced.'

Another pause.

'She is rather exquisite, your latest playmate.'

'Not a word I would choose.'

'Tell me more.'

'More like addictive. Like opium.'

'Dangerous. Is she a player?'

'Possibly.'

A long pause.

'Not long now. The endgame is still in place.'

There was the sound of someone walking, shuffling of chairs, a couple of sighs.

'No sudden moves, Philip.'

'I can wait too.'

The tape whirred to a stop.

Tsura rewound it in case Luca wanted to listen to it for a fourth time. He sat with his eyes closed, fingers in the high church position.

'An exquisite addiction?'

'Like opium,' she murmured.

Luca smiled. Marko made a face. Luca toyed with the black lighter, flipping the tiny secret compartment from which they'd retrieved the micro recorder.

'So? Philip? Is he white or black?'

'Either or both. A Janus. Ice for blood. He's on a one-man mission.'

Luca nodded.

'The Queen's knight is the detective?' said Marko. 'And the warder, the Italian?'

Tsura shrugged. Luca's eyes opened. They were staring directly at her.

'Neat, as in appearance?'

She said nothing.

'Or style?'

'Probably both. You're both,' she said, showing her white teeth.

'Um.'

'The King?'

'Nellis?' she said.

'*Si*. How much do you think he knows or suspects.'

'More than he'd say. He's feared.'

'Then we must allay someone's fear, so that they can talk more freely.'

She looked at him. 'The girl? Alex?'

'I'm sure Marko could be just as addictive, but we don't want to wear him out riding two fillies at the same time.'

She didn't look at him, knew that he'd have that curious little boy smirk; she'd see to him later.

Marko ignored her. He was looking forward to tangling with the young police officer. 'What about Hadden?' he asked, looking straight at her. 'Black or white?'

'Another Janus, but with a black heart.'

'The wife?' asked Luca, although he was enjoying the rising temperature.

'She is probably insane.'

'No matter. We'll consider it.'

He stood up and stretched his back. 'Time for dinner.'

\* \* \* \* \*

The operation had begun. Sam had passed them at the main gates. They watched as his tail lights disappeared into the trees. They counted ten and set off on foot. They were in full gear. Both of them had secreted army rucksacks and other equipment long before they were decommissioned. Charlie carried the Kalashnikov low. Roger had refused the offered alternatives. He'd reasoned that most people would be incapable of dealing with a fourth Dan.

He'd had second thoughts, of course, and third and fourth, especially after the Shirley Thomas starter for ten followed by fish and chips. He tried to shake it from his mind.

Marcus had left him a message. It didn't make much sense. 'Keep an eye out for ordnance.' What was he supposed to expect? Nuclear missiles in the garage? Anti-aircraft guns in the attic?

They came to the edge of the trees. The blaze from the building was, as usual, lighting up every nook and cranny. They waited for Sam's signal. His first job was to disengage the outside cameras. A torchlight blinked from one of the downstairs windows.

'Come on,' said Charlie, who made for the first of five vehicles parked out front.

They'd done this plenty of times before. The big knives tolerated little resistance.

They reached the front door and crouched down listening for the clicking of the lock mechanism. The door swung open. Quickly they were in and heading for the stairs. Sam lumbered back down to the security room, where sat the terrified figure of his colleague, gagged and tied to his chair. He'd not offered much resistance. He didn't want to have his windpipe crushed or his guts pulverised. Sam went back to the screens.

Charlie and Roger had reached the door to the second floor. Charlie took off his rucksack and found the semtex. Roger watched nervously as his friend's fingers deftly applied it to the lock and attached the detonator. He looked at his watch, twiddled with the dial and gave Roger the thumbs up. They both scrambled down the stairs and crouched either side of the stairway opening. Ten seconds and there was a soft whump. Smoke rolled down the stairway as Charlie and Roger headed upwards, omitting to use their usual battle cry. It would have sounded daft.

At the top they pushed in the damaged door and stood in the hallway. As well as Roger's own memory of the upstairs suite, for which he and Sam had spent four hours searching, they had a detailed drawing from the security room. Charlie was to deal with the nurses and Hadden if he appeared, while Roger was to make his way straight to Mrs Hadden's room along to his right.

On his signal, Charlie kicked open the nurse's bedroom and Roger went quickly along the corridor. So far it had gone like a well-oiled machine. Roger felt great. His head buzzed with the excitement of it and he knew Charlie was getting off on it big time. His eyes were blazing. Roger had a nagging doubt that this wasn't entirely down to adrenaline, but . . .

The plan imploded.

The nurse's room was empty. Charlie backed out, intending to go to the next room. Roger had disappeared. He heard a soft noise to his left. It was the lift door closing. The occupant who'd just stepped out onto the thick carpet was standing not three yards away.

Charlie raised the barrel of the gun.

'Stay right where you are. This gun is loaded and I know how to use it.'

Hadden didn't move.

'I know that Charlie, which is why I won't take any risks.'

'Good,' said Charlie, and momentarily lowered the gun as he struggled with the fleeting memory of whether he'd seen this man before.

Just as he realised this was a mistake, it was too late. Hadden's two steps and the kick to the gun were quicker than Charlie's drugged reflexes could cope with. As his finger was on the trigger it did fire a couple of rounds, but harmlessly into the floor. Unfortunately the next two kicks caused him a lot more harm. The first was to his chest, catapulting him against the wall. The second was to his head as he fought desperately to gain control of the gun. He was unconscious before he hit the floor.

Roger had reached Mrs Hadden's room and opened the door. The lights were on in the bedroom. His eyes were instantly drawn to the woman's naked body lying spread-eagled on the bed. First, the nakedness; second, the look in her eyes; third, the gunfire behind him, and fourth, the figure of Miss Ridley standing to one side. The combination of shocks was too much for him. His mind went into closedown.

Miss Ridley extinguished the light.

\* \* \* \* \*

By the time the police arrived, everything was sorted. Charlie was lying on the carpet where he'd fallen, with his hands and feet tied with tape. The head wound had been attended to by one of the nurses and the bleeding had stopped. He was groaning. Sam had replaced his colleague on the chair. His hands and feet were also taped, but a gag had been pronounced unnecessary unless to stop his embarrassing weeping.

Nothing else had been touched or moved.

Once this had been achieved Mr Hadden had assembled the whole staff, apart from the two nurses attending to Mrs Hadden, in the foyer to await the arrival of the police and ambulance. The Grange station was a little depleted as many of the staff had been called in to help with a murder investigation in Barrow. Mr Hadden was most understanding.

The police surveyed the scene. Charlie was taken off to hospital accompanied by two officers. Sam was arrested and taken off to the police station, still weeping.

Mr Hadden and his staff were interviewed quickly and their statements taken. Charlie's gun and other equipment were taken away for further examination. The damaged door was examined and photographed. Officers took the tapes from the security room and it was locked securely by the police until they could examine it properly in the morning. No-one mentioned a third man.

The police finally left at about three thirty. The staff returned to their duties and gradually silence descended.

In her bedroom, Stephanie Hadden lay huddled in the corner. She was still naked and very cold. The door opened and a figure in white entered. She stared as it moved towards her. She didn't scream. She didn't resist. She welcomed the comfort the needle promised. She embraced it and fell into the warmth of dreamless sleep.

In a room which the police hadn't searched and of which they were unaware, lay a naked man. He was unconscious. A quick inspection would have revealed the small bump on his right temple, but the cause of his unconscious state was more to do with the tiny puncture mark in his left arm.

The administrator of this medical intervention was currently enjoying the vigorous attention of a man accustomed to pulling off meticulously planned events. They would deal with their hidden captive later.

\* \* \* \* \*

Unbeknown to any of these players, the occupants of the house, the unsuccessful 'special ops unit', the two naked victims, the coupling pair, the police or anyone else, one other person had watched the entire proceedings.

Jimmy Beck had come to stake out an intervention of his own. He had only just settled down in the cleft of one of the ancient oaks on the edge of the car park, at the edge of the floodlights, as Sam rolled up in his car. He was subsequently treated to a grandstand view of the entire event. He'd seen the two brightly-lit 'soldiers' scuttling amongst the cars, stabbing the tyres. He was puzzled that no-one responded. This was clarified when the front door opened for the first man to let them in. He didn't wait long before he heard the muffled explosion. From his position directly opposite the front door he was perfectly placed to see the two men appear in the middle window on the second floor. One of them reappeared in two more windows as he moved along the corridor towards where Jimmy knew Stephanie Hadden was kept under lock and key. The muffled gunfire brought his attention back to the central window. He saw Thomas Hadden briefly, before he bent down out of view.

Lots of other figures appeared on every floor of the building and outside. The ambulance arrived followed by the police. He watched all the coming and going: the first man taken away in the police car and another in the ambulance. Eventually Hadden had stood at the front door as the police cars left and the house lights went out one by one, leaving only the outside lights blaring into the night.

He'd had to adjust his position quite a few times throughout this, but now he dropped to the ground and stretched his aching limbs. After some thought, he came to the conclusion that the hut was his best option and, untying the dog from where he'd left him, set off back. His mind was full of the story he'd watched unfold. He had a lot of questions. Not least being the whereabouts of the third man. He smiled to himself in the darkness of the hut. The Harry Lime tune drifted into his head and found its way to his lips. What on earth was that all about?

# CHAPTER 10

*Friday 26th June. Evening*

Alex was thoroughly pissed off and frightened. First, she'd spent virtually all Friday afternoon and much of the evening at the police station. It wasn't as if they'd given her a hard time; they'd just left her alone for hours on end. The person she'd most dreaded coming through the door and asking her questions, Irene, hadn't materialised. Although her second worst nightmare – that creep Aston – had been in a couple of times.

He'd been careful to arrive with a woman officer. She'd worked out a little plan if he came alone. She'd scream blue murder and claim he'd put his hand on her tits or something. Anyway, he was too clever for that.

'Where were you last night between nine and eleven o'clock, Miss Henning?' As if he didn't know.

'Out with my friends.' If only.

'And can you give us their names, please?'

'Can't be sure they were always there, can I? We were in and out of clubs? Sometimes in the loo.'

'I see you've included Tina Goodwright on your list?'

'Yeh, so?' Fucking daft tart.

'Were you there when she was involved in a fracas with another girl?' Fracas? Swallowed an effing dick-shunerry have you, Dave?

'No, I wasn't. Shame really. Time someone twatted the fat bitch.'

'Oh. I thought she was a friend of yours?'

Not bloody likely. Evil little dwarf. 'Like you, eh, Dave?' That made him blink. Sad bastard, who on earth would shag him?

'I'm not your enemy, Alex. But someone out there has a pretty nasty way of dealing with the people he doesn't like.'

Is that a threat? What's that look mean? Oh my God! He knows who it is! 'Well. You'd better get out there and find him quick hadn't you?' Instead of frightening the bloody life out of me.

This must have been replayed at least three times and that wasn't the worst of it. She came out of the cop shop at about six o'clock. One of Eric Nellis's men was waiting for her; straight in the car, round to the Majestic, upstairs to his office and the door shut quietly behind her. Nellis sitting in front of the bank of TV screens. Four for the Majestic and another five or so for his other places.

'You been playing away, Alex?'

'What do you mean, Eric?'

'You know well what I mean.'

She went up behind him and put her arm on his shoulder. 'Why would I do that, Eric?'

He was silent.

She went past him, stood against one of the screens and adopted a page three pose, complete with pout.

He didn't look at her for a few moments, which allowed her to stare at this monster who controlled her life. God he was ugly:

bald scabby head, little beady blue eyes skipping from one screen to another, suit too small, even if it cost a fortune. Sweaty shirt. Lower down she didn't want to think about, but knew damn well she was likely to have to face up to it soon enough. That's a terribly bad joke, Alex.

He looked at her. That was actually worse than what he made her do: the way he looked at her.

He pushed back his chair and indicated one of the screens. She bent forwards so she could see. Oh! God! You sick bastard! He was watching a screen which was connected to one of the many rooms he rented out to his army of prossies. She'd been one once. She thought she recognised the wallpaper. No expense spared. There facing the camera was the agonised face of Julie Carter, while behind her, humping away was some fat slob in a rugby shirt. Behind him she could see other T-shirts waiting their turn. Even as she watched, the lad was pushed aside and one of his mates took over.

'At least she died happy, eh, Alex. Doing what she did best.' You sick, sick bastard. One day. One day.

He reached out and grabbed her wrist.

'Just like you, eh. Alex. Doing what you do best.'

He pulled her towards him and forced her to the floor between his fat thighs. He leant back and grabbing her by the hair, pulled her face towards his crotch.

It never lasted long and he always let her go straight to the loo. Generally she just spat into the sink, but tonight she threw up. There was nothing in her stomach, but it didn't matter.

As she washed her face and saw herself in the mirror, she knew that she wasn't going through that again. She thought of what Irene had said. Tomorrow she'd go and find her. She needed to get out.

She knew the affair with Keane had been doomed from the start. Even if Nellis didn't care about it, she did and she couldn't bear it.

She went back to the office. He wasn't there. She slipped out through the door and crept down the stairs. She could hear him talking to someone. She went out through one of the side doors and as fast as she could towards the streetlights. She didn't see the glint of well-polished shoes as a figure stepped back into the shadows. She got a taxi and went back to her flat.

Nellis had set her up in a nice suite in one of his little hotels. No other women. The other rooms were rented out to businessmen. All legitimate.

She changed her mind about Irene, packed a bag and took one last look round. As a final thought, she sat down and wrote a note, put it in an envelope and found a stamp. Rang for another taxi and while she was waiting posted the letter.

At the station she bought a ticket to Lancaster. She wasn't going to stop there; she'd see what was on offer when she got onto the platform. She didn't see anyone she knew get on the train and closed her eyes as it slowly drew out of the station. Again the figure slipped back into the shadows. Unseen, but the plan was in place.

She also didn't see the two men get on at Ulverston. But when she saw one of them coming down the central aisle, she recognised him. Why wouldn't she? He'd been in the class above hers at school. She'd even been out with him. She'd stood him up on the second date. He'd not forgotten that. She didn't wait to discuss it with him now, so she got up and made her way towards the toilet.

As she shut the intervening door and stepped into the space between the two carriages, a strong hand grabbed her by the throat. She struggled. The door opened. The other man stood in front of her.

'Remember me, Alex?' he asked.

He didn't wait to hear what she was incapable of saying. He reached out and ripped her dress like it was a piece of tissue paper. The man behind her put his hand over her mouth. She struggled. He twisted her arm up her back. The man in front, she remembered his name: Derek. She squirmed in terror. She didn't see the other man's hand come up or the flash of a blade.

Suddenly the door was swinging open. She grabbed at Derek's shirt; it ripped as the other guy pushed her through the gap and she was out into the night air, flying like a rag doll. The speed of the train flung her against the bridge railing; the whiplash broke her spine and dropped her over the edge and into the mud twenty feet below. The knife splashed into a pool forty yards away. Her blood soon stopped seeping from the gaping wound in her neck.

The train sped on to Cark, where the two men got off and got into the car waiting for them. In the back seat sat Nellis's lieutenant. Money changed hands. The man didn't say a word. They knew better than to try and engage him in conversation. They were back in the pub well within an hour of receiving the call. They told their mates they'd been down to another pub, but the beer was crap, so they'd come back. By the end of the evening they'd made sure those mates would have no memory of whether they'd even left the pub, and the landlord knew better than to remember anything – ever.

Alex's body was investigated by a few crabs and other creepy crawlies which would have made her scream like a banshee if she had been alive. The water rose and soon was lapping gently at her side, lifting her thin dress and sticking it to her cold limbs. Eventually stronger currents rolled her off the mudflat and carried her carefully upstream. Later she got entangled in the bigger limbs of a motherly oak branch which had been stuck in the mainstream for some weeks now, waiting for the high tide which would release it and dislodge the pitiful remains of her once-enviable beauty.

\* \* \* \* \*

Maliverny was back amongst the crowd baying for blood. The executioners cut and hacked. Babington screamed his piteous pleas for mercy. '*Parce mihi Domine Iesu!*' The screaming which had seared into Maliverny's head had lived there since that day. He fought those around him to get away. A hand held his arm. He turned to take one last look. The young man's eyes were closed. He'd escaped, gone to his heaven or his hell.

He fought the hand from his arm and tried to run. A face appeared above him. A young girl. What was she doing here? She was calling his name.

'Maliverny! It's me! Cora! It's alright!'

He stared about him. No! Not the dungeon! Was it the Tower? The girl was talking to him.

'Maliverny. You're alright. You were having a nightmare.'

He stared at her. Memory flickered. Someone's daughter? He didn't know her. She was wiping his face with a cool, damp cloth. His clothes were sticking to his body. He shivered. A wave of heat passed through his body drenching him in sweat, followed by a wave of cold deep in his chest. He coughed and spluttered, spat out the phlegm. The girl wrapped him with a blanket. He shivered uncontrollably. From the corner of his eye he could see a fire, its flames lighting up the cavernous room. The panelling had gone and the stars shone through where the window used to be. He knew this place. A heavy drowsiness spread though his limbs like a draught of honey ale.

The last he saw was the girl's face. Who was she?

Cora was scared. The strange man had woken her with his groaning and cries. This worsened into a tumult of screams and curses and piteous mewling. He fought with unseen attackers, pushing her arm away as she tried to comfort him. She could feel the heat from his body. He was burning up. He'd got a fever or something. She wasn't sure what to do. What was that saying? Feed a cold or starve a fever? But she knew he was losing a lot of liquid sweating like that. So: keep him warm and make him drink a lot of water.

She emptied his sack of the horrible honey stuff and filled it from the little stream she'd found making its last few yards towards one of the river channels. When she got back he'd thrown off the sleeping bag and her coat, and was writhing about on the floor. He was a big man and, with his heavy coat flailing about, it was difficult for her to do anything with him. Thankfully he suddenly seemed to give up and fall back against the wall, banging his head on the way down.

Cautiously she approached. He'd stopped breathing! She reached out to touch his hand only to jump back like a scalded cat as he jerked and gave an almighty snore, before settling down again.

It was a good minute or so before she dared try again. His breathing was still uneven, but she managed to clean the graze on his forehead and get some water into his mouth. After a while he seemed to relax, the twitching stopped and his breathing became more regular.

She sat a few feet away and stared out at the approaching dawn. What was she going to do? She couldn't leave him, but she was starting to worry about her mum. And Mrs Trencham! She'd forgotten all about her. She went to get some more water.

When she got back, he hadn't stirred. She felt his face. He was a lot cooler, but damp. Maybe he didn't need any food, but she did. She decided she'd find her way back to the hut as soon as it was light. It couldn't be far. He'd said he'd carried her here. She'd just wait a bit longer. She looked across at him again. She'd been unable to make out much of what he'd said or shouted when he was rambling on, but one phrase had been loud and clear:

'Jesu, forgive me . . .'

**\* \* \* \* \***

### *Saturday 27th June. Morning*

All Fletcher wanted to do was go for a long walk with Laura, a picnic on Kidsty Pike and the sight of an eagle or two. Instead he had to settle for a meal out last night and some gentle lovemaking. Grace timed her return from the cinema to coincide with a final drink before bedtime. All in all, a happy family night, slightly spoilt by the driving rain going back over Shap at half past seven. Still, it was June and he was in the Lake District.

He arrived at the pathology lab a few minutes past eight to find Sykes looking a bit red-eyed and dopey.

'Youngest is teething. Wife and me argued from the moment I got home. Eldest is in trouble at school. Happy families, eh?' he managed a weak smile.

'No sign of Irene?'

'Not yet.'

They went down the corridor to where they could see some lights on. John Fox was talking to DI Aston. They both turned as the latecomers arrived. Aston nodded at Fletcher and shook the pathologist's hand.

'Not stopping, Inspector?' asked Fletcher in his best 'let's be friendly to the natives' voice.

Aston gave him a stony look from the doorway. 'I've got too much on my plate to hang about waiting for you. When we say bright and early here we mean it.'

'OK, so you were early and we're doing the bright bit. See you later.'

Aston would have snarled if he was a dog, but bit his tongue instead and left without another word.

'That's what I like to see,' said the pathologist, 'professional camaraderie!'

'Yeh, right,' said Fletcher. 'I'm not sure I can manage either. Well not with the old Aston Martin there. Shit off a shovel, eh?'

Fox ignored this and waved them into his lab.

Julie Carter looked a lot better than the previous morning and the doctor's stitching was a work of art, but she was still dead. Fletcher had lost count of the number of dead bodies he'd seen, but realised that no matter how many Sergeant Sykes had set eyes on, he was never going to be able to convince his stomach that it didn't need to evict any undigested food. Sykes exited stage left, to be replaced by a doe-eyed Irene Garner. Doe-eyed? No! Not possible! Unless. . . ?

She made a face at Fletcher and followed it with a huge grin. 'I should say I'm sorry I'm late, but . . .'

'You won at bingo last night?' said Fletcher, laughing.

'And you've already pissed off Inspector Stone-face big style. Couldn't be better, thank you, sir.'

'When you two have quite finished,' said Fox, 'I would like us to resurrect a proper respectful atmosphere in here for you to listen to my report.'

They both tried hard not to look like troublesome school kids and listened very attentively, not daring to catch each other's eye.

'Cause of death: heart stopped following violent blow to the chest. As I suspected when we found her, it's difficult to be certain about the choice of weapon. My guess is some kind of serrated knife. Butcher's or fisherman's, I'd suggest. The force of the blow suggests a very powerful person, almost certainly a man. There's a slight upwards thrust, but it's virtually horizontal, so someone slightly taller than the victim.' He paused. A proper atmosphere had descended upon the room.

'There are other injuries. Notably a blow to the face which would have been disabling in itself and a knife wound to the left cheek. This was a different weapon, a very fine, sharp blade, probably a Stanley or surgical knife. It wasn't a slicing wound, more likely caused by applying pressure to force it through her cheek, which would have been extremely painful and would have filled her mouth with blood. The absence of a large amount of blood in her throat or on the ground would imply that the killing blow was administered very shortly after the smaller knife wound.'

'Which suggests either someone carrying two weapons or two people with a weapon each?'

Fox gave Fletcher a sideways look. 'I'd be very surprised if it was the former, but I can't discount it.'

Fletcher nodded.

'Time of death: between nine and eleven thirty, Thursday night.'

He hesitated. Fletcher and Irene waited. 'She'd had at least one abortion and had decidedly unhealthy internal organs, which is not surprising considering the level of alcohol and amphetamines in her system and the complete absence of any food in her stomach. Her arms are covered with ancient and much more recent injection scars.'

Fletcher looked at the floor. Irene's doe eyes had been replaced by the more familiar fierce avenger look.

'Finally, this woman's body shows signs of multiple injuries going back to childhood. Broken bones, some not properly treated and therefore badly healed, cracked ribs, head injuries, burn marks, broken fingers, you name it she's had it done to her.'

Fox's voice had descended to a barely audible whisper as he finished. Silence filled the brightly-lit room, heartlessly bright somehow.

'In my humble opinion, not my medical opinion, you understand, I can imagine this woman wouldn't have regarded death as something to be feared – more like a blessed relief.'

Fletcher looked up at him.

'There may have been two people present when she died, but they were only the last in a long line of violent attacks and abuse this woman has suffered. You won't be able to find or convict them all, but I sincerely hope you put someone away for this.'

With that he walked from the room, leaving the two detectives to contemplate the task ahead of them.

Irene reached out and touched the woman's face and stroked her hair. 'No wonder you gave me that look, Julie.' She walked away.

Fletcher gave a big sigh and followed her. Found her outside with a white-faced Sykes. None of them could think of anything to say. So they got in the car and headed to the station.

\* \* \* \* \*

They didn't see Sadie Swift sitting in her car, waiting for them to leave. Doctor Fox was less than pleased to have to repeat his findings to another officer so soon after he'd explained them to this young woman's colleagues. Her warrant card didn't convince him either, and he insisted on ringing the number she gave him. The conversation didn't last long. He put the phone down and raised his eyebrows at her.

'Well, Inspector. Curiouser and curiouser.'

She didn't smile. He repeated his findings. She was thoughtful after he'd finished.

'The second person? The killer. How tall would you say?'

Fox shook his head. 'I can't be certain but no shorter than you and not as tall as me. Unless, of course, he bent down or stood on a box.'

She gave him a stern look. He shrugged his shoulders.

'But strong?'

Again he shrugged.

'Or heavy.'

Her eyes pierced him. 'Heavy?'

'Strength and/or weight would cause a similar effect.'

She nodded. 'And the knife?'

'As I said, butcher's or fisherman's, serrated and heavy duty.'

'A common choice of weapon locally?'

He gave her a wry smile. 'Not really. No.'

She waited.

'The thugs tend to use their fists or a blunt instrument, while the husbands and wives the kitchen knife. Smaller knives occasionally, flick knives or, like the first weapon in this case, the Stanley. I understand it's the weapon of choice for the big city villains.'

She turned to go. 'If you had to bet: butcher or fisherman, which would it be?'

'Fisherman: he was gutting not cutting.'

She gave him a final stare as chilling as his prognosis.

\* \* \* \* \*

There wasn't much fun back at the station either. The huge enterprise was fast beginning to look like a complete waste of time, which didn't reflect well on Chief Inspector Mancini. Fletcher went to see him, but was back out in a few minutes.

'Nothing,' he shrugged. 'Tight-lipped lot, these Barrow folk,' he added in a poor imitation of the accent.

Irene and Sykes shared a look, but couldn't disagree with him.

'Forensics came up with a big fat zero. No evidence of any value in the alley. Nothing on the clothes or anywhere else.'

'What about Dyer? He must be the obvious suspect.'

'Disappeared. Mancini's put out a national alert. Pictures to press and TV. Don't hold your breath. I suspect chameleon tendencies will be one of his more likeable qualities.'

'So what now?' said Irene, looking at her watch. What was she? A bloody school girl?! It wasn't even midday yet?

'Got something better to do?' asked Fletcher archly.

'As a matter of fact, I do, sir,' she smiled sweetly, which was enough to cause Fletcher to roll his eyes.

'Well. There's no sign of Miss Swift and with all this fuss no-one's going to be talking to us about anything.'

He gave Irene a meaningful look. 'May as well go and get fucked, the pair of us.'

Sykes gave them a forlorn look.

'You make your own decision, mate,' said Fletcher. 'You're not answerable to me.'

Sykes now looked even sadder.

'But if you were, I'd tell you to go home, fix up a babysitter and let her suffer, while you take the trouble and strife for an Indian or something. Here, get herself a bunch of proper flowers.'

Sykes stared at the tenner in his hand and immediately began to bluster. Too late. Fletcher was already getting into his car. He wound the window down and shouted: 'And not bloody carnations – I can't stand the cheery little buggers.'

Sykes watched as Fletcher drove away. Irene put her arm round him.

'He's not all good, you know. If he doesn't get what he wants, he'll knock you out the way as though you were nothing. Take his advice. I intend to.'

Sykes followed her with his eyes. She was one sexy woman and there was a swing to her hips which even he could recognise as that of a woman looking forward to seeing a man. He headed for the flower shop. It could only go completely wrong.

\* \* \* \* \*

### Saturday 27th June

Roger opened his eyes. Was he in heaven? Was it the white tunnel which people remembered after near-death experiences? Except it wasn't a tunnel. Everything was white. A creamy soft white. He was lying on his side against a wall. Where the floor met the wall it was a continuous padded curve. The soft light was coming from transparent circles in the ceiling, which were too high to reach. He struggled to his feet. He wasn't cold, but he was naked. Naked? Why? How?

Memory flooded back in a series of staccato images. Charlie stabbing tyres in the glaring floodlights. The whump of the explosion. Rushing up through the smoke. Running along the corridor. The distant gunfire. The naked woman. Miss Ridley. Miss Ridley?

Who had materialised inside the soft white room!

How did that happen? Was he dreaming? Where was the door? He backed away.

She was looking at him, leering at him. He felt the wall behind him. He remembered he was naked and covered himself. He felt a ridiculous smile sneaking onto his face. She was still looking at him. Not moving. Just standing there, wearing a peculiar set of clothes: one piece, all black, close-fitting like a dry wet suit. Ballet shoes. Although her hair was even shorter, it was pulled tightly back into a twist held by two short sticks. All this in a blink. What the fuck was going on? He opened his mouth to speak, but it was too dry, only produced a croak like a stupid frog.

She spoke instead in that curious neutral voice. No accent. 'Well. Roger. Here we are.'

He stared back at her uncomprehending.

'I'm afraid your little rescue plan has gone terribly awry.'

He twitched nervously. She moved slowly to her left. His eyes followed her like a rat. He began to realise that something very weird was going on.

'Your two friends have been arrested and taken away by the police.'

He angled himself to face her as she went further to his left like she was circling him.

'Unfortunately the police don't know about you and we didn't feel like telling them.'

She began to come back into the centre of the space, pacing methodically. Stopped and put her hands on her hips.

'We thought we'd administer our own justice as far as you are concerned. Plus we've got a few questions to ask you.'

His body was beginning to generate the adrenaline it decided it was going to need in what was definitely turning into a fight, not flight, scenario.

She began pacing from side to side. He watched, trying not to become mesmerised.

'Mr Hadden tells me you're a fourth Dan?'

He stared at the small, round black hole with the glistening lens set high on the wall on his left, which she had indicated with the slightest lift of her head. He looked at her, she was smiling: a cat smile.

This wasn't happening. He shook his head. Not a good idea. Everything whirled. She was still there. She stopped dead centre and bowed towards him.

'I am only Jinyin san duan. Gold Eagle.'

He'd heard of it. It was Chinese. He couldn't remember the rankings.

'Are you ready?' she whispered.

He shook his head and forced his dry throat to find some way of communicating even if it was by croak. Only a gasping sound came out, but it was the nearest to 'No!' he could manage.

She began to pace again but this time getting nearer and nearer. His training took over even though his head rebelled. He shifted position, came away from the wall, his hands out from his body.

She moved fast to his left, feinted and spun round. Only some residue of instinct saved him as her left foot arced past his chest. He stumbled backwards and ducked to his right as the punch thudded into the wall-padding behind him. He scuttled away and turned to face her. She was standing back in the centre, perfectly composed as if nothing had happened. She bowed again.

'Good. I'm glad to see your instincts have remained intact. It's not often I get to fight properly.'

He shook his head slowly and made a response, this time managing to produce a few intelligible words.

'I don't want to fight you.'

'What? Because I'm a woman?'

'No. Well, that's part of it.'

'You think you're going to lose?'

'You can't do this.'

'Really? I think you'll find we can, Roger.'

He tried a different tack. 'What if I win? What if you get hurt?'

'That's my problem. My risk.'

He shook his head again. 'This is ridiculous.'

She laughed. 'No, Roger. It's you who look ridiculous.'

He felt both shame and anger. Heard his master saying these were the two worst things to let into your head or into your heart or into your body.

He stood erect. Hands by his side.

She nodded and bowed again. He didn't bow, didn't want to give it any respect. He waited.

She began pacing again. He moved in a mirror image of her moves. She stalked, he went with the wave.

When the attack came he realised straight away that she'd misled him about the ranking level. She was far better. Quicker than him, and included a move he'd only ever watched, never achieved. He ducked and parried the first four but the last one clipped his right shoulder and her foot caught his ankle. Just in time, he swung away and regained his balance. She backed away and stopped. He could hear his breathing, but not hers. He knew he wasn't going to win.

She bowed again and came forward. This time he was caught by the third move, fell heavily and couldn't roll away before she crashed down on his chest. The pain was intense, her eyes glistening above him. Her arm was a piston blur as she withdrew it and hammered it back towards his face. He expected the crunch of broken bone and blood spurting into his eyes, but she'd pulled the punch millimetres from his nose. He tried to wriggle away, but suddenly her weight lifted and she stood up and away. He rolled onto his side and tried to get up.

The kick caught him in the ribs. He cried out, but managed to roll away, still trying to escape. The next kick was into his exposed lower back; before he could move she had her arm around his throat and began to slowly strangle him. He thought he was going to die. He stopped struggling. She let him go, stood up and hovered over him.

'Not yet, Roger; I'm not going to kill you just yet.'

He lay still looking up at her.

'Not until you've tried a lot harder.' She kicked his leg. 'Get up!' she hissed.

He crawled over to the wall and sat against it.

'You're pathetic,' she said.

He closed his eyes. How was he going to get out of this? It was bizarre.

'Toy soldier,' she said. He could tell she was nearer, could almost feel her breath on his face. He opened his eyes. She was crouched down in front of him, a smirk creasing her face, eyes gleaming with – what? Lust?

This close he could see her make-up and the edge of the lipstick. He could see the way the tightly-pulled back hair was held in place by clips and smell the hairspray, see the slight sheen on her muscled neck. Her hand reached out and grasped his dick; began to crush it. Despite his fear he could feel it responding, growing larger as she gave it a couple of gentle slaps.

'You sorry little worm; can't help yourself. Has that Barrow tart been giving you lessons?'

She stood up. He looked up at her. 'You're sick. You and Hadden both. Perverted monsters. Locking that poor woman away. Sick.'

She raised an eyebrow. 'Oh, dear? Are we getting a bit cross?'

Without any back lift she kicked him hard in the balls. He yelped and curled up against the wall. She grabbed him by the hair and dragged him a couple of feet into the room, kicked him hard and, bending down, grabbed him by the throat.

'You know what, worm? I'm going to give you one more chance. Now get up and fight.'

He lay where she left him, holding his aching crotch. 'I'm not fighting you,' he muttered.

She came over and put her foot on his shoulder. 'So what do you want?'

He ignored that, tried to push the foot off his bruised ribs. She dug in harder.

'Mr Hadden thinks you've come here for other reasons.'

He grabbed at her foot. She kicked his hand away and bent down. 'Are you working undercover, toy soldier?'

He tried to muster a puzzled look on his face.

'Taking orders from a certain Mr Pole?'

This time he knew he failed to hide his surprise. 'Don't know any Mr Pole and I don't take orders any more,' he managed with a gasp.

She kicked him hard again. 'What did you say?' she demanded.

He grabbed her foot as she kicked him this time and yanked hard. As she lost balance he brought his own foot up fast and kicked her in the ribs. She fell backwards onto the floor. Quickly he rolled on top of her and fought the writhing, flailing hands until he was able to straddle her and force her hands onto the floor.

She went still, looking up at him with a smile. 'That's better, Roger,' she said. 'What are you going to do now?'

He knew this wasn't going to last long, could feel the strength in her arms.

Before he could reply, her legs came up from nowhere, crossed in front of his neck and forced him back. Within seconds he was gripped in a python-like scissor hold, fighting for his breath. She wriggled round and forced both his arms round his own neck, so that she could strangle him with one hand whilst the other was free to grab his balls and squeeze them till his eyes watered and he screamed. She rolled him over and let go, kicking him hard as she backed away.

He scrabbled to get away. She followed him, until he got to the wall. He managed to lever himself up a bit. His insides felt like they'd been pulverised. She grabbed him by the neck. He gurgled. His eyes bulged.

'Time for a walk.'

She reached up and flipped open a hidden panel, turned a handle and he fell backwards into a dark recess. She forced him back until he was out onto a metal grill. Looking through the gaps he could see a fire-escape staircase descending into the darkness. She flicked a switch above him and fluorescent lights stuttered into life.

'Down you go, Roger. You can walk or I'll kick you down. Your choice.'

He hesitated and then began to struggle to his feet. She kicked his leg away. 'Sorry. I meant crawl. Not walk.'

He slithered down the first few steps. They were wet and scraped against his skin. He regained some control and began to crawl down. She didn't follow him.

He had figured that the staircase dropped the full height of the house and wasn't surprised to find a metal door about halfway down. He scrabbled at the door which swung open.

'Take a quick look, Roger. It's not locked. I think it fits the bill. Some very nice boys' toys I'm sure you'll recognise.'

Roger didn't need to look or need a light on. He could smell the guns. Caught a glimpse of dull metal. Ordnance. Not the big sort, but plenty of it. Guns. Grenades. Maybe rocket launchers. He'd been in a weapons store before. He staggered to his feet and looked back up at the woman who shone a torch in his face.

'There's only one way out and that's at the bottom,' echoed her voice from above.

He dragged himself to the next flight and stumbled down to the bottom. As he got to the final landing, he heard a metallic noise from above and looked up. The water knocked him down. The jet followed him whichever way he tried to scramble. Just as quickly as it came on, it stopped. He lay in a sodden heap and listened to the water draining away.

Looking up, he thought he saw a body heading through the air towards him. He tried to get out of the way, but the soft bundle flopped off him and landed in the water next to him. It was his clothes.

'Put them on, Roger. We're going for a little expedition.'

He realised he was shivering. He fumbled with the bundle. It was already wet. He struggled into the trousers and fought his way into the anorak, but he was still shivering. The clothes were cold and soaked through. His teeth began to chatter.

'Sorry about your nice shiny boots,' said a voice close by.

He looked up. She was standing only five steps above him. 'I couldn't find them.'

He tried to get up. Her boot clipped the side of his head, knocking him against the rail.

'Not yet, Roger. Wait for the order to advance, soldier.'

He groaned. His head was bleeding, blood seeping through his fingers.

'Right. Open the door and push it outwards.'

It seemed to take an age, but eventually he managed to force the heavy door out into the cold air. Before he had time to take in the view, she pushed him forwards and he fell onto the grass.

Half pushed, half kicked, he stumbled out onto the sand. The light was fading, but he could see they were heading out onto the estuary sands. Over to his left he caught sight of the lights from the building. She had the torch, which she shone in his face if he looked back at her. As they got further out, he stole another look back and could see a silhouette in the last window on the top floor.

'Get a move on, Roger,' she said, pushing him hard in the back. 'The audience is getting impatient for the final scene.'

He fell into a hidden channel. She dragged him out. Even though he was already shuddering with the cold, the fresh water was icy. He'd lost track of how far they'd come. All around him the sand stretched in every direction.

'This will do,' she said.

He fell to his knees. Her face appeared in front of his, torch beneath her grinning face like some grotesque ghoul.

'This is it, Roger. The final curtain. You need to stand up and take a bow.'

She dragged him to his feet, took a couple of steps back and stood looking at him. He staggered to his left. Her foot whacked into his stomach. He did his bow and crumpled to the ground without a sound. She bent down beside him.

'Well done, Roger. I'm disappointed I wasn't allowed to break a few limbs, but that's not how we want your body to be found. A few bruises here and there are fine. Goodnight, Corporal. Sweet dreams.'

She stood up, dragged him a few feet and rolled him into a deeper channel. He fought his way to the surface. He could feel the bottom beneath his knees and the slight surge of the current. He looked up. She was standing at the edge, where the water had bitten away at the collapsing sand. She stamped on it and a whole edge fell on top of him, weighing him down. He'd got sand and water in his mouth. He struggled to fight his way out of his sodden, sucking grave. His ears were blocked, so he couldn't hear her final words, but saw her blow him a kiss and disappear.

Somehow he managed to find enough strength to claw his way out of the channel, shivering and spitting out the clogging sand. Twice the bank collapsed back in, taking him with it, but finally he felt flat, solid sand beneath him. He rolled onto his side. He couldn't see a thing. There was no moon. No stars. No lights to guide him.

He staggered to his feet and looked around: total darkness. No wind. No direction. The sound of sand plopping into the channel behind him. He turned and felt his way. Nearly fell back in, lay down and put his hand into the water. It was flowing towards his left much stronger now. The tide was coming in. He needed to get to dry land. He got up and set off alongside the channel, sometimes stumbling into it. No idea where he was heading, a grey figure in the vast expanse of grey sand; all the while the soft plopping and slushing of the banks collapsing into the ever widening and deepening channels.

\* \* \* \* \*

## Saturday 27th June

Fletcher felt strangely disconnected from the events going on around him. There was plenty to make him angry: the sickening violence, the smirking villains, the incompetent colleagues; all the things that normally pushed his buttons, but . . . ? He'd not gone home, but found himself parked at the end of the road near the caravans where they'd tried to catch Jimmy Beck.

He walked the length of the beach and back again, dawdling, beachcombing. Pockets full of shells. Head empty. Well, not empty. Not at all. He'd been here and there in his head: up on the tops at Todmorden wearing his new outdoor gear; standing on the viaduct with a mad man; lifting the dead body of that young police officer lying on top of Sadie, couldn't remember his name; running like hell to get out of the tower, the explosions rocking the building as he flung himself to the ground, and always returning to that scruffy little pub in Bacup. Louisa Cunninghame in a Sophia Loren hat.

He spent the rest of the afternoon in the car looking through the collated summary Mancini had given him. He had to hand it to Aston who'd done most of the work. Zero.

Why did that trouble him? Was it that he just didn't like the man, or was there something else? He couldn't put his finger on it: something to do with zero. Nothing. Not possible, surely. Nellis couldn't have that much control. OK, most people were terrified of him, but it must be relative. There must be someone, somewhere, who was either too stupid or innocent or had a grudge against him. The impossible gave birth to the inevitable. As Holmes would have said (the master detective not the naive Barrow namesake): *when all other possibilities are discounted the answer must be the one staring up at you from every page.* No matter how implausible. He

227

shook his head. But how to expose it? And how would that help them find the IRA hired hands in all this mess?

'Ay there's the rub . . .' he said and started the engine.

He stopped at the service station on the M6, even though it meant he had to come off and go back south for a few miles. He knew he could get out via the no exit service road and continue his way north.

Saturday afternoon it was nearly deserted. Most weekenders were already back in their escape holes, making the best of the second day away, drinking themselves stupid, away from work and bosses and reality. Whereas his reality was looking at the dead body of a woman who'd been abused all her life, before being killed in a back alley and left as bait for the rats and other vermin.

He'd reached a conclusion he couldn't begin to suggest to Mancini or anyone else, certainly not Sadie or Adversane. Yet he was strangely detached? Why? He should be still there, unearthing and following leads which others had missed or deemed irrelevant or, what he was now thinking, deliberately covered up. Secrets and lies. Instead he'd decided to go back to his own escape hole. He'd not phoned Laura. She probably wasn't expecting him.

He stared across at a gang of youths who were trying to liven the place up a bit. Laughing and throwing things at each other. A young woman came out from behind the counter and remonstrated with them. One of the lads threw his drink at her, which splattered down her uniform. She stared at it, burst into tears and ran back to the kitchen. The youths took this a signal to start the wild rumpus and began running round the canteen area, knocking people's drinks over, tipping plates into their laps. One of them grabbed a woman's handbag and they scattered, whooping and yelling. One of the lads, bigger than the rest, came thundering towards Fletcher. As he got level he swung out intending to hit the man in the face – arrogant twat, sitting there in his leather coat.

Fletcher ducked the blow and, half standing, punched the lad hard in the guts. He fell like a dead weight, all the wind knocked from him, and lay gasping on his side, fighting for breath. Fletcher got up, calmly stepped over him and went to his car. Five minutes later, he was heading north through the Howgills. He felt nothing. Numb.

When he got to the house, he sat outside watching the woman and the stepdaughter he loved passing backwards and forwards in the brightly-lit kitchen. Tears crawled down his face.

\* \* \* \* \*

Irene was back at the conference hotel. She had butterflies in her stomach. When was the last time that had happened? Would he turn up?

She'd spent the whole afternoon having her hair done and a manicure and a full body massage – the works. She knew she looked absolutely stunning. Other men looked at her as she sat waiting in the bar. One even made his way towards her, until he saw her shaking her head and mouthing 'No'. He shrugged and gave her a 'well it was worth a try' puppy-dog look. She checked her watch. Stop it! Teenager!! And, no! You can't have another drink, yet!

The conference was mainly men, which was why Matt had chosen it for her – something to do with the construction industry. The few women who were present were having a difficult time not looking smug. A ratio of ten to one in their favour meant the selection process was entirely in their hands. Who wouldn't be smug? Irene had been last night. But she still thought she'd got lucky.

And here he was, slipping through the crowd. Dark hair, dark eyes, a slim but, she knew, muscular body, a suit which fitted, crisp white shirt, Italian shoes – sheer elegance and his smile was heading straight to her. Look away! Play hardball!

No way. She returns his smile and stands to kiss him as he comes up close, the warmth of his body mingling with her heady perfume. People stop and stare, smiles on their lips too. Brief lives entangled in one visceral moment of bliss.

# CHAPTER 11

*Saturday 27th June. Midnight*

Roger stumbled once more and lay still. He could feel willpower ebbing away in direct ratio to the strength of the incoming water. He'd crossed the channel before it got even wider because he sensed it bearing left, taking it nearer to the main channel.

In this he was entirely mistaken. The channel had weaved this way and that until he'd no idea which way he was going. Some of the channels in this stretch took the incoming tide in a huge curve back on itself. He'd actually not gone very far at all.

He lay there, bringing his knees up to his chin. At least whilst he was moving he'd kept some body warmth, but as soon as he lay down his temperature started to drop. His eyes closed.

A small ripple swept under his foot, followed by a bigger one.

Suddenly he heard a different sound: sloshing and glugging to his right. He tried to get up, tried to see through the darkness. A torchlight flashed towards him, found him and bobbed up and down as it came nearer and nearer. He groaned and fell back into the sand. She'd come to finish him off. But first there was some rapid splashing and a hairy snout sniffed at his face. There was a low growl and more splashing all around him.

A hand grabbed him by the arm; the light was in his face. He shielded his eyes. A voice swam into his head.

'What the bloody hell are you doing out here?' it said.

Not her. His heart lifted.

The man was strong. He helped Roger up and turned back the way he'd come. It was actually only a hundred yards or so. A rock loomed out of the darkness. They staggered through a channel up to their thighs and then a grass bank, solid land. Twenty more steps. Some straggly trees fingered their way out of the gloom. A building. The man helped him round to a door. They went in and shut out the cold night. Inside a stove was burning. The room was thick with smoke, but it was warm.

He fell onto the floor and lay there soaking up the warmth, coughing the sand out of his throat. The dog gave him another inquisitive sniff and went to lie down near the stove.

His rescuer didn't have much to say but concentrated on getting him out of the sodden clothes and into a sleeping bag. Roger realised that he had stopped shivering out there on the sand, but now he shook with a vengeance.

The man busied himself with a cooking stove, brought him some scalding tea and poured the contents of a packet into a pan. Cursing, he went back out into the night, returning a few moments later with a bucket full of water. Some of the water went into the pan and he began to stir it. The dog had raised his head as the man went out and growled at Roger, but settled down again as soon as he came back.

Roger's teeth had stopped chattering and the shudders were coming in waves, rather than continuously, which was a good sign. He was gradually able to focus on the stranger in the flickering light of the stove. He wondered vaguely why there was no light, but he could see well enough to know it wasn't her, nor Hadden or any of his men.

'You saved my life,' he coughed.

The man looked at him. 'You're not the first. It's the dog who heard you,' he said.

Roger couldn't think of anything to say to that. He coughed.

The man was still staring at him, until his face broke into a gap-toothed smile. 'You're the third man, aren't you?'

Roger didn't understand.

'You were one of those soldiers breaking into Hadden's palace.'

Roger's eyes widened. Fear surged back into his body. He started to shudder again.

'I was watching. I saw three of you go in, but only two come out.'

The man turned, took the pan off the stove and poured the contents into a large mug. 'Here. Drink this. Tomato soup. Warm your insides.'

Roger took it and sipped at it greedily. The man sat on the floor, looking into the firelight.

'What were you doing in there, anyway? He's nowt worth stealing, unless he's changed.'

Roger concentrated on getting the soup down.

'Unless?'

Roger put the mug down. 'Who are you?' he asked.

The man weighed up the odds. 'Jimmy Beck. And you?'

'Roger Skeldon.'

Jimmy eyed him thoughtfully. 'So what were you doing out there? By rights you should have drowned by now.'

'They knew we were coming. I heard Charlie's gun go off, but someone knocked me out. Next thing I know I'm in this white padded room.'

'Uhuh,' said Jimmy with a nod.

Roger looked at him. 'You know it?'

'I know of it.'

'Well, then this woman – Ridley, she's called – she was there when I came round. She . . . she . . . beat me up. Martial arts stuff.'

Jimmy gave him a puzzled look.

'I know, but she was really good. I couldn't . . .' Roger trailed off. It sounded ridiculous.

'So then she took you down the fire escape and abandoned you in the middle of the sand?'

Roger stared at him. 'How do you . . . ?'

Jimmy got up and filled the kettle again. 'Someone told me about the fire escape. She wouldn't have to take you very far in the dark, especially if you'd had a beating. The house is only round the next headland. Can't be more than a mile, but on the sand in the dark it may as well have been on the moon.'

Roger gave this some thought. 'So what are you doing here?'

Jimmy looked into the flames, stroked the dog. 'We're not very popular just now, are we, boy?'

Roger left it at that and snuggled down in his bag. He suddenly felt incredibly tired. When Jimmy looked across at him a few seconds later he'd dropped off. Jimmy sighed and quietly got into his own bag. Sleep didn't come so easily to him.

\* \* \* \* \*

### Sunday 28th June

It rained all Sunday morning. Laura brought Fletcher tea in bed. He didn't stir. She decided to leave him, see if sleep did him any good.

She sat by herself watching the rain. She couldn't figure out what was wrong with him. She'd never seen him like this. She'd seen him cry before, but this was different. He seemed to be suffering from some sort of depression. She had to keep telling herself it wasn't another woman – in particular a certain young lady whom she didn't trust, mainly because she was no lady. Although strangely, she didn't really think the woman was the cause, there was something else.

She started to peel some potatoes, hoping that food might cheer him up. She knew he didn't eat properly when he was working. Grace had got up early and left with some friends to go to a festival somewhere down south. She hoped the weather would be better there. At least one person was happy.

'Hi,' said a hoarse voice from the doorway. 'Can I tempt the young lady back into a warm bed?'

She went willingly.

Later, after he'd got them both another brew, they sat up in bed. Not much was said and she thought it best to give him time.

The rain was easing off when he spoke. 'Have you ever been to Barrow?'

'Once, when I was a child; I had an aunt and uncle who lived there. All I remember was the beach. They've been dead a long time. Not been near since.'

He stayed silent for a few minutes, then said, 'Can you imagine a place where everyone is afraid? Where no-one dare speak out?'

'Sounds medieval.'

'I said "tribal" to Irene.'

Laura ignored that.

'The thing is, I don't believe it.'

'What?'

'That one person can have so much power.'

She couldn't think of what to say to that, other than to think of people like Hitler and Stalin.

'The alternative is worse.'

'How come?'

He got out of bed and went to the bathroom. She heard the shower running. He put his head round the door. 'Do you fancy a drive?'

'Where to?'

'Sunny Rochdale.'

She laughed and then realised it wasn't a joke. Three hours later, they pulled up outside a large stone-built house at the end of a track high up on the side of Holcombe Moor beneath the Peel Monument.

The door was open and a large, heavily-built man filled the space.

'Well,' he said. 'You're the last person I was expecting to see on a Sunday afternoon.'

Chief Inspector Frank Worthington, still in charge at Rochdale nick but counting the days to the finally agreed retirement date in October, showed them into his mill-owner's residence. Mrs Worthington – archetypal farmer's wife, nearly as large as her husband, no-nonsense Yorkshire Dales farming stock – provided tea and freshly-made scones, pronounced with a short 'o', nodded a curt hello and took Laura off to show her round the garden.

'You've got half an hour, gentlemen, before you've to git tha'selves down to t' Rabbit and Dogs, back in time for dinner at five,' were her parting orders.

Worthington settled himself into his huge armchair and steepled his fingers in expectation. Whatever brought Fletcher here wasn't going to be good news.

'So? What's to do?' he asked.

Fletcher put the china cup down, relieved to get it back on its equally delicate saucer in one piece. 'Sleeping with the enemy. No. Lying with the enemy or even shagging the enemy, sir.'

'I would ask you not to use such words in my house, Inspector,' said Worthington.

He paused. 'Are we talking about colleagues?'

'I'm afraid so, sir.'

'Evidence?'

Fletcher shook his head. 'You know that if I had evidence I wouldn't be here, sir.'

'Circumstantial?'

Fletcher shook his head again.

Worthington looked at him sternly. 'So what have you got?'

'A feeling. An instinct. A gut reaction. Sixth sense. Call it what you like. I just know a bent copper when I see one. I can feel it in my bones.'

Worthington was shaking his head all through this. 'Come on, Fletcher. You know me better than this. Tell me something solid.'

'It's too perfect.'

'How perfect?'

'How can one man hold an entire town in a state of such fear that no-one, not one person, will dish the dirt? There must be tens, no hundreds, of people he's hurt, upset, destroyed or otherwise pis . . . annoyed. But no-one is willing to give us a single left-over scrap of a half-gnawed splinter of a bone of a clue. Chief Inspector Mancini brought in over eighty people after a prostitute was murdered outside one of this man's clubs. I thought it a clever strategy, because it didn't include the prime suspects. Lots of people knew the victim. She was a sad, abused woman, but someone must have cared about her. Someone knows what happened or, more to the point, who would want her dead – but, nothing. Complete waste of time, and God knows how he's going to square the cost with the chief constable.'

Worthington waited to see if there was any more. Fletcher had been unable to remain seated and paced up and down Mrs Worthington's best Wilton. He was going to wear a hole in it.

'Why not a dissatisfied punter?'

'She was attacked by two people. The first was probably only threatening her. We've got a more than likely suspect for that, but the second one meant her to die. Used a gutting knife.'

Worthington stared at the younger man. He'd seen him angry before, but this was a level of righteous vengeance he'd not witnessed. 'So who is it you suspect of the cover-up?'

Fletcher hesitated.

'I've no evidence . . .'

Worthington waved it away like an irritable fly.

'He's a local DI. Miserable bastard called Aston. Dave Aston. As in Martin . . .'

Worthington waited.

'And he spends most of his free time at the end of a fishing rod.'

The chief inspector put up his hand. Fletcher was silent. The ladies returned. The two gentlemen strolled down the lane to the pub, returning on time for a traditional Sunday roast that Laura could only marvel at: Yorkshire puddings with thick gravy as a first course, followed by meat, roast potatoes and three veg; upside-down jam sponge pudding, which Mrs Worthington called 'railway pudding' with a bucketful of custard; Wensleydale to finish. Coffees and brandy for the men, Laura to drive home. Fletcher had one final brief conversation with the chief inspector as they shook hands. The only word Laura managed to catch was 'proof' – a concept she knew caused Fletcher a lot of grief.

Fletcher hadn't cheered up much, but Laura could sense a grim determination had overtaken his depression. He was gone before she woke up in the morning. On the kitchen table she found a note. One slip of paper folded into four. All it said was 'I love you Fx'.

\* \* \* \* \*

Cora and her father didn't meet up on Saturday, even though they were not half a mile apart. She thought he was still hiding out in Barrow. He thought she'd run off to Manchester. He was putting off the inevitable need to leave his favourite places, and she was seeing the smoke from the chimney, not daring to approach. She watched for about an hour. He was out with the dog, catching rabbits and collecting various items from Hadden's gamekeepers' hut and the other outhouses. She gave up in the end and went back to see how Maliverny was getting on.

She needn't have worried. He slept most of the day, only waking late on. She'd managed to catch a couple of fish, so that's what they ate. He was quiet, thoughtful and kept staring at her. She was restless. Not sure what she should do, first resolving to go back and face the music, before wavering and thinking plan B was better. Hour on hour, she changed her mind this way and that. Very little was said.

Evening came and despite – or because of – the desultoriness of the day, they were both tired. Maliverny was still recovering from his latest bout of the sickness and Cora from restless indecision. They settled down in separate corners, listening to each other's breathing and watching the fire slowly die.

It was long after the sun had gone down and Cora's eyes had closed when he began to speak. She blinked and looked across to where he was leaning up against the wall. He was staring into space and she couldn't be sure he was even aware of her.

'Father, forgive me for I have sinned,' he began, and after a short pause continued with what Cora knew her mother called a confession. She had long ago stopped going to church, but still wore a cross round her neck.

'I have told lies. I have blackened the good names of righteous men. I have taken the thirty pieces of silver and betrayed those who thought I was their friend. John Savage. Robert Barnwell. Chidiok Tichborne. Many have died because of me. Lord forgive me.'

Cora held her breath. She could see the sheen of sweat on his face. His eyes stared resolutely at the wall.

'God have mercy on their souls,' he whispered, his voice becoming hoarse. 'Jesu, save me. Jesu save me from such a death.'

Cora watched as he repeatedly crossed himself until his head sank onto his chest. It was some time before she moved. Without regard for his fever or the stench of his body, she put her arm round his hunched shoulders and rested her head on his arm. Her head filled with images of her own transgressions before she cried herself to sleep.

* * * * *

Steve Nellis didn't do Sundays – well, not before late afternoon. But today was an exception.

He found Grim, who was helping his dad with his nets. Albert Grimshaw didn't like his lad knocking about with the likes of Steve Nellis, but they'd been friends since primary school. He shrugged when he saw the lad standing at the door of the boat house. The Grimshaws were not given to wasting any words. He glanced up as his son walked away. He had the same deliberate step as his, same big hands hanging by his side. He went back to his nets.

No-one apart from school teachers called him William and he didn't listen to them anyway. He'd ended up in the remedial department, even though they knew very well there was nothing wrong with him. He could read, write and do sums. He didn't like gym or football. Never brought a note. Just wouldn't do it. Happy to watch, well maybe not happy; the Grimshaws didn't smile. He didn't want to do anything but draw and he *could* draw. Only with a pencil and no colouring in, but the drawings were startling in their accuracy and fine shading. He wasn't bothered if they put them on the walls or not. Only drew what he fancied, mainly natural things, but occasionally a chair or an object which interested him. Never people and certainly not girls. They didn't exist, as far as he was concerned; not that many would approach him anyway. He was just too big. A strange solid presence.

He and Nellis didn't say much to each other either. Sometimes Nellis would ask him things, but he didn't expect an answer. But, for whatever reason, they were inseparable. Once or twice older lads would think Nellis was asking for a slap and needed putting in his place, but faced with Grim they backed off.

His reputation rested on one incident. Nellis had called some bigger lad a name or something. The lad had punched him in the face and knocked him down. Grim had simply grabbed the lad by the scruff of his neck and slammed his face into the nearby wall again and again and again. The lad was in hospital for months and still bore the scars.

No-one said a word.

Now he followed Nellis as he called on the other members of the gang: Hodge, Naylor, Trev and Ozzy. Indie had gone missing. No-one asked why. The six of them waited outside the King George. A battered transit drove up. Two men in shell suits: one driving, the other by his side. He didn't need an introduction. Trev had been told about the boots and tried real hard not to look at them. 'If you can see your face in them you're about to die,' said Indie's voice in his head. He wished he hadn't come. Nothing was said, he got in with the other lads and the van turned round and headed across the bridge.

On the way the younger ones looked out of the windows. They didn't often leave Barrow. They stared at the fields and the sheep, looked at the distant hills. They'd never been there. Might as well have been a foreign country.

The van trundled through Ulverston. One or two had been here, giving the locals a bit of stick. The van continued out of town and didn't stop until after they'd seen the old railway bridge rusting away above the innocent looking river in its wide, sandy bottom. They parked up in Greenodd and the two older men went into the pub. Nellis pulled a bag from under one of the seats from which he produced a set of golf clubs and silently handed them out. The men came back out with a crate of beer, from which the young ones took a bottle each – apart from Grim.

'What we doing out here, Nellis?' asked Naylor, aware of the darting glances of the others.

Nellis sneered at him. 'What's the matter, Nails? Don't you like playing golf?'

Naylor laughed, but no-one else did.

Nellis stood up and began to slash at a bed of nettles by the roadside. 'The Farah tart has told me where the teacher basher might be hiding out. So we're going to get our stash back. You got a problem with that?'

'Out here?' asked Naylor, looking around.

'Not here, you daft sod. Over there beyond the woods.' He pointed out over the estuary with his club. 'Her dad's got a little hideaway apparently, so we need to go and hack them out of the rough.'

Naylor looked towards the distant trees and back at the assembled gang. 'So what's with the heavy artillery?' he asked, nodding at the two men sitting on the wall.

'You're always asking questions, Nails. If you don't like it, you can fuck off home.'

'I didn't say that. I just wonder why we need their help, if it's just Cora and her dad.'

Nellis walked up to him and looked up into his face. 'Because, you nosey bastard, there may be more than just them, OK?'

The man with the army boots stood up. 'Are you lot ready? We're not hanging about while you have a girly spat. We need to get going. The tide'll be turning soon.'

Nellis glared at him. 'It's alright, Baz. It's nothing. Is it, Nails?'

He pushed Naylor against the wall. Naylor pushed him back and raised his six iron. Nellis went up close. 'Are you thinking of using that, Nails?'

They eyeballed each other for a few seconds, until Naylor lowered the club. The driver, Frank, laughed, stood up and followed Baz as he made his way towards the old bridge. Both of them were carrying bags over their shoulders. The five lads trailed after Nellis, Naylor bringing up the rear. A couple of the locals came out of the pub and watched as the gang ignored the warning sign and clambered across the bridge.

'We ought to tell the police, Ken.'

'Not bloody likely, Stan. They're from Barrow. Eric Nellis's lad. You saw nothing, mate.'

He walked away, leaving his friend to consider the dilemma.

\* \* \* \* \*

### Sunday 27th June

Roger came to with a start. Light was streaming though cracks in the walls. His memory surged back. He looked over to the other side of the hut. The man's sleeping bag was rolled up. He'd gone.

Roger got out of his bag and peered through the slats of the shutters. It was daylight, looked like it had been raining. He'd no idea of the time. Turning back into the room, he bumped into his trousers hanging from the ceiling. He felt them. They were dry. So was his shirt and anorak. He put them on. In the corner was a pair of boots – a bit big, but they'd do.

He went outside and looked around: no-one in sight. The estuary twinkled at him through the trees. He shuddered, but made himself walk through so he could see it stretched out in front of him. Away to his right he could see the road. It must be Sunday, he thought. He couldn't see the main channel, so reasoned it was low tide. He looked again at the road. He needed to get back. He thought of Shirley.

It started to rain heavily.

There was a sound behind him. The dog was just four yards away, growling deep in his throat. Roger didn't move. Jimmy Beck appeared through the trees.

'Thinking of getting off, Roger?'

Roger nodded.

'Get some breakfast inside you first though, eh?'

Roger's stomach gurgled. He followed the man and the dog back to the hut. The smell of bacon made his stomach even more excited. Jimmy was crouched down shaking a sizzling pan. 'Courtesy of Mr Hadden himself,' he said.

'What?' asked Roger, fear rising above his hunger.

Jimmy looked round and grinned. 'It's alright. He doesn't know. I got it from one of his gamekeeper's sheds.'

Roger gave a sigh of relief and sat down on the bench. Hunger replaced fear. 'What's the time?'

'Late morning. Tide's on the turn.'

Roger took the proffered sandwich and burnt his tongue wolfing it down. 'I need to get back,' he said, with his mouth full.

Jimmy ignored this and offered him a second helping. They both sat munching and gulping mugs of tea.

'So what are you doing here anyway?'

His rescuer narrowed his eyes. 'I'm not stopping. My daughter's in a bit of trouble. I thought she might be hiding out here, but she's not, so plan B.'

Roger considered this, considered asking what sort of trouble and what plan B might be, but came to the conclusion that he was in enough trouble himself without having to cope with anything else right now.

'So what are you going to do about what happened to you last night?'

Roger shook his head. 'Don't know really. It's not sunk in yet.'

'They meant you to die.'

'I know – but what can I do?'

Jimmy nodded, thought of adding something, changed his mind. Nothing else was said for a few minutes. Each one of them had plenty to think about.

Roger got to his feet. 'I don't know what to say. You saved my life.'

Jimmy smiled. 'I told you. It was the dog.'

Roger put out his hand. 'I know, but still . . . thank you. If you ever . . .' He thought how stupid that was, offering such a self-possessed and competent man his help. He went to the door, couldn't think of anything else to say and stepped outside. Jimmy followed him and pointed away to his right.

'Stick to the grass on your right; in half a mile or so you'll be able to see the old railway bridge. Ignore the sign. It was built by the Victorians. They'll have to blow it up before it falls down. You'll be able to get a bus from Greenodd although there won't be many today. It's Sunday.'

Roger thanked him again and set off. The rain had eased to a drizzle, but the clouds were low. He'd be lucky to get to the road before it rained again. When he got to the corner he turned to wave at the man, but he'd gone.

Roger carried on. He'd seen the fog gradually thickening further down the estuary. He crossed over a gully which came out from behind a farm inland. There was a small outcrop of rock in front of him covered in gorse and a few wind-ragged trees. He opted to struggle through the branches rather than scramble over the sharp rocks and splash through the little gullies.

As he climbed up a steep-sided rock to reach the other side of the outcrop, he slipped and nearly lost his balance. Taking it again more carefully, he clambered to the top and peered over. Immediately he ducked down and huddled against a tree trunk.

Not thirty yards away, coming towards him, were six or seven men. It wasn't the sight of the incongruous golf clubs in their hands which astonished him, nor the inappropriate townie clothing and footwear, but the fact that he recognised one of them instantly. One of the last people he'd expect or fear to see in such a place as this. He sneaked another quick look. No mistake.

Now only twenty yards away, striding along with a bag over his shoulder, was the unmistakable hulking shape of Private Barry 'Baz' Smith, late of the Lancashire Fusiliers, dishonourably discharged for the rape and assault of a Cypriot woman more than three years ago. Barry Smith, who Roger knew to be currently in the employ of one Eric Nellis. Roger hunkered down, looked to his right. There was cover if could make it. He ran, crouched down and disappeared into the thicker grove of trees.

A more observant bunch would have noticed the giveaway footprints and broken branches as they clambered across the outcrop, but they were too busy complaining about their trainers getting wet to pay attention to sheep-shagger stuff like that.

Roger watched from his hiding place. They crossed the gully and set off across the sand towards the hut. It was obvious that they must know where they were going. Jimmy had said he wasn't too popular right now and that his daughter was in some sort of trouble. But what could he do against eight thugs, carrying golf clubs, and not a ball in sight? He watched as Baz ordered them to fan out. That confirmed it. He had to do *something*.

He started to move through the trees. He figured he could get all the way there without going out onto the sand. He had to help. The man had saved his life. He wasn't to know that things were just about to change for the worse back at the hut.

\* \* \* \* \*

The reason Jimmy hadn't been there to wave back was that, as he stood watching Roger crossing the sand, the dog growled a warning before inexplicably racing off into the trees.

Jimmy knew better than to give his position away by shouting after him. Cursing the dog, he hurried into the hut, picked up his bag and headed for the wood, but to the left of where the dog had run. He knew that if he could get to the track, he could be long gone before anyone appeared. He didn't pause until he was into the old yew trees.

Then he stopped and gathered his breath. In the distance he could hear the dog barking, yelping. What on earth had he found?

He slapped his forehead! Stupid! There was only one person the dog would run to, who he'd yelp at like that! Cora! He broke cover and began to run back along the track.

* * * * *

That same morning, Cora had left Maliverny muttering and grumbling as he reassembled the remains of the fire. She hadn't mentioned last night and neither did he. She'd said she would fetch some more firewood, but had only gone a few yards when she heard something rushing towards her through the woods. She hid behind a tree, but that was useless. The next minute she was rolling around being kissed and licked, laughing and giggling with happiness.

Her father leaving was bad enough, but taking his dog was heart breaking. She'd been about nine when he'd come back from the races with a tiny puppy in his pocket. She loved the little bundle of wriggling warmth. She'd spent hours with him on the beach or chasing rabbits on the North End. When they'd both calmed down, she set off with him at her heels back to the hut. Her dad must be there.

As she got near, the dog went on ahead. She approached carefully. The dog came back. It barked once. She put her fingers to her lips. It would be fun to surprise her dad. She fondled the dog's ears and held his collar. They walked down the slight slope to the hut. No smoke. The door was open. She pushed it ajar and looked inside. No-one there. She stepped back out and thought of calling his name, but something stopped her. The birds had stopped singing. The only sound was the breeze in the trees. The dog growled, sniffing the wind. She knelt down, holding onto him. They both heard a sound. Someone was coming. Not someone.

Five, six, seven people came out of the trees all around her. Her heart sank. She clung to the dog.

Nellis swaggered towards her. 'Hi, Cora. Good to see you. Nice dog you got there.'

The dog growled. His hackles were rough against her arm.

She watched as the others spread out. The lads she recognised, but not the older man.

'We've come for our stash, Cora. Where is it?'

'It's not here,' she said, trying to stop her voice wavering and hanging onto the dog for grim death. She knew he'd go for them, but they wouldn't hesitate to use the clubs.

'Oh. No. That's a shame.'

'It's not far. I hid them.'

'Clever girl. So let's go.'

A voice came from behind her. 'She's not going anywhere, Nellis.'

She turned to see her father at the gate. Her eyes widened at the sight of the gun in his hands. It was pointing at Nellis.

She looked back at Nellis. The grin had left his face. 'Hey. Jimmy. Long time no see,' he said.

'Not long enough, you little shit. Now back off, before I remove one of your nobbly little knees.'

Nellis looked nervously round. The gang was there but their eyes were flitting from one to the other.

'I'm not joking lads. I'm not going to miss from this distance. He's the first. If you run, I'll get another two for certain. So just put the clubs down and piss off back to Barrow.'

Nellis didn't need to look; he knew they weren't up for this.

Neither was he. They all knew Jimmy Beck could use a gun. Where the fuck was Baz?

'Right here, Stevie,' said a voice off to his right. Baz appeared from behind the hut, his gun pointing at Jimmy. 'Put the gun down, Jimmy or I'll kill the girl . . . or better still shoot you and kill the girl later.'

Jimmy held his aim. 'You wouldn't want to do that, Barry,' he said calmly. 'The way I see it, by the time you've fired at me, young Stevie here will have a gaping hole where his head used to be and that would take some explaining to Doreen – whatever you do next.'

Baz considered this for a while and changed his aim. 'You're right, Jimmy. So I'll kill the girl first. Whatever happens after that will be all down to you. A dead daughter and Doreen to deal with sounds worse to me.'

Throughout this exchange, the others had stood as still as extra trees. There was a terrible silence. Wisps of fog began to creep through the trees: arboreal and human.

Jimmy slowly lowered his gun, tears of anger in his eyes.

Baz stepped forward. 'Throw the gun this way, Jimmy,' he said, still pointing his own gun at Cora. The dog barked. Nellis jumped, raised his club to protect himself. Jimmy threw the gun down the path.

Baz nodded towards his mate Frank, who edged across to pick it up.

At which point, a centre-back burst out from behind the hut and brought Baz down with a charging tackle. The gun went off. Naylor and Hodge ran. Ozzy and Trev froze, dropped their clubs to the ground. Trev passed out and slumped to the ground in a puddle of his own making. The charging figure grappled with Baz on the rough ground. Frank had reached Jimmy's gun only to be knocked aside by Jimmy. The gun flew off into the bushes. There was a scream of agony from Baz which ended abruptly as a fist crunched into his mouth. He slumped onto his back and his head lolled limply to one side.

Roger slowly got to his feet. Jimmy and everyone else stared in astonishment. Except for Nellis, who stood centre stage, holding Cora by her hair, a knife to her throat. The dog struggled in her grip. Nellis kicked it away. It came back for him, but Jimmy's call stopped it in its tracks. It stood confused, barking and growling.

'Frank, get the bloody gun, you stupid twat!'

Frank looked up at Jimmy, who was glaring at Nellis. 'If you harm her, you're dead, Nellis. If the dog doesn't finish you off, I will.'

Frank was scrabbling in the bushes.

Nellis calmly raised the knife and cut a thin line across Cora's face. She screamed. The dog barked and leapt at Nellis. He kicked it away again. 'Call it off, Jimmy, or I'll do the other cheek.'

Jimmy yelled at the dog which withdrew a few feet, but was still barking. Frank had found the gun and shakily pointed it at Jimmy.

'OK, everyone. Let's just stay calm, eh,' said Nellis.

Throughout all this Grim hadn't moved.

'Just you and me, eh, Grim?' said Nellis, recovering his arrogance.

Grim said nothing, but didn't take his eyes off Cora.

'OK, Cora. Where's the stash? I've run right out of patience. Tell me or I'll cut you again.'

'Let her go.'

Everyone stared at Grim. Nellis looked at him in disbelief. 'What? What did you say?'

Grim didn't move. 'I said leave her be.'

'Grim. This is me, Stevie. Your mate.'

'Let her go.'

Nellis stared at him. 'Frank, shoot the stupid bastard. He's lost it.'

Frank looked at everyone and raised the gun.

From out of the fog came a huge black shape. It bellowed into their midst, heading straight for Cora. Before Nellis could do a thing, the figure's arm extended into a longer bladed slash which caught the hand holding the knife to Cora's face. Blood spurted into the air. The figure followed through the cutting swipe with a bludgeoning punch into the open-mouthed face of Nellis, whose brain had yet to register the pain screaming up his fingerless arm. The scream disappeared into the eager jaws of the vengeful dog. The figure carried on over the falling Nellis and powered into the uncomprehending Frank, knocking the gun into the air. It exploded. The black shape faltered and fell to its knees. Before anyone could move, it struggled once more to its feet and thrashed onwards into the woods.

It was as if time had stopped.

In the middle, with fog creeping round his legs, stands the rock-like statue of William Grimshaw. At his feet lies the inert crumpled form of Steven Nellis, bleeding profusely into the mud. Beside him cowers Cora Beck, the dog licking her face, with the blood of her attacker dripping from his teeth. Roger Skeldon kneels astride the body of Barry Smith. Trevor Foster, who hadn't witnessed a thing, is still lying in his own piss. Ben Osborne staring at Grim. Jimmy Beck with his hands over his eyes. Frank Burnham spread-eagling in a thorn bush, his eyes staring sightlessly at the tree tops. Two other young men running for their lives through the encroaching water.

The frozen image unfolded, the arrested film stuttered into motion.

Jimmy rushed to his daughter and carried her into the hut, found water and a cloth to wash her cheek. Roger went into triage mode and checked on Baz, Trev, Frank and Ozzy in that order, before returning to Nellis and fetching a bandage from the hut to stop the bleeding from his hand. He couldn't see the missing fingers in the churned-up mud and blood. He decided to leave Grim where he stood.

In the end, it was Roger who went to the farm and told the tale – well, some of it. It was nearly half an hour before the ambulance and police arrived.

\* \* \* \* \*

Marko's first act was to take Irene by the hand and lead her out of the conference hotel and find the taxi he'd ordered. Five minutes later, they were walking into a new Italian restaurant down on the dockside. They sat by the window and watched the boats bobbing about in the swell. He was a good listener. Normally she didn't tell people she was a police officer, even if it included telling outright lies, but with Marko she felt different. He made her feel special.

After the meal, he suggested they go for a walk. He was a gentleman. No roving hands, no sloppy kisses on her neck. No peering down her cleavage every time she looked away. As it got late, she began to think perhaps he was just going to put her back in a taxi and send her home like Cinderella. Instead he stopped outside a city centre hotel, nothing flash or expensive, and asked if she'd like to spend another night with him. She did want it very much and she wasn't disappointed.

He was gentle but forceful, with expert fingers and a delightful tongue. She melted into a haze of pleasure. They didn't stop until dawn. It was nearly midday when she woke as his fingers dextrously aroused her from her dreams.

Afterwards he ordered a very late breakfast, which they ate like a couple of piranhas. It was nearly getting dark when he told her he needed to go. He said he had a meeting in London the following morning and had a long drive ahead of him.

It was only as she looked in her purse for some money to tip the taxi driver that she found the thin black box. Unable to wait, she opened it and gasped at the contents. Oblivious to the waiting taxi driver looking in his mirror, she lifted the bracelet out and put it round her wrist. It was a perfect fit. Not wide or flashy, neither too heavy nor flimsy. Smooth glimmering silver. In the middle opposite the clasp was a single small stone. Was it a real ruby?

She gave the driver a ten-pound note and walked away on a cloud. Marko had said he'd ring her when he had time tomorrow. She couldn't wait.

# CHAPTER 12

***Monday 29th June***

The Grange police hadn't been so busy since . . . since . . . no-one
could remember. First there was the overtime call from Barrow.
Complete waste of time, but the extra pay was welcome; except
no-one had spent a penny of it, because there was the break-in at
the Hadden place. Not as if they were required to do very much,
or spend for ever on the forensics. The culprits had been
apprehended by Hadden and his staff and confessed without
complaint. Charlie Conroy was still in hospital nursing some very
sore ribs and a splitting headache. He and Sam White had told the
story the three of them had agreed if anyone got caught. They said
nothing about Roger. The police didn't mention him, so neither
did they.

The only slight niggle for Chief Inspector Ross was the
security tapes. Somehow or other they'd been wiped. Hadden
shrugged his shoulders and pleaded technical ignorance, despite
the fact he owned an electronics firm. Sam White denied that he'd
done it, but he was the only one with the technical know-how,
motive and opportunity, so they charged him with that as well.
It didn't feel right to Ross though, especially as the big soft lump

kept bursting into tears. They'd only started to put the paperwork together when the third event hit them . . . and if the first two were a waste of time and a bit strange, this one was way out there with UFO sightings and serial cult murders.

The first Ross knew about it was getting a call at half past seven on Sunday evening as he was reading his youngest a bedtime story. As the event unfolded and he listened to the contradictory and unbelievable tales the different participants told, he began to feel he was in one of those night-time fictions his six year old asked for time and again.

In reality it had everything. Guns, golf clubs and knives, ex-soldiers, an ex-gamekeeper and gangs, a fifteen-year-old runaway and seventeen-year-old gangster and, at the bottom of it all, the largest haul of drugs he'd seen since he'd left Leeds. Three of them had been taken to hospital. One had been taken straight into surgery. The rest had been held overnight for questioning – including the four younger ones who'd been taken to a special unit outside Lancaster.

The following morning he'd called a team meeting and assigned tasks. Now he stood looking at the incident room boards trying to compose a sensible narrative from the disjointed stories the participants had offered. As most of the suspects were from Barrow, he'd contacted Chief Inspector Mancini who'd agreed to send over a couple of officers who could provide background and additional information which might clarify things a bit. A phone rang and Ross was informed that they'd arrived. Two minutes later he was introducing his team to DI Aston and DS Sykes. He began to tell them his concocted version of the event.

He pointed to the photos of the two men who had police records, Frank Burnham and Barry Smith. Aston and Sykes exchanged glances and nodded to acknowledge that they knew them. Sykes was also able to identify all the youngsters and Jimmy Beck. They only person they didn't know was Roger Skeldon, although Ross had already received confirmation of the ex-soldier's honourable discharge and service record.

'Nellis and the other young lads have been giving us a lot of trouble for some time,' said Aston.

'Is he the son of your Mr Big?' asked Ross, grateful that he had left that sort of confrontation behind him.

Aston pulled a face. 'He's only Mr Big in Barrow, sir. This might prove to be his downfall.'

Ross sighed. 'Well, good luck to you. His son will be lucky if he can use his right hand again and the rest of them are saying nothing – or rather they're telling us tales about fishing and golf.'

'Golf?' asked Aston with a frown.

'I assumed it was the gang's latest favourite enforcement equipment although, of course, they claim they were only practising and had unfortunately lost all their balls.'

Aston suppressed a smile. 'Our chief inspector mentioned guns?' he asked.

'Well, yes, that will be a bit harder for them to explain. Mind you, the most likely gunman, Smith, won't be saying anything for some time.'

Aston raised an inquisitive eyebrow.

'Someone mashed his mouth into a pulp. It will require some complicated surgery, although I don't suppose his looks were ever his main selling point. His arm is broken as well.'

'Do we know how that happened?' asked Sykes.

Ross gave him a doubtful smile. 'Good question sergeant. Take your pick. As I say, the victim will have plenty of time to come up with his own version, but unless he did it to himself we've no-one stepping up for that. Although the injuries weren't inflicted by a gun or a golf club, so I'd be inclined to suggest Beck or Skeldon. The attacker would have had to be very strong.'

Aston gave Sykes a baleful look. He hadn't asked for him, but Mancini had insisted.

'So what did happen in your opinion, sir?' he asked.

'For what it's worth – and it's only conjecture at this point – I'd say that the young girl had somehow or other got hold of the drugs and run off with them. Whether this was with the connivance of her father, I'm not sure. But they both admit the fishing hut is somewhere they frequented. The father and Skeldon claim they were on a fishing weekend together and didn't know about the drugs. To be fair, they were actually found in Smith's bag, but if they'd already been handed over I don't see why everyone was still hanging around. Beck has a bona fide gun licence and no criminal record, although I believe you might have some other thoughts about that. Skeldon is clean. Commendable service record. Although . . .'

Aston looked at him.

'It may only be a coincidence, but he was in the army at the same time as Smith. We're carrying out further investigations into that.'

'So what happened to young Nellis?' asked Sykes.

'Another insightful question, sergeant,' said Ross and smiled at Aston. 'Unfortunately that's the most difficult bit to pin down. The fact is that he's only recently come out of surgery. He's also going to need a new set of teeth and won't be a pretty boy any more. But the worst injury is to his right hand. It appears that someone cut his fingers off.'

The two Barrow officers looked at each other and back at Ross.

'Don't ask me who or why. A knife was found at the scene, but forensics tell me it's too small to inflict the injury he sustained. They're talking about swords. To be specific, a rapier.'

'A what?' said Aston, in genuine astonishment.

'A rapier, Inspector, a long, thin-bladed fencing weapon, not found at the scene. No-one admits to seeing it or can explain the injury.'

The three men were silent, lost in their own thoughts.

'So what are the charges, sir?' asked Aston eventually.

Ross turned to the board and went through the photos. 'Barry Smith: possession of an illegal firearm, possession of a large quantity of class A drugs. Frank Burnham: the same. I dare say we might get them to grass each other up, but I doubt it. Neither of them is going to even admit knowing Eric Nellis. Cora Beck: handling Class A drugs but we'll probably not pursue that, she's still a minor and we've no hard evidence. I understand you'll be looking to interrogate her regarding an assault on a teacher?'

Sykes intervened. 'The teacher doesn't want to press charges, sir, so . . .'

Ross nodded diffidently and continued. 'The young lads: possession of an offensive weapon, at best they'll get a warning. There's no evidence they used them. Beck and Skeldon? We've nothing. No charges. They'll be released later this morning, along with the lads and the girl.'

He confirmed that forensics were still searching the scene, but so far had nothing else to report. Aston thanked him for his time and the two officers set off back to Barrow.

They were followed an hour or so later by a series of cars carrying some very chastened young men not looking forward to being reunited with their families.

Roger and Jimmy said their goodbyes outside the station, both knowing that their stories would not change. Each owed the other his life. Blood brothers. They would be in touch. They both had unfinished business with a mutual enemy. Roger got a taxi back to Ulverston.

Jimmy, Cora and Tig had been taken in a police car back to Barrow. The three of them were deposited on the pavement outside the small terrace house. The door opened and Maggie rushed out. She shepherded her daughter inside. Jimmy hesitated before being brusquely beckoned in, the dog at his heels. The door was firmly shut. The neighbours knew nothing yet, but the reunited family at number seventeen knew they soon would.

*  *  *  *  *

### Monday 29th June

Fletcher didn't find out about the incident until after Aston and Sykes got back. He'd asked the desk sergeant to tell Sykes to get in touch when he returned.

He'd spent some of the morning with Sadie Swift. She'd suggested they go for a drive. She drove out of Barrow, the same way Sykes had taken them on the ill-fated nature walk, but as they reached the estuary, she turned right down to a strange neck of land which led across a causeway to Roa Island. As they got out of the car, seagulls swept low, competing with the nearby school playground to see who could make the most noise. There was a pub and it was open. They asked for tea and a bacon sandwich, which were served with a smile and a brief weather forecast.

Fletcher looked into Sadie's pale-blue eyes. She knew something he didn't know, he was sure, but he was damned if he was going to ask her.

'What are we doing out here?' he asked.

She pointed through the window. 'Have you seen the castle?'

He turned to look. 'I hope you're not going to tell me it's got a locked tower and secret tunnels. I've had enough of that, thank you.'

'Well I don't know about that, but it was where Lambert Simnel landed with his army.'

'Ah, 1487, the Yorkist pretender,' said Fletcher.

Sadie stared at him. 'How do you know that?' she demanded.

'Same way as I know that's not the reason you brought me here.'

She sighed. 'DI Aston? What d'you think?'

Fletcher took a sip of his rather strong tea. 'Miserable bastard, counting the days to his pension, but will hopefully snuff it beforehand from a heart attack brought on by eating too many bacon sandwiches, smoking too many fags and sitting on his lardy fat arse all day.'

Sadie considered this heartfelt diatribe and pushed away her half-eaten sandwich. She wiped her lips with the paper napkin and gave him a stern look. 'But is he on the take?'

Fletcher finished his sandwich and wiped his mouth with the back of his hand. 'Who would be doing the giving?'

'Nellis. Obviously.'

'Why?'

'You mean why more than just the money?'

He nodded. She shrugged.

'It would explain a few things,' he said, leaning back against the wall.

'Such as?'

'Such as according to his summary, no-one – not one single person – is prepared to talk about who might have killed Julie Carter.'

'You think he knows?'

Fletcher looked out of the window.

'You think he did it?' she asked.

'Why would he do that?'

She had no answer for that.

'I'm pretty certain the first cut was Ian Dyer. It's his style, but not the gutting knife. That's a bigger, stronger man.'

'The pathologist suggested that,' she murmured.

They pondered the consequences of their conversation so far.

'What did Julie Carter know which could have harmed Aston or Nellis?'

'Maybe it's not her. My money is on Jimmy Beck.'

'Why?'

'Because he's still alive.'

'You mean they can't kill him, because he knows something and has a safety clause?'

Sadie considered her perfectly manicured nails.

'So they kill Julie as a warning?'

'Possibly, or maybe she knows as well and was trying to blackmail them.'

Sadie stood up and he followed her outside. The children had gone back into school, while the seagulls were squabbling over their leftovers.

'Symbiotic,' said Fletcher.

'What?' asked Sadie as she ducked under a seagull being chased by another.

'Kids and seagulls. They feed off each other.'

'What do the kids get out of it?'

He shrugged. 'Pleasure. Not being alone.' He wandered off towards the slipway. At the top he stopped to stare out at the castle perched on its rocky plate.

She joined him, holding her hair back from her face. Wind was not her favourite thing. While Fletcher's leather jacket seemed to be out of place everywhere, her immaculate suits and appearance worked best indoors. Now both her hands were trying to exercise some control: one restricting the damage to her hair, the other stopping the wind whipping up her skirt.

'So where does this get us in our search for your party poopers?' he asked.

'It was your idea to upset the apple cart. There are plenty of apples on the road. A fair number of bad ones, but I've only seen a couple of possible exploding ones.'

He walked back to the car to put her out of her wind-blown misery. They sat looking at the boats teetering at odd angles on the seaweed and mud.

'So who are they?'

She told him about spotting Keane and how she'd followed him. 'Your type of woman, I think,' she said.

He grinned. 'You mean a certain married lady?'

'No, I was thinking of that school teacher in Rochdale, Frances something.'

'Diamond,' he said softly.

'That's right: shiny black hair in a pony tail. Although Keane's lady was shorter and more muscular.'

'So what do you know about this Keane?'

'Not much. Wealthy family, public school, dropped out of University. Black sheep. An elder brother who was a captain in the army, killed in Northern Ireland nearly two years ago. No record other than a multitude of speeding fines. Not sure why he's on Adversane's list, but he went quiet when I mentioned I'd seen him.'

'His brother was killed by the IRA?'

'No love lost, apparently.'

'Um,' said Fetcher. 'And the woman?'

'I imagine she's his comfort blanket.'

'Where did you see him?'

'Well, that's what was interesting. He's staying in the same hotel as me. I followed him the other day, Friday. They went to another hotel. He waited in the car. She went in, came back out with a bag. They drove to that big pub on Walney . . .'

'The King George?'

'Yes,' she paused, waiting for him to comment. He grunted, but his eyes were concentrating elsewhere.

'They were only in there for half an hour. It's the next bit which got me really curious.'

He didn't speak.

'They drove out of town, through Ulverston and took a right signed to Grange. I passed them about three miles later. He'd pulled off the road. It wasn't a lay-by, some kind of farm gateway, I think. I drove on and waited for about ten minutes, went back to see if they were still there. I thought they might have spotted me, but they'd gone.'

'So they'd turned round and gone back?'

'That's what I thought at first, but . . .'

'But what?' He still wasn't looking at her.

'I'd spotted another turning. Not a track, a proper road. I followed it, came to some big gates. Long drive disappearing into the trees, couldn't see a house or anything. I waited for about an hour, but they didn't come out. Maybe you're right. Perhaps they'd turned round. When I got back to the hotel that evening, he'd checked out. Gone.'

'Was there a sign on the gates?'

She nodded. 'Private Property – Keep Out – Hadden Estates.'

He sighed. 'And?'

She gave him a look. A look which he hated. Secrets and lies. Adversane.

'Why didn't you tell me this before?'

'Hah! When have I seen you?'

He looked at her then. She returned his gaze. She'd straightened her hair and was back to her immaculate best.

'I haven't heard from Adversane. But as you know, he holds his cards close.'

He looked away. She started the car.

'The King George is where Eric Nellis hangs out,' he said quietly.

'Ah,' she said. 'I didn't know that.'

'So let's go and see this Mr Hadden.'

* * * * *

Irene had arrived at the station with an even dreamier look on her face that made the women officers grin and unsettled the men. In addition, she was sporting her latest jewellery in such a self-conscious fashion that the older women shook their heads. In their experience, men giving you expensive presents generally meant they were after something more than your body.

This dream-like state lasted until she opened the letter personally addressed to her. Her face changed dramatically. She went looking for Fletcher to be told he'd gone off with the Darth Vader spook, as Sadie had been christened by the local station comedian. Even this didn't bring a smile back to her lips. She put the letter back in the envelope and scribbled a message on the outside. There was only one person she felt she could trust to give this to Fletcher when he returned. She needed to get going.

So it was that Fletcher found Sykes waiting impatiently in the office when he and Sadie returned. First he gave them a quick summary of the fishing-hut saga and suggested they get round to Maggie Beck's pronto or they'd miss catching up with Jimmy. Then he gave Fletcher Irene's letter.

Sadie watched as Fletcher read the letter. His face gave nothing away, which in her experience was a bad sign. He handed it to her to read. It was only a few words but it was enough. She handed it back. He gave it to Sykes, whose eyes went big as he read it. He looked at Fletcher.

'Did Irene say where she was going?'

Sykes shook his head.

'Bloody hell,' cursed Fletcher.

'Can't imagine who taught . . .' began Sadie, but Fletcher's glare cut her short.

'Right, Sergeant. Get some back-up and bring Jimmy Beck in. Inspector Swift and I are going to pay our friend Nellis a visit.'

He looked round the office and summoned Watson and Holmes over, telling them to get their coats and follow him.

On the way out, he told the desk sergeant to tell Sergeant Garner where they'd gone and that if she buggered off again on her own, she'd be going back to Penrith sharpish. Neither he nor Sykes had seen the fierce look in Fletcher's eyes before but they knew not to question it. Without another word, Fletcher and Sadie got in her car and drove round to the Majestic with the two younger officers close behind.

At that time of day the Majestic was closed to punters, but the cleaners were hard at work. Nightclubs always look sad and dingy places in ordinary lighting with the odd shaft of daylight peering through open windows or doors, but the Majestic was as bad as they come. Even after a couple of hours of sweeping and cleaning, the four women were nowhere near finishing, but had stopped for a well-earned break. They didn't look surprised to see the police arrive. One of them shouted across, 'There's only us here at the moment, but we could put the music on if you wanna dance!'

The other women laughed, but went quiet when Fletcher came over.

'Sorry, ladies. We'll have to give the last waltz a miss this time. Is there no-one else here at all?'

'Nah,' said one of the older ones. 'Mr Nellis doesn't normally show his face till we've nearly finished; but in any case I don't think he'll be coming in today, 'im and 'is missus 'ave gone over to Lancaster to t'ospital. Their Steven's been given a right going over apparently; 'ad 'is fingers cut off.'

Fletcher nodded. 'So I heard.' He looked round. 'So where's his office.'

'Out the back, up the stairs, but it'll be locked.'

Fletcher smiled. 'Thank you, ladies. Nice talking to you.'

Their smiles disappeared as he set off towards the back door. Sadie and the two local officers followed.

'Hey,' said the older woman. 'I just told you. It'll be all locked . . .' She didn't finish the sentence because they'd left the room. She looked round at the others. They all started talking at once, but went silent again as they heard the crash of a heavy door being broken open. Their voices dropped to whispers.

Upstairs, Fletcher had been the first to reach the door. He gave it an exploratory push. Holmes and Watson were looking distinctly uncomfortable.

'Sir, we've not got a search warrant . . .' tried Watson, knowing straight away he was wasting his breath. Fletcher didn't even glare at him, just picked up the fire extinguisher and smashed it into the lock. It took three blows, but finally the door surrendered and swung uselessly on its hinges.

'Right. All the tapes and any suspicious packages. I reckon we've got five minutes maximum.'

While Holmes stacked the cassette tapes lying around and those he found in cupboards into a box, Watson went through each machine and extracted the ones in use. Fletcher went through all the drawers, while Sadie did the toilets. Fletcher found nothing he thought of any use, but Sadie came up trumps: two handguns and a plastic package.

'Too easy,' she said. 'You'd think they'd have hidden them somewhere less obvious than that.'

'I suspect he never thought it would happen to him,' said Fletcher.

He grabbed a couple of newspapers off the desk, crumpled them up and threw them in a rubbish bin by the desk. Before Holmes and Watson could work out what he was doing, he'd set fire to another one and thrown it in with rest. They backed away.

'What are you doing, sir?' asked Holmes. This did get a glare.

'What do you think you daft bastard? Haven't you done your basic fire training?'

The flames were taking hold. Smoke was starting to billow up towards the ceiling. Fletcher threw more papers onto the blaze. He picked up a chair and threw it at one of the screens, which exploded and fizzled with electric sparks. Finally he picked up the fire extinguisher and threw that at a different screen. Again a loud bang and a shower of sparks. The extinguisher exploded into action but merely drenched Watson who dodged out the door. Holmes and Sadie followed, clutching their respective prizes. Fletcher stayed a few more seconds to watch the fireworks, before calmly walking through the door and following his colleagues down the stairs.

At the bottom the women were gathered at the open doorway, too scared to stay but reluctant to miss the action. Fletcher strode across the dance floor heading for the door.

'I'm sorry ladies – I think you need to leave the building. There seems to have been an electrical fault upstairs and I think I can smell burning.'

The sarcasm was lost on the ladies as the latest explosions erupted, sending plumes of black smoke out into the main room. They screamed and fought each other to escape. Fletcher calmly waited, before smashing the little window on the wall and pressing the fire alarm. Nothing happened. He shrugged his shoulders and followed the ladies out onto the street.

His three colleagues were waiting. He ignored the yelling and the distant explosions.

'Holmes. Put those tapes into Inspector Swift's car. Go straight back to the station and tell Sykes to hang onto Jimmy Beck until I get back. Watson, you wait here until the fire services arrive. You know nothing. You tell them nothing. Is that clear?'

Watson nodded like a clockwork doll. Holmes hesitated, looked at Sadie, realised she wasn't going to help, got in the car and raced away.

Fletcher and Sadie got in her car and drove more calmly from the scene.

'I assume you know somewhere which has the facility to play these tapes?'

She nodded. He looked out of the window.

'Where the bloody hell is Irene?'

\* \* \* \* \*

Sykes had not had a successful morning. First he'd had to endure the silent treatment and glowering looks from Aston, to and from Grange. Then he'd hung around waiting for Fletcher. Now he was back at the police station having failed to catch Jimmy Beck. A sleepy-eyed Cora had eventually answered the door to say both her mum and dad were out. He sent the other officers to check. She wasn't lying.

She'd gone into the kitchen and filled a bowl with cornflakes.

'Do you know where they've gone?' he asked.

She looked at him sadly. 'I think my mum's at work. She won't be back till tea time. I don't know where my dad's gone.'

Sykes gave her a stern look.

'Honest. I don't know. He'd gone before I woke up.'

He looked at the constable standing in the doorway. He shook his head.

'OK, Cora. If you see him, tell him he's got to talk to us. Soon. Yeh?'

She nodded. They left.

He didn't know what to do next.

\* \* \* \* \*

The door opened. Holmes came in and stormed over to his desk, throwing his coat at the chair. It fell to the floor. He hadn't seen Sykes standing in the corner, kettle in hand.

'Cup of coffee, Ian?'

Holmes nearly jumped out of his skin. 'Yeh, please, Sarge,' he stuttered as he regained his composure.

Sykes pretended not to have noticed how upset his colleague was, thought it best to give him a few moments.

'There you are,' he said putting the coffee on Holmes's desk. Holmes had his head in his hands. He looked up.

'Problem, Ian?'

'It's DI Fletcher, Sarge.'

'Why? Where is he?'

'Er . . . I don't know . . . now. Gone off with DI Swift.'

'Now? You mean you did know where he was before?'

'Oh God! What a mess.'

'Well. Are you going to tell me or what?'

Holmes looked at him, got up and went to close the door. 'Right. We went to the Majestic. Nellis wasn't there. Just the cleaners. But Fletcher . . . he . . . well, we went upstairs. He broke the door down with a fire extinguisher. Told us to collect the security tapes. DI Swift found a couple of guns and some drugs.' He hesitated, thinking, did she? Could she have?

'Go on,' said Sykes quietly.

'Fletcher. He started a fire. He's wrecked the place – threw a chair at one of the screens. For all I know the place is still going up in flames. I heard the sirens.'

He looked at Sykes.

'Sit down, Ian. OK. Write it all down and give it to me. No-one else. Not a word. Understand?'

Holmes nodded. Sykes gave him one more look and walked out of the room. He ran downstairs, got in his car and drove to the Majestic. Three fire engines, smoke belching from the roof at the back. He saw a fire officer he knew.

'Hi, Gordon. What's the situation?'

The fire officer made a face. 'Well I don't think you'll be rocking and rolling in there for a while, that's for sure.'

'Are you going to be able to save it?'

'Hard to tell, there are a lot of electrics in there. All them neon lights, disco stuff. There'll probably be a building left. It's old, well built, but it'll be gutted. Not as gutted as Mr Nellis though.'

'Why's that?'

'Fire alarms didn't work. Wiring's knackered. Fire doors locked. He'll not get a penny from the insurance. Good job for him it didn't happen at night – doesn't bear thinking about – two hundred and odd people in there on a weekend.'

Sykes thanked him, stood watching for a bit, but he could see the firemen had got it under control. He went back to the station.

* * * * *

Jimmy Beck hadn't stayed long at his wife's house. They didn't have much to say to each other and neither of them wanted to argue in front of a tearful Cora. Maggie fussed about making a meal, putting off the serious conversation as long as she could. But eventually she sat at the kitchen table and listened to their stories. Neither Cora nor Jimmy told her even half the truth, although Cora couldn't hide the large plaster on her cheek. She didn't mention Maliverny and Jimmy didn't expand on what had happened to Roger; they both stuck to the tales they'd told the police.

When they'd finished, Maggie told Cora to go and get some sleep. For once in a long while her daughter went upstairs without a murmur. When Maggie came back down, Jimmy was ready to go. He went up and kissed Cora goodnight. She didn't ask if he'd be there in the morning and he didn't say.

Downstairs he gathered his things and stood at the door.

'Is that it then?' asked Maggie.

He shook his head. 'No. I've got a few things to sort out. But I am coming back.'

'Yeh,' she sneered.

He looked at her hard. 'I mean it, Maggie. Cora needs us both, but right now I need to do something I should have done a long time ago. Something I've never told you about, something the police won't do anything about. But it's wrong and I can do something to change that.'

She stared at him; she'd never heard him speak like this before.

'Look after her. She's had a terrifying experience, worse than she's told you, believe me.'

She managed a nod. He sighed and went. The dog followed.

Maggie sat at the table for some time. Tears rolled down her cheek. Why did she have to sneer?

Jimmy got the train to Ulverston. Half an hour later he was knocking on Shirley Thomas's door. She let him in and took him through into the front room. Roger got up to greet him. The three of them talked long into the night.

\* \* \* \* \*

*Monday 29th June*

It took Irene only an hour to find Amy Dobson.

She knocked on the door of a semi-detached house in Roose. There was no reply. She heard a noise and rushed round the side to see the unlikely sight of Amy 'Dobbo' Dobson trying to scale the garden fence. As Irene watched, Amy lost her grip and fell backwards into a bush.

Irene walked over and helped her up. Amy was covered in scratches, but came up fighting. Irene slapped her so hard she fell onto the grass and lay gasping for breath.

'You fucking cow. You can't do that.'

Irene dragged her to her feet and slapped her again, this time not so hard and hung onto her so she didn't fall. 'I think you meant to say "Hi Irene. Would you like a nice cup of tea?"'

They went back into the house.

'Nice house,' said Irene, as she watched Amy put the kettle on and find a couple of cups.

'It's not mine,' said Amy.

'I think I'd worked that out.'

'It's a friend's. His wife's left him.'

'Found out about you, did she?'

Amy looked at her. 'She was a cow anyway. He's better off without her.' She poured the tea.

'Sit down, Amy. I'm not going to tell anyone about your little secret, except I think you'll find it's not that much of a secret. But that's not your most pressing problem.'

'What d'you mean?'

'Did you know Alex has done a runner?'

'Alex who?'

Irene banged the table with her fist, knocking her teacup onto the floor. 'Don't act the innocent with me, Amy Dobson!'

Amy's mouth fell open.

'You know damn well who I mean. Alex Henning, who's been servicing another friend of yours for the last few months.'

Amy nodded, close to tears.

'OK, Amy. I'm not going to hurt you, but you've got to tell me what you know.'

She waited. Then: 'So you don't know where Alex has gone?'

Amy shook her head. Her mascara had run and made her look a bit like Alice Cooper towards the end of a show.

'What do you know about Julie Carter?'

'Nothing,' said Amy vehemently. 'I don't know anything about that.'

Irene gave her another severe look. 'You were there on Friday night, with Tina Goodwright and the other girls.'

'Yeh, but we didn't know what was happening. We were over the other side of the square.'

'But Indie spoke to you didn't he?' Irene said quietly.

Amy's eyes went huge and filled with tears. 'I didn't. Honest. Irene.'

'Alex says otherwise.'

Amy shook her head violently.

'Alex says she saw him grab you and stuff some money in your hand, told you to find out who the new girl was. The one who threw Tina over her shoulder.'

Amy was still shaking her head.

'Alex says you followed the girl; saw her go off with one of Nellis's men. Someone called Keane: blonde guy, flash car.'

Amy tried to hide her look of terror behind her trembling hands. Suddenly Irene grabbed Amy's handbag and pulled out her purse, from which she took a wadge of notes.

'You've been busy Amy, what's this? Five a day? Does your lover boy know he's just a B and B?'

Amy was back to shaking her head. Irene leant across the table and held the money to Amy's face.

'Do you know what the word "indelible" means, Amy?'

Amy looked at the money, which Irene was sliding back and forth.

'It means you can't wash off the invisible dye we put on these notes.'

Amy looked at Irene and shook her head.

'I'm betting that some of this money is the same money which I gave to Julie Carter, which Ian Dyer took from her before she was killed.'

Amy was paralysed.

'All I have to do is take it back to the station and there's a special machine which will prove that these are the same notes.'

Irene gave Amy some time to understand what she was saying, but just in case it wasn't clear, she added, 'Which means, Amy, that you'll be charged with receiving money from a murderer and hiding evidence from the police.'

She let this lie sink in. 'You'll go to prison, Amy.'

Amy was crying openly now.

'Do you know what they do to fat girls in prison, Amy?'

Amy screamed, 'Stop it! Stop it!'

Irene leaned back in her chair and waited. Amy shuddered uncontrollably.

'What did you see, Amy?'

Amy wiped her face like she used to do at school, on her sleeve. 'I saw you and Julie go into the alley. You came out and got in a car. A few minutes later Indie came out. He grabbed me and gave me the money. Later I told him about the girl and Keane. That's all I know.'

'Did you see anyone else come out of the alley with Indie?'

Amy closed her eyes and clenched her fists.

'Was it Keane?'

She opened her eyes and stared straight at Irene. 'No.'

'Who was it, Amy?'

'I . . . I . . . don't know. An older man. His face was in shadow. He was wearing a cap. Indie grabbed me. When I looked again the man had gone.'

Irene considered her next question carefully. 'Amy? Could it have been Inspector Aston?'

Amy's head came up. She frowned. The name puzzled her. She fought hard to keep the surge of relief appearing on her face. 'You mean Dave Aston?'

'Yeh.'

'No . . . No . . . I don't think so. No, I'm sure. He wasn't as fat.'

'You're sure?'

Amy couldn't stop the rueful grin. 'I should be.'

It was Irene's turn to frown. 'You mean . . .'

'Yeh. Quite a few times, but not recently.'

Irene laughed. 'That fat bastard? You're kidding?'

'No. A bit sad really. If you knew his wife, she makes his life a misery.'

Irene put the money carefully into a plastic evidence bag. The stuff about indelible dyes was something she'd seen on the telly. She didn't think it was scientifically possible yet, certainly not out here in the back of beyond. But she did know that if it was the money she'd given Julie then her fingerprints would be on it and so might Indie's.

She told Amy to get her coat and took her back to the station. She wasn't expecting praise from Fletcher, but he might forgive her going off on her own.

# CHAPTER 13

***Monday 29th June. Late morning***

'Where the fuck have you been?'

Irene had been right. Fletcher was at his surliest and it didn't get any better. She knew it was best to stand up to him – especially in front of Sadie, who was standing at the window, arms folded, looking as cool as ever.

'Finding and bringing in for questioning a potentially crucial witness, sir. Without the aid of a fire extinguisher, sir.'

'Don't get clever with me, Sergeant. I'm sick enough of your town's half-arsed attempts at a police force.'

'Well, don't include me. I told you I'm from Askam and that's what I'm doing.'

Sadie produced a delicate cough to attract their attention. 'Good to see your training techniques haven't altered, Inspector. She's doing really well.'

They both glared at her.

'Perhaps you'd better tell us who this "crucial witness" is, Sergeant?' she added, smiling through gleaming teeth.

Irene continued to glare at Fletcher.

'OK, Irene, I give in,' he said, slumping into a chair. 'Who is it? Doreen Nellis?'

Irene laughed. 'Same shape, but a lot less scary.'

'So what's she know that Doreen doesn't know?'

Irene opened her handbag, took out the notes she'd taken from Amy and put them on the desk.

'What's this? Your takings from last night?'

Anyone else but him and Irene would have given his arm a tweak, but she bit her tongue. 'I'm afraid my "takings from last night", as you so quaintly put it, weren't financial, sir. More a down payment in kind.'

Sadie sighed.

'Will you two stop it, you're like a bad trailer for a *Coronation Street* meets *The Sweeney* Christmas show.'

Irene gave Fletcher one more glare. 'That's some of the money I gave Julie Carter.' She let this sink in. 'If I'm right, you'll find Julie's, mine and Ian Dyer's fingerprints on them, as well as Amy Dobson's.'

'Who the hell is Amy Dobson?'

Before Irene could answer, the door opened and Chief Inspector Mancini stepped into the room. They all stood up. They could tell he was not a happy man. He ignored Irene and nodded at the other two.

'My office now,' he said, and turned on his well-polished heel and walked away. Fletcher and Sadie looked at each other. He shrugged and she sighed. The pair of them set off after the senior officer.

Irene was left frustrated. What could she do? She went in search of Sykes.

\* \* \* \* \*

The two detective inspectors stood in front of the chief inspector's desk. He was sitting behind it with both hands clasped in front of him. His desk was the epitome of the organised man. A telephone, a clean ink pad and two pens. Nothing else. Normally, clear desk equals clear mind, but Fletcher could see that this wasn't the case. He thought he'd better get stuck in.

'I realise, sir, that my methods may seem a little heavy-handed, but I think we needed to do more than just upset the applecart. We have only a day to go before the launch. The security teams are already crawling all over the place . . .'

Mancini held up his hand and Fletcher stopped.

'Don't patronise me, Inspector. I know about your "methods" and I am well aware of the security issues, which incidentally are being conducted outside and above my and your remit. They will be the ones making the decisions about what happens on Wednesday; irrespective of whether you've burned down half the town centre or not. That's not the issue here, is it?'

Fletcher looked into the dark eyes which betrayed the anger held back by the grim expression. He decided to let the chief inspector say his piece.

'Afterwards, when this is all over, you and your colleague will be dispatched elsewhere, and, if I have any say in it, it will be a long way from me.' He paused. 'However, from now on, even though it will be only for two days, you will agree to inform me of all your intended actions before – I repeat *before* – you carry them out.' He paused again.

Fletcher opted for silence.

'Is that understood?'

Fletcher and Sadie both nodded without looking at each other. Mancini continued to stare at them, which Fletcher judged was probably the only chance he was going to get. Mancini looked down at the envelope Fletcher placed in front of him.

'I think, sir, with due respect, that the contents of that letter will prompt you to consider the next course of action indisputable.'

Mancini ignored the comment, picked up the envelope, pulled out the note and read it.

Fletcher chanced a glance at Sadie whose grey-blue eyes danced beneath her raised eyebrows. A look which said it all: 'you lucky bastard'. His blue eye winked at her.

Mancini looked up from the letter. 'When did you get this?'

'About five minutes ago when we returned from the "accident", sir.'

Mancini ignored that as well. 'But I suspect it arrived a lot earlier and it's addressed to your colleague, who . . .'

'Acted on her own initiative, sir,' said Fletcher, adding, 'as I've always encouraged her to do, sir.'

'Meaning?'

'That she read what Alex Henning wrote about Nellis and went to find Amy Dobson, whose younger sister she'd interrogated yesterday.'

'Alone?'

'We were otherwise engaged, sir, and given the other information provided in the letter, sir, I imagine she thought it was the best course of action, sir.'

Mancini chose to ignore the repeated use of the patronising 'sir' routine and leaned back in his chair. 'So, can I assume that your sergeant has – what's that English expression – "saved your bacon", Inspector?'

'If you mean has she brought home the goods, sir, then yes, she has.'

Mancini got to his feet and handed the letter back to Fletcher. 'I want a transcript of the interrogation before you leave the station, Inspector. No more impulsive moves without my explicit approval. Is that clear?'

Fletcher nodded and turned to leave.

'That includes Sergeant Garner as well,' added Mancini.

'Understood, sir,' he nodded, already beginning to calculate how much he could trust Sykes to operate on his own.

Fletcher opened the door, expecting Sadie to follow him, only to hear her speaking quietly to Mancini. 'If you don't mind sir, I have something to ask,' she was saying. She looked at Fletcher and widened her eyes at him. He read the sign and hurried out.

He reappeared downstairs in time to catch Irene and Sykes in conspiratorial mode at the back of the canteen. He gestured to them to stay put and grabbed a coffee.

'OK, what's the plan?' he asked as he sat down.

Irene looked at him suspiciously. 'It depends on what happened upstairs, sir.'

Fletcher shook his head. 'You and me grounded. No further actions without seeking permission to leave,' he grinned.

'So? What next?'

'You and me with assorted plods to interview your Amy, whilst Eric will be acting on our behalf elsewhere.'

Sykes gave him a baleful look. 'Not funny, sir.'

'No. I'm sorry, Sergeant, but neither is our strong suspicion that your boss is up to no good with our burnt-out friend.'

Sykes was shaking his head.

'I know. It's not good, but we need to find him before Mancini gets his hands on him.'

Sykes looked from Fletcher to Irene. 'Look, he's never been my favourite colleague either, but I don't think he's bent. Honestly.'

Fletcher gave him a sad look. 'My instinct says otherwise, but it's best you talk to him first; otherwise we'll learn nothing. You get him to meet up with me and I promise to give him a fair hearing. If Mancini gets to him first, he'll just deny everything.'

Sykes continued to stare at him. Fletcher could see the arguments going on in his head. Local loyalties versus hard-headed calculation. He added a penny to tip the scales.

'Inspector Swift is buying us time as we speak, Eddie, but the fan has been turned on and there's already a bit of a whiff in the air. Aston's not in the station. His shift doesn't begin for another two hours. That's all we've got and it's all down to you. I expect he's gone fishing.'

Sykes couldn't be sure whether Fletcher was guessing about Aston's preferred wife-avoidance pastime or whether someone had told him, but it helped him make up his mind. 'I know where he'll be. I'll give you a ring within the hour. I'll take Watson. You've gone too far for Holmes.'

Before Fletcher could question this, Sykes was gone, leaving the canteen door ajar.

Fletcher turned to Irene. 'Come on, Purdey, let's go and see what your young lady can tell us.'

Irene made a face at him, but followed him down to the interview room.

\* \* \* \* \*

### Monday June 29th

Cora was at a loss what to do. Her experiences during the last few days had left her somewhere between numb and paranoid. She'd told no-one about Maliverny, although she was pretty certain it was him who stormed through the midst of the stand-off. She kept hearing the swish of the sword as it passed within a hair's breadth of her nose, followed by the splash of blood over her face. All she'd wanted to do was wash it off as quickly as possible and even now she shivered with disgust and horror at the thought of it.

She broke down and cried the following morning when her mother told her that her father had gone. Why did he always have to disappear when she needed him most? She needed to tell someone about Maliverny Catlin. Someone who wouldn't laugh at her. Her mum had made no effort to comfort her, although when she'd stopped crying, she'd offered her a tissue – but then she'd got up without a word and gone to work.

Cora couldn't watch the television; it was unreal. She didn't want to see anyone, couldn't settle anywhere. The police came looking for her father and searched the house. She'd nothing to tell them and they seemed reluctant to press her about anything. They were only there half an hour. Afterwards she wasn't even sure it had actually happened. Eventually, having wandered aimlessly round and round and up and down the small house, she found herself staring out of her bedroom window at the back of the house on the other side of the alley. The opposite window stared sightlessly back at her offering no comfort or answers. She lay on her bed and stared at the ceiling. What was she going to do?

She must have dozed off and came to with a start to see her mother standing at the doorway with a can of Coke in her hand.

'Do you want this?' she asked.

Cora sat up on the edge of the bed and held out her hand for it. Her mother leant against the door jamb. 'Do you want to talk about it?' she asked.

Cora looked at her, checking to see whether this was a world-weary question or a sneer. It was neither. She could see the lines on her mother's face and the dark eyes staring at her, but nothing else. She pushed back on the bed so she could lean against the wall.

'That teacher's going to be alright and she's told the police she doesn't want to press charges,' said her mother quietly.

Cora had heard this already, but looked down at the can and nodded. 'It was an accident. I only pushed her, but she banged her head when she fell. I panicked. Didn't know what to do. So I ran.'

Her mother didn't say anything or give her one of her sighs, but didn't move either. Neither of them spoke for what seemed an age.

'Your father said he would come back. Soon.'

Cora raised her head and looked hard at her mother, whose face was still devoid of expression. 'Meaning?' she asked.

Again, instead of a disinterested shrug her mother merely shook her head very slightly.

'I don't know. Except he wants to see you again soon.'

Cora's spirits crept out from the deep hole they'd descended into, hope stumbling into the light. 'Did he say when?' she asked, trying not to sound too eager.

This brought a smile to her mother's face. 'When has he ever said when?'

Cora couldn't deny this, but was startled by the smile.

'But I think he means it this time. He said he's got to sort something out; something he should have done a long time ago.'

Cora tried to read what this might mean. 'Did he say what it was?'

Her mother shook her head slowly. 'No, but I might have an idea.'

Cora moved to edge of the bed. 'What?'

Her mother shifted her position and went to look out of the window. Cora held her breath. Her mother put her arms round her thin body and took a deep breath. 'Your friend Ian.'

Cora gave her a sharp look. 'He's not my friend. He's a vicious, mean bastard.'

Her mother came and sat on the bed. It was the nearest she'd been to Cora for as long as she could remember. 'That may be true. The police are looking everywhere for him. It was on the telly and front page of the *Mail*.'

Cora gave this some thought. She had an image of him walking away from the gang on the seafront, his untied laces whipping about his boots, the final savage glare and a contemptuous gob of spit flung into the wind. She looked back at her mother, who was fiddling with the ring on her right hand. Cora remembered the day when she'd torn her wedding ring from the other hand and thrown it across the room. She'd never asked her about this other ring.

'He wasn't with Nellis at the hut,' she said.

Her mother looked up. 'That's not why they're after him.'

Cora frowned. 'So what's he done?'

'Julie's dead.'

'Dead?'

'She was found in the alley down by the Majestic. The police haven't said how she was killed, but they have said she was murdered.'

Cora's head was full of conflicting possibilities. 'Does Dad know?'

Maggie looked away. 'I'm not sure. He didn't say and he didn't seem upset that way, but . . .'

Cora was making connections. 'So Indie's gone missing?'

'Yes.'

'They think he did it?'

'Looks like that.'

'So Dad might have gone looking for him?'

Maggie did give a sigh at that, but not a sarcastic one. 'Perhaps, but . . .'

'But what?'

Maggie shook her head trying to get the right words. 'But like you, he's been out at the hut. I don't think he knows and I couldn't find the words to tell him. Maybe the police told him.'

Cora frowned again. 'But? Oh, so that's why they came looking for him this morning.'

'Did they?'

'Yeh. I did think it was a bit over the top. There were loads of them. They searched the whole house and the shed out the back.'

Maggie stood up and began to pace up and down. 'Why didn't you ring me?'

'What for? They were only here five minutes. As soon as they figured out I didn't know where he was, they were off.'

Maggie stopped and thought about this. Cora's stomach rumbled. Both their serious faces broke into smiles.

'I think you need some late breakfast, girl. Come on.'

Quarter of an hour later they were both tucking into egg and bacon.

'So what's the connection with Indie?' asked Cora with her mouth full.

Maggie wiped her plate with a piece of toast and got up to pour herself another cup of tea. She sat down again and took a sip. 'It's a long time ago. Just before you started going to school,' she said with a wan smile.

Cora wiped her mouth with the back of her hand and waited.

'Your dad's not a bad man,' Maggie said.

Cora nodded, biting her tongue on a rush of very direct questions. Maggie glanced at her to see if they would be forthcoming, but decided to continue. 'He had a good job, doing what he loved working on the big estate.'

Cora had vague memories of the house in the woods where they used to live with the grey-blue windows and doors.

'But Eric Nellis dragged him back into some trouble or other. He never told me what exactly. He'd say he was going fishing, but actually he was coming back to Barrow. Anyway, whatever it was they were doing, it all went wrong one night and your dad came back in a terrible state. He wouldn't tell me anything, but took all his clothes off and burnt them.'

Cora was spellbound but horrified, while Maggie carried on, determined to tell it now she'd started. 'Every time I asked him to tell me what it was, he got angry, told me to leave it be. He'd never spoken to me like that before. He spent hours at work, wouldn't speak to me for days on end. I was really scared . . . and then the police came for him. Took him back to Barrow.'

She stopped, buried her head in her hands and sobbed. Cora got up and put her arms round her. Her mother clung to her until the shuddering stopped and she wiped her face on a tea towel. Cora sat next to her and held her hand. It was cold. She waited, too worried to speak.

'I got someone to look after you and went to the police station, but they wouldn't let me speak to him or tell me what was going on. A woman officer told me that it could be days before they let him out – if at all. I went back to the house, but it wasn't days, it was the same afternoon. He came back and went straight out again without saying a word.'

Cora got up and put the kettle on. Her mother sat and stared at her hands on the table.

'The estate manager came round the next day to say we had to leave by the end of the week. Jimmy didn't tell me what had happened until weeks later. We'd gone to stay with my mother and he eventually got a job, but it was in a factory. He hated it, but it was all he could get.'

Cora poured the hot water into the teapot.

'One night he came back from the pub. It was late – he was drunk. Just sat there and cried, saying he was sorry, over and over. I didn't know what to do.'

Cora couldn't imagine her dad crying, but didn't interrupt.

'It must have been the middle of the night when he calmed down and told me – told me what that bastard Nellis had done to him.'

Now she was angry, but it didn't stop the tears. Cora held her close. Maggie pushed her away.

'They'd been in a pub, Nellis and his gang. There'd been an argument. I don't remember what it was about, a woman I think. Anyway, Nellis and this other bloke went outside to settle it. Jimmy followed them, probably trying to stop it, the fool. He didn't see who pulled a knife first, but he did see Nellis stab the other man more than once. When they realised that he was dead, they panicked. The pub was on the dockside, so it was easy to put him into the water. It was high tide. Nellis insisted they went back into the pub and pretend that the bloke had run off.'

Cora stared at her mother in disbelief. Maggie got up and walked to the window. Neither of them spoke for a long time. The late afternoon sun crept into the room.

'The police couldn't prove anything. The body wasn't found until three days later, by which time the fish, rats and birds had destroyed any clues. They got a tip-off from someone and arrested your dad and Nellis and a few others, but they'd had time to practise their story. And in any case there was only Nellis and your dad who knew exactly what had happened. The story was in the paper for a few days, but the police had nothing, so they had to let them go.'

Cora waited to see if there was anything else. Her mother couldn't look her in the eye. 'But what's this got to do with Indie?' she said.

Maggie looked up, her eyes were red. 'The man that Nellis killed was Ian's real father, Duncan Wallace.'

Cora stared.

'His mother left Barrow soon afterwards, taking Ian with her, but they came back a few years later with another man, Alan Dyer. I don't think they were ever married. He was a nasty piece of work, always in fights and in trouble with the police, used to beat Jean up all the time. Got into drugs, turned her into an addict. She's dead and he's in prison.'

Cora thought of how Indie had changed after primary school. He'd always been in trouble, but when he was younger it was only mischief; at secondary school he became violent and unpredictable. A question popped into her head, but before she could ask it, her mother gave her the answer.

'I'm pretty sure he doesn't know.'

Cora nodded. 'But Steve Nellis does . . .'

Now it was her mother's turn to frown. 'Why do you say that?'

Cora bit her lip. 'I only agreed to hide the drugs because he said he knew something that would put my dad away for a very long time.'

Maggie thought about this. 'But why would he tell anyone about what his father did?'

Cora knew why. She didn't know how she knew, but blurted it out. 'Because his dad's told him a different version.'

Maggie looked at her in surprise, but then realised the possibility and all it meant. The two of them sat and considered what they knew and what, if anything, they could do about it.

Cora began to form a plan while the rest of the afternoon passed in a blur. Eventually Maggie cooked a meal and they sat in front of the telly but without registering what was flickering away in front of them. As the news came on, Cora got up and went to get her coat.

'Where are you going?' asked her mother, trying hard not to sound aggressive.

'I thought I'd go and find Robbie. We've a few things to sort out,' she replied, looking her mother in the eyes.

'Well, don't be late.'

They both knew it was a lie, but neither of them wanted to damage their new-found closeness, so they let it go. Maggie didn't know where Cora was going, but she knew it wasn't to Robbie. She had her fears, but knew she'd have to let Cora sort out things her own way. Equally, Cora wanted to tell her mother the plan but knew she wouldn't approve, so she went.

Maggie stared at the telly and wondered what she could do.

*Monday 29th June*

The message was clear. Abort main target. A further secondary target. Luca didn't like it. He could understand that the first target might be dropped because the security services had got wind and replaced the high-profile royal with someone not worth the same risk, but the extra second target didn't make sense. Well, not immediately. He was pretty certain that Keane was part of some drugs connection Nellis had made. He obviously wasn't a local and was playing a dangerous game of double cross.

Hadden, on the other hand, not only had wealth and status, but from what Luca had found out, his sadistic treatment of his wife deserved a suitable punishment which Tsura was more than keen to administer. He'd already decided it would be just the two of them. He hadn't needed to be told the nature of the punishment: it carried its own distinct signature. But his instincts told him there was something odd going on. He didn't like it. There was another hand at work and he'd a pretty good idea whose that might be.

Luca hadn't heard from Nellis regarding his, now unnecessary, request for a suitable site, but he had heard that the obnoxious man was having trouble with a series of disasters. Although this gave him some limited satisfaction, it left him feeling they were wasting their time here. The new secondary target would be easy enough and the fee more than covered their costs, but it felt wrong. The new instructions said the timing would be beneficial if it coincided with the launch for publicity reasons, but this wasn't essential. This left him even more uncomfortable. It was the oxygen of publicity that the IRA craved, whilst the other hidden hand preferred silence and oblivion.

He listened again to the tape which Tsura had brought back from her journeys with the young man. What else was he up to? He needed Tsura to have some more time with Mr Keane, but the instruction to disappear for the time mentioned on the same tape seemed to have been followed to the letter.

Equally, the information received through Marko's device was of little use other than to confirm the ongoing determined pursuit of Nellis and all his works. He had to admire Fletcher, the little corporal who seemed at the heart of this mayhem; he liked a man who didn't play by the rules and his two assistants were delightful.

A man after his own heart. It would be a shame to spoil the party, but that seemed to be the intention of the new instruction.

He looked at his watch. They were late as usual. It was as well he always included that extra time for them. Indulgent – but worth the pleasure they brought.

\* \* \* \* \*

It had been a long night and most of it spent trying to persuade Jimmy not to carry out his plans. Roger and Shirley were all for going straight to the police, but Jimmy was equally sure that wouldn't change anything. 'He'll have covered all the options, don't you worry,' he said.

'Yeh, and that will include making sure no-one will get anywhere near her again,' argued Shirley.

'Which is precisely why now is the best time to go in. Just when he thinks no-one would dare to try.'

Roger could see both sides of the argument, but it was Jimmy's final card which turned the tables.

'He's forgotten about me,' said Jimmy. 'It's over ten years since I left and I don't think he even knows I've been upstairs.'

'What about the cameras?' asked Shirley.

'It was after a storm. All the electrics went off and it was two or three days before everything was back to normal.'

'But there's a generator,' she added.

'Not then there wasn't. He had it installed soon afterwards, because he didn't want to be caught like that again.'

This silenced Shirley for a bit.

'But how are you going to get in and, more to point, get out again?' asked Roger.

'Well, you gave me the idea for that.'

'Me?'

'Yeh, or rather Miss Ridley. I'm going in the way you came out.'

Roger nodded, but still couldn't see how that would work. 'I'm sure it's locked and alarmed like the rest of the house. And there's definitely a camera in the white room.'

'That's where you come in,' said Jimmy.

'I'm not going back there again,' said Shirley and Roger in unison.

Jimmy sighed. 'But it's the only way,' he said.

They both shook their heads.

'Listen. He thinks you're dead and that Shirley will be too scared to do anything.'

'Exactly,' she echoed.

'So what will he do when you both turn up with a couple of police officers accusing Miss Ridley of trying to kill you?'

'They'll deny it. It's my word against the two of them and the rest of his staff.'

'But it's recorded on their cameras.'

Shirley looked at Jimmy as if he were crazy. 'He's not going to let them look at the cameras, is he?'

Jimmy smiled. 'That's when the alarms will go off.'

Roger was struggling to follow the plan. 'You mean that's when you'll be breaking into the fire escape.'

Jimmy was shaking his head and laughing. 'No. That's when I blow up the generator!'

'*What?*' they both cried.

'It's in one of the outbuildings and I can get in through the roof.'

They stared at him in disbelief, until it dawned on Roger. 'Classic counteroperational tactics,' he nodded. 'Divert the enemy's attention while the main attack comes from another direction.'

Shirley looked from one to the other. 'You're crazy! Both of you.'

'It might just work,' said Roger.

'No, Roger. I can't let you do it,' wailed Shirley.

Roger didn't seem to be listening. 'How will you blow it up?' he asked, wondering if he could get Charlie to tell him where he'd hidden his explosives supply. But Jimmy was already grinning.

'I helped install it. The electricians told us exactly what not to let happen. It's got a manual override which allows you to make it reach a point where it will automatically cut out, leaving everyone in the dark. No alarms. No lights . . . and this is the best bit. All the fire doors unlocked!'

'So you'll be waiting at the bottom of the fire escape?'

'Up the stairs, through the white room, fireman's lift, down and away.'

By this point Shirley was banging her fists on the table, but it was no use. Roger was up for it.

It took another few hours to bring her round, but they had an answer for every argument, so eventually she had to give in. Jimmy pointed out that the following night the tide would be going down around eight o'clock and showed them the timetable he'd worked out. Her final doubts were settled when Jimmy explained about how he was going to get the police there.

'Eddie Sykes and I were best mates at school. We don't see each other much since I was in trouble with the law when Cora was just a little kid, but I know he'll not let me down.'

The talking finished about half past three and they all went to bed. Jimmy didn't sleep much. He'd other plans to make, more deadly than the one he'd shared with the other two. Eddie had told him about Julie and who his superiors thought was responsible. They both knew otherwise and Jimmy wasn't going to let the bastard get away with it this time. Equally, he knew someone else who would be the perfect ally once he knew the truth – but that could wait. He'd waited all these years. Another few days wouldn't matter.

Roger didn't sleep much either. He lay next to Shirley's warm body and went over the plan time and time again, each time coming back to how he would deal with that woman who had so humiliated him. He also wondered whether he should have told them about the weapons store. He'd not heard from Marcus although he had left a suitably oblique message confirming what he'd asked him to look for. Ordnance? If it was Special Branch, why and how had they become suspicious of Hadden, and what was he intending to do with all those guns?

His mind took him back to that moment in the ambush when all hell broke loose and he hit the deck. He shuddered at the thought of all those dead bodies. It occurred to him that he must have a charmed life. With that somewhat discomforting thought he drifted off to sleep.

\* \* \* \* \*

### Monday 29th June

Fletcher stopped Irene outside the door of the interview room.

'So how did you know it was Amy Dobson?'

'Ah,' said Irene. 'I went to the horse's mouth. Well she's more like a Shetland pony really. Although her father was probably a gorilla.'

Fletcher made the connection. 'Tina Goodnight!'

'Very good, Inspector,' she laughed.

'And she told you who?'

'And someone else told me where.'

Fletcher put his hand on the door handle. 'So, what's the approach?'

Irene put her head to one side. 'Er . . . you bad cop, me bad cop?'

He grinned and opened the door. They signalled to the uniform to leave. He'd heard the stories and vanished. Amy looked from one to the other and began to cry. Irene gave Fletcher a shrug. He ignored it and dragged a chair from the wall by its front legs, making a terrible scraping noise on the wooden floor. He brought it up next to Amy and sat down. Irene took his cue and sat opposite her. Amy looked from one to the other and began to squirm in her seat. She opened her mouth to speak, but Fletcher put his finger to his lips.

'This is how it goes, Amy. No, you can't go to the toilet. Nor can you have a fag or a cup of coffee.'

She looked beseechingly at Irene, who glared back at her. Amy looked back at Fletcher whose face had come even nearer.

'We could take you to the mortuary and let you see Julie Carter's body. . .'

She gasped and stared at this monster, transfixed by his scary eyes. Yes, it was true. One green and one blue.

'Or we could go and see Mr and Mrs Nellis together, nice and cosy, afternoon tea, cucumber sandwiches, cakes. . .'

Amy had large eyes, but now they had expanded from saucer to dinner plate.

'Or you could continue this story . . .'

She gulped and nearly swallowed her tongue.

'Once upon a time . . . dah di dah . . . and then the little man with the scar came out of the alley and grabbed the little girl by the arm. "Take this gold and go and find the gypsy girl," he said, but before she could run away another man came out of the darkness and she saw that it was . . .'

The two eyes glittered and Amy felt warmth in her knickers which she knew wouldn't go away. She wept with shame and fear. The nose beneath the eyes wrinkled in displeasure. The mouth crinkled into a sneer of disgust. She wanted to die and she knew it was more than likely with every breath she took. She burst into tears.

Fletcher had lied. Even he couldn't bear the smell of such liquid fear. He nodded to Irene and she took the poor girl to the toilet. While she was gone, he went and found a mop and bucket and cleaned up. He had felt worse, but not that much worse.

It was a good seven or eight minutes before they came back, during which time Fletcher contemplated what he knew. It was a big mess. He thought it unlikely that Nellis would have carried out his own dirty work, but despite what he'd said to Sykes he didn't think it could be Aston. Not if what Irene had told him about the poor sap's wife was true and, in any case, his initial instincts had been bone-idle slob not killer. So who was it going to be?

What about the young blonde guy Sadie had told him about? He didn't fit the MO. Dr Fox had said strong or heavy. Hang on. What had Sykes said about the guns and golf clubs affair? Some big lug who'd ended up in hospital with a mashed-in face? What was his name?

The door opened and Irene helped Amy back to the chair, unable to keep the look of surprise appearing on her face as she took in the state of the floor and the smiling face of the 'bad cop' as he sat leaning back in his chair. Amy sat down and looked at the table; her face was red raw, but her seat was dry, so she opened her mouth to confess all, only the words wouldn't come. And in any case another mouth was uttering them.

'. . . and she saw that it was him . . .' she looked up at the face of her torturer, who continued and finished the sentence '. . . Mr Smith. Known to his friends and enemies everywhere as "Big Bad Baz".'

She stared at Fletcher open mouthed.

'It's alright, Amy. You didn't say a word. Did you?' he said. He shook his head until she joined in like a zombie. He stood up and leaned forward onto the table.

'I think you need to take a holiday, Miss Dobson. Fortunately, you've come to the right travel agent. Miss Garner will take you home to pack your bags and arrange for you to be picked up and whisked away to a happier place, while we tidy up here. Maybe in a few weeks or months you'll be able to come home or maybe you'll find a nicer place to live happily ever after.'

And so it came to pass – or would have done if Cora Beck hadn't spoilt the end of the story.

# CHAPTER 14

*Monday 29th June. Evening*

Stephanie Hadden could sense the excitement in the air and feared the worst. No-one had said anything to her but their unusual smiles told her that he'd organised some sort of further humiliation – or even what he'd recently promised. There was a part of her which wished this would be true. Since her last failure, any lingering hope had been extinguished. If there was a hell, it couldn't be any worse than this.

She stood back from the window, watching the sun go down into the glimmering water. She knew that it was beautiful, but felt nothing but weariness. In the window to her right which faced the wood, she could see her reflection. She knew that she had been beautiful once but that meant nothing either. A wan smile appeared on the reflection's face.

'I am half sick of shadows . . .' she whispered to herself.

She became aware of unfamiliar sounds. Heavy engines. Lots of muffled but metallic clattering. She went over to the windows looking over the car park. Towards the end of the building were a couple of large trucks. Several men in dark clothing were moving quickly back and forth, carrying boxes and other bulky things.

Her husband and Miss Ridley were standing to one side, talking to a man she didn't recognise. She watched until the men climbed into the cabs. Her husband kissed the woman and she climbed up as well. The vehicles drove slowly away into the darkness beyond the brightly-lit courtyard. There were a few moments of expectant hush.

From somewhere Stephanie found the willpower to move. It occurred to her that this was her chance. Seeing everyone getting into the trucks and hearing the empty silence in the house, she figured that her husband was the only person left – which meant only one thing.

Without a sound, she tiptoed to the doorway into the next room. The door was open, which confirmed that he was coming this way. She slipped through and ran across the thick carpet, opened the door into one of the side rooms and pulled it to, leaving it slightly ajar.

She was right. She tried to stop her heart from pounding and held her breath. She heard him come through the door from the other side and saw the briefest of movements as he passed through into her room. He'd soon realise that this was the only place she could possibly be. She turned round and looked around her hiding place. This was where they kept the medical equipment. There must be a knife or a pair of scissors in here. She reached out towards the nearest drawer and froze. He was back out in the corridor.

'I know you're here, Stephanie. There's nowhere to hide.'

Her fingers reached inside the drawer and found a large pair of scissors, but before she could retrieve them he burst through the door and knocked her back into the room. She staggered back against a cupboard, sending bottles and boxes tumbling onto the floor. He was quick and forced her back against the wall. Within seconds he'd squeezed the breath out of her and she meekly slipped down. He let go of her neck and stood up. She stared at the floor. Her whole body went limp.

He pulled over a chair and sat down close to her. She looked at his shoes. Black and shiny as always. She could see her distorted left eye reflected in the sheen. She knew she was going to die.

At first all she could hear was his breathing, but then he began to talk in a slow, quiet voice.

'It's over, Stephanie. I have to go.'

She looked up into his dark eyes. For once they looked sad. There was no smile. She held his gaze. He reached out, picked up her hand and held it. He carried on in the same tone.

'I still love you,' he said. 'I always will.'

She stared at him.

'But you betrayed me. Making me believe you'd given me a daughter when all along you knew it was that filthy hippie who was its father.'

Her eyes widened as his face filled with hatred.

'So now I'm going to take you to him. So that you can spend eternity together.'

With that he stood up and, grabbing her arm, pulled her to her feet. Even though she was expecting it, the blow to her face still knocked her head backwards. She cowered away from him, only to feel him release her. She flinched, expecting the next attack, but nothing happened.

Instead she became aware of the inexplicable presence of two other figures. Dark shadows which had appeared without a sound and now fanned out as her husband backed towards them. He seemed oblivious to these shadows and Stephanie was beginning to think they were some kind of vengeful inventions of her own – but then one of them spoke.

'I'm afraid that it's you who has a more pressing engagement, Mr Hadden.'

Her husband's body stiffened. She could see his face in half shadow, his deep-set eyes widening in consternation. He swung round to face the intruders. He didn't speak. How long had they been there?

He backed towards her, but the figure to his right cut off the route with a lithe elegant movement. He was distracted by Stephanie's sudden gulping cough. It was sufficient for the figure to his left to make his move, which was fast and brutal. The kick to Hadden's chest sent him hurtling into the wall and, before he could gather his wits, a punch thudded into his throat. He slid down to the floor, gasping for breath. They quickly hustled him out into the corridor. The last Stephanie heard of him was a hoarse cry as the outer door of the fire exit clanged back against the metal staircase.

The two figures were gone and she was left staring at the empty doorway.

She forced herself out into the corridor and made her way through what had been her prison for so long. Soon she was out in the cold night air. Without giving it a second thought she set off towards the ruined house. She knew exactly where she was going. She'd held it in her heart for seventeen long years.

*Monday 29th June*
There was no need to hurry to capture Julie's murderer; he was still under sedation following the knock-out blow he'd received during the golf tournament, which Fletcher still hadn't fully

understood. The punch had been administered with such force that it had dislocated Baz Smith's jaw, an unfortunate condition which meant that if he was conscious he wanted to scream, but couldn't without further damaging his mandibles – hence, the continued enforced slumber. Not exactly sleeping beauty, and in for a devastating press release when he was allowed to come round, which had now gone front page in the *Mail*.

Equally, Fletcher and Irene were deemed inappropriate as volunteers for the interrogation of DI Aston. Chief Inspector Mancini had co-opted his colleague from Lancaster to conduct the interview and neither of them even saw Aston come back into the station with Sykes. So, having arranged for Amy to be taken to a safe house in Newcastle and completed the relevant paperwork, the two of them took themselves off to the pub.

Irene could see that Fletcher was descending into one of his reflective moods and was wondering how to escape, when she was astonished to see a dark figure step through the door. Her heart missed a beat but she managed to indicate to him that this was not a good time or place. His inky black eyes smiled at her and a jerk of the thumb told her where he'd be. Irene picked up the two glasses and went back over to Fletcher, her mind reeling with potential get-out clauses.

'Someone you know?' asked Fletcher, with a wry smile.

She bit her tongue. No point in lying. 'Yes, but I wasn't expecting him to turn up here,' she said, trying for the same level of nonchalance but knowing it wasn't going to happen.

'No-one expects the Spanish Inquisition,' said Fletcher, the smile broadening into a grin. At least he wasn't sinking into his grim or angry depression.

'What do you want me to do?' she asked, still standing.

Fletcher laughed. 'I don't think you need telling. Bugger off and get on with it. There's nothing for us. Thirty-six hours and it'll be all over. The best news would be that the royal gets her head blown off and we don't get asked to do any more dirty work ever again.'

She sat down and took a big gulp of her pint. 'Who told you it was a "her"?'

'No-one. Just my preferred option.'

Irene considered the alternatives he might mean and decided she didn't care. She took another gulp and stood up. 'Are you sure?' she asked.

'Oh, are you still here?' he said. 'I thought you'd be up against a wall by now.'

She glared at him. 'It's not like that, actually. He's . . .'

Fletcher gave her a surly look. 'Piss off, you daft tart, before I change my mind.'

He picked up her half-empty glass and poured the contents into his own. She didn't need any further encouragement, grabbed her bag and coat and set off towards the door.

At the doorway she turned to look back at him but he'd picked up the local rag and was pretending to read it. She smiled to herself and pushed her way out into the night.

Fletcher threw the paper down and finished the pint. He stared across the pub at a group of blokes who had kept looking over at him and Irene, presumably wondering why she'd want anything to do with him. His mind drifted back to the pub in Bacup. Sophia Loren.

He made an odd connection. What was it Sadie had said about that young man, Keane? 'A multitude of parking tickets'? Once the idea popped into his head, it flowered.

He drove round to his hotel, went up to his room and picked up the phone.

It rang for some time before a quiet voice announced that he'd got through to the residence of Mr and Mrs Cunninghame-Knox. He gave his name and waited. Another long pause until he could hear her steady breathing.

'Michael. It's a Saturday afternoon and our guests are about to arrive. You have two minutes.'

'Good afternoon to you, Louisa,' he replied.

'I'm reliably informed you've re-activated your pyromaniac tendencies as a means of annoying the local criminal fraternity,' she said.

'Nothing like gathering round the campfire to loosen a few tongues. Sing a few old songs.'

She sighed. 'One minute, Michael.'

'Two names,' he said.

She waited.

'Philip Keane.'

'Black sheep,' she confirmed. 'An ancient Anglo-Irish family. Fourteenth or fifteenth Baronet fell at Balaclava, I believe. His brother was killed in Northern Ireland over a year ago. I met his father a couple of times. Handsome man, but an arrogant womaniser.'

'Anglo-Irish? What does that mean?'

'Absent landlords living in London, who own vast estates in Ireland managed by local bailiffs.'

'So not popular with the natives?'

This produced another sigh.

Fletcher changed tack. 'What about Thomas Hadden?'

This time there was no sigh – more an intake of breath.

Fletcher heard a voice speaking to her. She turned away from the phone and he could hear a muffled conversation.

'I'm sorry, Michael, but I must go.'

'Of course,' he said.

'But I can tell you this,' she said sharply. 'It's only a rumour, but it's said that his wife's state of mind is not what it seems.'

'Do you know her?'

'I met her once. Not your type at all. Delicate skin, one of Titania's fairies, but now I hear merely a husk, positively ethereal.'

'I see,' murmured Fletcher, expecting to be cut off.

'But you must know,' she said. 'She's a Keane. Philip's cousin.' She paused. 'And Hadden isn't his real family name. He's a Holden. Old Lancashire family. Recusants.'

'What?'

'The Catholics who kept trying to get rid of Good Queen Bess and put a Scottish Queen on the throne.'

'Ah,' said Fletcher. 'I see.'

'Less said the better,' said Louisa.

With that, the phone went dead. He put it down and considered himself in the mirror on the dressing table opposite.

Now it made a sort of sense. This was an ancient battle. Hadden could be the IRA connection. It all came back to religion. Old hatreds nurtured long and deep in priest holes and secret coded messages. What was it Mr Chapman, his disgruntled old history teacher, used to say? 'It was the Elizabethans who invented the secret service. Codes. Double agents. Four hundred years before James Bond,' he used to sneer.

But what about Keane? Not so much a black sheep as a wolf in a 'turncoat'? Was he the assassin? He didn't fit the Nellis's gang prototype. Sykes had muttered something about a Manchester drugs connection, but suppose that was only a cover? And where was he? Disappeared along with Dyer. Were they working together? Bloody Adversane!

He gathered his few belongings and calculated the time it would take him to get to Penrith and when he'd have to get up tomorrow morning to get back, as opposed to spending the night on his own. It wasn't really a debate, so half an hour later he was heading up the main road.

He was not really concentrating on his speed until a car flashed its headlamps in his mirror. Cursing, he accelerated and left what looked like an old Cortina for dead. Five minutes later, he slowed down to let it past as they reached the dual carriageway at the top of Lindale hill. It took some moments before his brain had processed the information, but he made the connection. Red and white Cortina with a hand dangling out; a hand that belonged to a certain young man who was wanted for questioning and was nowhere to be found.

As it went past him, he looked across. In the passenger seat was a young girl and beyond her was a young man giving him the finger. He pretended he hadn't seen anything and allowed the car to speed on ahead. It wasn't Ian Dyer, but it was one of young Nellis's gang. He pictured him in the King George, looking at Nellis with all the venom a bad loser at pool could produce. His second thought was that he'd bet a week's salary that the girl was Jimmy Beck's daughter, Cora. He watched as the tail lights sped away from him and juggled the thought of Laura's warm body against a potential career-boosting arrest. It was tough and he knew he'd never tell Laura, but he pushed his foot to the floor and set off in pursuit.

\* \* \* \* \*

Irene found Marko leaning against her car in the car park. He stood up as she approached and they embraced, but he was a bit surprised when she pulled him into the shadows and backed up against the wall. She put her hand in his thick curls and smothered his mouth with her own. His hand went snaking down and found the hem of her skirt, while her hand quickly unzipped his trousers. A few more seconds of fumbling and he was inside her, pushing her up the wall. Whatever Fletcher thought about her, she'd never done this before and she was astonished at how exciting she found it.

She took him back to her hotel room, all thoughts of Fletcher wiped from her mind. Eventually, they washed each other clean in the shower, put some clothes on and went out for a meal.

When Irene woke in the morning he was gone, but the bracelet had now acquired a companion piece: a necklace of the same solid silver with an even bigger ruby setting, which she decided even she couldn't wear to work.

$$* * * * *$$

### Tuesday June 30th
The following morning Marko had woken Luca early and they'd listened to the tape which he'd extracted from the 'ruby' in the bracelet while Irene slept. There was little to interest them. They were amused by the references to the 'accident' which Tsura had gone to take a look at. She'd seen Irene tracking down Tina but lost her in the back streets whilst she was hunting the girl who they now knew had the identity of the whore's killer.

The whereabouts of Tsura's amour and the young thug were still unknown, but Luca could see how both of them might be involved. The previous tape had hinted that Hadden was running them and that they were both operating as double agents for him and Nellis. Whether they knew each other or not wasn't clear, and neither of them had yet reappeared.

As the two of them sat in the hotel dining room trying to drink what the English seemed to think could be called coffee, Tsura joined them. They brought her up to date.

Then they told Marko how they'd arrived at Hadden's house to find men filling trucks with assorted weaponry. They couldn't be sure who they were, but when they'd gone they'd found it easy to gain access and surprise Hadden attacking his wife. They'd carried out their contract with a more than usual sense of moral justification.

'So what now?' he asked.

Luca looked from one to the other. They waited. He looked out at the lake, which was finally appearing from behind a fading screen of morning mist.

'We've two choices. Either we carry out the reduced commission or we cut our losses and go home.'

They continued to wait. Neither of them had an opinion either way.

'I'll be honest with you,' he said. 'I'm intrigued by the low status of the new target. He's not someone to put on our curriculum vitae, but he must know something someone doesn't want him to share. Perhaps a brief encounter before elimination might answer a few questions.'

Marko nodded. 'Today?'

'I think so, don't you? Under the noses of the security services might bring us some kudos? Assuming he turns up.'

'The contact assures me he will be here.'

'Where to look?'

310

'Well. A visit to the scene of the crime seems the obvious place to start.'

Marko looked at Tsura, who shrugged her shoulders.

\* \* \* \* \*

It didn't take long for Cora to find Nails. He lived in a squat near the middle of town. She was relieved to find he wasn't out of it or pissed up, and a little perturbed by his willingness to help. He was the only one in the gang who could drive legally. His dad was a garage mechanic and Nails had passed his test as soon as he could. He knew where Nellis's Cortina was kept and didn't need a key, so within an hour of leaving her mother's they were heading out of town.

'Why do you think he's in Lancaster?' she asked.

'Loads of student squats. He's got a stash of good stuff and they've got more money than sense, so he'll be able to keep on the move and keep out of trouble.'

'So how will we find him?'

Nails laughed. 'I've got a few readies as well, and he's hardly unnoticeable. It just depends on whether he wants us – me or you – to find him. If he doesn't want us to we won't find him. End of story.'

He didn't have much else to say.

In the past, he'd have done a lot of showing off when he was driving, weaving in and out of the traffic and stuff, but tonight he only hassled one other driver who gave way fairly easily: a middle-aged bloke day-dreaming his way home to a wife and kids after a hard day at the office.

In Lancaster he drove confidently from one squat to another.

Cora sat in the car while he strode from candle-lit houses to darkened front rooms full of deafening Wagner. Nobody was saying anything. After about an hour he said he'd done enough to spread the word and suggested they found a bar and waited. He parked up outside one on the dockside and she followed him through the door. He bought himself half a pint and an orange juice for her. Without saying anything he went into the pool room and put some coins on the table. She sat and watched, her mind a blank.

Nails was on his second attempt to get on the table, when a shadow fell across her table and a voice she'd never liked came over her head.

'Red in the bottom corner you daft twat,' it said.

Nails looked up and sneered. 'When I want your advice, I'll be in an old folk's home.'

He took his choice of shot and the ball bounced off the side cushion and left his opponent with an easy finish.

'Fat chance, you scumbag! You'll not live that long,' said the voice, and Cora felt his slim fingers crawling round her neck. She froze. He pushed her along the seat and sidled in beside her, putting his small glass of something colourless onto the table. He stank of unwashed clothes and pot. She glanced towards him.

Indie had made some effort to disguise himself: shaven head, funny little gingery beard and dark clothes, but there was no mistaking the thin line down his cheek and the scary eyes which she'd always thought were just too impossibly blue to be real.

'What are you after, Scrag-end?' he asked.

Nails came over towards them. Indie looked up at him.

'Fuck off, Nails and find your own shag,' he growled.

Nails took one look into his eyes and went back to the pool

table where, as a habitual loser, he was accepted with the offer of making it interesting: they'd fallen for his act. It generally ended in a fight, but that didn't bother Nails; he was a very fast runner.

Indie swivelled the blue gaze back at Cora. She had given it some thought, but now that she was scarred face to scarred face with him, she couldn't remember any of the cautious introductions she'd constructed. So she stumbled straight in.

'You know what Nellis is always saying to me about my father?' she blurted.

For once in his life Indie was caught by surprise. 'You mean that he's not your real father? That you're a little bastard!'

'Yeh and that he knows something about my father that would put him inside?'

'So? You come all this way to tell me something I already know?'

She looked at him hard. Did he know already?

'What *do* you know?'

He rolled his eyes, which was bizarre, like two blue snooker balls.

'That you're a bastard and your dad killed a man.'

'Who?' she couldn't stop herself asking.

'Who?'

'Yeh. Who's he supposed to have killed?'

Indie frowned at her which was always odd, like one side of his face was trying to make a cross. He shrugged. 'I don't know, do I?' he said and returned the hard look.

She was determined to see this through, although now she'd begun to tremble. 'But I do,' she said.

'So what? Some loser's dead ages ago. Why do you need to tell me?'

She reached over and took his glass. He was too startled to stop her as she took a sip. She screwed up her face as it scorched the back of her throat. 'What's that?' she croaked.

He laughed: 'Polish vodka, you silly bitch! Do you want another one?'

She shook her head in disgust, but the words still came out. 'It wasn't my dad who killed someone. It was Nellis.'

Indie made a face. 'Nellis! That soft twat! He couldn't kill a mouse.'

'No, his dad.'

Indie did that crinkly thing with his mouth to show he grudgingly agreed that was possible. 'So who did Eric kill?'

Nails chose this point to put the black down by doubling it across the table. The room went silent. The lad he was playing swung his cue up into his other hand and glanced at his mates.

'You two-faced bastard! You're a fucking hustler.' He started to make his way round the table and his three mates stood up.

'Leave him,' said Indie in a quiet voice.

The four of them glanced over at the skinhead sitting with the girl.

'What the fuck has it got to do with you, you bald twat?'

'Nails, give the "boy" his money back,' said Indie.

The pool player squared up to Indie. 'Who are you calling "boy"?'

Indie looked up at him. 'You. . . and if you don't take the money and back off, you'll not get to grow up.'

The lad laughed, but the blue eyes made him check out his mates. He was disconcerted to see that they weren't a hundred per cent on his side. He looked back at the skinhead and saw why. A long blade dully gleamed on the table top, gripped in the knuckles of a grimy hand. He took a step back. 'Hey . . .' was all he could manage.

'Nails. The money.'

Nails placed two five-pound notes on the side of the pool table. His opponent looked at them and took the right decision. Without another word spoken they backed out. When Cora looked down the blade had disappeared.

'Nails. Get me another drink,' said Indie. Nails went out into the main bar.

'Your dad,' said Cora.

Indie looked down at his empty glass. 'What did you say?'

'Eric Nellis killed your real dad. He was called Wallace. Duncan Wallace.'

The next few moments were the stillest, the most silent and the most terrifying of Cora's life.

Nails appeared in the doorway, read the signs, placed the drink in front of the stiffened effigy of his friend and backed out with a worried glance at Cora.

'Who told you this?' Indie asked.

'My mother,' she said.

He picked up the glass and after a short pause lifted it high and drank it in one gulp. Unlike Cora, he didn't gasp for breath or feel his throat to see if had scorched a hole through his flesh. He put the glass back on the table.

'Why should I believe your mother?'

'Why should she lie? Why wait until now? I believe her.'

'How did it happen?'

She told him. He listened intently. When she was finished he sat very still. She held her breath. He reached up to his jacket pocket and, undoing the button, pulled out a small photograph and handed it to her. It was a black and white shot of a couple at the seaside. They were sitting on a bench, both smiling at the camera. The young man had his arm round the girl's shoulder and her head was tilted in towards his neck.

'Look on the back,' he said.

She turned it over and read the words. It said: Canny and me. Blackpool June 1962.

'It was all that was left in her handbag, hidden in a side pocket. I'd seen other pictures of my mam when she was younger, it's definitely her, but I never knew who the man was. He doesn't look anything like my stepdad. Fucking ugly bastard, he was.'

'I guess "Canny" might be short for Duncan,' she offered.

'I think you guess right . . . and I remember my granddad. We went to see him once. Just me and my mam, in Glasgow in one of them big tenement houses. I was scared stiff of him, couldn't understand a word he said but I remember his name. Charlie Wallace. My mam told me it was her uncle, but . . .'

Cora couldn't think of anything else to say. Indie let out a sigh as though he'd being holding it in all his life. 'Come on, Cora,' he said. 'We're back to Barrow.'

He got up and walked out of the room. She followed. They went out onto the street and found Nails sitting in the car. Indie got in the passenger seat without a word and Cora squeezed into the back. Nails turned on the engine.

'Where we going, Indie?' he asked.

'Barra.'

Nails thought of a lot of things he might say or ask, but didn't. Instead he revved the engine and did a noisy three-point turn, before heading back up into town and taking the road to the M6. They were turning off onto the A591, before Indie spoke.

'I need to go and see someone first,' he said. 'I need a gun.'

Nails glanced at him, but said nothing. He'd already decided that as soon as they got to Barrow he was going to make himself scarce, but the closer they got the more he understood that it wasn't going to be that easy. He'd no idea where or how to get a gun, but he didn't doubt Indie would know and he would get it and he would use it. But Nails didn't know what Cora had told Indie, so he didn't know who the victim was going to be. He didn't expect Cora to speak up next.

'I know where there's a gun,' she said.

Both of the young men turned to look at her.

'Watch the road, you daft twat,' said Indie.

Nails swerved back onto his side of the road and straightened up.

'Where?' asked Indie.

'It's near my dad's hut. I know where it's hidden.'

'What sort is it?'

'A shotgun.'

Indie was silent for a few minutes. 'OK. I know the way,' he said.

The red and white car began to ascend the hill in the moonlight. The occupants didn't speak again until Indie told Nails to take a left. It was then Cora knew that Indie knew far more than she did. She sank into the battered old leather seat which stank of old sex and spilt beer.

Roger slowed down as they came to edge of the trees which hid the house from the drive. Despite the thickly-gathered firs, they could see the bright wall of lights glaring out into the darkness. He glanced in his mirror to see Jimmy's face, eyes blank and his mouth a thin, grim line of determination. He looked across at Shirley, who was staring straight ahead. He knew she was scared, but felt proud that she'd not let him come without her.

Jimmy leaned forward and put his hand on Roger's shoulder. 'We'll wait for Eddie. He won't be long.'

Shirley gave Roger a meaningful look. 'We're not going in without him are we, Roger?' she said.

He shook his head. Jimmy sat back in his seat and wound down the window. The night air was sucked in bringing with it the smell of the estuary. Wisps of fog were already floating between the trees.

Headlamps approached from behind and were doused as the car drew level. The three occupants of the first car looked across to see that Eddie Sykes had brought a friend. Jimmy got out of the car and went to the driver's door as Eddie opened it.

'Who's the back-up, Eddie?' asked Jimmy.

Eddie got out of the car and stood face to face with Jimmy. 'He's a colleague, DC Gary Watson. I've filled him in. He'll be OK.'

Jimmy wasn't entirely convinced, but there wasn't much else he could do. 'You give me ten minutes to sort the generator. I'll set it to cut out another five minutes later, which will give me time to get round to the bottom of the fire escape. I'll come back this way and give you the nod. OK?'

Eddie had been through all the arguments with Jimmy and knew there was no point in revisiting them, so he nodded and watched him set off at a brisk pace to their left. He thought of having a quick word with Roger, but realised it wouldn't make any difference and got back in his car. They waited. It seemed a long ten minutes. As they'd got their windows shut against the fog, they didn't hear the third car pulling up with a scrunch of worn tyres behind them or hear the doors shutting or see the two shadows creeping behind them through the woods.

\* \* \* \* \*

It was only because of Indie's natural caution that they didn't come roaring up behind the two parked cars sitting on the drive with their lights off. He'd told Nails to kill his lights as they turned off onto the drive. Cora didn't know this road, but knew it was heading down towards the estuary not far from the hut. She thought of Maliverny and the ruined house, and shivered.

Nails pulled up as they caught sight of the two dark shapes ahead of them on the drive. Indie whispered to him to reverse back behind a large bush and told him to wait or he'd cut his balls off. Nails didn't say a word.

Indie told Cora to get out of the car and follow him. She zipped up her jacket and thought of her dad; she'd no idea how near he was. Indie made his way over to the right of the lights which filtered through the trees from the house, which must be the house she'd seen from the ruin. Indie stopped, bent down and signalled to Cora to do the same. They had got to the far end of the main building. Cora could see, through the bushes to her left, a large gravelled area in front of the main entrance from which all the lights blazed. Indie gave her a look.

'Do you know who lives here?' he asked.

She shook her head.

'He's an evil bastard, but he's the only person who frightens Eric Nellis.'

Cora knew there was more, but didn't ask. Indie seemed uncertain what to do. 'I was going to ask Mr Hadden a favour. He owes me big style, but I'm not sure what's going on with the two cars. Looks like they're trying something on – although this guy's got everything lit up, alarmed and covered by hundreds of cameras, so I don't rate their chances.'

He'd no sooner said this than the two cars' lights came on as they drove through the trees and pulled up in front of the house.

Three men got out and approached the front door. Indie drew his breath.

'Coppers,' he sneered. 'The one at the front is Eddie Sykes and the other's some young twat. Don't recognise the third guy.'

'I do,' said Cora. 'He's the one who took out Baz Smith when Steve's gang came looking for me.'

Indie turned to look at her, his face half in shadow. 'What? That little guy took out Baz? You're kidding!'

Cora nodded. 'Well he did. He's ex-army I think.'

'So's Baz, but . . .'

Before Indie could say anything else, they both ducked down as they heard someone moving fast through the trees behind them. They couldn't see him, but heard the rustling heading further away beyond the house towards the ruin. Cora wondered if was Maliverny, but it didn't seem like his blundering style. As they watched, they saw a dark figure slip out from the trees and run across towards the other end of the building. Cora knew instantly it was her father.

'That's my dad,' she whispered hoarsely to Indie.

'What the fuck is going on?' was all he said. They kept their heads down, not knowing what to do next. Their heads turned as they heard one of the three men banging on the front door.

They watched. The three men waited. One of them backed off and looked up at the first-floor windows. No-one answered their knocking. The lights continued to flood the scene. The one Indie had identified as Sykes stepped up again and hammered on the door. There was still no response. In the distance they could hear a whining noise that slowly got louder until there was a loud bang and all the house lights went out, leaving the three men lit up by the headlights of the two cars. Sykes hammered on the door again, before trying the handle which opened without any effort. He turned to the other two and the three of them produced torches and went into the building.

Indie grabbed Cora by the wrist and dragged her back into the trees. 'I don't know what's going on, but it looks like Hadden's not there. How far is it to your dad's hut?'

Cora didn't know what to do. Should she go after her dad or carry on with Indie? Two things settled it. First the torchlight under Indie's chin scaring her witless, followed by the dull gleam of the knife which appeared in front of his scar.

She nodded him in the direction of the ruin and led the way. She told him they didn't need the torch because she knew her way in the dark, but she'd seen a dull flickering of a fire reflecting off the old stone walls of a dark silhouette jutting out above the trees. She headed towards it. If Indie had seen the firelight he didn't ask, but he kept up close as she hurried along the path between the rhododendrons.

\* \* \* \* \*

Back in the house, Roger was leading the way as they charged up the stairs. At the top the door, which they'd had to blow open the first time, stood ajar. Roger hesitated, remembering what had happened to Charlie, but Eddie pushed past him and shone his torch in both directions.

'Along there,' said Roger, indicating the way to the woman's rooms.

They walked through the rooms unhindered until they stood in front of Mrs Hadden's bedroom door, which was closed. Eddie looked back at Roger who nodded. Sykes turned the handle and the door opened without a sound. The room was empty. Roger indicated the door to their right. They stepped into the white padded room and shone their torches onto a scene from hell.

Standing in the middle of the room was the figure of Jimmy Beck, torch in one hand and shotgun in the other, frozen to the spot. As the others moved forward, they could make out a shape on the floor. It was like a giant starfish, but as each one of them focussed on its real identity they put their hands to their mouths. Watson was the last to take it in and dropped his torch.

This was not a starfish but a once human body. A female body, its neck a deep red colour. Not blood. There was no blood.

Nevertheless Eddie Sykes backed out of the room and emptied his guts elsewhere. Roger, who had probably seen more dead bodies than the other three put together, pulled the two other unheeding men back through the door and, helping Eddie to his feet, guided them down to the cars.

Eddie recovered sufficiently to explain how to use the car radio, before heading for the bushes to bring up the rest of his innards. Roger found himself talking to a night-shift sergeant who calmly acquired the relevant information and assured him that help would arrive within minutes. It did – surprisingly in the person of DI Fletcher, dragging a struggling youth by the scruff of his neck.

\* \* \* \* \*

Cora and Indie had reached the ruin well before the sirens and flashing lights told them that they'd have to seek a different route back to Barrow. If Indie had noticed anything odd about the cold, black hulk before they approached, the firelight had gone when

322

they stumped up the embankment and stood looking out over the estuary. The earlier threat of fog had proved false and now a full moon stood high in the western sky. The water surging down the channels twinkled and glittered between the glistening sand like quartz veins in a marble floor.

Cora glanced back at the ruin, which remained a dark mass of surly rock and shadows, refusing to offer any lighter surfaces to reflect the glory of the moon. There was no sudden movement or bursting forth of sword-waving attack, and Indie seemed indifferent to the splendour all around even though it glinted in his eyes.

'Where now?' he asked.

Cora indicated the slightest of tracks and set off towards the hut. He followed. They soon came to the large barn and Cora clambered across to the trapdoor hidden under the corrugated iron. She told Indie where to shine the torch so that she could pull it back to reveal the old wooden planks, pulled at the heavy iron ring and showed him the steps descending underneath. Indie followed her as she stepped carefully down, and heeded the warning to mind his head. Cora confidently stepped over to the old table and dragged out the old bag . . . which was empty.

She stared at it in disbelief. Indie grabbed her by the shoulder. 'What's your game?' he demanded, his face close to hers.

She was lost for words. He shook her hard. She looked him dully in the face. The penny dropped.

'My father,' she said. 'He must have taken it to the big house.'

She couldn't see Indie's face, but knew it would be consumed with rage. To make matters worse, in the distance they both heard the sound of sirens. He grabbed her by the arm and dragged her back up the steps.

Back on the path they could hear the sirens getting closer. Through the trees across the estuary they could see them racing along the coast road. Indie shone the torch in her face.

'If you've set me up, you'll wish you'd never found me,' he yelled.

She fell to her knees unable to speak, but when she looked up he'd gone – vanished. Another face loomed up in front of her and a stench of rotten teeth filled her nostrils.

'Maliverny!' she said.

'At thy service, milady,' he said.

She stood up and nearly tripped over the crumpled body at her feet. She looked down. It was Indie who, to her relief, began to groan and reach for the back of his head. Maliverny raised his sword arm, but she shook her head.

'No! No! Maliverny, he's my friend!' she shouted. The giant hesitated. She knelt down and helped Indie sit up. The back of his head was bleeding slightly but it didn't look serious. He groaned and opened his eyes, which slowly focussed on Cora. Despite his confusion, he glared and reached out to grab her by the throat, only to find a thin, sharp blade biting into his hand. He winced and let her go, looking up to discover the bearded face grinning at him.

'If he be thy friend, my pretty, thee needs to choose with better care.'

Indie's eyes went big. He looked sideways at Cora, who laughed. 'It's alright Maliverny, he means me no harm. Let him be!'

Maliverny reluctantly withdrew his sword and took a step back. Cora helped Indie to his feet and guided him down the track to the hut. Five minutes later, the three of them were huddled round the stove as the kettle began to rattle.

It took Cora a long time to tell Indie her tale and, as he never saw Maliverny Catlin again as long as he lived, Indie eventually thought it must have been the blow to the head and not for real. He wasn't the sort of person to listen as intently as he did that night, but it changed his thinking about Cora for ever.

The sirens had stopped for the moment, but could be heard later on their way back to Barrow. The moon filtered through the shutters until it was nearly dawn. Indie snored and Cora slept and Maliverny Catlin slipped out and away.

# CHAPTER 15

***Wednesday 1st July***

The launch ceremony on Wednesday the first of July went off without a hitch. The sun shone and the town's locals, visitors and traders had a wonderful day. The champagne bottle broke on the first hit and the crowds cheered as the black hulk slipped gently into the waiting tugs in the deep channel. The day's festivities continued well into the evening, and no-one seemed to have noticed that four of the invited guests' places at both the launch and the Mayor's banquet had remained unfilled.

Fletcher wasn't even in town; he'd driven up the M6 late the previous evening in a slightly sullen yet resigned sort of mood. He'd only just breasted the top of Shap summit when the police car came up fast, blue light flashing and indicating him to come off at the junction. He sat in his car and watched as the slim figure of his erstwhile protégée made her way back to him, the wind playing havoc with her fringe.

Sadie only looked him once in the eyes after telling him the tale. He imagined that she'd elaborated more than Adversane would have approved of, but it was clear. She reminded him that the documents he'd signed in Todmorden still required his silence and that he should take satisfaction from the fact that his 'good work' had helped prevent a 'major incident'. He merely nodded, his hands never leaving the wheel and the engine still running.

Her car drove off in a flurry of spurting gravel and he watched as it crossed the bridge and surged back onto the southern carriageway. In seconds it disappeared back over the hill.

Weary beyond measure, he put his car into gear and continued his journey north. He'd made himself spend a good half hour in the Fox trying to cheer up a bit, but knew he'd not be right until he'd spent a day up on the fells. He went home and Laura eventually heard the full story. Well, not the full story – she knew that.

* * * * *

### Monday 29th June

It had begun so well. On the Monday night, he'd followed the red and white car to Lancaster, but lost it in the maze of little streets that the driver seemed to know really well. Only mildly dissatisfied with himself, and knowing it was now too late to go home, he decided that his best chance was to go back to the South Lakes junction and wait for the car to come back. He based this on Irene's conviction that Barrovians always came back sooner rather than later.

In the event, he didn't have to wait long for her to be proved correct. The car accelerated past him as he lurked half asleep in the first lay-by, and he caught up with it as it turned off at the A591 roundabout. There were few other cars about, so he stayed well back thinking he knew where they were going and would catch up after Ulverston. He was fortunate to see the brake lights coming on near the old railway sidings at Backbarrow and the car veering off the main road to the left. He took the same turning, signed to Cark, and set off down a road he didn't know. Again he was nearly caught out as the car swerved abruptly to the right and disappeared into the woods.

He went past the lane end and pulled in a few hundred yards further along. He got out into the cold night air and looked back to the turning. He was sure there was no sign, but a memory stirred. Was this where Sadie followed that young man? Keane? He got back in the car and reversed back to the junction. Sure enough there was no sign. He drove the car as quietly as he could until he came to the gateway: 'Private Property – Keep Out – Hadden Estates', just as Sadie had said. He pulled into the hedge and set off down the drive.

Minutes later Fletcher saw the car. At the same moment there was a muffled explosion and the lights he could see through the trees went out. The driver of the car opened his door and got out. He was alone. Well, he thought he was, until a hand grabbed his wrist and forced it up his back until he yelped.

'Good evening, sir,' said Fletcher as Nails foolishly attempted to kick back against his attacker's shins. The next thing Nails knew, he was spitting gravel and blood from his mouth as he struggled to get his face out of a muddy puddle.

Fletcher allowed him to lift his head, before shoving it back in and rubbing his face in the mud and grit until he could hardly breathe. The young lad gave in. Fletcher pulled him up so that Nails could see who it was: that bloody mean bastard copper who'd roughed Nellis up. He spat a mixed soup of blood, gravel and mud onto the ground.

'So? What's to do?' asked Fletcher with surly grin.

'Dunno, copper, and I wouldn't tell you anyway. Bloody aggravated assault that was!'

'Ooh! Get the little lawyer! I think you'll find it was resisting arrest whilst trespassing on private property,' said Fletcher, giving him a hefty push. Nails managed to retain his footing and considered making a run for it, but Fletcher read his thoughts and grabbed him by the collar of his jacket.

'Of course we could go and check out whether you're an honoured guest instead, couldn't we?' he said. Before Nails could say another word, he began dragging him down towards where the lights had been extinguished.

Thus it was that Fletcher and his captive arrived as the familiar figure of Eddie Sykes stumbled into the trees and ullocked his insides into the undergrowth. The two car headlights enabled Fletcher to half recognise the other ashen-faced officer and another man holding a shotgun. He didn't seem intent on using it but rather as if he'd forgotten it was in his hand.

Fletcher held onto the young thug and was about to begin negotiations with the gunman, when yet another man stepped out of one of the cars with the coiled wire of the police radio reaching back inside. Momentarily confused, Fletcher stood and stared, but the man offered him the radio and explained:

'I think you'd better take charge now, Inspector. I'll go and look after your colleague.'

Fletcher's brain whirred into action. He realised that the white-faced youth was looking at him and remembered his name.

'Watson!' he said. 'Get some handcuffs on this young lad and put him in a car. Watson came out of his trance and did as he was told. Roger fetched Sykes out from the bushes and handed him into the care of a young woman who'd appeared from nowhere but seemed calm enough. The gunman had broken the barrel of his shotgun and was sitting on a low wall staring at the house.

Watson realised that Fletcher had never met Jimmy Beck, so he introduced them. Neither of them could think of much to say.

Roger Skeldon managed a statement of sorts, which left Fletcher understandably incredulous. He spoke to the sergeant on the other end of the radio and confirmed that all three emergency services were on their way. They could be heard wailing up the coast road as he put the radio back in its slot.

The next few hours or so passed in a flurry of activity: police cars, ambulances, SOCO vans all crowded onto the gravel in front of the house. Jimmy Beck was accompanied back to the out-house where he showed them how to rectify his procedure and bring all the lights back on, although it took a little longer to stop all the alarms from bellowing in their ears.

Fletcher needed one glance to see the poor wretch upstairs was well past first aid and left the professionals to do their jobs. Dr Fox arrived and spent only a few minutes examining the body, before announcing that he didn't think the death had happened long ago and that it was probably as bad for the victim as it looked. Fletcher figured that his real work wouldn't start till everyone else had finished, so he took himself off back to the hotel to see if he could get some sleep.

### Tuesday 30th June

The following day was one of those occasions which Fletcher recalled as best described by his English teacher, Miss Elphinstone, in her sonorous rendering of 'When sorrows come, they come not single spies, but in battalions.'

He'd come awake slowly. The dream was something to do with water, but it faded. He took in his surroundings. He'd spent a lot of his working life in hotel bedrooms and this was no worse than any other, but he suddenly had a deep longing for Laura's room. He remembered that last night he'd nearly gone there, but events had intervened and now he must get up and make himself go and look at a body on a cold slab.

He groaned and pulled the bedclothes back over his head. There was a knock at the door. It could only be one person: Irene, with her recently acquired doe-eyed look. He yelled to her to damn well wait and struggled out of bed.

He'd been right about the person, but the doe had disappeared, to be replaced by the avenging Cumbrian harpy he preferred. 'Bastard,' she kept repeating.

Fletcher was trying hard not to snigger or make any comment at all, although plenty came to mind. The doe had been comparing the ruby stones on the two gifts she'd received from the gentle hunter, when her sharp eyes had detected a dark spot in the centre of the one on the bracelet. Her regularly sharpened nails quickly solved the mystery and she had angrily shown Fletcher the tiny device secreted underneath what she now suspected was only a piece of tinted glass.

'But why me?' she asked.

Fletcher had already asked himself that question, along with many others, but she'd work it out for herself soon enough. They took it to the technical guy, who mumbled something about 'bloody spooks' and took it off to his lab. No word as yet.

They'd called in at the path lab on the way to the station, but Fox had only done his preliminary investigation and refused to speculate, other than that the poor woman had been strangled by someone intent on causing maximum pain. Why the murderer had done this was beyond his remit, he reminded Fletcher.

Knowing who might be the principal suspect didn't help, but at least they had an idea about who they needed to question. Except he'd disappeared.

A thorough search of the enormous house had produced absolutely nothing, even with the ex-soldier's help. Roger Skeldon had merely confirmed that it was a *Marie Celeste*. Everything was as he remembered it – minus the people. He decided he'd keep quiet about the weapons store which he'd only smelt anyway. Whether Marcus or Hadden had arranged their disappearance, he decided he had enough of undercover work, unless it was under Shirley's bedcover.

They'd managed to track down one of the chefs recovering from a monster hangover in bed with two equally hung-over girls who were now in desperate need of their next fix and willing to confess to anything if they could get it. But all he'd been able to tell them was that the entire staff had been told to leave on the Saturday afternoon, all with substantial bonuses and a threatening lecture about professional loyalty.

Fletcher went to see Mancini, but he hadn't arrived at work yet and wasn't answering his phone. So Fletcher rang the ACC and brought him up to date. His superior agreed with his suggestions and initiated a nationwide search including air and ferry ports. Infuriatingly, they could find no photographs of either Hadden, his wife or Miss Ridley and were reduced to employing a local art teacher to do his best with the help of Skeldon, Shirley and the chef.

When Mancini arrived, Fletcher suggested he ask the ACC to send them reinforcements, which was grudgingly agreed.

By this time Irene had worked herself into such a rage, Fletcher told her to fuck off and find out as much as she could about her 'Marko'.

'I'll fucking "marko" him. Smooth talking bastard!' she spat, as she stormed out.

These may have been the single spies, but the first battalion arrived in the station as Mancini was bringing the reinforcements up to speed in an incident room that was fast running out of boards. The Nellis entourage included Mr and Mrs, an assortment of Nike-clothed and booted attendants and a Manchester lawyer. In other circumstances Fletcher would have relished the exchanges, but Mancini invited DI Roberts from Millom to take on the task. Fletcher didn't quite understand the expression of pleasure this brought to the little man's face. Maybe it was his introduction to the now spiked-up and vengeful looking DS Garner that was ringing his bell, but Fletcher thought it might be something else.

By the time everyone was busy, he realised he hadn't set eyes on Sadie. This was rectified immediately by her appearance in the outer office. It was obvious that she was getting herself up to speed by asking all and sundry before she got to him. That made him smile; he knew who had taught her that trick. She finally arrived in Aston's office, which Fletcher had commandeered, and closed the door behind her.

'Your usual level of mayhem, I gather,' she said as she folded her arms and leaned back against the glass door, blocking anyone's view of their encounter.

Fletcher sighed. 'Why me?' he asked in an innocent voice.

She snorted and ignored that; Fletcher didn't do innocence at all well.

'Well you've roused Adversane. He's on his way. Should be here by noon.'

Fletcher gave her a glowering look.

'Not me,' she said. 'Plenty of suspects around though. There's half the UK Special Branch within a mile of this office.'

Fletcher didn't pursue that; it was a complete waste of time.

'So what do you know?' she asked.

'Not much. We found Mrs Hadden's nurse's body. She'd been strangled. Hadden and his wife have disappeared without trace, as they say. National alert on all ports and airports. Mancini has taken over and has arranged for a press conference in about an hour's time.'

The first seemed to surprise her less than the second of these two announcements, but he was used to her ability to hide her thoughts and feelings.

'We've had to call in reinforcements, but we're a bit short of anyone to question just yet.'

She decided to take a seat, which required adjustment to the knee-length skirt and a quick check on the gleaming black bob. He tried to keep a straight face.

'So what's with the Nellis mob?' she asked.

'No idea,' he shrugged.

She smiled. 'You mean the insurance company is questioning your close encounter with a "majestic" conflagration.'

'Dodgy electrics is my guess.'

'That doesn't help me, does it? What am I going to say to Adversane?'

Fletcher put his feet on Aston's desk. 'I've no idea. We haven't got the slightest lead on any Paddie plans, have we? Unless . . .'

He clicked his fingers as a thought struck him. 'Follow me, madam,' he said.

She traipsed after him down into the technical labs housed in the cellars. She couldn't think what had come into his mind, but it might be something to keep Adversane happy. He'd not been himself recently: big fleas on his back, as he put it. She caught up with Fletcher downstairs who cornered a younger man with long greasy hair. He gave her a longer look than she liked, but pointed them to a stack of photographs on the table in front of him. Fletcher picked one up and looked at it, put his head to one side and finally turned the picture through 90 degrees.

'No. You've got me. How about the inside of a Star Trek phaser gun?' he said.

The technician grinned at him. 'Not bad. Not bad at all. For a copper,' he added with undisguised contempt, which Fletcher ignored.

'Actually, it's a state of the art recording device and given the Cyrillic lettering, I'd say KGB or Stasi. Although considering what's recorded on it, I'd say it's fallen into the hands of some East European porn merchant.'

They stared at him, waiting to see if he'd got any more to say. He hadn't, and reverted to fiddling with a minute piece of equipment with surprisingly nimble fingers.

'So it doesn't mention anything to do with submarines?' asked Fletcher.

'Sorry,' he said, without looking up.

Sadie asked if she could take away the device which the technician had extracted from Irene's bracelet, the blown-up photos and the recordings. He shrugged and agreed with complete disinterest.

'Presents for the boss, eh?' said Fletcher, as they made their way back upstairs.

She ignored him and went out of the door, no doubt heading for the same place where she'd watched the Nellis tapes. They had revealed nothing other than the most sordid and sickening images of sexual violence. This time Fletcher suspected she'd just get an eyeful of Irene's best moves, although how she would react to that he couldn't imagine.

Fletcher was pondering this as he passed the interview rooms on the first floor. He'd gone two steps beyond, when he heard the raised voice of Doreen Featherstone yelling at the little man from Millom. He stopped, considered the protocol and made up his mind. Bugger the protocol.

He opened the door of the room and found himself face to face with the Glaswegian Gorgon in full flow – not a pleasant sight. His appearance was sufficient to stop the stream of invective being directed at DI Roberts who, Fletcher was pleased to see, was struggling to keep a straight face. Fletcher took the opportunity presented to him, and even without the aid of a shiny shield launched his attack on the snake-headed monster.

'I'm so sorry to interrupt, Detective Inspector,' he said with a smile, which was greeted with a gracious nod of the head. 'However I'd feel now would be a good moment to mention that not everything was lost in the terrible disaster that has occurred. My colleagues and I were able to rescue a substantial number of tape recordings from Mr Nellis's office and after giving them a good clean, we hope to be able to return them within a day or two.'

He allowed only a few seconds for this to sink in, before clapping Roberts on the shoulder and exiting to thunderous silence.

He couldn't stop himself from laughing and guffawing all the way back up to the incident room, where the assembled teams stared at him with puzzled faces, before shaking their heads and getting back to their work. He went into Aston's office and, picking up the phone, ordered two bacon rolls and a large mug of tea. Things could only get better.

\* \* \* \* \*

Indie was used to waking up in places he didn't recognise, with only fleeting memories of the previous day's events, but the image of the giant's face looming over him was enough to jolt him awake with an abrupt shock. He rubbed his eyes. Daylight slanted through the shutters. He remembered where he was and looked across to where he thought the man might be, but there was only the huddled form of Cora with her blonde hair sticking out of the top of the sleeping bag on the floor.

He shrugged his way out of the bag she'd given him and fumbled in his pocket for a fag. It was only when he opened the door that she stirred and, like him, sat up with a start. She too looked round for Maliverny, only to focus on Indie giving her a serious look as he sparked his lighter into life.

She snuggled back into the warmth of the bag and returned his stare. 'What are you going to do now?' she asked.

He looked out at the woods. 'How can we get to the road?'

She knew not to ask any further, his face had a hardness to it she understood only too well. 'Quickest would be round the edge of the sand and over the old railway bridge.'

He looked back at her. 'Did I dream that big bastard or is he for real?'

'He's real,' she said, 'but I'm not sure when or why.'

He cocked his head to one side, but didn't say what she saw in his eyes.

'OK. You show me the way and then I'll split. Yeh?'

She said nothing.

Five minutes later they were scrambling round the rocks heading for the bridge. The tide was in, lapping on the grass turf. In the main channel three swans glided alongside, letting the strong current do most of the work. Cora stopped to watch them, but

Indie strode on. He could see the bridge and the houses beyond. His mind was ahead of him, planning the where, the when and the how. The what and the why were fixed and final.

Across the bridge, it only took him a few minutes to find a car and get it started. Cora stood and watched as he adjusted the seat. She opened the passenger door and got in. He gave her a stern look. 'OK. I'll drop you in the town, but after that I'm on my own.'

She fastened the seat belt and stared straight ahead. They drove in silence all the way. Indie took the coast road from Ulverston which brought them to the Vulcan Estate, where he parked up in a side road. He got out and pulled up his hood. Without another word, he set off towards the town centre.

She watched him go until he turned the first corner and disappeared. She set off quickly in the same direction, but at the corner she kept straight on. There was more than one route to where he was going and she was determined to be there. Her advantage was that the police and lots of other people weren't looking for her.

But they both ended up at the same place at the same time.

# CHAPTER 16

t was Tsura who suggested a way of leaving their calling card loud nd clear, more out of sympathy with the woman concerned than ny financial gain. Luca wasn't sure that they would gain any benefit beyond a grim satisfaction, but found it difficult to resist er argument.

The tactics were quickly agreed and they grabbed a few hours leep. Apart from Luca, of course, who continued to turn over he Rubik cube of interconnections in his head. He suspected a double- or even triple-cross, and was increasingly certain that the UK Special Branch was the main player in this game of blind man's bluff, which made him think they might not get paid at all.

They drove in two cars to Barrow and began searching for heir prey. It wasn't difficult, but they were surprised to see the Nellis clan, accompanied by their latest target, Keane, walking bast the Town Hall heading for the burnt-out skeleton of the Majestic.

Luca dropped Marko off and continued on to be sure that was where they were going. Tsura parked her car as she saw Nellis angrily earing at the police tapes which barred their entrance to the remains of his property. Two of the thugs stopped at the doorway and turned to face the world, while the other three and Keane followed Nelli and his gesticulating wife into the blackened interior.

Tsura glimpsed Marko heading down the side street to her left and took that as the signal for her to make the frontal assault. She took a couple of shopping bags from the back seat and took a deep breath. Her distinctive black hair was hidden beneath a colourful scarf she'd bought on an Appleby market stall only a week ago. She gathered herself and walked over until she was level with the two men standing outside the club door, adopting the pose they normally only performed in the dark. She could see that they felt awkward, not least because the torn tapes fluttering in the breeze quite clearly stated police no entry signs. She took this as her cue.

'Hey,' she shouted as she stopped, putting down one of the bags.

They pretended to ignore her, but she made that impossible by stepping towards them and holding up a bit of tape. 'What are you doing? You're not supposed to be in there,' she demanded.

One of the men looked at her as though she'd crawled out from the drains. He glanced around. There weren't many other people within hearing distance; it wasn't exactly on a shopping route.

'Fuck off, you nosy cow,' he said.

She took another two steps forward. 'Hey, watch your language. You can't talk to me like that.'

The other guy made the mistake of going down the two steps to speak to her. 'Are you fucking deaf?' he said through gritted teeth. 'Fuck off or I'll break your fucking neck.'

This was nothing if not prophetic, but not what he meant.

Tsura took one more step, put down the bag and turned into a whirling dervish. Her first kick broke his left leg below the knee. She grabbed him by the hair as he began to fall and with a blur of a pirouette brought her arm round his neck and gave it a fierce jerk. Before he hit the floor, she was onto the other man who was so astonished he didn't have time to offer any resistance. The leap from a standing start ended with her right foot crushing his windpipe. She cartwheeled back, skipped over the prone bodies and slipped through the open door.

In the square opposite, there were only three people who saw any of this. One of them, an old man sitting on a wall with a bottle in his hand and a dog at his feet, stared in disbelief. The dog barked, but stayed where it was. Another was Luca striding across as though he had somewhere important to go. He continued on as though nothing had happened. He reckoned they had about two minutes. More than enough. The third was Jimmy Beck sitting in a borrowed car parked in the shade of the Town Hall.

The two thugs lay still and had ceased to be visible to anyone unless they were close enough.

****

Marko had found the side door from which Indie had emerged to deal with Julie. It was firmly locked, but in the empty alley he was free to use maximum force. It took three kicks. Fortunately both the doors they'd used to gain entry had small entrance spaces before opening out into the main hall, so they were unseen and the noise muffled.

As if connected by some sixth sense, the two of them waited for one another. Tsura inched open the heavy inner door so that she could hear the torrent of complaints being spluttered by Nellis's wife as she shouted that their ineffectual lawyer needed to get his finger out and sort. She heard the quiet sound of Marko gaining access. The shouting stopped and she heard Nellis tell one of his men to go and see what the noise was, but he only got halfway there. Another voice came from up above. 'Stop right there, Jed,' it said.

Tsura saw the man look up above the door she was peeping through.

'What the fuck?' said Nellis, who now came into view. 'Dyer, is that you?'

'No it's my fucking dad, come to finish the job.'

She could see this startled Nellis, who looked to his left, where she guessed his wife must be. He looked back above her. 'What the fuck are you on about?' he asked.

'You killed my dad, Duncan Wallace. Fifteen years ago.'

'You're fucking mad, Indie. Where d'you get that from?'

'Me,' said another voice.

Tsura's eyes went wide. What was all this about? She wondered whether Marko was getting any of this. If he wasn't, he might make his entry any second now.

Nellis laughed. 'Ah. I get it now. Cora Beck. I expect your dad told you that tale, did he? Lying bastard.'

'No he didn't. It was my mother.'

Nellis looked back at his wife, who Tsura could now see edging towards her husband.

'Same difference. She's only saying that to protect him because she believes his lies.'

'Too bad, Nellis,' said Indie. 'I believe them and I'm going to finish it here and now.'

Nellis laughed and looked around him at his three men who'd all produced guns and grins. 'OK, Dyer, when you're ready.'

Tsura held her breath. There was a metallic sound and the whoosh of something heavy falling through the air. A black shape swung across in front of Nellis, who ducked in time as it flew onwards, only to see it catch one of his men a crunching blow on the side of his head. He fell like a skittle, his head snapping awkwardly as he hit the ground.

Before Nellis or anyone else could move another shape hurtled across the space . . . and another. Indie had somehow tied up the blackened heavy stage lights which were now operating like giant pendulums. The two other men had begun firing wildly, while Nellis and his wife were scrabbling across the floor towards the bar at the back of the room. One of the men followed them, while the other made for the door where Marko was hiding. He reached it and, as he stood there trying to find his target, an arm snaked out and dragged him through the doorway. He didn't reappear.

It was at this moment that Indie descended like Peter Pan, clutching one of the ropes he'd used to tie the lights. The scene was like nothing else Tsura had ever seen outside the circus. The lights were still swinging back and forth while Indie stood centre stage. The metallic clanking and whooshing slowed to a few creaks. Nellis and his surviving bodyguard came out from behind the bar and came at him from either side. Neither of them was grinning now. They kept looking up to see if they could spot Cora. As well as the bodyguard's handgun, Nellis had now acquired a sawn-off shotgun from behind the bar. Indie didn't move.

'OK, Dyer. Game over, I'm afraid. You lose.'

Indie drew his knife. Not his usual weapon. Something much heavier.

'You're a coward, Nellis. You put your guns down and I'll not use the knife.'

Nellis gave a hollow laugh. 'Like father, like son. Let's make it a fair fight, eh? You prick. Do you think I was going to give that cheeky bastard a chance? He'd had a go at Doreen. I wasn't having that . . . and now I'm not having this, either.'

The woman concerned raised her head above the bar. Her face was white and her hair was a mess.

Tsura thought it was time to intervene. The odds were far from even, but Indie had one last card to play. The final stage light wasn't on a rope. It fell straight down onto the last bodyguard's head.

Nellis looked up involuntarily to see Cora's pale face. Instinctively he raised the gun to point it at her, forgetting that the more dangerous enemy was only a few steps away. He didn't get chance to correct his mistake.

Indie was fast. The knife was big but it travelled unerringly towards its target. It thudded into Nellis's neck an inch above his collarbone. The gun went off, but Nellis slowly toppled backwards, blood gushing from his neck like a burst pipe. He hit the ground, shuddered and gurgled for a few moments, his back arching in a final rictus of agony before settling amidst a flood of blood. Indie's knife slowly toppled out of the gaping wound and clattered to the floor.

For a moment no-one moved or spoke. Nellis's body managed a few more spasms, but they all knew he was dead. Doreen was the first to move, coming out from behind the remains of the bar, bottle in hand. The noise of it splintering as she smashed it against the bar top made Indie jump, while Tsura came forward out of the shadows.

'You murdering wee shite, I'm going to cut your evil guts out.'

Indie had instinctively taken a couple of steps back and glanced towards his knife. Doreen was quick on her feet for her age and weight, and now he could see he wouldn't reach it before she reached him. He backed further away.

Tsura moved forwards from the doorway, but she knew she was too far away. Where was Marko? More worryingly, where was Keane?

Before she could call out, she heard a grunting noise behind her and the door crashed open. She turned and instinctively rolled to one side, to avoid the thug whose neck she'd crushed staggering into the room. His face and shirt were covered in blood, but he managed to point his gun at Indie's back and the shot echoed round the cavernous building. Tsura blinked and flung herself at the thug's tottering body, which collapsed as his leg buckled and snapped when her two-footed challenge crashed into him. She rolled and came up with his gun in her hand.

Indie had dropped to his knees, but beyond him Doreen was gasping in amazement at the giant red hole which was flowering in her chest. With one final effort, she flung the bottle at Indie before collapsing onto the inert form of her husband. The broken bottled smashed on the floor and the pieces skittered away.

Again, silence fell upon the scene. Tsura was first to move, running lightly to the two bodies and checking their pulses before returning to the groaning figure crumpled against the half-open door. He would live, but probably never talk again. The weight of the gun told her it was empty. She dropped it by its owner.

Cora appeared from a door behind the bar and ran over to Indie, who was lying shivering on the floor where he'd fallen. Tsura came over to them. 'We need to get out of here fast,' she said.

Cora looked at her with an odd expression. Tsura couldn' know that Cora was wondering if she knew a giant of a man with a long coat and broken teeth. The two of them helped Indie to hi feet. Tsura was worried about Marko, but figured the side doo was still the best escape route.

She guided them across, put her finger to her lips and pushe at the door. It only opened a few inches before bumping up agains the heavy body of the man whom she had assumed Marko had dealt with. She pushed it wide enough to slip through. The oute chamber was in darkness. She scuttled through, kicked open the outer door and sprang out into the alley.

Marko's non-appearance was instantly explained. She took in the intensity of the battle raging with only the slightest hint of a soundtrack. Marko hit the wall with a bone-crunching groan She saw that his left arm was limp and useless. His knife was lying three or four metres away, whilst a small handgun nestled agains the doorstep beneath her feet. Marko's assailant stopped in mid lunge and glanced at Tsura. Their eyes met. There was the glimpse of a smile as he whirled away and hurtled down the alley. Tsura had only a second to pick up the gun, take aim and fire. It wasn' a gun she would have chosen, but she rarely missed.

At first she thought she *had* missed but, although he managed another two steps, Keane faltered and he stumbled against the wall. His hand reached out to take hold of the drainpipe and he swung round to look back at her. She saw the grimace of pain, but then he gathered himself, winked at her and was round the corner She stepped across to Marko who gave her an apologetic grin before his eyes rolled upwards and he slumped onto the ground.

Luca was nowhere to be seen. Tsura left Cora with the two incapable young men and fetched the car. Five minutes later, she was driving out of town heading for the hotel. She knew how to set a broken arm. She was less sure about the young man who stared sightlessly through the window, although she thought the girl was made of strong stuff. They would all live. She didn't fear for Luca.

* * * * *

Luca had doubled back to the car and only just made it as he saw Keane running in an awkward fashion across the square. The silver car took off at speed and continued erratically towards the Walney Bridge, but then turned right and began heading out of town. Luca kept his distance but was surprised to see it pull off to the left towards a farm building.

Luca stopped at the main road, figuring there was no other way out. In the distance he saw Keane get out of the car and run towards the large spoil heap which ran for over a mile along the far side of the fields. He wasn't moving so easily now, occasionally stumbling but always getting up again. Luca got out of his car and made his way down the lane. Keane was now halfway up the sloping disused lorry track. Luca broke into a gentle trot.

Unusually for him, he hadn't noticed that he'd been followed from the Majestic. The pursuing car had turned to the right as Luca had pulled up and had parked outside a house near the pub opposite the lane end. The driver, Jimmy Beck, watched as Luca jogged up the path and disappeared over the summit. He waited for a minute or two before getting out and walking up to a nearby house, kicking an old football into the untended garden full of bikes, scooters and other boys' toys. Without knocking, he pushed open the door and went in.

As Luca got closer to the summit, he took care to cut off to the right of where he'd seen Keane disappear. At the top he raised his head warily. What he saw made complete sense. He shook his head in disappointment. Below him was a small dilapidated shack clinging to the hillside. There was nowhere else his quarry could be. He made his way down, gun in hand. He didn't need it.

He reappeared five minutes later carrying something long wrapped in his jacket, came back down the track, got back in his car and drove away.

Inside the house Jimmy stepped back from the window and picked up the cup of tea he'd been offered. Three pairs of dark eyes stared at him. Five minutes later he was heading up the track to the top of the spoil heap.

* * * * *

It wasn't the body count that upset Fletcher, although even by his standards it was pretty excessive. He recalled Dr Fox reciting the list in his methodical, professorial voice.

'A severed jugular, one gunshot to the chest, one broken neck and leg, a second broken neck, one fractured skull caused by heavy flying object, one crushed skull caused by heavy falling object and one strangled nurse.'

Fletcher could only offer him a shrug when the furious doctor complained angrily about the removal of remains of the woman's body from his lab by a tight-lipped crew of men in white coats who wouldn't answer his questions. He was left with a piece of paper signed by a high court judge containing thinly veiled threats concerning his ongoing employment and pension prospects.

The surviving victim, as Tsura suspected, would only ever speak again with the aid of a mechanical voice box. His evidence, given many weeks later, was worse than useless. His description of a flying woman in a headscarf was not helpful and, quite frankly, seemed deluded.

Fletcher didn't find the carnage involving a group of people responsible for the suffering of so many others much worry to his soul. They wouldn't be missed. He was briefly interested in the identity of the strangled woman, but Roger Skeldon had unflinchingly identified her as a Nurse Birch. He told them about what had happened to Miriam, but couldn't tell them where to find her. Meanwhile the Haddens and the private secretary Roger said was called Miss Ridley had proved to be Lucan-like in their complete disappearance.

He couldn't even get annoyed with Irene. She'd arrived back in a sullen mood. She'd been unable to find any trace of Marko. He'd not been on the delegate list for the conference and he'd paid for the hotel rooms with cash using her surname, which she didn't find at all funny.

No. It was the arrival and instructions from Adversane which got up his nose.

The 'old boy' had arrived late in the afternoon having stopped off for 'a decent lunch, considering how far north it was'.

'Hadn't realised the place was so damn far away,' he'd said, as he breezed into the police station where officers, SOCOs, hospital staff, journalists and even the mortuary attendants were still trying to come to terms with the scale, brutality and variety of the killings.

Fletcher had walked away before he hit the bastard, so it was Sadie who brought her superior up to date. To say that Adversane wasn't that interested was an understatement. He cut short the descriptions of the victims' injuries and a list of possible suspects and insisted on getting Sadie to round up the ACC and the chief constable for a private meeting at an undisclosed venue. Fletcher, of course, was not invited.

It didn't take long. Adversane didn't return to the police station and Fletcher was summoned with everyone else to the incident room, where they were informed by the chief constable that for reasons of state security, particularly at this time and place, the killings were to be put down to an argument between Nellis and his underlings which had got out of hand. They weren't pursuing any other leads and, as far as the press was concerned, the case was closed.

Equally, the disappearance of a local high-profile businessman, his wife and his secretary was deemed a private family matter. Roger, Shirley and Jimmy Beck were released without charges at midday, but had all been given severe warnings about taking the law into their own hands. Two or three days later Charlie Conroy and Sam White were also released under similar conditions. Fletcher suspected that the chief constable had also spent some part of the afternoon with the editor of the local rag, as the massacre didn't even make front page. The TV crews who were already in place for the next day's big event were easily dissuaded from disturbing their carefully planned schedules.

They'd also had to let young Naylor go. He'd managed to come up with a story about feeling so tired after a party that he'd just driven off the road and stopped for a rest. He knew nothing of the whereabouts of Ian Dyer or anything about the Haddens.

The final act of that 'busy day at the office' was the arrival in the station of a woman who asked to speak to 'that copper from London who's shagging Irene Garner'. Her determined face persuaded the desk sergeant to ring upstairs, although he hadn't the nerve to tell the 'London copper' the full message. Fletcher didn't mean to pick up the phone, but he was glad he did; at least because of that he gained some sense of grim satisfaction. He went from the office without saying a word, but downstairs told the desk sergeant to tell Inspector Swift where he was going.

He listened to the woman. He wasn't sure he believed her, but drove her back to her house. He sat and listened as the two young lads told him their story. They often played on the spoil heap across the road from where, on a fine day, you could see the Isle of Man rising out of the mists like Avalon.

He looked at her dark eyes and black hair and asked her only one question.

'Do you know Jimmy Beck?'

She gave him a sly look. 'You're not so daft as you're stupid looking. He's my brother, but I haven't seen him for ages,' she added, with a quiet smile.

Fletcher drove his car down the farm track and parked next to the silver sports car. He added two and two and got Keane. It was obvious when you knew. Up the sloping path in the wrong sort of shoes. Five minutes later he was standing looking across the muddy channel where he could see the northern end of Walney Island and the busy scurrying of the security teams scouring every inch of the small airstrip. Beyond it he could see the West Shore caravan site and beyond that the beach he'd walked along only a few days ago. No-one had thought of this. But the man lying on his side a few yards away must have worked it out. From here it was a difficult shot, but Fletcher suspected he would have been able to make it. The weapon the two lads had described the older man carrying away was 'long and had a telescope on it'.

It was at this moment, Fletcher knew they had used him. Perhaps they'd known all along about Keane as well. Used him as well, poor bastard.

Fletcher had assumed the man was dead, but a gasp of pain startled him. He looked down at him. His eyes were open, but unfocussed. He was trying to turn over, but gave up. Fletcher slid down the gravel and knelt down beside him. The man's eyes settled on him.

'Fletcher?' he shivered.

Fletcher nodded. He could see the dark patch on the side of Keane's jacket. He thought it best not to move him.

'Shame really, but there it is . . .' He coughed blood and closed his eyes, the dark-red liquid dribbling from his mouth.

Fletcher couldn't think of anything to say. Keane's eyes opened again. A look of panic was replaced by a weak smile.

'Tell my moth . . .' His words stopped. A black hole had appeared at his temple. His eyes lost their smile. Fletcher heard the 'phut' sound and looked up. Five figures in black surrounded him, all with guns pointing at him. Hard eyes stared out from black ski-masks. The one with the elongated pistol gave a slight signal and the guns were lowered. He stepped down to where Fletcher was kneeling.

Fletcher stood up. The man looked out towards the airstrip. 'Not many guys capable of that shot,' he said. One of the others bent down and picked up a discarded round and showed it to him.

'Dragunov SVD?' he suggested.

The first man nodded. 'Accurate over a thousand metres in the right hands,' he added.

Fletcher looked down at the still figure huddled on the gravel.

'Just in time, Inspector,' said the man. 'Well done you. No one else thought of this. Probably get a medal from the Queen.'

352

The black figures departed as silently as they'd arrived. Fletcher was still there, looking out at Avalon, when the others arrived. His mind had floated back to that evening less than a month ago when he and Laura had watched that film star at the airport whose name he couldn't remember. He knew of at least one person who would have made the connection: Excalibur to Avalon. If only he could read those hidden signs.

Fox didn't need much time to confirm cause of death. The shot to the head had prevented the slow death the man would have endured from the abdominal wound. Less than an hour ago, he guessed from the amount of blood. He didn't expect to conduct the autopsy and he was right.

Sadie confirmed that this was Philip Keane, but Fletcher had already walked away. He'd had enough.

The afternoon dwindled towards a glorious sunset. Mancini was invited to take extended leave and Aston was reinstated without censure. Sadie had gone without a word whilst Irene said she had a few friends to look up, so Fletcher ended up on his own in the car park. He took one last look at the big sheds looming over the police station and set off home. There were traffic jams on the A591, but all coming the other direction, heading towards the next day's jamboree.

He hadn't intended it, but as he drove out of Ulverston he saw that the tide was out in the estuary, so pulled in to take one last look. It was too far away to see but he knew that on the other side was Jimmy Beck's hut and further down the huge house which had been all closed up. As he watched, he thought he could see a figure way across the glistening expanse: a dark speck moving quickly, leaping across channels and reaching the far edge before disappearing into the woods. He turned to get back into the car, just as three swans flew low across the wet sand and swung to their left down the main channel. He was reminded of Louisa's wedding night. He sighed and got into the car, but the two images stayed with him for a long time.

* * * * *

The missing businessman turned up three days later. The tide thoughtfully deposited him on a little beach just up from the Ulverston canal. It took some time to identify him but the injuries were instantly recognisable. Although Thomas Hadden had eventually drowned, it was obvious that any attempt to escape the tide and the treacherous sand had been rendered useless by the destruction of both his knees and his ankles. Dr Fox was minded to write 'in the IRA style', but thought better of it. As he half expected, the tight-lipped crew returned and he signed the relevant documents without demur.

* * * * *

Roger Skeldon was surprised to get a phone call a week after the event. He'd moved in with Shirley and spent most of his days recovering from their night-time exertions, which didn't seem to be letting up.

The man introduced himself as a Mr. Welch, who worked for VSEL, and he was inviting him to attend an interview for a senior post in the security team at the yard.

Roger found himself standing on the Walney Bridge two days later with his new badge and a cheque for a month's salary in advance in his wallet. He'd been pinching himself every hour or so, but here he was and it was true and not a word from Marcus Pole.

He walked back to the yard and got into his new car. He'd told Shirley to get herself to the hairdressers. He was taking her out tonight and it wasn't going to be the local Chinese either.

He continued to ignore the small voice trying to to tell him he'd signed up with the devil, put the car in gear and set off towards Ulverston.

* * * * *

Stephanie Hadden, her frail, skeletal body wrapped in the flimsiest of summer dresses, was found three weeks later following an anonymous phone call. The police took dogs and cautiously entered the ruined hall. They found her body in a small room which a local historian later told them would have been a priest hole. She'd managed to open the heavy door and squeeze inside. They also found another body. A young man; eventually identified as Kenny Baxter, who'd worked for the Haddens as a gardener and gone missing fifteen years earlier. The two bodies were examined by Dr Fox, who declared that Stephanie Hadden had died of hypothermia, although there was evidence of numerous older injuries and that the young man had been tortured and that many of his bones had been broken. After fifteen years Fox was unable to detect that the young man's innards had been removed whilst he was still alive using a fisherman's gutting knife.

He was as capable as anyone at constructing several dreadful scenarios, but in truth no-one would ever know.

Only Jimmy Beck, watching from his hiding place in the trees, gained some satisfaction from this. His silence was no longer necessary.

He and Maggie had promised each other they'd tell Cora the truth eventually but after all that had gone on that wasn't going to happen anytime soon, and anyway, how do you tell your teenage daughter that her real father had been murdered and her mother had been imprisoned and tortured for fifteen long years? And how do you explain all the lies they'd told. Still, most of the people who knew or suspected the truth were now dead. Maybe they wouldn't tell her.

He dropped down from his hiding place and took one last look at the ruined house before setting off back towards the hut. The dog ran on ahead, glad to be free to chase the scents.

The old house settled on its rocky outcrop; the wind rustling through its open windows, while it muttered its rosary of lies and secrets in dark corners until a kind silence overwhelmed it.

* * * * *

### Friday July 3rd

Two days after the launch, Indie walked into Barrow police station, but although they had some circumstantial evidence they had to let him go. His fingerprints weren't on the money Irene had given Julie. No-one had seen either him or Cora enter or leave the Majestic the afternoon the Nellis gang was decimated. No-one knew of his motive. He hadn't been involved in the battle at the hut. No-one, not even Baz, when he was eventually able to speak, was prepared to say a word against him; although in his case Baz knew the silence was mutually protective. He and Frank Burnham had been given six years each, but neither of them ever came back to Barrow. Amy Dobson refused to testify. She couldn't see any advantage to be gained in telling them the truth, even when she found out that Hadden was dead. Aston knew he was beaten and went back to his previous operational mode: inactive. Indie walked out. He didn't smile until he was three streets away.

The following morning, he and Cora sat on the rock watching the dawn light shimmering on the water. Neither of them had anything more to say. The night before they'd been in the ruined house where they'd fumbled with each other's bodies until it seemed to be right. They'd found each other's nakedness both awkward and surprising, but they fitted neatly enough.

She'd taken him there partly because she hoped that Maliverny would reappear, but there had been no sign of him. They'd even gone to look in the dilapidated and desecrated mausoleum. The lid on the tomb which Maliverny had forced open lay in broken pieces and the inside gaped dark and empty in the dim light coming through the cobwebs. There was no treasure and no bag of chess pieces, so Indie was only partially convinced when she showed him the ivory soldier biting his shield.

Oddly enough, the one person who could have made the connection for her was back in London in the basement of a large Edwardian building interrogating Susannah Ridley, who had been arrested with several others when the trucks were stopped just ten minutes after leaving the big house. She couldn't help him much.

He could have explained to Cora in far more detail than Fletcher's old history teacher about the numerous attempts to kill and replace Elizabeth the First, including the Babington Plot.

Anthony Adversane had got a First at Cambridge in History and both knew and admired the Machiavellian intrigue and double-dealing of Elizabeth's favourite, Sir Francis Walsingham. He knew about the army of informers and agents and envied his predecessor's powers and budget. Unfortunately he had to be even more devious in this respect.

But he still wouldn't have believed her.

\* \* \* \* \*

Later Cora watched Indie walking away across the shining sand, his thin loping figure dissipating into the dazzling light. She didn't know whether to believe him when he said he'd be back, but she knew she couldn't make him stay.

It was only when the train was pulling into Preston station and he searched for his ticket that he found the ivory figure nestling in his top pocket.

She hadn't given everything away. In her room that night, she took out the unusually thick and textured paper on which were the words which Catlin said was a poem written by one of the conspirators he had betrayed. The handwriting was all curls and whirls and she didn't know who he meant or understand every word, but she found it unbearably sad.

> *My prime of youth is but a frost of cares;*
> *My feast of joy is but a dish of pain;*
> *My crop of corn is but a field of tares;*
> *And all my good is but vain hopes of gain:*
> *My glass is full, and now my glass is run;*
> *And now I live, and now my life is done.*

**\* \* \* \* \***

### Saturday July 11th
*Arena di Verona, interval between Acts One and Two of Verdi's opera* Nabucco.

Luca and Marko remained in their seats while Tsura went in search of pizzas. The first act had been as wonderful as ever. They watched as the army of technicians crawled all over the set, transforming it from the temple of Jerusalem to the palace of Babylon. Marko pointed with his good hand across and above the main stage at a tiny figure inching his way along a gantry on which hung twenty or so lights. When he reached the end, he bent to disengage a connecting rod and the whole gantry swung over to the right, where his colleague gathered it in with a rope and attached it to its new position. Luca thought of the young man who had engineered a similar if more lethal sequence back in that strange town with its badly dressed Mafioso.

The opera was his treat. He'd been astonished to receive a phone call the previous Monday from his bank asking him into which account he wanted them to put the large payment they'd received on his behalf that morning. The source was undisclosed, but the manager was able to say that it hadn't travelled far and so no further questions were necessary.

He smiled.

Verona. Verdi. Vivace.

# HISTORICAL NOTES

1. Maliverny Catlin is mentioned briefly in records connecting him to Sir Francis Walsingham, Elizabeth I's Secretary of State, who was instrumental in exposing the Babington Plot in 1586. This was a Catholic plot to assassinate the Queen and put Mary, Queen of Scots on the English throne. The chief conspirator was Sir Anthony Babington (1561–1586), a young Catholic nobleman. The plot was used as the main evidence against Mary and led eventually to her own trial and execution.

    i. Babington and many others were interrogated, tortured and sentenced to death. The sentence for conspiracy and treason was to be hung, drawn and quartered.

    ii. There is evidence that Catlin spent time in the 'northern counties' in the summer of 1586, trying to uncover connections between the conspirators and the Earl of Northumberland. He was one of a number of spies and double agents employed by Walsingham who is considered by many to be the first spymaster.

iii. Many North Lancashire families were well known for their recusant Catholic sympathies and involvement in numerous conspiracies during this period. Many of them lost their lives and property.

iv. 'My prime of youth is but a frost of cares' is the first line of a poem written by Chidiock Titchborne, one of Babington's co-conspirators, in the Tower of London during his interrogation and torture.

2. Lord Mountbatten, Elizabeth II's uncle-in-law and several other relatives were killed by an IRA bomb on 27th August 1979 at Mullaghmore, County Sligo. On the same day the IRA ambushed and killed 18 British soldiers at Warren Point, County Down.

3. The first *Trafalgar* Class submarine was launched at Barrow-in-Furness on July 1st 1981. The ceremony was performed by Lady Fieldhouse, the wife of the commander-in-chief of the fleet, Sir John Fieldhouse.

4. 'The Lewis Chessmen have long been associated with mystery and romance.' Although their origin is now widely believed to be twelfth-century Scandinavian, their discovery on the Isle of Lewis is the subject of much controversy. I took the liberty of passing them into the possession Maliverny Catlin in a previous short story, *The Boundary*, www.attheedge.eu so could not resist including then once again. For the most up-to-date analysis see *The Lewis Chessmen Unmasked* by David H. Caldwell, Mark A. Hall and Caroline M. Wilkinson, published by the National Museums of Scotland, 2010

5. The Furness Railway ran from Lakeside on Lake Windermere to Barrow. It crossed the River Leven near Greenodd. The line was closed in 1967 and the bridge was dismantled sometime later. I have taken the liberty of extending its afterlife so that my characters didn't have to go all the way round via Haverthwhaite. Today there is a footbridge. This estuary and Morecambe Bay are notorious for their deceptive and fast-moving tides, which have claimed many victims.

# About the Author

ick Lee was born in North Yorkshire 1948, went to study History in ondon in the late 60's, but spent most f his time going to Jimi Hendrix and ream concerts, whilst squatting in a ries of elegant but condemned dwardian mansions.

He became a drama teacher in 1974 and later studied for a Ed in Education through Drama with Dorothy Heathcote. He orked in a variety of secondary schools, colleges, special needs partments and residential homes - including a 4 year spell as nior Advisory Teacher with Leicestershire LEA – after which he turned up north to be a Head of an Expressive Arts Department Barrow-in-Furness, followed by 5 years working for the Barrow ducational Action Zone and as an education consultant. As well classroom drama, he was also writing and directing plays with udents including several successful Edinburgh Fringe productions.

He has an MA in Writing Studies from Lancaster University d written many short stories and has already published two lumes of poems. His involvement in outdoor education, taking ty kids into the wilds of Snowdonia, the Lake District and the ountains and islands of Scotland, have provided the backdrop r his London cop's adventures.

He moved to France in 2006 to enjoy retirement – although rious bouts of DIY and gardening have kept him busy!

He began writing the Mick Fletcher suspense thrillers two ars ago and has not been able to stop since!

# Daughter of the Rose

ISBN: 978-1-908098-47-4

Detective Mick Fletcher has been sent even further north to Penrith after his unacceptable behaviour in West Yorkshire. Never mind he and his sergeant were both awarded commendations for their bravery and dogged persistence in preventing a national disaster.

New cases include a dead prostitute and a missing wife – but Fletcher has got family troubles of his own.

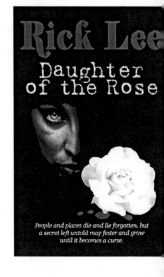

People and places die and lie forgotten, but a secret left untold may fester and grow until it becomes a curse.

Octavia Hutton and her National Trust colleagues are excite when they gain access to an abandoned Gothic mansion. Little d they know how their expectations will be overwhelmed by wh they are about to uncover.

These investigations at first seem to be unconnected – bu will a serial killer weave them unexpectedly together . . . and b the catalyst for a final act of terrible vengeance?

A suspense thriller . . . with a supernatural edge.

Lightning Source UK Ltd.
Milton Keynes UK
UKOW050629111112

201982UK00001B/4/P